The Natural Causes Of Murder

a Francis and Alicia Mystery #2

by

Geoffrey Hild

Cover design: SelfPubBookCovers.com/RLSather

2

ACKNOWLEGEMENTS

Thank you to Angela Bayes, M.A., M.Ed., for having at her fingertips, whenever I called, the relevant details of all things feminine, pertaining to religion, or currently in vogue. And thanks also for being my trusted and intrepid first reader.

Thank you to Cheryl Carter, M.A. for your critique of an earlier incarnation of this story, which also served as a brief, intense course on writing the modern novel.

The Natural Causes of Murder

d

Chapter 1

October 2011

Maybe I'd been hanged in a previous life, I don't know. But I do know for sure that I don't like anything even a little snug around my neck. So, I waited until the last possible second to fasten my collar button and cinch up the knot on my tie, before pulling open the front door of the Wrigley Community Church and going on in.

Family and friends, recently returned from the cemetery, filled a spacious room in the basement of the church. Some sat at the small round tables, others stood in tight conversational groups. Diagonally halved sandwiches were set out near the large stainless steel percolator that filled the air with the bitter aroma of overheated coffee. The solemn part was over now, and normal, although not yet convivial, conversation had already returned.

I spotted Alicia. Her dark brown hair customarily fell as a lush cascade onto her shoulders, but was for this occasion restrained by a black ribbon, tied in a bow at the nap of her neck. She sat at one of the small tables with her sister Ellen and Ellen's husband, Roger. In a contrast of styles, Ellen, who was only a year Alicia's senior, wore her hair in the coif of a much older woman, cropped short with tight curls. Roger, the insurance salesman, was a man of indeterminate age in a suit.

"Well, look who finally shows up," Roger greeted my approach.

1

"I just got in from Spain," I said.

I then expressed my condolences to Alicia and Ellen on the passing of their mother, and they concurred that it was sweet of me to come when I could.

I set up for a quick exit, by saying, "I can't stay. I have to get right over to the office. I wasn't supposed to stop anywhere."

"Just sit down for a minute," Alicia quietly detained me. "You have a minute, don't you?"

As I sat down, Roger spoke up again, "Spain, eh? What's it like in Spain?"

"Sunny and warm, Roger," Alicia nipped at him, while keeping her green eyes fixed on me. "Francis, I need to ask a small favor of you."

"Trouble?"

"No, not this time. I just need you to go with me to Puerto Rico."

"Tell me that's a club in Humbolt Park."

"No, the island in the Caribbean," Alicia said. "They're going to tear down some old monastery, before it falls down, and I've scored a little contract to fly in and give an opinion on which musty old paintings are worth saving. You know, how much restoration work would be needed, how to box them up for shipment – that sort of thing. It's easy money and gets me out of the basement of the Art Institute for a few days."

"What's my part in this?"

"The Bishop said that I needed a man to accompany me up at the monastery. And I think your Spanish will come in handy. The Abbot doesn't speak English."

The favor was hardly small, but after a few moments of thought, I started warming to the idea. Despite our long-ago divorce, in recent years Alicia and I had fallen into a friends-with-benefits relationship. However, as a field service engineer, I traveled so much that there tended to be rather lengthy time spans between the benefit allotments. So, it readily occurred to me that a few nights with Alicia on a Caribbean island could hardly help but prove to be mutually beneficial.

"It's after lunch and a Friday," I said. "So, my boss will be pretty heavily lubricated. But if nothing much is going on, I'm sure I can wrangle a few days off. When do we leave?"

"I was supposed to be there now, but Ellen and I were still tied up with tag team Mom-sitting. Could you leave Monday?"

"Actually, that'd be best. Less chance of something popping up." This could definitely work out.

"And Ellen is going with us."

My heart sank. Roger slapped down his paper cup and rose from his seat.

"Sit down." Ellen's voice was low, but firm. "Don't embarrass me here, now."

Ellen's eyes, still reddened from the wiping of funeral tears, followed Roger's bespectacled ones, as he lowered himself back onto his chair.

Roger also kept his voice down, but still demanded, "What have the two of you been cooking up? Damn it, Ellen, every time you get around Alicia you start to go crazy. Her flighty lifestyle and this open marriage—"

"We're divorced, Roger," Alicia broke in. "It's okay for me to date whoever I want. Including Francis."

"Alicia and I have spent the last three weeks, day and night, taking care of Mom, watching her slowly die." Ellen kept her voice low and controlled. "I'd just like to take a few days to lie out on a beach, while Alicia does her monastery business. I'll be sharing a hotel room with her, if it makes a difference to you."

I didn't know about Roger, but Ellen's staying in Alicia's hotel room sure as hell made a difference to *me*. However, I could only sit there, glumly aware that I'd been tricked.

I studied Alicia's pretty face. It was the soft, unlined face of a woman in her mid-thirties who applied sunscreen daily, even in the winter. She could afford to back off on her makeup, allowing herself only a touch of color on the lips and just a little drama of mascara around the eyes.

Ellen, whose makeup looked applied with heavy strokes from a loaded brush, continued to manage Roger's objections, concerning who's going to mind the children, what's he supposed to eat, and sundry other difficulties encountered when the wife is away.

Alicia didn't join in the argument. As Ellen responded to each of Roger's protests – responses that came rather too quickly to have been unrehearsed – Alicia calmly observed the competition, like a riding coach watching with approval, as her pupil lifted the horse over each successive fence.

With the tide of the marital battle now safely turned in Ellen's favor, Alicia leaned against my shoulder and spoke softly. "I tried to reach you all week."

"I lost my cell phone right after I landed in Spain," I matched her subdued volume. "Either in Valencia, or Almussafes. Maybe somewhere in between."

"What's in Almussafes?"

"A Ford engine plant. I was troubleshooting a machine breakdown."

"But somehow you got word of Mom's passing and the funeral arrangements."

"I stopped by my apartment on the way in from O'Hare and listened to my messages," I said. "But I was supposed to bring the specs for a new machine order straight to the office, the minute I got back to Chicago. The Proposal Department's hungry. They'll be working the weekend on the bid. So, I'd better get moving."

"I'll e-mail you the flight details."

I stood and stretched my chin high in an attempt to gain some relief from the grip of my fastened collar and knotted tie. On the opposite side of the table, the domestic quarrelers, now reduced to intermittent sniping, were oblivious to my departure.

I plotted a course through the maze of tabled and free-standing relatives and family friends. And although impeded at one point, while I waited for a large man to scoot his chair in, I eventually managed to gain passage and emerge into the open area near the exit.

As my hand pushed against the door, another hand with a set of polished almond-shaped nails (trimmed for manual dexterity, while retaining just enough length to tear flesh) lightly came to rest on my forearm.

"Francis, a little heads-up about the trip." Alicia's chosen route to the exit had evidently taken a more favorable line. "The Bishop actually said he wanted my *husband* to accompany me up at the monastery."

I turned to face her and waited for the rest of it.

"Well, you know how the Pope feels about divorce. And I never did change my last name back. No sense bitching the deal for a technicality."

"I think lying to a bishop trumps getting a divorce on the road-to-hell-o-meter."

"I won't actually *say* you're my husband. I'll just message him that Francis Elton will accompany me. You could be my brother, for all he knows."

"By the sound of the hotel accommodations, I might just as well *be* your brother."

"Oh Francis, you'll be right in the room next door. And Ellen might go home early, if she starts missing her boys. And is that all you ever think about?"

Alicia moved in closer, loosened my tie, and unfastened my collar button. Bringing her lips close to my ear, she whispered, "We'll fit it in somehow. I promise."

I recognized the fresh apple scent as her body wash. It lingered for a moment, as Alicia walked away, returning to her table. She walked well in heels.

***

At the San Juan Airport on the following Monday, the evening was already dark, but the early October air was still noticeably warm. Alicia, Ellen, and I moved with the herd along a lengthy concourse, heading toward the baggage claim area.

Alicia stopped abruptly. "Oh my God, it can't be him."

A trim, middle-aged man, wearing a sports jacket, stepped toward us.

"Lieutenant Dodd?" I asked, pulling the name and face out of storage. "Phil Dodd from the Marietta?"

"The finest damn Destroyer ever to tag along behind a Carrier. Hello, Francis," Dodd said. Then to the ladies, "Alicia and, uh, Ma'am."

"What's going on?" Ellen asked.

"I don't know," Alicia said. "We barely get here and some old drinking buddy of Francis's shows up." Alicia's eyes hardened. "Lieutenant, we're very busy right now. Why don't you call Francis in a few days? We'll be at the Caserio Inn."

"Actually, I'm here to meet you on official business," Dodd said. "Here to present you with a rare opportunity to serve your country. We *are* at war, you remember."

"*You* are at war, Lieutenant," Alicia said. "Shooting up the Arab countries may be your business, but it's not mine. Now the three of us are going to continue on through those doors and simply pretend this nasty little surprise never happened."

"I'm not a lieutenant, anymore." Dodd produced a small leather-bound folder from an inside jacket pocket and opened it for us to see an official-looking identification card featuring his stoic face. The card identified Philip Dodd as a Special Agent of the Naval Criminal Investigative Service. "I need to discuss some things with the two of you on the ride into town."

When Dodd stowed his ID, I caught a glimpse of a pistol grip, under the cover of his sports jacket.

"I think it'll be alright," I said to Alicia. "We can at least listen to him, while we wait for the luggage."

Alicia's eyes remained hardened and fixed on Phil Dodd, as she fired back at me, "This will be on *your head*, Francis, if your old lieutenant screws things up for me on this project."

"Again, I am no longer a lieutenant."

"But I'm warning you, Lieutenant. If that little credential you just flashed at us turns out to be from a Cracker Jack box, I won't hesitate to call the *real* police and have them put you where I've always thought you belonged."

***

We stood back, out of earshot from the ring of people who were gathered around the baggage claim carousel, waiting for the feeder conveyor to start up.

"What's with the Naval Criminal business?" I asked Dodd. "I thought you weren't in the Navy, anymore."

"We're civilians, kind of."

"So, what crime's been committed?"

"Nothing yet. I'm working anti-terrorism, right now. And before you ask what that has to do with you, just relax for a minute and let me tell you a little story."

"Oh, God." Alicia rolled her eyes. "Not one of his sea stories."

"There's this Engineman Second Class," Dodd began. "He works on the launches that putter around out in the harbor at Guantanamo Bay. You know, the Navy Base in Cuba where we warehouse our excess intake of terrorists."

"We keep up with the news, Lieutenant."

"Okay, good. So this Engineman is of Arab descent and a Muslim, and he's volunteered many times to be there to whisper in a Chaplain's ear to get him through whatever Muslim ritual that comes up, like a funeral or some Ramadan thing. So, he's a fine young sailor, willing to help out in a pinch, and everything's peachy."

"That was a lovely story, Lieutenant. Now, can we—"

"Then one day, one of the Chaplains is here in San Juan on leave for a few days and strolling along, and he sees the Engineman – in civilian clothes – sitting in an outdoor café at a table with this well-fed Arab, who's wearing a jacket and tie, but also these white tennis shoes. And off to one side is another Arab, a big one, also in a suit, but with dark sunglasses, who's just standing nearby next to a wall, like he's a bodyguard or something. The Chaplain tries to catch a little of their conversation, as he passes by, but it's not in English. The Chaplain thinks, well, maybe it's the sailor's dad, down from Detroit to see how Navy life is treating his boy. But then again, there's that bodyguard. The Chaplain wonders, what's the deal? So, back at the Officer's Mess, back in Gitmo, the Chaplain mentions all this to a Warrant Officer who's in base security, and he passes it on to the NCIS."

"That's where you come in," I said.

"Not just yet. So, a watch is set on the café, and Mr. Tennis Shoes shows up again, sipping tea and munching a cookie, with the bodyguard once again standing nearby. He's followed back to his hotel, and we find that he's registered as Jaspar Rahim of Paris, France. With a little more snooping we find that Mr. Rahim of Gay

Paree is here in Puerto Rico to buy an old monastery up in the mountains that's about to be torn down, so that he, or more likely the people he represents, can build a resort hotel, or something, there."

"You mean, the monastery where I'm going to appraise the paintings?" Alicia was now interested.

"The very one," Dodd said. "Well, it turns out that the Engineman's okay. After a little questioning, we find out he was in San Juan on R and R and had only sipped tea with Rahim as a favor to his old grandpa, who rode camels, or something, together with Rahim's father back in the Old Country. So, some family stories are swapped, and the dutiful grandson sails out of the picture. But now, we're worried that Jaspar Rahim is maybe going to build an Al Qaeda training camp up in the mountains. And so, how are we going to get a man into the monastery to scope it all out on the sneaky?"

"Is that my suitcase?" Ellen plunged into the crowd.

"Then we catch a break," Dodd continued. "A structural engineer, who was hired to go up to the monastery to discover that the crumbling old foundation is indeed crumbling, he gets a visit afterward from the NCIS, and he tells our guy he's heard that an art restorer from the Chicago Art Institute is coming down to have a look at the monastery's crumbling old paintings. So, the Southeast Field Office up at Mayport does a check on who that art restorer might be."

Alicia looked up to the vast reaches of the Terminal's ceiling. "How can this be happening to me?"

"That's right, it's pretty Miss Alicia Elton. And who's her able-bodied assistant for this little expedition? Why it's Francis Elton, whose heart Alicia broke by putting him out with the trash, twelve lonely years ago. Now Mayport thinks it's kind of odd that Alicia would employ her ex for this adventure. So, just for fun, they run a background check on broken-hearted Francis and find that, long ago, he was an electronics technician in the Navy, and lo and behold, his old lieutenant was none other than yours truly, Philip Dodd, Special Agent for the NCIS, who is languishing away at his desk right there in Guantanamo Bay, Cuba. Just a short hop away."

"It wasn't my suitcase." Ellen returned from the fray. "Some old lady got all kinds of nasty about me touching her bag."

"So," Dodd concluded, "that's why we're all bunched up here at the SJU baggage claim discussing our patriotic, post-nine-eleven duty to stamp out Islamic Extremists everywhere. Well, that's not quite right. I have no idea why the schoolmarm here is with us."

"Her name is Ellen, and she's with me, and that's all you need to know," Alicia said.

While Alicia was reflexively defending her sister, I was thinking about Dodd's use of the words: our patriotic duty. That could mean anything from voting to putting your life on the line for little or no pay. And I knew that whatever Dodd was about to propose was sure to upset Alicia's plans. And that she was not going to take it well.

However, further discussion was interrupted by the arrival of our suitcases. It was like seeing familiar old friends come sliding down the chute to begin their ride on the carousel.

***

Phil Dodd rode with us to the off-site rental car lot. He sat up front with the shuttle-bus driver and seemed to be keeping his attention mostly on the side rearview mirror. Alicia and Ellen chatted together in the middle seat. I sat in the rear seat and thought about Dodd. He was from the deep past, my Navy days. Dodd was a career Navy man who'd worked his way up through the ranks to his commission. But he didn't make it to retirement. And I knew why: the incident in the Philippines. I wouldn't have guessed that Dodd would start a new career as a Special Agent, even if it was for the Navy, but I was pretty sure that the ID he flashed was real. They don't let just anyone walk around an airport boarding area, packing a concealed handgun.

At the rental car lot, we waited outside the tiny glassed-in building for the people in line ahead of us to numbly sign multiple times within the stapled sheaves of fine-printed rental agreements. Dodd stood off to one side and spoke short sentence fragments into his cell phone. When he put it away and stepped back to us, Alicia was ready for him.

"What is it that you want from us, Lieutenant? It sounds like you're hinting around about going up to the monastery with Francis and me."

"Something like that. But see, we can't arouse suspicions by having another guy just unaccountably show up with you two." And then Dodd came out with it. "I want to take Francis's—"

"Absolutely not!" Alicia anticipated him. "You can pal along. I'll do that much for my country. But you're not going to screw up this project. I'm scheduled to meet with the Bishop first thing tomorrow morning, and then Francis and I are going on up to the monastery. You can ride in the backseat, if you want. I'll introduce you as my other assistant. But that's it."

"It won't work that way. I'd be blown immediately. I have to be Francis."

"I can't lie to the Bishop." Alicia caught the look I gave her. "Shut up, Francis."

A little smile briefly came and went on Dodd's face. "Alicia, I need very much to get inside that monastery when Rahim is there. We know he's been up to the monastery practically every day since he arrived, and we don't think he's just been scoping out the best spot for the tennis courts. But nobody can know who I really am. I have to be inconspicuous, to be nobody in particular. I have to be Francis."

"No. I need Francis. I need him to translate Spanish for me. The Abbot doesn't speak any English, and for all I know, nobody else at the monastery does, either."

"I can speak Spanish," Dodd said.

That surprised me. "Since when?"

"Go ahead. Ask me something in Spanish. I took a course."

I said, in Spanish, "What is the color of Ellen's shirt?"

"Wait a minute." Lines formed on Dodd's forehead. "What color, then something about a shirt. *Camisa* is shirt, isn't it? Wait a sec. What color...shirt...from Ellen...Just say it once again, will you?"

"Is there something wrong with my shirt?"

"I didn't say I was fluent."

"Better stick to English," I said. "Lots of people here are bi-lingual. Well, in the cities, anyway."

Alicia looked off toward the darkened horizon. "All I wanted to do was go up to the monastery, look over the paintings, write out my report, and get my check."

"Alicia, these are perilous times," Dodd pressed his appeal. "Potential threats cropping up all over the place. And you know the heavy price we pay when we get complacent. This could be nothing, or it could be the real deal. I can't know, unless I'm actually there to check it out."

Dodd watched Alicia's face, as she now seemed to search for a coded answer in the flashing lights of stacked aircraft, broadly circling in the night sky.

In a subdued tone, Dodd added, "I can't promise you the Navy Cross. But you could do your job, and I could do my job, and you'd be helping your country."

It took a full minute, but finally Alicia lowered her gaze to our level. "Oh, all right, Lieutenant. But you'll be paying for what it cost me to bring Francis down here. For nothing."

"Well, that's settled, then." Phil Dodd beamed at us. "Francis, from now on, I'm you."

***

I was at the wheel of the rental car for the drive to the Condado district. Exiting the expressway, I ramped down to the hazards of the city streets. There, the flow of cars slowed to a crawl. Which was a good thing. Because I quickly discovered that even the most basic traffic laws were flouted with impunity. A stop sign was merely a suggestion, the use of a turn signal a display of weakness. Red lights were obeyed eventually, but only when the cross traffic on green encroached insistently enough. Seemingly, no violation was deemed worthy of a horn honk, much less a traffic ticket. Driving faster than ten miles an hour would be insane.

Nighttime added to the tension of navigating the perilous streets, but guided by the map app on Alicia's smart phone, we, at last, found the Caserio Inn. The 1940s era Bed and Breakfast (the result of Alicia's online search for a modestly priced hotel with an additional discount for the hurricane season) was a three-story dwarf wedged between two giant steel and glass towers. I was unimpressed, but Alicia pronounced it "quaint," and that settled it.

Dodd helped me unload the luggage, while Alicia and Ellen went in to the front desk. Then Dodd was on his phone again. This time I caught his end of it.

"Yeah, the little buggers stuck with us right to the hotel...Both Middle Easterners, not locals. Got a good look this time...No, keeping their distance. For now, just eyeballing...Well, if needs be, I'll tidy up the playing field. But I'd prefer to wait till after I've been up to the monastery. Don't want to spook the Sheik...Yeah, it's a go. I had to wave the flag a little. But as it stands now, I'm her new date for the prom...Okay. I'm going to tuck them in and call it a night."

After I returned from squeezing our rented economy car into a tight spot on the left side of the broad one-way street, Dodd helped me haul the luggage up the three steps to the guest lounge and then on up a full flight of stairs to the second floor rooms. I separated my satchel from the women's several suitcases, and after Dodd and Alicia agreed on a launch time in the morning, we left the women to their unpacking.

As Dodd and I entered the room next door, I caught a whiff of old-building smell that air freshener sprays never seem to completely mask.

"For two people who, according to the airline, are traveling as Mr. and Mrs. Elton," Dodd observed, "the hotel accommodations seem a little strange."

"Yeah, about that." I tossed my satchel on the nearest bed. "The Bishop also assumes Alicia and I are still married. So, you'll have to stretch your acting abilities a little further tomorrow."

"Well, well. You know, I *thought* there was a little secret going on."

"We're just letting them think what they want."

"No problem. You bring along anything to drink?"

"No."

"Then I've got things to do." Dodd gave me a firm handshake and left me alone in my hotel room.

I sat on one of the two double beds and brought out the prepaid flip phone that I'd bought from a vending machine at O'Hare, before we flew out. From a small spiral-bound notebook, I keyed in names and numbers I'd need during our stay. Dodd hadn't given me a contact number, but that wasn't surprising. Running a parallel course, but always a little apart from the group, was Dodd's style. In any case, this was a government operation now. I'd been relegated to watching from the sidelines.

***

The next morning at the prearranged time, Phil Dodd pulled to the curb in front of the Caserio Inn. Ellen and I waited with Alicia on the sidewalk, there to see her off, trying not to show any anticipation of our planned day at the beach.

Alicia's unconcealed look of annoyance was perhaps the result of having had too much time to think about what she'd agreed to. She wore no makeup and had again restrained her lush hair with the black ribbon. There was a military cut to her tan shirt and brown trousers. I supposed this was meant to downplay her feminine attributes, while up at the monastery – as if something shy of a nun's habit would have achieved that.

"We'll take your car, Alicia," Dodd said. "I've already had to deal with some interest we've attracted, so we have to begin our matrimonial debut the moment we cast off."

"I have the keys," I said.

As we exchanged car keys, Dodd mused, "I think I'll like being you, Francis. You know, takes some of the pressure off."

"You're not going to act like this in front of the Bishop, are you?" Alicia warned.

"Don't you worry your pretty little head. I know exactly how to play the role of the faithful husband. You won't even know I'm alive."

"Francis, this is all your doing."

Dodd and Alicia walked off side-by-side in an uneasy truce, toward where I'd parked the night before. It was, of course, senseless to hope that Dodd would wait in the car when Alicia went in to talk to the Bishop.

***

Provisioned with hotel bath towels and dressed for the beach, Ellen and I started off in flip-flops for the wide sandy shoreline a block behind our hotel. Ellen demurely wore a white cotton blouse over her bikini, and I was togged out in swimming trunks and a t-shirt, along with a ball cap to shade my eyes from the morning sun. Just as we reached the end of a narrow side street, where the concrete gave way to sand, my phone erupted in a shallow version of music.

"A slight change in plans." It was Alicia's voice. "I'm going to be riding up to the monastery with Monsignor Cabrera, so we can talk over my assignment. Dodd – I mean, my other Francis – is going to follow us in the rental car. Monsignor Cabrera can't stay, but he said it would be better if he personally introduces me to the Abbot. I get the impression that the Abbot is kind of old and not altogether with it."

"Who's Monsignor Cabrera? Is he the Bishop?"

"No. He's on the staff of the Archbishop. I'd been hired by one of the Auxiliary Bishops. I know. I got confused too. But Monsignor Cabrera was assigned to my project, so I was handed off to him. But listen, the reason I called is that we could all meet for lunch. The only one at the monastery who's allowed to dine with guests is the Abbot. And Monsignor Cabrera says the Abbot is in really poor health and lately hasn't really been up to the lunch-with-the-guests thing."

"So we're lunching with a priest?"

"The Monsignor will be gone before lunchtime, but he suggested that my husband and I go back down the mountain to Luquillo for lunch. He gave me the name of a good restaurant. And he said there was a really nice beach there, too. So, I thought, since you two were going to a beach today anyway, you and Ellen could drive out to Luquillo Beach, and later we'll all rendezvous for lunch at the restaurant. I'll phone you with directions to the restaurant from the beach as soon as I get them."

"Sounds like a lot of fuss just for lunch, but…"

"Okay, I forgot to spray my allergy medicine up my nose this morning. And apparently, we have to hike up a path through the rain forest to get to the monastery. So, mold is pretty much a given. I'm just hoping it won't be too bad. Tell Ellen the nasal spray is in my suitcase. She knows what it looks like."

"All right, Luquillo Beach, nasal spray, and lunch. Got it."

I told Ellen about the revised plan, and we retraced our steps back to the hotel to change out of beachwear and into street clothes for the journey – and also, to sweet talk the desk clerk out of a road map of the island.

***

The water at Luquillo Beach was so warm and calm that it was hard to believe it was the Atlantic Ocean, and not a giant heated swimming pool. What little wave action there was gently lapped at the sand, as through being careful not to disturb anything. Ellen and I floated lazily, staring up at light blue infinity, about halfway out to a sweeping arc of discretely spaced wood pilings that poked out of the water, delineating the perimeter of the swimming area and supporting a single resting pelican each. The mountains of El Yunque Rain Forest, where the monastery was located, loomed in misty heights above the tall palm trees that somehow managed to thrive in the dry sand. The beach curved inward along the shore of a large bay that went on seemingly forever in either direction.

After a languid swim back to shore, I planted myself on a towel, toes plunged into the sand, just within the shade of the palm trees. I took the occasional swallow of a rum and coke, purchased at a refreshment stand up the beach. Five feet in front of me, Ellen sat in full sun on her towel and applied lotion to her stomach. Her drink, resting on the hot sand next to her, was mostly gone. And the tight curls of her rigorously styled hair were now mostly relaxed – rollers and setting spray being no match for the tranquil warm waters of a Puerto Rican bay.

"I think I'll come out here every day." Ellen now lay, facing the sky. "It's so deserted, not like the beach back by the hotel. This is just what I had in mind when I told Alicia I'd come down here with her and kick back a little."

"It sounded like you both deserve some downtime."

"The past couple of months with Mom were a load. I mean Alicia and I traded off, but then I still had to rush home to take care of Roger and the boys. So now, it's time to have a little adventure, a little fun. You know, before time runs out. It's my chance to be more like Alicia, more of a free spirit. On this gorgeous deserted beach on this gorgeous day, she'd be laying out stark naked, soaking up the sun."

"I doubt she'd be out in direct sun," I said. "Her skin is her pride and joy."

But Ellen was almost right about the beach being deserted. It was a weekday morning during hurricane season, and we shared the beach with only a few other people. And they were indistinct figures, far down the long curve of sand.

Ellen sat up, finished the last of her solar-heated rum and coke, and repositioned herself onto her stomach. "Could you slather some lotion on my back?"

I moved out into the sun and set my drink on the sand next to Ellen's towel.

"Undo my strings, so I don't get lines."

I untied the still-damp strings on the upper half of Ellen's bikini and applied the coconut-scented lotion. Smaller and slimmer than Alicia, Ellen's skin was tight, her backbone well defined. I'd spent the previous month in Spain, where at the beach the upper half of a woman's bathing suit was optional, so by comparison, a couple of untied strings on a woman's bare back was not especially provocative. But then again, in Spain, for me anyway, it was all look and no touch.

I finished smoothing on the lotion and wiped the excess off my hands on a corner of her towel, before downing the rest of my drink. It was now warm and sugary, no longer refreshing. I felt a headache coming on. Squinting with the pain, I pressed the heel of my hand to my forehead.

"You okay?" Ellen asked.

"Too much sun and too much rum. You don't have any aspirin in your bag, do you?"

"No. But aspirin's too slow, anyhow. Get back into the shade and sit with your legs crossed Indian-style. I'll show you a trick."

I retreated to the cooler sand, beneath the palm trees. Ellen followed, holding the top half of her bathing suit in place with one arm pressed across her chest.

I sat crossed legged on my towel, while Ellen got into position behind me. Her knees appeared on either side of my hips, and the aroma of coconut from her suntan lotion washed over me. Ellen placed one hand on the back of my head and other on my forehead. She held my head tight.

"Now lean back against me and relax," Ellen said. "Think of your happy place."

"Actually, this beach *was* my happy place, right up until I got the headache."

"Shush. Just relax and stop fighting me. You're all tense, just like Roger. This is what I do when he gets a headache from looking at his insurance papers too long."

As I leaned back, I felt the warmth of Ellen's breasts on my back and quickly realized that she couldn't have both hands pressing on my head and hold up her bikini top too.

"This has to be the best headache treatment in the universe," I said. "Even my back feels good. I envy Roger."

"Roger hasn't had the bare breast part yet. This is the start of my new freedom. I'm trying it out on you, because that's what Alicia does. It's easy for her to be the flower child. You're there to protect her. But today she's up at a monastery, being all Miss Prim-and-Proper, not taking any risks, playing it safe. So, I'm borrowing you for the day, while I loosen up a little." Ellen released the pressure. "How's that head?"

It took a moment to realize it. "My headache's gone."

"I thought it would be."

"That's amazing. Where did you learn to do that?"

"My mother would do it for Alicia and me when we were little girls. It always worked. Then when she was getting near the end and the pain meds weren't working anymore, Alicia and I took turns holding her head. I don't know how much it helped in that situation, but she seemed to like it."

"That had to be rough."

"Actually, Alicia has taken it a lot harder than me. She just won't let on. She keeps it all suppressed."

The smart phone in Ellen's blouse pocket began to chime. Ellen scampered the short distance out to her towel, dropped to her knees with her back to me, and brought the phone up to her ear.

"Hello…Alicia, slow down." Ellen began repeatedly switching hands to keep the phone at her ear, while she struggled back into her blouse. "You mean the guy with the tennis shoes, *that* Arab?"

Ellen twisted around to look at me, with concern on her face. I couldn't imagine what this was about.

"Well, what reason did the police give to keep you there?"

What the hell? This didn't sound like Alicia was 'playing it safe.'

Ellen listened for a long time. Too long for it to be anything minor.

"We're at Luquillo Beach, Francis and me…Yes, yes, I've got your nasal spray. You sound all stuffed up. How bad is…It'll be all right, we'll bring it to you. We're leaving right now. I already have my top back on." Ellen's hand quickly rose to her mouth. "No, no.

We went swimming, and then Francis had a headache. I'll tell you about it later."

There it was, the number one reason not to make a move on your ex-wife's sister. Those six little words: I'll tell you about it later.

Ellen got to her feet, slid her phone back into her shirt pocket, and returned to the shade, where I was now also on my feet.

"You know that Arab guy with the white tennis shoes that you're friend Dodd talked about? He was up at the monastery. And he died. The police are there, and maybe somebody killed him. They won't let anyone leave. Alicia said they've been talking to Dodd for over an hour. And she snuck her phone out of her purse, and she called me when they weren't watching her. They wouldn't let her call out, otherwise. She said her head is about to explode, and she's all tears and snot. She needs her allergy spray. So, we have to go up there."

Ellen's words tumbled out so quickly that I had to struggle to arrange them in my head. Alicia's reaction to mold wasn't anything new, but a dead Arab certainly was.

"Did Alicia say why the police were questioning Dodd? Do they think he killed the Arab?"

"Alicia told the police everything about Dodd. That he was with Naval Intelligence, or whatever, and he was after the Arab with the tennis shoes. And that Dodd made it like her obligation to American freedom that she let him substitute himself for you, so he could get into the monastery. She said she wasn't going to lie to the police and get herself into trouble, just to cover for your old lieutenant."

"So, now the police are grilling Dodd, but not letting her go either," I said. "That was some fine bargain, she made."

"You think Alicia's in trouble?"

"If Dodd killed the Arab, yes."

Chapter 2

Following a hasty outdoor rinse-off and a quick change back into street clothes inside the cement block bathhouse, Ellen and I abandoned the ocean and struck out for the mountains.

Because the sign for El Yunque National Park was partially obscured by the ever-encroaching greenery, I almost missed my turn, off of Highway 3. After a short bridge over a deep drainage ditch, the road took a jog through an unkempt village, before starting to gain altitude. At the park's Welcome Center, a clerk in the gift shop marked a general location for the monastery on a handout road map of the park, while pointedly informing us that the secluded monastery was not considered a normal destination for tourists.

Undeterred, we drove on, climbing up through serpentine curves within the dense tropical forest. Breaks in the towering vegetation, where the asphalt road skirted a drop-off, allowed occasional spectacular views of the Caribbean Sea. At times, a ramshackle souvenir store or a doubtful-looking restaurant, roofed with mismatched scraps of tin, would appear just beyond a shallow dirt parking area off the side of the road – each one looking as slipshod and out-of-place as a gypsy camp.

Much higher up the mountain, we came upon a large group of cars, several of them police vehicles, parked on a sparsely graveled area just off the other side of the road. And although the parking area fronted no visible roadside attraction, curiously, it hosted the activity level of a county fair.

Slowing the rental car to a crawl, I studied the busy scene. A cameraman shouldered his equipment from out of the rear of a white van that featured a transmitter dish on its roof and proclaimed WAPA-TV and NOTICENTRO in bold colors along its side. A ravishing, on-the-spot reporter pivoted the van's passenger-side mirror toward her flawless face and touched up her lipstick in its reflection. Beyond the TV news van, several uniformed policemen blocked all access to a packed dirt-and-gravel pathway, cut diagonally into the mountainside and leading upward through the trees and undergrowth. In close proximity to the police presence, a waiting ambulance was backed into position. Standing apart from the uniformed police, two men, wearing light windbreakers, kept their pale heads in the shade and maintained a steady vigilance through mirrored sunglasses. About a dozen assorted onlookers milled about the rest of the parking area, snapping pictures with phones and cameras, while waiting for something to happen.

I nosed the little rental car into a narrow open spot within the array of parked vehicles and consulted the park's road map. The gift shop clerk's X seemed to generally coincide with where I figured we were.

"What's Alicia gotten herself into?" Ellen asked, as we left the car and blended in.

The beautiful newscaster had now staged herself, so that, in the background, the ambulance and the knot of policemen were each just over their own teasing bare shoulder for the camera shot. Her rapid-fire Spanish was a little too fast for me to pick up everything, but the gist of her report was that an Arab businessman from France had unexpectedly died, while up at the monastery, and that the police were investigating, but would give no further comment.

The newscaster, still reporting, and her cameraman, still recording, then worked their way nearer to the policemen at the base of the path leading up to the monastery. I pressed my hand on Ellen's back, and we followed closely behind the cameraman. My hope was that the police would assume we were part of the TV crew. But my plan fizzled, when the uniformed officers refused to let even the actual newspersons pass.

While the beautiful newscaster scored a few dramatic sound bites of policemen staunchly denying her access, I drew Ellen back a few paces and quietly said, "It doesn't look like they're letting anyone through at all."

"Tell them that we have to get Alicia's medication to her. That it's a medical emergency. Here." Ellen pulled a plastic bag out of her purse, reached into it, and withdrew a small, plastic, squeeze bottle with a pharmacist's label glued to its side. "Show them the nasal spray. Tell them that Alicia had no idea what your crazy friend was going to do."

I knew confronting the police with a demand would be futile. And I didn't think much of the odds that the medication would actually get to Alicia, if I were to hand it off to the officers to relay up to her.

"The policemen will just follow their orders," I said. "They won't listen about Alicia's allergies." I gently tugged Ellen out of earshot of the crowd. "Let's drift on up the road a little on foot. Maybe we can find a place where we can go up through the trees, do an end-around, and pick up the path a little higher up the mountain."

We strolled together in the direction of the rental car, as though we'd lost interest and were leaving. Instead, we walked on past the car and continued up the road on foot.

The blacktopped road snaked relentlessly upward. Cars coming down from the summit would appear unexpectedly. So, we walked single file, ready to step quickly off the asphalt and onto the narrow band of gravel and weeds that separated the road from the wall of damp vegetation. When we were well out of sight of the policemen, I started scanning for a way up through the steep and dense tropical forest. At first, nothing looked promising, but about a quarter of a mile up the road, we came upon a shallow scenic pull-off where a tall, narrow cascade of water splashed onto some large rocks, before disappearing into a culvert that ran beneath the road and reappearing out the other side.

"This looks doable," I said, "but it'll take a lot of heart."

Ellen lifted the long strap of her purse off her shoulder and transferred it over her head to hang more securely across her body. Tilting a defiant chin up to the rain forest, she said, "Let's get up there."

I picked out what looked like a feasible line of attack and went first.

The climb was tough from the start. I needed to use both hands and feet to propel myself up through the robust and slick-leafed plant life that crowded the rocky edge of the waterfall. The damp air was heavy with the smell of working compost. Ellen struggled along behind me, complaining but keeping up.

Above and beyond the top of the little waterfall, the pitch of the mountain wasn't quite as steep, and the undergrowth, spindly and starved for sunlight beneath the high canopy, put up much less resistance to our progress. I used the stream that fed the waterfall as a reference to keep from wandering too far afield. As we persisted in our upward slog, our sweat-soaked shirts clung to our bodies, and relief from the heat and humidity came only in the short sporadic bursts of cool rain. With her initial determination spent, Ellen held onto the back of my belt. Towing her sapped a lot of my own stamina, but I was afraid that if I stopped to rest, I wouldn't be able to convince myself to start again.

After about ten minutes, I figured that, since we hadn't come upon the pathway up to the monastery yet, it probably rose by means of switchbacks, zigzagging its way up the mountain. I now angled to the left, while still trudging ever upward. Soon, I crested a rise, but halted when I heard voices from below and in front of us.

Ellen must have heard them too, because she drew up alongside me. Together we peered down through the undergrowth, attempting to locate the source of the weary Spanish beneath the chirping of tropical birds.

Initially, I saw only fleeting bits of white descending through the screen of leaves and branches, about thirty feet below our position. Then through a break in the foliage, two paramedics, struggling to guide a small-wheeled gurney down the dirt and gravel pathway, briefly passed in full view. Puzzlingly, the light blue sheet, draped over the gurney, lay flat on its surface. No covered rotund form lay beneath it; no white tennis shoes poked out one end.

After the EMTs moved out of our view, Ellen asked in subdued volume, "Why was that gurney empty? Weren't they supposed to bring the dead guy down?"

"I don't understand it, either," I also kept my voice low. "I'm sure I heard the TV reporter say the Arab businessman was dead."

Ellen undid the clasp on her purse and dug a hand in. "I'm going to call Alicia."

"She had to sneak that call out to you," I said. "If she forgot to put her phone on vibrate and the police hear the ring tone, they might confiscate her phone. And she'll lose her only way to contact us."

Ellen's eyes narrowed for a moment, but then, without waiting for me to forge the way, she abruptly started down the steep slope toward the pathway below. Immediately, Ellen's heel placements became sliding grooves in the damp soil and her flailing grasps at the spindly branches became increasingly more desperate, as she descended through the steeply pitched undergrowth – perhaps, more rapidly than she may have wished.

I allowed some extra space to form between us, to minimize the risk of crashing down on top of her, and then followed, doing a lot of sliding and grasping of my own.

***

The humidity level remained oppressive, and the smell of decay pervasive. But compared to groping up through the hot, wet tangle of the rainforest's lower strata, ascending the mountain on the modestly graveled pathway was an airy walk through a leafy cathedral.

We actually were climbing up a wide and well-trodden, middle depression in the pathway's roughly three-foot width. Two narrower and shallower ruts, one on each side, ran along at the pathway's edges, where the rain forest seemed anxious to inch in and reclaim its rightful territory.

I hadn't noticed how dark it was under the forest canopy, until we rounded the last switchback and daylight beamed down through the trees from a wide opening at the pathway's upper end. As we neared the opening, the corner of a large white building came into view. It stood on a portion of cleared mountain ridge and was set against a blue sky.

"We should get off the path now," I said. "I don't want to run into any police."

"If we don't go through the front door, how are we going to get in?"

"I just want a sneak peek at what we're walking into, first."

Once again we were off the path and stumbling up through the undergrowth in a steep climb. But this time it was only for half a minute.

We halted just within the edge of the rain forest, alongside of which ran a continuation of the three-parallel-grooved pathway. On the other side of the pathway and taking up most of the rest of the cleared area on the mountain's broad shoulder was a long, densely-planted, vegetable garden, surrounded by an unpainted picket fence.

To our right stood the large, two-storied structure, the corner of which I'd glimpsed, just before we left the pathway. Undoubtedly, this was the main monastery building. Its exposed post-and-beam timbers framed the cracked and failing, white stucco facing, but, at least, the tall, narrow windows looked intact.

I caught a whiff of cigarette smoke floating past and cautiously inched my head further out, seeking its origin. Beneath a covered entryway at the front of the main building, which faced the pathway's broad left turn at the top of the climb, two uniformed police officers smoked, as they languidly guarded the front door. I absolutely did not want to give them something to do.

Off to our left, several outbuildings were nestled on the opposite end of the long garden. My attention was drawn to the largest of the tin-roofed buildings. It had a stone chimney, out of which dark smoke floated up, drifted sideways, and was absorbed by the treetops.

"Let's go talk to the folks in that big shed," I whispered.

"As long as it's not uphill," Ellen whispered back.

Now, as old hands at picking our way through the foliage, we maneuvered across the side of the slope keeping well back from the clearing. This brought us around to the far side of the outbuildings, where, shielded by the height of the garden's trellised plants, we were out of the police officers' view.

As we passed along the side of the big shed, I looked through each of its two un-shuttered and unglazed windows in turn and could see all the way through to the greenery just outside the windows on the opposite wall.

I did not, however, manage to catch a glimpse of anyone within the structure.

Ellen and I rounded the corner of the big shed and stopped just outside the its closed front door. The three-grooved pathway swung around the end of the fenced garden and terminated at the hard-trampled area beneath our feet. The big shed's front door was also the final destination of a well-worn footpath that cut straight through the center of the extensive garden and looked as though it originated at the rear of the main monastery building – which strongly suggested a back door. And from what I could see, there appeared to be no policeman posted there.

I had just made up my mind to skip talking to whoever might be inside the big shed and simply proceed on up to the unguarded rear entrance, when the shed's weathered door creaked inward.

A tall, robust man in a heavily stained, brown robe now filled the doorframe and demanded of us, in Spanish, "Who are you?"

Startled, I had to find my voice, before responding in Spanish to what I assumed was the king-sized version of a monk, "I am Francis Elton, and this lady is Ellen Van Kemp. We are bringing some urgently needed medicine to a woman who is working at the monastery today. The woman who needs the medicine is the sister of Mrs. Van Kemp."

"Am I to believe that you did not see the monastery's front door, when you arrived at the top of the cart path?"

"We avoided the policemen at the front door, because they may not understand how urgent the need for the medicine is, and—"

"Give it to me." The big monk held out a beefy hand.

"Give him Alicia's medicine," I relayed to Ellen in English.

"Why should I?" Ellen brought her purse up tight to her chest and put a protective forearm in front of it.

"Because he asked for it, and he looks like he could easily take it from us without asking."

With evident misgiving, Ellen opened her purse, withdrew the white plastic bag, and held it out. The big monk took the bag and looked inside. He pulled out the squeeze bottle of nasal spray, held it up in front of his eyes, and examined the pharmacist's label on one side and the drug manufacturer's printing on the other. Apparently satisfied, he dropped the nasal spray bottle back into the bag and returned it to Ellen.

"I am Brother Hugo," the big monk now spoke in surprisingly unaccented English. "Tell me why the need for this medicine is greater than the risk you undertook to bring it up here."

Ellen's response came forth in a flood. "Alicia was already blocked up when she phoned me. And if it becomes a really bad episode, she'll start to have trouble breathing. It's her allergies. Something around here must have triggered it." Ellen took a sweeping look around her. "Well, everything, really."

Brother Hugo silently studied us from his superior height. He studied long enough for me to worry that he was deciding whether, or not, to take Ellen and me, each by the arm, directly up to the front door of the main building and into police custody. But, to my relief, the big monk, finally, said, "Come inside."

***

Despite the open windows, the odor of decomposing pineapple, at once both pungent and fragrant, was definitely present at nose level, as we entered the big shed. Uncovered crates of wine bottles – some open and empty, others stopped with corks and full – surrounded a cramped central work area. Crowded on a stained and scarred worktable were numerous lidded, plastic pails and glass jugs, all fitted with air-locks. Within the glass jugs, the liquids ranged from dark amber to pale yellow. Evidently, the monks shunned retail outlets as a source for their table wine.

The smoke we'd seen wafting from the chimney came from a wide-mouthed stone fireplace at the far end of the shed. At first, I was amazed to see a wood fire burning beneath a metal beer keg. But then I saw the copper tube poking out of the top of the keg and bending downward, next came the cooling coils, and finally the delivery point of the copper tube, from which successive drops of clear liquid fell into a waiting pewter pitcher.

I knew a still for producing homemade liquor when I saw one – though, perhaps, if I were not so acquainted with the concept, I would have completed my degree in Engineering on the first try.

Working nearby the still, was the shed's only other occupant: a short and youthful-looking monk, wearing a toil-worn robe that looked a couple of sizes too big for his slight frame.

Brother Hugo extended one of his big hands in the direction of the little monk. "This is Brother Emilio. Our task here is to make wine for our table and rum for barter with the local merchants."

Brother Emilio briefly smiled at us and then returned his concentration to pouring a measure of thick black liquid into a glazed vat. I suspected that he'd merely responded to his name and didn't understand the English his fellow monk had just spoken.

Brother Hugo eased himself onto a tall stool. "That is about us. Now, about you." The big monk settled his focus on Ellen. "I believe the part about bringing medicine to your sister. I know there is a woman at the monastery today – the art expert who is to appraise the paintings in the dining hall. I see her family in your face." Brother Hugo shifted his attention to me. "But an honest man does not avoid the police."

I had to delay my response, while I selected a place to start. Brother Hugo patiently waited, closely watching me.

"We avoided the police down at the base of the, ah, cart path, as you call it, because they were not letting anyone up here," I began. "And I couldn't be certain, if I gave the medicine to the policemen to pass on to Alicia, that she'd actually get it. So, our only option was to make the climb up through the rain forest. And after all that effort, we didn't want to just be escorted right back down the mountain again by the policemen at the front door and be right back where we started."

I paused for a breath and also to gauge the big monk's reaction, so far. But his facial expression was about as animated as the Sphinx.

I went on, "Now, I fully understand that an Arab businessman has unexpectedly died at your monastery this morning and that the police don't want anyone else coming up here, until they're finished. Nevertheless, we absolutely do need to get the nasal spray to Alicia before her respiratory situation becomes critical. I promise we'll leave immediately afterwards."

Brother Hugo remained on his stool, keeping his eyes on us, as he addressed his diminutive fellow monk in Spanish. "What do you think, Brother Emilio? These people hide from the police, and yet they bring much needed medicine to the woman from the Art Institute. This woman here says that she is her sister. What do you think, do we help them?"

"Surely, we must," Brother Emilio responded in pleasantly light Spanish without hesitation. "It would be a simple matter for me to take the medicine to the woman from the Art Institute."

"No," Brother Hugo said. "We do not know what fluid the medicine bottle actually contains. We cannot simply assume that it is the medicine stated on the label. That is why the police would not have delivered it to her. And that is also why you, or I, should not."

"Then I will lead this woman to her sister," Brother Emilio said. "Does either sister speak Spanish?"

I spoke up in Spanish. "No, but I will accompany you and translate for the women."

I saw Brother Hugo run an eye over Ellen's wet, clinging blouse and shorts, before saying to Brother Emilio in Spanish, "We have our good robes here. Wearing them, these two will pass as monks." Brother Hugo now locked eyes with Brother Emilio. "There is no need for anyone to bother the policemen. They are busy."

Brother Hugo then turned back to us and spoke to Ellen in English, "Brother Emilio has decided to help you. It is his kind nature. You will need to wear a robe."

Brother Hugo moved across the interior of the shed, took the two robes from their pegs, and brought them over to us. The one that was about the size of a pup tent, he handed to me.

It now dawned on me that these monks were wearing their work robes, and the robes on the pegs were what they wore when they weren't brewing things up in the shed. That seemed practical. I couldn't imagine there being laundry facilities on this remote shoulder of the mountain.

"Mrs. Van Kemp, you are about the same size as Brother Emilio. You will wear his robe." The big monk handed the smaller robe to Ellen. "Raise the cowls over your heads, when you leave this shed, and keep them there, until you return."

"Francis, give me a hand with this," Ellen said.

I flared out the bottom of the smaller robe and brought it over Ellen's head.

When her hands didn't appear out of the sleeves, I said, "You didn't get your arms through."

"Just a minute. I have a little adjustment to make."

There was a lot of movement under the robe, and when Ellen's hands at last emerged from her sleeves, one of them held a white bra.

"Here." Ellen stepped in close to me and jammed her bra into my front pants' pocket. "There shouldn't be anything too perky-looking in a monk's robe."

***

With the cowls of our robes shrouding our heads, Brother Emilio, Ellen, and I were ready to be three monks making our way up to the main building.

Brother Hugo again filled the open doorway of the shed, as we formed up outside. In Spanish, he said, "Brother Emilio, the police have instructed the art expert to remain in the guest quarters. Take these people there, but do not remain. I need your assistance back here."

"I will return quickly."

Ellen and I thanked the big monk and followed Brother Emilio single file through the gate and up the narrow garden path. After passing through the extensive vegetable garden, the three of us entered the rear of the main building by way of a sun-bleached door. Brother Emilio led us along a dark hallway and then into the light of an open inner patio area at the building's center, before plunging us into the gloom of another long hallway, which, I saw to my alarm, led directly to the front door.

However, at the hallway's midpoint, Brother Emilio turned and led us up an impressive staircase, broad enough for two people to pass. Along a hallway on the second floor, Brother Emilio stopped at the first door on the left. Like a doctor entering an examination room, the little monk lightly knocked and then, without pause, opened the door and entered.

We stepped into an austere room, furnished only with two single, bare-mattress beds, a table, and four chairs. Alicia was perched on a deep window ledge, hugging her knees and keeping watch through the divided panes.

Ellen broke ranks and rushed forward, her cowl falling back. Alicia slid off the window ledge, and with mutual squeals of delight, the sisters fell into an embrace. With her chin resting on Ellen's shoulder, Alicia's puffy, watery-cast eyes winced through the tight hug.

When I turned to thank Brother Emilio, he had already vanished. I closed the door, as soundlessly as I could. We were, after all, still sneaking around, and the reunion had caused enough commotion already.

Alicia took the nasal spray from Ellen's hand, pecked a kiss on her sister's cheek, and rushed through a door off to one side. It embarrassed Alicia to repeatedly clear her nose in front of anyone, prior to spraying the medicine up each nostril.

Ellen smiled at me. "Thanks, Francis. I couldn't have done this alone."

While I was trying to think of something gallant to say in response, the door, that I had just moments before closed, opened. Before I could turn to look, I was roughly shoved deeper into the room, toward Ellen, and then three men had us corralled in the center of the guest quarters. A hand from behind me roughly jerked back the cowl from my head.

With weary eyes regarding Ellen and me through wire rim glasses, the man who stood directly in front of us announced, in English, "I am Detective Sergeant Alvarez of the Puerto Rico Police. Keep your hands where I can see them."

Chapter 3

Only the tallest of the three policemen was in uniform. Of the two in plainclothes, Detective Sergeant Alvarez was the fat and balding one. His badge, displayed face out from its folder, sagged the pocket of the straight hemmed, un-tucked shirt that covered the conspicuous bulge at his hip.

"Where is Mrs. Elton?" the Detective Sergeant demanded.

As if in response, there was the sound of a nose being repeatedly blown, interspersed with coughing.

We all looked toward the door through which Alicia had gone.

Detective Sergeant Alvarez gave a slight head nod to the uniformed officer. The officer stepped over to the door, gave it three quick raps, and called, "Señora!"

"*¡Ocupado!*" Alicia shouted through the door with one of her few Spanish words. Strangely, her congestion helped with the pronunciation. In English she added, "You're a man. Use the back yard."

"Señora, come out, please," the uniformed officer requested in passable English.

"Hey!" Alicia's raised voice again pierced through the door. "Give me a minute to wash up, will you? I'm not as pretty with snot on my face."

The sound of water splashing sporadically in a basin went on for half a minute. It belatedly occurred to me that Alicia was in a bathroom, and of course, that was why the uniformed officer did not just open the door.

But then I wondered, this centuries-old place stuck way up on a mountain has indoor plumbing?

His hand now grasping the doorknob, the uniformed officer looked again to the Detective Sergeant. Alvarez waved him off. The officer's hand dropped away, and he stood back.

Alvarez moved his attention onto Ellen. "Dear lady, who are you and what are you doing here."

Visibly taken unaware, Ellen managed to say, "I'm Ellen Van Kemp. Alicia's sister."

"And?"

"And I came here to bring Alicia some medicine," Ellen's voice rose in strength. "Some nasal spray. She has allergies. She said it was the rain forest, but this old building is pretty musty smelling too."

"Nasal spray," Alvarez said. "A need that could easily have been fulfilled by one of my officers."

"It's prescription," Ellen now almost scolded.

Alvarez let this drop and returned to his initial concern. "You will show me some identification."

"My purse is under this robe."

"You are fully clothed under the robe?"

"A blouse and shorts."

"Then simply remove the robe."

As Ellen struggled to pull the monk's robe up over her head, Alicia came out of the bathroom. "What the hell's going on?"

"Please stand there quietly, Mrs. Elton," Alvarez said. He turned to me. "And you, sir. What is your name? And why do I find you standing here?"

"I'm Francis Elton. Alicia's former husband. I escorted Mrs. Van Kemp up here to deliver Alicia's—"

"Stop. Did you say that your name is Francis Elton?" Alvarez raised his eyebrows above the rims of his glasses.

Alicia broke in, "Francis, I—"

"Mrs. Elton, you were instructed to remain quiet." Alvarez returned to me. "Mr. Elton, you will also show me some identification. And it would be better if you also removed your disguise. I assume this will not startle the ladies."

"I'd be more than happy to get out of this hot-assed thing."

I began to wrestle my way out of Brother Hugo's voluminous robe. While blinded for the time it took for the coarse material to clear my head, I felt something leave my front pants' pocket. When my vision was restored, I saw Ellen's white bra at my feet.

I looked up to find everyone else's attention intently focused on the lifeless bra.

"Oh, thanks for bringing that too, Francis." Alicia swiftly moved in and scooped up the undergarment from the floor. All policemen's eyes were now fixed on Alicia. "What? You guys never sweat?"

Wishing to quickly move past the errant bra event, I said to Alicia, "You sound much better. The nasal spray must be working."

"Thanks entirely to you and Ellen. The guardians of public safety here just tossed me into this stifling room and forgot about me."

Ignoring Alicia's swipe at him, Alvarez directed the other detective in Spanish, "Montero, see what other surprises you can find in this man's pockets."

Obligingly, I quickly emptied my pockets onto the table and stood still to let Detective Montero pat me down. Meanwhile, Alvarez ordered the uniformed officer to go un-cuff the suspect and bring him to the guest quarters.

By the time the officer brought Phil Dodd into what was already a crowded room, Alvarez had dumped Ellen's purse out on the table, next to my stuff, and was thoughtfully perusing both her driver's license and mine.

The uniformed officer had halted Dodd at a respectful two pace distance from Alvarez and continued to maintain a grip on Dodd's upper arm. While Alvarez was engaged with his rather prolonged study of the licenses, Dodd made a business of massaging his right wrist and flexing the fingers below it. But above this activity, Dodd's eyes darted from face to face – lingering, it seemed, somewhat longer on mine.

Evidently now satisfied with the amount of time he'd made Dodd stand and wait, Alvarez held the driver's licenses on display and spoke in English. "It appears that I have found the real Francis Elton, the man whose identity you, sir, for an extended period of time, confused with your own."

"As I explained to you," Dodd said, "Mr. Elton was unable to accompany Mrs. Elton when she was scheduled to attend to her work up here at the monastery. I simply took his place. It was easier just to let the priests and monks think I was him. No big deal."

Alvarez hardened his look toward Dodd. "And when an Officer of the Law asks you for your name, is that also an occasion where is it easier to say that you are someone else?"

"At the time, I chose not to complicate things."

"The sudden death of Jaspar Rahim *complicated* things," Alvarez said. "Unlike you, Mrs. Elton wisely chose to help us *un*-complicate things by telling us your real name."

Alvarez paused to hand the two driver's licenses to the other detective, who dutifully began writing the information in his notebook.

"However, during the course of confirming your identity, I have produced a further complexity. My inquiry triggered an undesired reaction from the Naval Criminal Investigative Service. There are now Special Agents from the NCIS at the bottom of the cart path. They insist that they be allowed to speak to Special Agent Philip Dodd. Naturally, I am reluctant to comply with their request, until Special Agent Philip Dodd has answered all of my questions to my full satisfaction."

"You are holding me prisoner here," Dodd said. "Against my will. That's unlawful restraint, or something."

"I do not believe we are in the realm of habeas corpus, just yet." The Detective Sergeant seemed pleased to point out. "And should I allow your fellow NCIS agents to come up here and interview you, I run the risk that a certain amount of, shall we say, coaching may occur. And even you – as a law enforcement officer, of a sort – should be able to comprehend why I cannot permit even the briefest rehearsal, when it is spontaneity of response that I require."

"Frankly," Dodd said, "I did expect you to extend at least a modicum of professional courtesy."

"Be happy that you are not still handcuffed to the prayer bench," Alvarez said. "This is a Puerto Rico Police investigation, and I am in charge of it. Therefore, until I am satisfied that you were not directly involved in the death of Jaspar Rahim, your fellow NCIS agents will remain down at the bottom of the cart path, and you will remain up here with me."

"The Special Agent in Charge at the Southeast Field Office will strenuously demand—"

"Yes, of course. Your superiors will strenuously demand of my superiors, in the clash of wills that they so perversely enjoy. But in the meantime, we will steal a few precious hours to investigate the death of Jaspar Rahim, unimpeded by their guidance. And if we find that the death of Mr. Rahim is, in fact, a homicide, quite frankly I will be looking hard at you, Special Agent Dodd. Exceedingly hard at you."

"Does that mean my sister and I can leave now?" Alicia asked.

"No, it does not." Alvarez turned to Alicia. "A female patrol officer will be summoned up from the road. She will search both you and your sister. I do not yet have a full accounting of all the items that have been brought in to contaminate my crime scene, but I intend to have one."

Alicia brought the nasal spray bottle out of her shirt pocket. "But, you can plainly see—"

"Mrs. Elton, had you not used your cell phone, after you were expressly told not to do so, none of this would be necessary. And you may well have been on your way back to your hotel by now."

Detective Montero tossed the driver's licenses on the table. Taking that as a signal that the local police had officially lost interest in my wallet, keys, pocketknife, and small change, I stepped in and stuffed them all back into their customary pockets. Ellen followed suit, restoring her belongings to her purse.

Alvarez addressed his men in Spanish, "Montero, call down to the Patrol Sergeant for a female officer and stay here with the ladies, until she arrives. Officer Saenz, bring these two men with us. Keep your baton at the ready."

As Dodd and I were herded out, Ellen clung to her sister's arm. Alicia's eyes questioned me, but I wasn't given a chance to translate.

***

With Detective Sergeant Alvarez in the lead and the uniformed officer as the rear guard, Dodd and I were taken across the hall and into a small, windowless room. A hand-carved crucifix hung on a wall that featured a jagged crack in the plaster that ran ceiling-to-floor behind the icon, like a lightening bolt. Below the crucifix, a pair of lit candles, the room's only light source, flickered on a shallow table. The smell of burning wax made the room seem even more airless. In the center of the room, a hard wooden bench with a set of handcuffs dangling from one armrest was positioned to afford an unobstructed view of the candles and crucifix.

The uniformed officer with baton in hand positioned himself a single pace away from the room's only door.

Dodd and I were relegated to the pitiless bench. Alvarez brought over a plain wooden chair, reversed it, and sat in front of us with his hairy forearms resting on the seatback.

The Detective Sergeant began in English, "I am very curious about you, Mr. Elton. When you are not delivering brassieres and nasal sprays in the rain forest, where do you live and what is your work?"

"I live in Chicago. I'm an industrial engineer. I do field service work for Windy City Machinery, troubleshooting and repairing machine breakdowns at customers' factories, when the problem can't be resolved over the phone."

"And you stated that Alicia Elton is your former wife?"

"That's right. She asked me to accompany her to the monastery. She said it would be more acceptable to the Bishop, if her husband were with her. I mean, I'm her ex, but…"

"And then you thought it would be even more acceptable to the Bishop to have Mr. Dodd secretly take your place."

"I told you," Dodd interceded, "that he couldn't—"

"I know what you told me, Mr. Dodd. And now I am asking Mr. Elton to tell me," Alvarez's eyes swung back to mine. "Well, Mr. Elton?"

"An agency of the Federal Government requested my cooperation," I said. "I complied. Nothing bad had to happen."

"And yet, it did." The Detective Sergeant shifted his attention. "Mr. Dodd, let me make something clear to you. As I am sure you are aware, certain elements within our shared Federal Government feel justified in persistently investigating and prosecuting corruption and misdeeds, variously attributed to every level of Puerto Rican law enforcement. Over the years, as you can imagine, this has led to a certain amount of resentment within our ranks. But now, in this particular situation, we find that our roles are reversed. So, let me take a moment to express to you that it is my strongest belief that if *our* sins are punishable, then, Special Agent Dodd, so too are *yours*."

"Okay now, let's not make this personal," Dodd said. "Sure, there've been times when some overly pious, applause seeking G-men have ridden rough-shod over you guys. But see, the NCIS and the Puerto Rico Police, we're reasonable people."

"Oh yes, Mr. Dodd, you and I are both reasonable men," Alvarez said. "And reasonable men, professionals like us, know that when you have a dead Arab businessman and an undercover Special Agent inexplicably at the same secluded monastery at the exact time of the businessman's death, a complete accounting of that Special Agent's actions and motives is required. However, thus far, Mr. Dodd, I have received only obviously evasive responses from you. And that has sorely tried my patience."

"Were they that obvious?"

The Detective Sergeant's face remained stern. "Fair warning, Mr. Dodd. Your window of opportunity is rapidly closing. Talk to me."

"All right," Dodd said. "I'll just lay it out. Francis let me take his place, so I could get next to Rahim and find out what he was really up to in buying this monastery."

"Alicia Elton has told me that much. I'm sure there is so much more that you can share with me."

"Like what?"

"Specifically, the immediate circumstances within which Mr. Rahim happened to die," Alvarez said. "Perhaps, it was while you were merely in the process of gathering information from him, and the particular tactic you were using – quite inadvertently – went awry. You can tell me. We are both professionals. I would understand. These things happen."

"All I did was observe him. I've told you that five times. I never touched him. I never even spoke to him, for God sakes. And he didn't do much of anything anyway, except lord himself around the place and sit in that big chair in the dining hall."

"Ah, yes, the Abbot's chair." Alvarez said. "The big chair upon which Jaspar Rahim was sitting, when he suddenly…simply…died."

"I didn't see any bullet holes in him. So I guess I didn't shoot him. No knife wounds, no blunt force trauma. So how was I supposed to have killed him? Make a mean face and scare him to death?"

"You have not yet exhausted the list of ways there are to kill a man."

"I'd happily help you narrow down that list, if you could tell me what made Rahim's heart stop beating."

"The Medical Examiner will tell us precisely that. Rahim's body was transported to San Juan by helicopter," Alvarez checked his wristwatch, "more than two hours ago. The Captain has ordered an expedited autopsy. We will have a preliminary report soon."

"You don't need an ME to tell you what a wound looks like," Dodd said. "If there aren't any marks on him, maybe he just winked out all by himself. He certainly wasn't the healthiest-looking specimen to ever trudge up that mountain path. And yet, here you are, charging ahead, unlawfully detaining people, accusing them of murder, when, for all you know, Jaspar Rahim died of polio."

"I am only holding you for questioning. Just as I am only holding Mr. Elton for questioning."

"I wasn't even here when the Arab died," I protested. "I was sunning myself on Luquillo Beach, drinking a rum and coke, when—"

"How can I know that, Mr. Elton?" Alvarez swung his attention back to me. He leaned in, bringing his face uncomfortably close to mine. "I know only that you suddenly appeared. When did you actually arrive? I can only speculate."

The Detective Sergeant leaned back, again bringing both Dodd and me into his field of vision. "Therefore, barring anyone's willingness to expand on his involvement, we will now patiently wait for the Medical Examiner's report – no matter how damning it may prove to be."

"So we're supposed to sit here in this sweat box, looking at Jesus nailed to a cross, for eternity?" Dodd asked. "How about a little refreshment. Catholics always have some wine around someplace, don't they?"

"It will not be long," Alvarez said. "It took perhaps twenty minutes for the helicopter to carry Mr. Rahim's body to San Juan for the examination. His bodyguard was taken with him, so that we may find an interpreter to take his statement."

Alvarez pushed himself up off his chair and placed it back against the wall. He returned to stand in front of us, but held what I was to recognize as his default glower exclusively on me for a discomforting half minute.

"Now what?" It was Dodd who broke the silence.

"Mr. Elton," Alvarez said, "you say you are an engineer? As it happens, I am in need of one."

"I told you my work is with machinery," I said, "I'm not an expert on structural problems, if that's what—"

"It is, I suppose, a type of structure," Alvarez said, "but some of its parts do not appear to be interrelated. I thought that, with your background, you might be able to identify the function of the unrelated parts."

Since I was all for getting the hell out of the oxygen-starved, little chapel room, I said, "I guess it couldn't hurt to take a look."

Alvarez lifted his gaze and spoke in Spanish over our heads. "Officer Saenz, you may retrieve your handcuffs."

After the uniformed officer removed the cuffs from the armrest, Alvarez said, "Stand up. Both of you will come with me."

The uniformed officer asked in Spanish if he was to handcuff the prisoner.

"The officer asks if it is necessary to put handcuffs on you, Mr. Dodd," Alvarez translated. "Is it?"

"Make it easy on yourself."

After instructing the officer to crack Dodd's skull open if he tried anything, Alvarez led an un-manacled Dodd and me along the upper hallway. The uniformed officer maintained a comfortable baton-swing's distance behind us.

As we passed the door of the guest quarters, I wondered if the policewoman had arrived for Alicia and Ellen's pat down. I harbored no hope that Alicia would quietly acquiesce to the procedure. I did hope that the policewoman would use her handcuffs, rather than her baton, to cope with Alicia's temperament.

***

Dodd and I followed the Detective Sergeant down the stairway to the main floor and continued our forced march out into the interior patio area. From somewhere in the open sky above us, I heard the air whacking sound of a helicopter.

"Your transportation is arriving, Mr. Dodd," Alvarez said. "I hope you won't mind my spiriting you off without a chance to speak to your cohorts down at the road."

"A chopper ride? It'll bring back fond memories," Dodd said. "I remember back in—"

"Please do not feel the need to entertain us with a reminiscence," Alvarez said, as we passed through another door and directly into a spacious dining hall.

Below a lofty ceiling, dim light filtered in through a series of tall, sooty windows that ran along the upper half of the far wall. Dark melancholy paintings, depicting a selection of New Testament events, hung in perpetual sorrow along the wall's lower half. Dominating the center of the dining hall was an exceptionally long wooden table, flanked by straight-backed chairs, ten to a side.

Half a dozen forensic technicians, dressed in light-blue paper jumpsuits and foot coverings, were variously engaged in dusting for prints, swabbing surfaces, and photographing everything in sight.

Alvarez again posted the uniformed officer just inside the room's only door, before leading Dodd and me further into the dining hall.

At the head of the table, but at a distance too far back to be of practical use for dining, stood a large chair, constructed of ornately carved wood with its armrests protected by hammered metal. As Alvarez brought us closer to the large chair, I visually identified the metal that fully covered the top of the armrests, as dull and heavily worn silver.

"This is the Abbot's chair," Alvarez said. "It is where the Abbot presides during the evening assembly, as he leads the monks in prayer. Also, I'm told that the current Abbot prefers to spend his personal daily periods of prayer and meditation in this chair, rather than up in the little chapel room."

"Jaspar Rahim was sitting in this chair when he died," Dodd said to me. "The Detective Sergeant can't seem to get to the point."

"If you can restrain your comments for a moment, Mr. Dodd, I was about to ask Mr. Elton for his thoughts on a significant peculiarity of this chair."

I followed Alvarez around to the rear of the chair, catching a whiff of pineapple en route. Strangely, the chair's side carvings that continued in an ornate pattern around the back of the chair made a detour to encompass a tall box, about six inches square on top and fully incorporated onto the back of the chair. The two-foot height of the box started at several inches above the floor and rose up to almost level with the armrests.

But it was *within* the tall box that Alvarez's "unrelated parts" resided. First and most obvious in the dim light was a section of three-inch diameter, white plastic pipe – of the kind used for modern household drains – sitting on end and extending slightly above the box's open top. Centered within the white plastic pipe was a two-inch diameter copper tube, and poking out of the center of the copper tube was a half-inch diameter, galvanized steel, water pipe. The bouquet of pineapple was stronger here, and I peered in and saw that a liquid (undoubtedly, pineapple wine made out in the big shed) filled the spaces between the nested sections of plumbing. Unquestionably, the white plastic pipe had an end cap glued onto the lower end to contain the wine. Unrelated chair parts, indeed.

"Well?" Alvarez asked.

I knew what it was, in general, since it was easy enough to identify the basic components. But it was the combination of the wine and the unique construction style of the steel pipe centered within the copper tube that triggered a memory.

"It's a Baghdad battery," I said.

Alvarez looked hard at my face, as though attempting to judge my sincerity – or sanity. But Dodd bent in for a closer look at the apparatus.

After a cursory inspection, Dodd straightened up. "A Baghdad battery. Stop clowning around, Francis. This is just someplace where they keep the wine after it gets all holy. And look. Look at the valve, down there near the bottom. The monks can hold their mugs under it, turn the tap, and draw themselves a little fortification. It's stuck here behind the Abbot's chair, so he can keep an eye on it, so the boys don't get too crazy."

"I was asking for Mr. *Elton's* opinion," Alvarez said. "You were saying that it is a battery?"

"It'll be a fairly weak one, I suppose, but it has all the right parts."

"It does not look like any battery that I have ever seen," Alvarez said. "And it is from Baghdad?"

"I read an article about it sometime back," I said. "Some archaeologists, who were shoveling around in Iraq, dug up a clay jar that had a tube, formed from a beaten-out sheet of copper, sticking out of it, and with an crude iron rod centered within the copper tube and held in place by a gob of tar. The inside of the jar tested positive for acidic fruit residue. It dated to about the time of Christ, so, of course, not all archaeologists were convinced that it was actually a battery that somebody was trying to make. You know, wine in a jar with a stopper is no big thing. But the cylinder of copper and the iron rod got some of them thinking."

"Why did they not just build a model of what they found and pour in some acidic juice?" Alvarez asked.

"They did. And when they tested it, they got about one volt of electricity from which they could pull something like half an amp of direct current."

"This is stupid, Francis," Dodd said. "What did they need a battery for, way back then? Did they have flashlights too?"

"For once, Mr. Dodd makes a valid point. Of what practical use could this have been?"

"I don't know," I said. "Some archaeologists speculated about electroplating gold onto silver, but others pointed out that the gold jewelry from that time was all gilded. I think they dug up a few other pots with the copper and iron remnants in them around the area later on, but nobody's ever found any wires. Hard to hook it up to anything without wires."

"I do not see the stopper that you said was part of it," Alvarez said.

"No, but that was just to keep the iron rod from touching the copper. See, here they've accomplished the same thing with this little bracket screwed to the wood of the chair, extending out, and clamped to the steel pipe with a U-bolt. Makes it a lot easier to pour fresh wine in at the top, after you've drained the old, depleted stuff out through the valve at the bottom, so you can keep a charge on it."

In the dim light of the dining hall, I now spotted the end of a bare copper wire, sticking out from within the grasp of the U-bolt. While I moved around for a better angle and strained my eyes to look for the rest of the wire in the shadows, Alvarez drew out his notebook.

Dodd tapped on the white plastic pipe with his fingernail. "Just some leftover plumbing parts stuck in here. Probably about a thousand years too soon to call in the archaeologists."

"I cannot have unknown objects in my crime scene," Alvarez spoke more to himself, than to Dodd or me, as he wrote in his notebook. "I must ask the Abbot—"

The door banged open. A man wearing in a light tan suit and a dark-tempered frown led two other official-looking heavies into the dining hall.

"Detective Sergeant Alvarez, the autopsy has been completed," the tan-suited man announced in Spanish. "Jaspar Rahim died of natural causes. As of this moment, your investigation is terminated."

Alvarez looked like he was about to protest, but evidently caught himself. "Yes, Captain," he responded in Spanish. "Did the Medical Examiner say what the specific cause of—"

"*Natural* causes." The Captain's eyes, small and fierce, defied his Sergeant to press the issue.

Alvarez stopped asking questions, but the temple near his right eye broke into a series of rhythmic spasms.

"Get everyone who is not a monk out of here," the Captain ordered. "Close down your crime scene."

Alvarez maintained a hard set to his features, as he looked at his superior.

The Captain continued, "I have ordered that Rahim's body be prepared for shipment. The bodyguard and the casket will be on the next flight to France. Rahim must be buried as soon as possible, out of respect for his religion."

With a hand motion, Alvarez summoned his uniformed officer over from his post at the door and ordered in Spanish, "See that the technicians do not leave anything behind and then sweep the building for stragglers."

As the uniformed officer went to gather in and herd out the scattering of light-blue jumpsuits, Alvarez ordered in English, "Mr. Dodd, Mr. Elton, you are to leave the monastery at once. Take the two women with you."

While the members of the Crime Scene Unit packed up their cases, the Captain, his two accompanying subordinates, and Alvarez moved away from us and went into a low-voiced conference, wherein the Captain was doing all of the talking.

"Francis, what's going on?" Dodd asked. "What's all the Spanish about?"

"Well, the guy in the tan suit with the big voice is a police captain—"

"I got that. What did he say?"

"Jaspar Rahim died of natural causes. Case closed."

"Uh oh."

"What? You're home free. I'd think you'd be—"

"I'm tickled to the pinkest extremity," Dodd said. "Except that full autopsies don't happen even close to that fast. You could grow a beard, just waiting for the toxicology results. But mostly, murdered people don't die of natural causes."

Chapter 4

Dodd sent me to round up Alicia and Ellen, while he went off to make a phone call. I didn't find the women upstairs in the guest quarters, but when I came back down to the entrance hallway, I heard a heated argument in English coming from outside the open front door. As I stepped out, I saw, at a short distance beyond the covered entryway, Alicia verbally holding two police officers at bay. Ellen stood nervously at her sister's side, as Alicia raged at the officers.

"If the police investigation is over," Alicia jabbed a finely honed fingernail in the officers' direction, "then *you* are the ones who should be leaving. *I* have to get back to work. The Archdiocese hired me to appraise the paintings in the dining hall. I can't *do* that, if I'm not actually *in* the dining hall."

"Captain Rivera has issued the order," the male officer asserted in English. "We intend to carry it out. By force, if necessary."

I saw the female officer draw a set of handcuffs from a case on her polished black belt.

"Look. True enough, I'm not a monk. But I work here. I have a contract." But at that moment, Alicia must have spotted the handcuffs coming her way, because she then quickly said, "Okay, okay I get it. I'm wrong. We're going."

I left the entryway and stepped into the sun.

"Francis." Ellen noticed me. "They're throwing us out."

The helicopter, resting on a thick carpet of mashed-down garden plants, fired up its engine in anticipation of churning up a whirlwind of vegetative debris.

Phil Dodd rounded a corner of the building and strode toward us. Over the noise of the helicopter, Dodd shouted, "All right. Come on, folks. We're cutting into their donut time."

"My God," Alicia again appealed to heaven, "won't he ever go away?"

***

Satisfied that we were complying with their instructions, the police officers disengaged where the cart path started down the mountain. The four of us – Alicia and Ellen out front and shouldering their purses, me lugging Alicia's tote bag of artist tools, and Dodd, unencumbered – continued on our own.

Dodd took a quick check back over his shoulder, before he spoke. "Francis, how did you get past the police down at the road?"

"We left your rental car in the parking area and walked up the road to a little waterfall," I said. "From there, we climbed up through the rain forest, for a while, following along the stream. Then we cut over to this cart path and walked on up."

"Great. I need to go back down along that stream. You folks just keep going down this path like everything's normal. When you get to your car – your car, not my car – just drive up to the waterfall. I'll be there."

Ellen looked back at Dodd. "I thought everything was over."

"I did too," I said. "Why can't you just—"

"Because my fellow agents are waiting for me down at the parking area. I've been on the phone with a friend of mine. A woman, very hip, in the field office up at Mayport. She says the NCIS thinks I'm responsible for Rahim's death. Like maybe I killed him, or something. And the Special Agent in Charge wants to pull me in. This is not good. I don't want to get yanked up to Florida and sit around on the hot seat, while a some stateside pinheads fumble around in my investigation and get stone-walled by the local police."

I tried again. "But that Police Captain said—"

"Natural causes, my ass," Dodd restated his earlier verdict. "Somebody got to that Police Captain. Somebody packing heavy political influence. And consequently, I now stand to get keelhauled by my own agency, unless I can make some sense of all this and pretty damn soon."

We rounded the first switchback and continued down.

Dodd asked me, "Do you remember where you got onto this path?"

"It was down there ahead of us at the next switchback. And the stream should be—"

"Stop, stop, stop." Alicia took two quick steps out ahead, about-faced, and planted her feet, bringing the rest of us to a halt. "Why, Lieutenant? Why does the NCIS think you killed the Arab?"

"Oh, they've just got their bureaucratic noggins stuck up their official bungholes."

"Don't try to blow me off. You did something *before* to make them suspect you *now*." Alicia's hands were clamped on her hips, her eyes fastened on Dodd's face. "I told you at the airport what I'd do, if you screwed up my job down here. And that Arab turning up dead has just screwed me up. And it's all the same to me, whether you're arrested at the bottom of a cart path, or at the bottom of a waterfall. So you'd better start explaining, Lieutenant. And it had better be damned good."

"Okay now, let's dial it back a little," Dodd said. "There's like this footnote in an old performance report. All based on a bit of speculation by some desk jockeys, sitting safe and cozy in Bahrain, back in oh-three. I was working a contact across the line in Iraq at the time. There was a nasty little turn of events, and it was alleged that I was involved. There's practically zero evidence."

"Not good enough," Alicia said.

"You were in Iraq?" I asked.

"It was just before the U.S. invaded," Dodd said. "We were slipping across into Iraqi territory and buying up whatever intelligence we could. Troop and tank movements, artillery positions and command centers. Stuff like that."

"And you were with the NCIS then?"

"You go where you're told to go and do what you're told to do. And I guess, since we decided to invade Iraq about five minutes after we invaded Afghanistan, military intelligence officers were getting kind of scarce. It's not like we had enough Army to go around, either."

"Get to the part where your own agency doesn't trust you," Alicia said.

Dodd hesitated. But there was no doubt that without our help, getting past the NCIS agents down in the parking area would mean that Dodd faced the prospect of abandoning his car and hoofing it all the way down the mountain road to Luquillo, not to mention jumping into the bushes at the sound of each approaching vehicle.

Dodd must have calculated along those lines himself, because after a few moments, he said, "Okay, I'm into Iraqi territory, a little deeper than I care to be, buying intelligence from this local tribal leader who's got a hundred sets of eyes in the area. I'm talking to him through this young Iraqi woman who's my interpreter. She's really a sweet woman, which is saying a lot, considering Saddam Hussein had her whole village practically wiped out for some, probably minor, offense against his regime. Anyway, being an interpreter paid enough to keep what family she still had left in food. So, everything's going along fine, we're getting good intel from the tribal leader, and he's loving the Saudi riyals I'm shoving into his pockets. But then, as the clock is running out, talk starts going around that Hussein's getting cold feet, looking to cut a deal. And at the time, none of us really knew if the military build-up wasn't just a big ploy to get the weapons inspectors back in. So, this tribal leader – and let's face it, he's just a thug – he gets nervous that the U.S. invasion isn't going to happen, and he's scared witless that Hussein will find out he's sold us information. So to cover his tracks, he has my interpreter, this sweet little woman, killed. A bullet in the forehead." Dodd allowed the mental image a moment of hang time. "You know the culture. She's just a woman. Then the next day, the tribal leader is found drowned."

"Drowned?" Ellen asked. "In the desert?"

"You waterboarded him." Alicia made the leap.

"You don't waterboard someone in a fountain," Dodd said.

The three of us just looked at him.

"I mean, from what I understand." Dodd quickly moved on, "See, I wasn't there. I'd gotten the word to head back to Bahrain with all due haste. It was later that I heard they found him face down in the fountain, the one in his compound. So, he must have, you know, slipped and hit his head, or something."

Dodd apparently saw on our faces that his explanation wasn't going especially well, because he added, "He killed that sweet little woman. Like she was nothing. So, don't get all teary-eyed about him. Okay? Anyway, the next day the invasion started. We came out, the Army went in. So, nobody knows for sure what happened."

"But the NCIS thinks you murdered the tribal leader," Alicia said.

"I can't help what people think. But you can see how this Rahim guy also turning up dead might look bad for me. You know, like maybe a pattern is developing. And it sure as hell doesn't help that the local police here have decided to sit this one out. So, I just need a little time and space to investigate Rahim's murder and get this all cleared up. Should do wonders for my career."

Alicia appeared unmoved. "Give Francis the keys to my rental car, and he'll give you yours back. And then you're on your own, Lieutenant. I knew I'd regret agreeing to any of this."

As we swapped keys, Dodd asked me, "Where's that stream?"

I pointed down toward the slope covered with spindly undergrowth just before the next switchback below us. "You can see where Ellen and I slid down. Just climb up and walk straight along the side of the mountain. You'll hit it."

"And you'll drive up and get me at the waterfall?"

I looked at Alicia. She turned away.

"I'll talk to her," I said.

Dodd gave me a hardy comrade-slap on the arm and strode off down the path. When he reached the switchback, we watched as he scrambled up through the rain forest and disappeared from view over the crest.

Ellen and I started out again. And when I was in range, Wham! Alicia smacked me so hard on the side of my face that my legs went two kinds of wobbly and the rain forest blurred into an over-soaked watercolor.

"That's for doing my sister," Alicia said.

"I never touched—"

Wham! This time I went dark for a second.

"That's for lying about it."

To my surprise, I found myself still on my feet and still holding Alicia's tote bag, but now a few steps back and, thankfully, out of the danger zone. The side of my head throbbed in cadence with my heartbeat. Alicia had struck the same spot with the second hit, just like a professional boxer would. And with headshots, even girl-hits add up.

"Alicia, that's not how it was," Ellen came to my defense.

"You just be quiet. I'll get to you in a minute. I'm dealing with Francis right now."

I tried to plumb the depths of Alicia's reasoning. "Where did you come up with—"

"Well, let me see. Oh, yes. Her bra fell out of your pocket." Alicia's green eyes had that National Geographic lioness-in-for-the-kill look. "And this morning, when I called for help, Ellen is just struggling back into her blouse. What was it, sex on the beach?"

"Look, you've got the wrong idea," I said.

"Oh, I've got the idea all right. The idea is that, since I'm all tied up and busy up at the monastery, you re-target 'Mr. Lucky' in the direction of my sister. What the hell, she's emotionally vulnerable too, after Mom's death. So, why not take advantage? You're beneath contempt, you know that?"

"Alicia, please listen," Ellen said. "We never had sex. I had my top off for a little while, that was all."

Alicia turned on her sister. "Don't you have a husband somewhere and a couple of little boys? So what were you doing prancing around on the beach, tits in the wind?"

"Like *you* have room to talk. Like *your* clothes never come off," Ellen shot back. "I know your allergy medicine makes you bitchier than usual, but that doesn't give you a pass for going off on me. For nothing."

The sisters faced off on one another. Light rain, which was never far away in El Yunque, began to fall, darkening the already slippery terrain.

Ellen pushed past her sister and marched on down the mountain with as much dignity as the slick, uneven cart path would allow.

The cool rain soothed the sting on my cheek. "Come on," I said. "There's no sense pretending we aren't all going to ride back to San Juan in the same car."

Before I reached the switchback, I heard Alicia tramping behind me.

***

Down at the bottom of the cart path, the uniformed policemen stood to either side to let Ellen pass between them. I came next, half a minute later, and then, maintaining a discrete distance, Alicia brought up the rear of the column. The three of us continued on across the noticeably depopulated parking area, as though we were unacquainted. The TV crew, busy with packing up, momentarily became alert, but just as quickly relaxed when they saw that none of us were newsworthy. However, the two men in sunglasses and windbreakers – who, I supposed, were the NCIS Special Agents that Dodd was avoiding – observed us with keen interest.

Ellen waited at our rental car, now one of the few remaining civilian vehicles. As soon as I unlocked and opened the driver's door, I pushed the button to unlock the rest of the doors. Alicia had arrived, but until a truce was agreed upon, I wasn't sure what seating arrangements would produce the least friction.

"I want to be as alone as possible," Alicia gave notice, as she opened the driver-side rear door. She climbed in and sat regally with her purse on her lap, waiting to be driven back to the city.

I reached the tote bag over Alicia's knees, deposited it on the hump in the floor, and closed her door. As I slid behind the wheel, Ellen took the passenger seat up front and remained righteously silent, staring straight

69

ahead through the windshield. Given the tense emotional atmospherics, I wasn't looking forward to my next errand.

After briefly assuring myself that no one was paying any attention to us, I checked for traffic and backed onto the road with the nose of the car heading uphill. At the edge of my peripheral vision, I saw the heads of the two NCIS agents turn.

There was no protest from the backseat, during the short drive up to the waterfall. I didn't know whether Alicia simply expected me to go pick up Dodd, despite her wishes, or if she was just disoriented about which direction led to the highway. In any case, I had enough sense not to open a discussion about it.

I used the narrow pull-off at the waterfall to complete a u-turn. When I came to a stop, the passenger-side back door swung open, and a sweaty and scratched up Phil Dodd dropped into the seat next to Alicia.

"Hi, gang. Go ahead, Francis. Drive casual. I'll just lie down back here. I could use with a little nap anyway."

"Get Away From Me!" Alicia screeched. "You damn, wet, filthy…"

I heard a heavy body-blow land, followed by Dodd's yelp of pain.

"I didn't agree to this, Francis," Alicia seethed. "If he rides with us, he rides in the trunk."

"Alicia," I said, "ease up, will you?"

"No, she's right," Dodd climbed back out of the car, then stuck his head back in. "My fellow agents will have seen you go the wrong way. They'll be at the edge of the road and scoping out the car's interior, as you come past. And we have to go down that way. We can't just keep going up the mountain. The road dead-ends at a hiker's trail going up to the summit."

I reached over and opened the glove box, pushed a yellow button, and heard the trunk lid pop. As I got out and walked back, Dodd was already bending himself into the trunk.

"You going to be okay?" I asked. "The trunk's kind of small."

"For a fairly short time, yes," Dodd answered from his cramped position. "The first store or restaurant you come to that's on your right, pull in and park way to the right in the lot. If my devoted friends start chasing after us, they'll have only a short glance as they whiz by. With any luck, they'll miss us."

I closed the lid on Dodd and climbed back behind the wheel.

***

As I rounded a bend and approached the wide shoulder at the base of the cart path, a uniformed officer with three-chevrons on his sleeve walked out onto the blacktop and signaled me to stop.

I noticed that the two NCIS agents waited until I'd braked to a halt, before committing themselves to advancing to the edge of the road and away from their chase car, the grill of which, I noticed, now faced out.

The policeman stepped around to my open window. On the opposite side, the Special Agents were already peering through their sunglasses into the passenger compartment.

"Is there some problem on the road ahead of us, Sergeant?" I asked in Spanish.

The policeman, who, up close, looked to be a veteran member of *La Uniformada*, responded in Spanish, "These men from the Federal Government believe that you may have picked up a passenger. A man with whom they wish to speak."

"I came down from the monastery with two ladies," I stayed in Spanish. "You see in this vehicle only myself and the two ladies."

"A moment, please." The policeman directed his voice over the roof of the car and switched to English. "It is apparent that no additional man has joined them."

I heard one Special Agent say to the other, "It looks kind of small, but maybe we should check the trunk."

In Spanish, I quickly said, "Detective Sergeant Alvarez ordered us to leave the monastery and immediately return to San Juan. We are attempting to comply with the orders of the Detective Sergeant."

"Why then did you, at first, drive *up* the mountain, instead of down?" the policeman asked in Spanish. "That is what has so excited these men from the Federal Government."

"I was confused in my directions." It's an effort to be artful, while speaking in a foreign language. It feels like telling your first lie. "I corrected myself at the first opportunity."

A Special Agent, advancing in my driver's side mirror, barked in English, "Okay, cut the gibberish."

The policeman visibly bristled and sternly frowned at the Special Agent.

"Get out and open the trunk," the Special Agent ordered.

I remained in my seat, held my eyes on the policeman's face, and stayed in Spanish. "When in Puerto Rico, I follow the orders of the Police of Puerto Rico."

My mirror now showed two carloads of tourists held up behind us. An oncoming car, whose lane was currently occupied by the policeman and the Special agent, also came to a stop. The policeman briefly surveyed the situation, slapped his hand on the roof of the rental car, and ordered in Spanish, "You are obstructing traffic. Move along."

I immediately accelerated down the mountain. There was shouting behind me, but I was just following orders.

***

I drove as fast as I dared down the curvy road. Behind me, the two carloads of tourists, who I now thought of as my blockers, no longer made sporadic appearances in my mirrors. Luckily, I had already slowed to a more appropriate speed, when I spotted cars parked in front of a rustic café ahead on my right. I had to brake almost to a stop in making the tight turn into the shallow lot. I nosed into an empty patch of dirt to the far right of three other angle-parked cars.

"How about a nice cold beer?" I asked my passengers, as I reached across for the trunk lid release.

"*I'd* certainly like a drink." Ellen opened her door.

"Why are we stopping?" Alicia demanded from the back seat.

"I want to free up some trunk space," I said.

Before I was out to give Dodd a hand in extricating himself, he'd already managed it on his own.

Dodd warily observed the two carloads of tourists going past, before turning to me. "Did somebody say beer?"

The café looked to be constructed entirely of salvaged-wood framing and floor-to-ceiling screens, assembled beneath a rusty corrugated metal roof. The structure precariously clung to the side of the mountain – the rear perched on a ledge cut into the steep slope and the street side propped up on tar-pitched pilings, which elevated the floor level about five feet above the parking lot.

The four of us trooped up the warped grey treads of the exterior stairway and entered through the screen door at the top. I settled Ellen and Alicia at a table and ordered drinks from a passing waitress. Dodd remained standing at a front section of screen, watching the road.

From my seat at the table I saw the transmitter dish of the TV news van go past. For me, that made the stand-down more official than the following sight of light bars atop police cruisers passing by in succession. The police investigation at the monastery was over, and the rain forest of El Yunque could return to the sleepy business of eco-tourism.

Dodd left his observation post at the screen and joined us, just as the waitress delivered two beers and two mojitos.

"Well, it looks like none of my fellow agents decided to follow you folks. Maybe they were short-handed. How many of them were there, Francis?"

"Just two, as far as I could tell."

"Probably had only one car," Dodd said. "Had to make a decision. Decided I probably wasn't jammed in the tiny trunk and chances were still pretty good I'd come wandering down the path and into their arms."

"Thank you so much for including us in your flight from justice," Alicia said.

"I'll pay for the drinks," Dodd said. "Does that help?"

"The only thing that would help now would be a nice fat check covering my expenses for this train wreck. But it looks like I'll be eating it, myself. As though *I* screwed it all up."

"No one's saying it was your fault," Ellen noted in a weary tone.

"You're damned right it isn't my fault. None of it is. It's Francis's fault. He's the one who can't say 'no' to his old lieutenant. Now, my whole project is a shambles, and we sit here having a party. Maybe I should shred my contract, so we can have a little confetti."

"I wasn't me or Francis who killed the Arab, okay?" Dodd said. "Yes, it happened on my watch. Just give me a little time. I'll figure out who did it. And everyone will be happy again."

"I'm not looking for closure. I'm looking for compensation."

From higher up the mountain, the unmistakable sound of beating helicopter blades rapidly gained volume. As the aircraft passed overhead, the whirling blades loudly hammered the air and rattled the metal roof. Then, just as rapidly, the reverberations diminished to a retreating putter.

"And there I go," Dodd said, looking off toward the fading noise.

"What do you mean?" I asked.

"Oh, after I got the lowdown on my newly perilous situation from my honey up in Mayport, I took a stroll out to the helicopter. You know, just to say hello to the pilot and maybe catch a ride back to San Juan without having to scramble down through a sweltering jungle, first. Well, the fabulous Puerto Rico Police were done with me, so obviously the helicopter ride didn't work out. But happily, I did manage to lose my cell phone, while I was confabbing with the pilot."

"And that's a good thing?" I asked.

"It is, if you consider that pretty soon my two colleagues back up there are going to have to call in and admit to the Special Agent in Charge that they have no idea where the hell I am. Then the SAC will have me tracked down by the GPS signal from my cell phone. And by calculating my course and speed, they'll figure out I'm traveling toward San Juan by helicopter. The two agents will be pulled off their stakeout below the monastery and sent scurrying back to the city."

Dodd paused for a swallow of beer. "When the chopper lands on the helipad on top of the General Stationhouse to drop off the Captain, they'll assume I'm still being held by the local police. But then, when I continue on to the old airport at Isla Grande, where they hangar the chopper, the two agents will be redirected to go grab me there. One can only image the collective slump in the shoulders of all involved when my cell phone is finally discovered under the co-pilot's seat."

Dodd smiled at us and signaled for another round. "So, that frees me up to get first pick at the low-hanging evidence and piece together who needed Rahim dead and why. Hopefully, my success will be rewarded with an assignment to somewhere other than a Quonset hut on the ass end of Cuba."

"Didn't you say there was a bodyguard, always lurking nearby?" I said. "Didn't anybody think to ask the bodyguard what happened?"

"Unfortunately, there's quite the language barrier," Dodd said. "Before the police got there I tried English, and that big monk tried Spanish and what sounded like Arabic, but I don't think the monk was very good at it, the Arabic I mean, because he had to use a lot of hand gestures. But nothing got through to him. It was like talking to your dog. Later on, one of Alvarez's men tried French, but he didn't understand that, either. So, I guess the bodyguard only knows whatever dirtball jargon they speak in whichever remote patch of camel country he and Rahim come from."

"Why couldn't the Arab have just died of a heart attack, like the police said?" Ellen asked.

"The police didn't specify a heart attack," I said. "Even when that Detective Sergeant asked, his Captain wouldn't go into any specifics at all. Just natural causes."

"And why not specify it?" Dodd said. "It wouldn't have taken a Medical Examiner long to find evidence of a routine medical condition or disease that's progressed far enough along to kill someone. They know their business. And if it was something rare, what became of that requisite month or two of testing and analysis of the body fluids and tissues?"

"They don't do an autopsy on everybody who dies, Lieutenant," Alicia said. "Our mother didn't have an autopsy."

"Then she was under a doctor's care. And her doctor would sign the death certificate. But for Rahim, the police investigation and the autopsy were already underway. Then suddenly it's declared a death by natural causes – like a studio press release when a celebrity dies of a suicide or accidental overdose. But Jaspar Rahim was no celebrity. So then, what's so important to the 'powers that be' that how Rahim died needs covering up? If you say 'murder,' you win the cigar."

A different waitress arrived with our next round of drinks. She examined us with open suspicion, expressed in her narrowed eyes and pursed lips, before returning to the small gaggle of employees at the bar, undoubtedly to report her findings. I wondered if they'd seen Dodd emerge from the trunk.

I returned my attention to Dodd. "How did your Special Agent in Charge manage to get those two NCIS agents already in position at the bottom of the cart path, ready to nab you, even before the Captain helicoptered in and shut down Alvarez's investigation?"

"I knew some additional Special Agents were due to arrive in San Juan this morning to set up a forward operation office, after I reported that I'd wormed my way into the monastery. So they were already in play for the SAC to send up to the monastery when the first phone call from the Puerto Rico Police came in, saying they were holding me for questioning about a dead Arab and asking for my bona fides. This, of course, was a direct result of Alicia ratting me out."

"As if anybody believed your freaking line of bull in the first place," Alicia commented.

"And apparently," Dodd went on, "the SAC had rashly leaped to the conclusion that I was the one who killed Rahim, despite the follow-up phone call from the Captain of Detectives with the update that, funny thing, turns out Rahim actually died of natural causes. Therefore, with the local police shrugging their shoulders and walking away, my own agency feels compelled to haul me back to Mayport for a reading of the list of my failings going back to my first birthday, followed immediately by my expulsion from the ranks of the NCIS."

"Are you saying that you have to prove that it was murder in order to prove that you didn't do it?" Alicia asked.

"Sounds tricky, doesn't it?"

The humming of tires from a fast approaching car brought Dodd quickly to his feet.

"And there they go," he said. "Make haste, my darlings, make haste."

I stood in time to catch a glimpse of a speeding blue car and a pale man in the passenger seat with a phone to his ear.

Dodd regained his chair and took up his fresh beer. "And since my trusted comrades feel the need to double-team me for my surprise apprehension, they must not know that Alvarez took my gun away from me." Dodd took a consoling pull from his beer. "The sad part is that with both of them chasing the dragged bait, my car is now sitting up by the monastery with nobody watching it at all. Therefore, I crammed myself into that damned trunk for nothing."

***

We drove back up to the parking area at the base of the cart path, where only two cars now remained. One was Phil Dodd's rental, and the other, in the process of being hitched to a tow truck, was, presumably, the rental of the late Jaspar Rahim.

Dodd climbed out and came around to lay a forearm on the roof and bend down to my open window. "Thanks for the lift, Francis."

"Where are you off to now?"

"While my pals are racing over to Isla Grande to capture me, I'll check out of my hotel, turn in my rental car, and take a shuttle to the airport."

"You're leaving Puerto Rico?"

"Leaving another trail. Got to keep the bright boys busy for the rest of the day, while I delve into some particulars."

Dodd paused at the door of his rental car to stretch his back and massage his shoulder, before getting behind the wheel and starting off down the mountain. We followed, but soon lost sight of him, as he sped down the twisting road heading for the highway back to San Juan.

"That guy is crazy," Ellen said. "He's just making himself look even more guilty."

***

As we neared the Caserio Inn, Ellen spoke without turning toward the backseat. "Alicia, we should go find something to chew on and talk." By the tone of her voice I knew a conciliatory "Please?" was not about to be added.

The response from the backseat was delayed, but finally Alicia said, "We need to go up to the room first and freshen up. I'm not going anywhere looking like this."

I pulled to the curb in front of our hotel. "Just let me park the car and change my clothes, and I'll join you."

"We're going to be talking about you behind your back, Francis," Alicia said. "It makes it hard to do with you sitting there."

With the ladies out and on their way into the Caserio, I found a place to park a few blocks away and hiked back to Ashford Avenue, heading for a small grocery store I'd spotted, tucked among the fashionable shops, global banks, and high-rise hotels of the Condado District. I was prepared for it to be expensive, and it was.

I soon returned to the sidewalk with a plundered wallet and a plastic sack containing a deli sandwich, two bottles of beer, and a five-pack of grocery-store cigars (machine-rolled floor sweepings, according to aficionados, like my boss).

As I entered the Caserio Inn, carrying my bag of groceries, the desk clerk lowered the handset of his house-phone into its cradle and signaled me over to him.

"I was just now calling your room, sir. You have a visitor. I asked him to wait out on the patio, where he could more appropriately continue with his cigarette."

I thanked the desk clerk and with a mixture of curiosity and apprehension walked out to a walled-in area, open to the sky and dotted with white ornamental-iron tables and chairs beneath gaily-colored umbrellas. There was only one person in the patio area, and he was seated at one of the tables, smoking a cigarette.

At my approach, Detective Sergeant Alvarez rose from his chair for a perfunctory handshake.

"Please, sit down, Mr. Elton," Alvarez spoke in English, as he regained his seat. "I ask only for a moment of your time. Naturally, this is concerning the death of Jaspar Rahim."

I set the grocery bag on the table and took a chair adjacent to his, so I wouldn't have to look and talk around the umbrella shaft.

"Is this an official visit?" I asked. "The impression I got from your Captain was that the investigation is no longer active."

"There are a several of points of interest that I wish to pursue with you."

"There's not much I can tell you. As I stated to you before, Rahim was dead, and you and your men were already up at the monastery, before I even heard about it. I don't even know which of his vital organs is supposed to have failed."

"The cause of death has not yet been determined by the Medical Examiner."

"But I thought—"

"I will be frank with you, Mr. Elton. The abrupt termination of my investigation did not sit well with me. I returned to the General Stationhouse in the helicopter, sitting next to Captain Rivera. During our flight, the Captain informed me that I need not trouble the Medical

Examiner any further, with respect to the unfortunate passing of Mr. Rahim."

"Well, that's it then. Nothing more you can do." I was wary of being taken into the Detective Sergeant's confidence.

"The Medical Examiner and I are not friends. He is friends with no one. However, our relationship is cordial. And shortly after my return to San Juan, I encountered the Medical Examiner – purely by chance, of course – while pursuing unrelated business at the Institute for Forensic Science."

While Alvarez paused to stub out his spent cigarette, I wondered why he was bothering to establish a plausible excuse for his forbidden visit to the ME's office, to me of all people. Hell, I'd be gone by tomorrow.

"I found the Medical Examiner in a bad mood," Alvarez continued. "Apparently, he had been pressured into rushing his autopsy. Worse, Captain Rivera had seized on his preliminary report, which stated the death as 'undetermined, pending confirmatory toxicology tests,' and used it to declare Jaspar Rahim's death to be by natural causes, which shut down the investigation. The Medical Examiner is furious about this. He now refuses to release the body for shipment back to France, or to sign any documents that state the category or cause of Mr. Rahim's death."

I felt uneasy. "Why are you telling me this?"

"I will tell you why. The Medical Examiner is a cautious man. In defiance of Captain Rivera, he instructed the toxicologist to proceed with the confirmatory tests. He does this because, if, for instance, the FBI, in one of their ceaseless probes into our affairs, were to decide one day to pursue their own investigation concerning Mr. Rahim's death, the Medical Examiner does not wish to be named as a co-conspirator in a perversion of justice. He suggested that it would be wise for me also to unofficially continue with my part of the investigation. Clearly, he is right. Selective amnesia can strike anyone's superiors without warning."

Detective Sergeant Alvarez paused to light a new cigarette. His next few words came out with the smoke. "However, I have a difficulty. Given the present circumstances, I cannot openly return to the monastery." He allowed the exhaled smoke to dissipate, before adding, "However, Mr. Elton, you can."

I wanted no part of this. "Listen, I don't think I—"

"There are more facts yet to be discovered at the monastery. You have a sharp eye. You saw a battery behind the Abbot's chair, when no one else did. I will need to know more about that, as well. You will educate me."

I groped for a way out. "Now that Rahim is dead, there is no buyer for the monastery. So, there is no need for the Archdiocese to go to the expense of having the paintings appraised, or cleaned, or anything. So, the Archbishop will just send Alicia home. And I won't be able to get back into the monastery without Alicia. I mean, what would I be doing there?"

"Then your first step is to convince the Archbishop that Mrs. Elton should continue with her work. The intention of the Archdiocese is still to close the monastery and to sell the property. The need for the appraisal of the paintings has not evaporated. And I am sure that Mrs. Elton would gladly embrace a renewed opportunity to complete her contract."

I sat there pondering whether a flat-out, heels-dug-in refusal would get me out of it.

But then Alvarez added, "And we wouldn't want that little matter of criminal trespass up at the monastery to hinder your ability to leave Puerto Rico whenever you wish." Alvarez ground out his cigarette in the ashtray with the same motion as turning a key in a lock. "You and Ellen Van Kemp both committed a felony by sneaking into a sealed crime scene."

"Now wait a minute," I said, as calmly as I could with my blood pressure banging in my ears. "According to your Captain, there was no crime. Therefore, there was no crime scene."

"It was a crime scene at the time you entered it. Police officers were clearly posted to secure the grounds and to preserve the evidence. You knowingly breached a restricted area in a willful violation of the law." Alvarez then opened the cell door, just a crack. "However, this matter can be overlooked, if you simply do as I ask."

The Detective Sergeant scraped back his chair and rose to his feet to deliver his departing words. "Do not attempt to disappoint me."

***

What I attempted, after Alvarez had gone, was a few bites of my lunch. But now, through no fault of the deli chef, the sandwich was tasteless, and I put it aside. Instead, I drank beer, puffed on a substandard cigar, and pondered my new circumstance.

Two beers and one cigar later, I decided that if my boss had an immediate assignment for me, I'd be on a plane to Chicago the next day with Alicia and Ellen, and to hell with Detective Sergeant Alvarez. I'd take the gamble that he was bluffing – that Alvarez wouldn't really hazard drawing his Captain's attention to the fact that he was still actively engaged in an investigation he'd been ordered to shut down.

On the other hand, if my boss had nothing immediately for me, well then I supposed it wouldn't hurt to talk the situation over with Alicia. After all, inherent with staying and assisting Alicia to reestablish her contract, there was that exceedingly desirable benefit in the offing. Clearly, an Alicia, happily completing her contract, would be an Alicia, more amendable to finding time to engage in what she'd originally hinted was in store for me when she'd first tricked me into coming to Puerto Rico with her.

I opened my cell phone and tapped in a number I knew by heart.

"Windy City Machinery, Sales and Service Department," a feminine voice efficiently answered.

"Sally, this is Francis. Is the Big Cheese in?"

"He's back from lunch, but I don't think he'll be coherent for a couple of hours."

"Probably forgot to order food again."

"I guess." Then without preamble, "Jack and I are separated now."

I instinctively went on guard. "Gee, that's…ah… that's too bad."

Sometimes, Sally and I would have after-work drinks together at a bowling alley, frequented also by our coworkers. Like as not, one or two of them would drop down into empty chairs at our table. Perfectly innocent. But there were other times when she'd suggest going some place else, and it'd be just the two of us. Those times felt more like a toe testing of less innocent waters.

"So, we're not living together anymore," Sally added.

I stayed in concerned-friend mode. "I guess it must be expensive then. Two separate households, and all."

"Oh, Jack stays in the basement. We couldn't afford two places on what he makes. He's got a bathroom, TV, mini-fridge, and microwave. He's fine down there."

"No offense," I was still being helpful, "but I don't think you've quite grasped the concept of a separation."

"It's a *trial* separation, and the living arrangements are the best we could do. But the important thing is that I'm a free woman now."

With an abundance of caution, I offered, "Well, I'm sure that after, say, a medium-length intermission, or so, the two of you will work it all out."

I listened to silence for a little while and then retreated to the reason for my call. "Well, if the Big Cheese ever gets on his feet again, I wanted to let him know I'm going to cut short this time-off he gave me. I wondered if he had someplace to send me right from here."

"Where's here?"

"San Juan."

"Puerto Rico? What are you doing there?"

"Well, there's this monastery that had some old paintings that had to be appraised and maybe restored, because—"

"You're with *her*, aren't you."

"Well, Alicia had to—"

With a dull click, the line went dead. I didn't think it was a technical glitch.

***

Entering my hotel room, I spotted a flyer for the Hard Rock Café, lying on my satchel. In a white area on the printed page were scrawled the words "Hope to see you there, Marietta." The number 8, in the restaurant's printed phone number, was circled. I wondered what Dodd wanted now.

Following a long shower, my ensuing nap was curtailed by a ringing telephone, the one provided by the hotel. I lifted the receiver.

"When was the last time you ate?" Alicia's voice asked.

The sack containing the deli sandwich with two bites out of it lay abandoned on the desk across the room. "I don't remember."

"We're about ready."

I pulled on slacks and a shirt and knocked on the door of the room next to mine.

Alicia, skirted and bloused in pastels, opened the door. Her face, framed by lush dark hair, glowed with a natural beauty, highlighted by the artistic application of cosmetics, from which she had abstained while among the clerics.

"I had to wake Ellen up, too," Alicia said. "You were snoring pretty loudly next door. I thought that anemic excuse for a painting was going to fall off the wall."

"We climbed a mountain." I entered the room and closed the door behind me.

88

Ellen appeared from the bathroom wearing a flower-patterned dress and holding a hairbrush. In pleasing contrast to the heavy facial paint she'd worn at her mother's funeral, Ellen's makeup now looked skillfully and reservedly applied. I took this as a sign that the two sisters were getting along together again.

When I announced that I was taking them to the Hard Rock Café for dinner and drinks, Ellen looked delighted. Alicia displayed less enthusiasm for burgers and fries, but seemed willing enough to dine out on my wallet, rather than her purse.

I drove us to Old San Juan and parked the rental car down by the harbor where several brightly lit cruise ships were tied up. At a pace dictated by women walking uphill in high heels, we tramped the block and a half up Calle Recinto Sur to the Hard Rock Café.

A long swathe of empty curbside parking spaces in front of the restaurant were reserved for arrivals of the limos, Ferraris, and 'Vettes of the swell people, but it was only just past eight, much too early for that crowd.

Inside, the requisite autographed guitars and performance costumes hung on the walls or were entombed reverently behind glass. A hostess led us up a short flight of stairs and into the dining area. As we passed the long bar, I spotted a lonely Phil Dodd, now sporting a ball cap and aviator sunglasses. It wasn't much of a disguise, but I supposed even a few seconds lead-time would be enough for him to slip out through the kitchen, if necessary.

Once we were seated and had drinks coming our way, Alicia said, "Why don't you go talk to him now, so we can eat in peace."

It didn't surprise me that Alicia had picked out Phil Dodd at the far end of the bar. She had a habit of sweeping a room for male reaction to her entrance. And I never noticed a lack for her fair share of attention.

I rose from my chair. "Just a regular burger for me. I'll try to make this quick."

"I can't say I'm surprised," Alicia confided to her sister. "I knew we wouldn't be rid of him that easily."

"Is it the crazy guy again?"

I left the table and made my way to the end of the bar.

"What are you drinking?" Dodd asked.

"Beer's fine."

"*Camarero*, a *botella* of Budweiser for my *amigo*," Dodd ordered. Then to me, "Hear that, Francis? Spanish."

"I only have until our food comes."

"Okay, I need you to go back up to that monastery for me. I need to know where everyone was just before the time and also right at the time that Rahim pegged out."

For a moment, I considered telling Dodd about my unofficial visit from Detective Sergeant Alvarez, but I decided that I really wanted to become less involved, not more.

"I don't have any further business up at the monastery," I said. "And I'm sure that's exactly what I'll be told, if I go knocking on their door."

"But they'll let Alicia back in. And she needs to finish her work in order to get her check. You heard her. And, more importantly, she needs an escort up at the monastery, so the monks aren't tempted to give in to their carnal urges, or something. And that escort is you."

"I think they've tumbled, by now, to the fact that neither of us is Alicia's husband." An opened bottle of beer appeared in front of me. I took in a cold slug of it.

"Go talk to that priest. What's his name? Let me think…Cabrera, that's it. He's a monsignor. That means he's a big shot. His word would get you and Alicia right back in."

"My boss is expecting me back for another assignment. I have to fly out tomorrow. And frankly, neither Alicia, nor I, are especially anxious to explain about lying to the Archbishop."

"A harmless white lie for a patriotic cause." Dodd airily waved his hand without taking his elbow off the bar. "It won't be so bad. And I'm not asking you to do all that much. There are only four regular monks left up there. That's in addition to the Abbot – but he can hardly move. Now, here's what I can tell you, from what I know. About twenty minutes before the hue and cry goes out that the Arab is dead, I'm in the kitchen with two of the monks – not the big one and the little one, I mean the two regular-sized ones – and they're fixing lunch. And I'm not saying my Spanish is great, but it's good enough to get across to them that the Monsignor, Alicia, and I are not going to be there for lunch."

Dodd interrupted himself for a quick swallow of his beer. "And then, Monsignor Cabrera comes into the kitchen and says to me that he's going to have tea with the Abbot before he leaves, and also that Alicia's ready to go to lunch. Cabrera then goes out to the patio area, and as I look through the doorway, I see him go off with two steaming mugs."

Dodd took another swallow. "Then I leave the kitchen through the door that opens onto the front hallway, en route to going upstairs to get Alicia to take her down to Luquillo and rendezvous with you and Ellen at a restaurant. So, that's where those two monks, the Monsignor, and I were beforehand. At some point ten to fifteen minutes later, Rahim is ushered off life's stage the hard way, while sitting in the Abbot's fancy chair in the dining hall. So, those fifteen minutes are the time period in question."

"As I mentioned before," I said, "I'll be flying out tomorrow with—"

"You're all I've got, Francis. And we were old salts together. Don't you remember the great times, patrolling the sea lanes on the Marietta, the baddest Rottweiler on the whole damned ocean. And occasionally sliding into port for a recreational piece-of-ass and drinking the local hooch until our tonsils caught fire. And then right back out to the open sea where a man can draw a decent breath of fresh air?"

"Were we in the same navy?"

"Those were the best years. I can't believe you don't prize those times. Don't you have any memory at all?"

"I remember you relentlessly angling to get into Alicia's pants, whenever we were tied up in San Diego. If you haven't noticed, she's still kind of pissed about it."

"Okay, okay, we were all younger then. Point taken. But you'll do it, won't you? You'll go back up to that monastery…for your old shipmate?"

"Is it still my patriotic duty, or are you just in trouble with your job?"

"Pick the one you like."

"Look, it isn't just me," I tried another tack. "You're talking about re-enlisting Alicia, too. And if she wants to cut her losses and go home, that's it."

"Talk to her. Romance her. For God sakes, pretty damn soon I'm going to have to surface again, a couple days at the most, and I'd better be lugging a big honking story, starring yours truly, as the hero, and who, against all odds and with tremendous fortitude, solved the murder of our favorite wandering Arab, Jaspar Rahim."

Dodd finished off his drink and signaled for another, before pressing on, "The thing is I'm rotting away in Gitmo. Shadowing Rahim and finding out what he was up to was my ticket back into the game. And as long as we're remembering things past, let's not forget that the reason I'm not still a career Naval Officer – and I could have been a full Commander by now – is because of that stupendous blowup in the Philippines, that was all your fault."

"*You* sent me up into the mountains on a search and rescue. How did *I* know that I was walking into a guerrilla camp?"

"I sent a Second Class Petty Officer into Olongapo City to find a Chief Petty Officer who didn't show up for his port watch and bring him back to the ship, all on the quiet. You get the Chief, I paper over his absence, end of story. It was that simple. Like returning an overdue library book. You didn't have to fall in love with a bargirl with a Kalashnikov in her closet. You didn't have to start a goddamn revolution. Just bring the

Chief back. Sober or drunk, I wasn't fussy. Next thing I know, it's goddamn D-day in Olongapo with reports of two *'Canos*, whose descriptions sound suspiciously like yours and Chief Mossman's, right in the thick of it. How could I paper over *that*? I couldn't. Nobody could. So I take the hit. And you and Mossman each get a fanny spanking, but I get passed over for Lieutenant Commander and tossed over the side. All because *you* couldn't focus on one simple task."

I took another swig of beer, delaying my response. It wasn't even much of a fanny spanking. Like erring priests, Mossman and I were spirited away. I was transferred off the ship and reassigned to the transient barracks at the Navy Base in San Diego, to wait out the last few months of my enlistment, and Chief Mossman, cashing in on his sleeve-load of hash marks, was hurriedly retired. So, Dodd was right. He took the brunt of it.

As though sensing my thoughts, Dodd said, "I'm guessing that the transient barracks were a lot more comfortable than the Filipino prison cell you were staring at." Dodd then added, "You owe me, Francis."

He needn't have appended the last bit. I was already thinking it.

"I'll see what I can do."

I slid off the barstool and headed back to our table. As I weaved through the intervening diners, I spied two men standing across the table from Alicia and Ellen. The waitress was also there, dropping off our food order, and one of the men was making hand motions at Alicia and Ellen's empty glasses.

As the waitress went off about her business, I dropped down on the chair in front of my burger, fries, and beer. "Sorry it took so long. He likes to reminisce."

"We've been having a swell time," Alicia said. "We've acquired boyfriends, while you were gone."

"Who's this guy?" asked the one with silver hair and a gold chain gleaming through his three-buttons-open shirtfront.

"My husband." Alicia placed a French fry just between her teeth and held it there, watching for my reaction, rather than that of the interloper.

I let her have her fun, while the silver-haired man was next presented with Alicia casually appropriating my beer and tilting the bottle to her lips.

"Is *her* husband around here too?" Silver Hair indicated Ellen with his chin.

"This is the night my husband stays home and cleans his gun," Ellen said.

Alicia quickly set the beer bottle down, brought a napkin up to her mouth, and coughed, while air slapping at her sister's shoulder. "Don't wait till I take a swallow of beer and then say something like that. I thought it was going to come out my nose."

Ellen covered a giggle.

"We ordered them drinks." Silver Hair was not amused.

"If you hurry," I said, "you and your silent partner can catch the waitress over at the bar and cancel the order."

Silver Hair and I locked eyes, but there wasn't going to be a fight. He broke first with a glance toward the bar. I knew he was trying to come up with a scintillating exit line, but time was his new adversary. He retired from the field, striding purposefully toward the bar. His sidekick followed.

Alicia gave a histrionic sigh. "My hero."

"Your entertainment."

Ellen had her compact out and was checking her face in its mirror. "I thought it was reaffirming to have a couple of guys hitting on us."

"As long as you have an escape route, it's fun." Alicia was taking her older sister to school. "You've been out of the rodeo a long time. You forget how tightly you have to hold the reins."

Ellen snapped the compact shut. "I think we pretty much covered this ground at lunch."

Alicia didn't push back, but the merriment of only a minute before was gone.

To revive the festive mood, while we ate, I brought up happier times: specifically, the year when Alicia and I were first dating. I was a Seaman, attending Electronics Technician School up at Great Lakes Naval Base. On weekends, I'd come down by train to Chicago, where Alicia shared a cramped apartment with Ellen. If Ellen didn't have a date for the evening, I'd take both sisters out to dinner and some amusement, or the three of us would crowd onto their lumpy sofa – our "amigo pile" – with delivery pizza and a six-pack, and watch a rented movie. I begrudged the Navy for the duty weekends I'd had to spend on base. But mostly for Alicia, Ellen, and I, it was our year of fun.

After a few post-dinner mixed drinks at the Hard Rock, we burst out onto the sidewalk, still recalling long-ago episodes, laughing and tipsy. Unsteadily, we maneuvered our way downhill through the evening crowd. It was like old times again, except that now I wasn't going to get to sleep with Alicia at the end of the evening. But for the present, I figured I had successfully paired good times with Puerto Rico. And hopefully, the feeling would spill over to the next morning, when I would attempt to persuade Alicia to stay on and complete her contract.

Chapter 5

Separately, first Ellen, then myself, and finally Alicia straggled down to the Caserio's kitchenette for coffee and toast. While such fare was far from an antidote for the intoxicants consumed the night before, it was, more or less, what could be kept down.

Like the other bed and breakfast guests who had filtered through the open buffet, we found shelter from the morning's sprinkle of rain under a festively colored umbrella at one of the tables out on the adjacent patio.

While the three of us were still bonded by the fellowship of the shared hangover, I attempted to take a measure of Alicia's willingness to petition the Archdiocese to let her continue with her project.

I began with, "Are you going to talk to the Archbishop before you leave?"

"I told you he's an Auxiliary Bishop, but he wasn't there when I phoned yesterday, while you two were napping. The clerk put me through to Monsignor Cabrera. I set up a meeting with him for later this morning." Alicia took a sip of coffee. "And I can look forward to having my ass handed to me for lying to him about your pal Dodd. But I can't just leave without doing a wrap-up. I have to at least try to maintain *some* semblance of professionalism. I'm just going to live through it, and then we can catch an afternoon flight out."

Alicia's having a meeting already set up encouraged me. "But maybe you could talk the Monsignor into—"

"After the lies I told?" Her eyebrows lowered. "The lies you made me tell. I fully expect Monsignor Cabrera to excommunicate me before I even...I mean, just as I was starting to..."

Alicia scrunched-up a paper napkin, and then, after a few moments, opened it up again, pressed it flat on the table, and began smoothing out the wrinkles. Without looking up from her work, she told us, "When I rode with Monsignor Cabrera up to the monastery yesterday, he was so...so down to Earth. Not all strict and magisterial, like you'd think. Now, I guess I'll be shown the other side of him." Alicia re-clenched the napkin and cast it aside.

"I'm sure he'll let you explain," Ellen soothed.

"And they're still going to sell the monastery property," I slipped Alvarez's argument in. "Soon as they attract another buyer. So, the paintings still have to be appraised. And you're already here, already started. We could suggest the option that you just go ahead with it. That it would be more practical."

"*We* could suggest."

"I'll go with you," I said. "I can explain to the Monsignor how we thought it was our patriotic duty to go along with Dodd's plan. How you, at first, rejected the idea, but Dodd's appeal to God and Country finally persuaded you."

"I'll go too, if it'll help," Ellen offered.

"Thanks, but it's going to be hard enough to explain a different pretend-husband standing next to me, without having to account for yet another member of the troupe."

"Does that mean I'm going with you?" I asked.

"If you want to apologize too, you can go with me."

"And you'll ask Monsignor Cabrera to let you continue with—"

"I'm just going to apologize and say goodbye. I've sullied the name of the Chicago Art Institute, and I've made a freaking fool of myself. How can I ask for anything, but forgiveness?"

I slumped back against the hard iron seatback.

"Francis is just trying to help," Ellen unexpectedly came to my aid. "And it would only take another day. And if it would make everything better…"

"And if Monsignor Cabrera agrees to it," Alicia said, seemingly thinking out loud.

I leaned forward in my chair, careful not to disturb her thoughts.

Alicia lifted her Styrofoam cup and gazed into the black liquid. "I suppose, it would be nice to salvage something from the rubble."

***

As Alicia and I crossed the causeway on our way to the Cathedral in Old San Juan, she continued to enthuse about Monsignor Cabrera, "I think you'll like him. On our trip up to the monastery, after we were done talking business, Monsignor Cabrera told me about how he and the Abbot were boys together growing up in Fajardo. He said they were just Sergio and Pedro then. But they were both going to be priests. And they actually were at the seminary together, but Cabrera dropped out and was then drafted into the Army and sent to Vietnam."

"Wait a minute. They drafted Puerto Ricans?"

"Evidently. Anyway, the Army trained him to be a Medic, because he told them he couldn't kill anyone.

Then after he got back from Vietnam, he completed his seminary studies and finally does become a priest. His first assignment was at the Cathedral, doing all the early morning masses and sorting out the piles of old documents that somehow survived the fires and hurricanes over the centuries. Meanwhile, his pal Sergio, who's been a priest a lot longer, took over as Abbot up at the monastery. Cabrera stayed on at the Cathedral to computerize the bookkeeping and records, back when it was still floppy discs, and he's been like 'Father IT guy' there, ever since. He says he loves being at 'Archbishop Central.' And he and the Abbot have remained close friends all these years."

"That explains why it was Monsignor Cabrera who drove you up to the monastery," I said. "I wondered why such a senior priest was given such a pedestrian assignment."

"A chance for a chat with his old friend, I suppose."

"Sounds like you had a pretty long chat with the Monsignor, yourself."

"It was a long trip," Alicia said. "But it got a little uncomfortable after that, because Monsignor Cabrera then says, 'I see that you are troubled.' Which jolts the hell out of me, because I was still lingering in *his* life story, and it seemed to come out of nowhere. But I recover enough to tell him that my mother had just recently died after a long illness. And then he throws another fastball at me. He says, 'You must give yourself permission to cry.' Just like that. Then he says, 'If not now, when you are with someone around whom you do not need to show strength, then when?'"

When she didn't go on, I prompted, "Then what?"

"I bawled my eyes out all the way up the freaking mountain, that's what. I've never spoken with anyone like that before in my life." Alicia turned her head away. "I shouldn't have told you this. I don't want to talk about it anymore."

***

Up on the high ground in the Old San Juan district, Alicia and I approached a large, architecturally plain church on Calle Cristo.

"That's it," Alicia said. "That's the Cathedral. Look for a parking place."

I had anticipated a familiar European-style cathedral with its vertical Goth and gildings, but the façade of the Cathedral of Old San Juan was so unadorned it was hard to put a name to its architectural style at all. When I pulled to the curb, I was still unsure that this was the right place, but Alicia insisted that it was.

One step through the tall double doors, however, revealed a completely recognizable, richly embellished, Old World Cathedral. We advanced deeper along a center aisle, beneath a barrel-vaulted ceiling, passing between the rows of hardwood pews set on a diagonal checkerboard of outsized marble floor tiles. On either side, beyond the barrel vault's arched supports, various marble side-altars featured statues of saints, stained-glass windows, overlabored paintings, and racks of votive candles alight with offered prayers. At the far end, a domed chancel area sequestered the stately main altar within a white railing.

Halfway up to the main altar, a slender, gray-haired man in a black cassock stood waiting for us. The Roman collar snugly encircling his neck caused me discomfort just looking at it.

"Monsignor Cabrera," Alicia greeted him. "Thank you so much for meeting with us."

The Monsignor took Alicia's offered hand and held it as he spoke to her. "The unfortunate event that engulfed our poor monastery flooded my thoughts throughout the night. I welcome the opportunity to express them." The Monsignor's gaze then fell on me, as he concluded, "Perhaps, it will prove to be cathartic for all of us."

Alicia's hand, released from the Monsignor's clasp, touched my shoulder. "This is Francis Elton. The real Francis Elton." Alicia took a breath. "We used to be married. For four years. I mean, when we were young. It's getting to be a long time ago now."

Without commenting on Alicia's tumble of words, Monsignor Cabrera reached out for the handshake. He had quite a grip for a senior priest.

"You are the industrial engineer," he said.

My face must have registered surprise, because the Monsignor then added, "A priest hears things." He continued with, "I had hoped that you were a structural engineer. We suddenly find ourselves in urgent need of advice on temporarily shoring up an unstable foundation."

"I'm afraid my expertise lies in a different area of engineering."

"So I understand."

"Monsignor," Alicia said, "I am truly sorry about the deception. How I led you to think the NCIS agent was my husband. I can only imagine what you must think of me."

"I confess that I was rather doubtful of the first Mr. Elton from the beginning," Monsignor Cabrera said. "Mostly, it was how he spoke to you. Not his words, but the manner in which he said them. But there was also your noticeable recoil at his touch and his lack of courteous regard for your comfort. The two of you actually bumped, while selecting your seats in front of my desk. In contrast with what I observed with *this* Mr. Elton, as he escorted you down the aisle toward me, the previous Mr. Elton seemed rather ill-at-ease with you."

The Monsignor's observations simply ended there. And for a short, yet awkward, time, there was only the sound of tourists shuffling around by the main door, snapping pictures, and murmuring among themselves.

"I feel so awful," Alicia finally said.

"Feeling shame, for having engaged in a deceit, is quite appropriate," Monsignor Cabrera said. "And yet, after our talk on the road to El Yunque, yesterday morning, I find I cannot cast you as a willing participant in the ill-considered charade."

I noticed that the Monsignor didn't include me in his absolution.

"And then," Monsignor Cabrera's words held a sigh in them, "to have it all turn out so tragically."

"I was still restricted to the guest quarters during all the excitement," Alicia said, "but it must have been horrible for you to find the Arab dead in the Abbot's chair."

"As it happened, I had left the monastery directly after delivering a mug of tea to Sergio – excuse me – to the Abbot. And because I have, so far, avoided the nuisance of carrying a cellular telephone, I was quite unaware of Mr. Rahim's unfortunate passing, until after I had returned to San Juan and Captain Rivera called me. I, of course, immediately drove over to his office and conferred on the matter."

"So," I said, "the last time you saw Rahim, he was fine?"

Monsignor Cabrera shifted his gaze back to me. "I believe I implied that." His dark eyes studied me for a few moments, before he added, "I spoke with Mr. Rahim briefly on my way to deliver the tea. Does that satisfy your curiosity, Mr. Elton?"

Without waiting for a response, Monsignor Cabrera returned his attention to Alicia. "But I am neglecting my duty. The distressing events at the monastery are nothing compared to the sorrow that still weighs upon Alicia's heart." The Monsignor took a pace back to make room. "Please, Alicia, would you step into the pew with me? Will you join us, Mr. Elton?"

Alicia pushed on my shoulder to get me ahead of her, and one-by-one, we entered the narrow space between the pews. Once all three of us were in, we sat shoulder-to-shoulder on the long wooden bench. The Monsignor swung a section of padded kneeler down into place, and following his lead, Alicia and I slid off the pew and onto our knees.

"We are going to pray for your mother."

After some preliminary ritual phrases, Monsignor Cabrera launched into a request to God that He look after Alicia's mother, just as Alicia and Ellen looked after her, during her final days. Subsequent to a few exit words, the prayer was over. And again taking our cue from the Monsignor, Alicia and I slid back onto the pew.

"Whenever you think of your mother," Monsignor Cabrera said, "I want you to say in your head your own version of the prayer we have just shared. Do this, until it gradually supplants your sorrow and you simply carry the prayer unspoken in your head, but always in your heart."

"Thank you, Monsignor," Alicia said.

"I accept your apology, Alicia, and I forgive you. But it is God that you must ultimately satisfy. Please do your best in the future to maintain a level of integrity in your dealings with others equal to that which you would wish from them." Monsignor Cabrera's voice was so soothing that I almost missed that he was now addressing me, when he said, "Let us leave Alicia alone with her thoughts for a few moments."

Monsignor Cabrera lifted the kneeler out of the way and Alicia pulled her feet back to let me sidestep past. I followed Monsignor Cabrera up the main aisle. At first, I thought he was going to part the flood of tourists who had ventured in as far as the vestibule and take me out through the double doors. But instead Monsignor Cabrera abruptly turned and led me crosswise through a section of pews to a deserted area along a wide side aisle, where red curtains covered the entrance to a confessional booth. There the Monsignor stopped and confronted me.

"When was the last time you attended Mass?"

I needed to take a minute to think back.

But apparently, patience was not one of the Monsignor's virtues, "You appear to be probing your long term memory."

Then it hit me. "How did you know I was raised Catholic?"

"I saw a slight genuflection, as you entered the pew. You started an ingrained behavior, but then caught yourself. When did belief in God become for you merely superstition cloaked in ritual?"

I tried a few responses in my head, but couldn't come up with one that didn't sound worse than not answering at all. Alicia was right. The Monsignor's questions came at you hard and fast, as though fired from a pitching machine.

"The day will inevitably come, when you are faced with a moral dilemma. When doing the right thing seems wrong, and doing the wrong thing seems right. What then, Mr. Elton? What procedural guideline will you use? What technical manual will you reference?"

Sparing me no time to respond, the Monsignor next demanded, "What caused the divorce?"

Okay, this was something I'd actually thought about. "It was years ago. I was in the Navy, out to sea most of the time. Alicia and I were married and had an apartment in San Diego. Alicia was so young and beautiful, and I wasn't there to protect her. And there was never any money, but Alicia was rabid about getting her degree in Fine Art. It was her dream to work at the Chicago Art Institute. Without telling me, Alicia took a modeling job, posing for art classes at the University. So, as a University employee, she got free tuition for her own classes. But this was posing nude.

Which was definitely not okay. When I found out, I about went nuts with jealousy. I ranted and demanded that she quit, but she refused. She ranted back that, if I made more money...well, you get the picture. It tore me up inside, especially when I was out to sea. The paperwork said 'irreconcilable differences,' but it was jealousy, pure and simple. That's one of the seven deadly sins, isn't it?"

"No, nor is posing nude for a university art class. Who took possession of the car?"

"What?"

"In the divorce settlement. Even underpaid enlisted men will have a car, if they are married and have an off-base apartment."

"Oh. I let Alicia have the car. It was just an old—"

"You were so consumed with jealousy and rage that you broke the sacrament of marriage. Yet, you then gave the largest asset that the two of you held in common to Alicia. Even though the car could easily have been sold and the money divided equally."

"That wouldn't make sense," I objected. "Then neither of us would have a car. Besides, I'd be living on the ship, and she had to get all the way over to the campus to attend her classes. It was only fair."

"Fair, in this circumstance, would be the equal division of assets. But you did not stop at fair. Your final gesture, upon dissolving your marriage, was to assist Alicia in her struggle to attain her dream, using the only means available to you. How do you explain this to yourself, Mr. Elton?"

The spacious interior of the Cathedral seemed to close in, and the cloying odor of incense began to nauseate me.

"I have to get some air."

***

Outside the Cathedral, a welcome cloud attenuated the sun's harsh rays, and an onshore breeze found its way inland from the high bluff, a block away, to cool the air. I wasn't sure how the Cathedral's great vault had become so suffocating. But I felt better, standing in the fresh air wafting in from the open sea, from which – I now conceded to Dodd – a man can draw a decent breath.

"The Cathedral is very beautiful...on the inside, I mean." Alicia's voice preceded her appearance, as she exited the open church doors.

"The Cathedral has been kept from showing its age by being continually burnt down or blown down, but always resurrected." Monsignor Cabrera followed Alicia out. "However, given its persistent susceptibility to destruction, it was finally deemed more prudent to just keep the exterior simple. Nevertheless, I personally find the façade rather elegant in its simplicity."

Monsignor Cabrera brought Alicia across the open pavement to where I stood, near the steps down to the cobblestone street.

He now faced both of us, but continued speaking directly to Alicia. "It is evident that Mr. Elton did not accompany you today for the purpose of adding his own apology. This leads me to I suspect that you have some other matter that you wish to discuss with me."

To her credit, Alicia came right out with it. "I would like to complete my appraisal of the paintings up at the Monastery."

Monsignor Cabrera nodded. "I had anticipated this. Unfortunately, with Mr. Rahim's death, the situation has become financially much more difficult. An agreement with the National Park Service forbids us from simply abandoning the monastery's main building. But there are presently no funds available, even to have it demolished and the site cleared, let alone rehabilitate it. Therefore, the Abbot and the few remaining monks will have to stay on and maintain the property as it is. We can only pray that the foundation does not catastrophically fail, before a new buyer can be found."

"But still, an appraisal of the paintings, and an estimate of the restoration costs, will have to be addressed eventually," Alicia pressed forward with my talking point. "And I'm here now."

"The money for your services was contingent upon the sale of the property. So, I'm afraid that—"

"I'm willing to pay for my plane ticket and my hotel room," I blurted out. "It'll reduce Alicia's expenses by something like fifteen hundred dollars. I'm sure she will adjust her final accounting to reflect this. Consider it a donation on my part."

I received stares, rather than smiles for my indulgence.

After a prolonged moment, Monsignor Cabrera said, "It is a generous gesture, and I will accept it. Also, it admittedly is my fervent hope that Alicia will discover a treasure among the monastery's paintings, a masterpiece hiding behind years of neglect."

"Then we have a deal?" I asked. "I mean...you and Alicia have a deal?"

"Call it the gambler in me. I must, of course, discuss the matter with the Archbishop." Monsignor Cabrera allowed himself an out. "Unfortunately, he is still in New York. And it has proven difficult to speak with him directly."

The Monsignor paused to consider for a few moments. "Perhaps, just a short update inserted in his daily e-mail would suffice," he then decided. "Let us assume that it will. Therefore, this afternoon, I will call Brother Hugo and leave a message, requesting that he inform the Abbot that the art expert will be returning to the monastery tomorrow morning to continue with her work." Monsignor Cabrera now focused on me. "And I will also ask Brother Hugo to do his best to explain to the Abbot, how it has come to pass that Mrs. Elton will have a *new* ex-husband, accompanying her."

The Monsignor, I noticed, was not above getting in a final kick.

Chapter 6

"Nice one, Francis." Alicia yanked her seat belt across and snapped the metal tab into the buckle for punctuation.

"What did I do wrong now?" I asked, as I cautiously eased the rental car out of the parking space across from the Cathedral grounds.

"First of all, you couldn't possibly bring yourself to apologize for deceiving the Archbishop, so you offer a bribe instead."

"I have never in my whole life spoken a single word to any Bishop whatsoever, let alone an Archbishop. I'd never even spoken to Monsignor Cabrera, before today. So when could I have lied to any of them? What would I be apologizing for?"

"You were complicit."

"Is that the legal term?"

"And why were you grilling Monsignor Cabrera about whether the Arab was still alive, or not, when he left the monastery? What's it to you?"

"I wasn't grilling him. And it was you who brought up the subject."

"And don't think I can't put together your little huddle with that reptile Dodd at the Hard Rock and your sudden desire to get us back up to the monastery. You're such a whore. What's he paying you? Or should I assume he's bankrolling that the fifteen hundred you're so obligingly coughing up, since you've never before in your life had that kind of money to splash around."

"Since we're salting old wounds from our marriage, why is it that getting your own way never seems to be enough?"

Throughout the years of our post-divorce on-again-off-again relationship, the baggage of our marriage was perpetually forwarded to our next destination. I could always count on it arriving at some point, but never precisely when.

With chastising silence from the passenger seat teaching me a lesson, I circled around through the congested streets of Old San Juan and headed back to the Condado District.

***

As Alicia and I entered the lobby of the Caserio Inn, the desk clerk called us over. Ellen had left us a message that she'd gone to the beach a block behind the hotel.

While Alicia was in her room changing into more appropriate attire, I was in mine donning shorts and sandals. A brochure for the San Cristobal Fortress lay on top of my satchel. On the line stating the hours that the historical site was open, the 5pm closing time had been circled and an "M" written next to it – as though "Marietta" wasn't code enough.

Alicia and I left the Caserio together and walked the short distance to the beach in search of Ellen. Having revitalized her contract (thereby avoiding a blot on her personal file at the Art Institute) and having imposed sufficient punishment on me (as far as I could tell), we were again on, more or less amicable, speaking terms.

And happily, the conversation stayed on neutral subjects, as we walked the narrow side road that ended in the wide beach that ran for miles along the towering oceanfront hotels of the Condado District.

Ellen was easy to spot. Her hotel bath towel was laid out in a lightly populated area of sand, and a rented wood-and-canvas backrest propped her up in a sitting position with her legs attractively posed and glistening with lotion in the late morning sun.

"I see we've kept our top on today," Alicia greeted her sister. "And with all those delicious-looking men just over there."

Ellen kept her eyes on the paperback Romance she was reading through sunglasses. "Look a little harder at the delicious men."

Alicia held a flat hand above her eyes for a second survey of the men – some tossing around a Frisbee, others sunbathing together, still others standing paired off with cool drinks and conversing tête-à-tête.

"Oh." Alicia dropped her hand.

"Sometimes they go frolic in the surf," Ellen said. "But right now the Saudis are chilling the party."

A group of four people stood almost motionless and thigh deep in the modest waves about ten yards from shore. The two Arab men wore knee-length swimming trunks on the lower half of their hairy torsos. Of the two Arab women, one wore a dark brown one-piece bathing suit – the kind my grandmother wore at the beach at Traverse City, when I was a boy. Still, the somber one-piece looked quite daring next to the sari-like affair covering the other woman, complete with a swath of the material draped over her hair.

Displaying slightly more animation than mannequins, the Arab group did not interact with the water any more than necessary, and they didn't appear to interact with each other at all. At the water's edge, their children, large eyed and topped with beautiful and abundant black hair, were busy scooping wet sand into brightly colored plastic buckets and building miniature desert fortresses. One of the Arab men kept a strict eye on the gays mingling on the beach; the other kept a lookout toward the horizon, perhaps scanning the waves for an assault from the sea.

Maybe, we'd all misjudged Jaspar Rahim. Maybe, he'd had the vision to identify a legitimate need for a quiet place up in the mountain rain forest, as a retreat for his fellow Arabs to enjoy themselves while on vacation. Maybe, the hot sand and salt water reminded them too much of home, and some time spent in a tropical forest, lushly green and smelling of refreshing rain, would help them relax a little.

"If you're done toasting your legs, I'd like to do some shopping," Alicia told her sister. "I've got the day off. And they're letting me go back up to the monastery tomorrow."

"Sounds like things went well with the Bishop."

"It was Monsignor Cabrera that we talked to. Francis laid fifteen hundred dollars on the table, and the Monsignor has dreams of untold riches hidden among the artwork. So, the contract practically rejuvenated itself. I just had to stand there and look pretty."

Ellen put her book down. "I never know when to believe you two."

"Then believe this. If Francis can afford to pay cash for his sins, he can afford to buy us lunch."

***

We lunched at the Parrot Club in Old San Juan, celebrating Alicia's born-again contract by washing down our sandwiches with Rum and Cokes. Alicia and Ellen, delighted at the prospect of their shopping trip, then went off on their own with the rental car. This left me with about three hours, before my rendezvous with Phil Dodd at the San Cristobal Fortress.

Leaning forward to maintain alignment with Earth's gravitational pull, I climbed a steep and narrow street. As the muscles in my thighs burned, I gave some thought to my assignment from Detective Sergeant Alvarez. Returning to the monastery and snooping for Dodd meant I'd have to do the same for Alvarez. No way could I avoid that. And since I'd probably have only one shot at it, I figured I'd better get a clearer idea of what the Detective Sergeant expected of me.

I emerged onto a thoroughfare, running along the top of the old city wall, where I stood a good chance of catching a passing cab. While waiting, I extracted the Detective Sergeant's card from my wallet and punched the numbers into my cell phone. I was informed that the Detective Sergeant was in his office and that I could leave a message. Nice, I thought, I didn't even rate being put on hold. My message was that I was on my way over.

It was a lengthy and expensive cab ride to the address on Alvarez's card, but thankfully once we were out of Old San Juan and onto an expressway, the cab driver could pick up the pace. We took a cloverleaf exit onto Franklin D. Roosevelt.

This disoriented me enough that I asked, "Where are we?"

"We are in Hato Rey," the cab driver responded in English. "It is the neighborhood of the very rich and the very poor. The banks, the University, the Coliseum, the FBI – and of course, for you, the General Stationhouse of the Puerto Rico Police – they all are here. And they surround themselves with their poor friends of the barrio."

Seemingly spanning the distance between the planet's surface and the lower stratosphere, the General Stationhouse loomed as an imposing mass of concrete, steel, and glass, garnished with a helicopter pad perched high above and extending beyond one edge of the rooftop. The cab made a sweeping U-turn and stopped in front of the entrance.

Having paid off the driver, I pulled open a heavy glass door and crossed a spacious lobby. After informing the uniformed clerk that Alvarez was expecting me, she made a phone call.

"Detective Sergeant Alvarez is in the building, but is not available." The clerk re-cradled the phone and took up her pen. "Would you care to leave a message?"

Damn it, it was Alvarez who had approached *me* for help. As far as I was concerned, being rebuffed twice marked the end of any cooperation on my part.

"Apparently, it is not that important," I managed to tell the clerk, without outwardly losing my temper. But if the hydraulic closer had allowed it, I would have slammed the heavy glass door behind me.

I stormed off in search of cold liquid solace. But I didn't make it as far as the nearest watering hole. About a quarter-mile away from the grandiose General Stationhouse, a Crown Victoria pulled to the curb alongside me. The passenger window descended with the whirring of a little electric motor, and Detective Sergeant Alvarez leaned across from the driver's seat.

"Get in, Mr. Elton."

I was still fuming, but this is what I'd traveled halfway across the city for. I climbed into the passenger seat, and Alvarez pulled out into traffic.

"You must not contact me," Alvarez dispensed with any greeting. "It cannot be known that I am pursuing this case. I was sure that I made that clear to you."

"How else could I let you know that I am going back up to the monastery tomorrow?"

"Ah. This is good. Very excellent. Now, I need—"

"Hey. It cost me a lot of money to arrange this. The taxi ride over here wasn't cheap, either. How about a little thank you?"

"Yes, of course. Thank you. I had every confidence in you. So what I need to know from you right now concerns what you said about the Abbot's chair. You said there was some type of battery attached to the chair. You must tell me more about this."

"All I know is what stuck in my mind from that magazine article about what was dubbed a Baghdad battery. And what I saw behind the Abbot's chair was functionally the same thing, just rigged up with scraps of modern plumbing. But, no question it would work as a battery, just like that ancient one they dug up. Although, as I said, only a handful of archaeologists thought people living sometime around the first-century actually built a battery on purpose."

Alvarez kept driving the neighborhood, driving Puerto Rican style: slowly, yet with single-minded aggression. "And what do *you* think, Mr. Elton?"

"I think it's easy to make a battery. Maybe, even to make one inadvertently, while you're trying to make something else. But I agree with you and Dodd that it's pointless to make one at all, unless you hook it up to something that can actually use its energy."

We ramped onto the expressway, and I got a taste of Alvarez's driving skills at speed. Soon, we were flying low across a long bridge over a sizable lake and heading for the SJU airport, but instead, Alvarez merged onto a different expressway, cutting through the countryside. I didn't get the impression Alvarez had a definite destination, but we sure were making good time.

"You say that it is so easy to make a battery, that even people living in the time of Jesus could do it," Alvarez said. "Then make one for me, Mr. Elton. I challenge you. Make me a battery."

I couldn't understand Alvarez's fascination about something that was so basic. It was like he was asking me to demonstrate that water runs downhill. "Okay, but I'll need a voltmeter to prove it to you. You don't strike me as a man who takes things on faith."

"You have not misled yourself."

We were well past the airport and out into the countryside. The Detective Sergeant took the last Carolina exit and waited in his car, while I ran into a Home Depot store and returned with a cheap, digital multi-meter.

Watching me cut the meter free of its plastic packaging with my Swiss army knife, Alvarez asked, "You buy the meter only? You need nothing else?"

I looked up from my work. "I need a lovely glass of wine."

Behind his wire-rims, Alvarez's eyebrows lowered. "Do not play with me, Mr. Elton."

"Wine is the one item I need for a battery that I don't usually carry in my pocket."

The Detective Sergeant's eyebrows stayed where they were, as he shifted the transmission into 'drive.' I felt fairly sure he was now considering what he was going do to my face, if I couldn't deliver.

* * *

The neighborhood bar that Detective Sergeant Alvarez selected would have needed a good floor-mopping to rise to the level of seedy. As we entered, a man in a back booth hastily swept his plastic bags of merchandise off the table and into a small plastic cooler on the seat beside him. His customer eased himself away and slunk into another booth.

Alvarez and I selected seats along the row of stools, and the bartender arrived just as my ten-dollar bill landed on the bar top. I ordered a glass of red wine, the cheapest they had. Alvarez waved the bartender away without ordering. Looking around, I saw that the attention we'd drawn on our entrance had not subsided. I felt uneasy, but the Detective Sergeant showed me a smile and an amused wink at the discomfort that the bulge at his hip under his shirt flap was causing the bar's patrons.

When the bartender returned with a stemmed glass of wine and a modest clutch of dollar bills, I pulled a small glass ashtray toward me. From the loose change in my pocket, I selected a penny and a nickel. I laid the two coins next to one another within the ashtray, but not touching, and poured in enough wine to just submerge them.

Alvarez watched, as I plugged the leads into the little digital meter and positioned the selector switch to read low voltage for direct current. When I touched the tip of one lead to the penny and the other lead's tip to the nickel, the LED's on the meter displayed a reading of just over four tenths of a volt.

"Voila," I said. "Not quite half a volt, but a battery, nonetheless."

Alvarez frowned and the bartender leaned in for a closer look.

"And this is the same principle as your Baghdad battery?" Alvarez asked.

"What you see behind the Abbot's chair is simply a scaled-up version," I said. "But given the greater surface area of the copper tube and the iron rod, it might achieve as much as a couple of volts."

"So the Baghdad battery could not have killed the Arab?"

The bartender's head came up. He looked at Alvarez, then at me, and quickly moved to the other end of the bar.

"No," I said. "A car battery is a thousand times more powerful, but you would feel nothing if you grabbed your car's battery terminals, one in each hand. Your body has too much resistance to direct current."

"But someone went to the trouble of constructing a crude battery out of scrap plumbing and installed it behind the Abbot's chair. Of what use can it be?"

"I didn't say that I know what it's for. I only said that I know what it is."

***

"I will no longer concern myself with your Baghdad battery," Alvarez announced, as he drove the Crown Vic away from the low-life bar. He pulled a few pages of folded paper from his shirt pocket and slapped them onto the console between us. "And this. This so-called preliminary autopsy report is equally useless. Now, everything depends on the toxicology results. Captain Rivera cannot control that. And while I wait for those results, I will focus my interest on my list of possible suspects."

I picked up the report and tried to make sense of it, but there were too many medical terms in Spanish, or perhaps Latin, that were outside my vocabulary.

"I had previously confirmed," Alvarez said, "after speaking with the two monks who prepare the food, that Special Agent Dodd and Monsignor Cabrera were in the kitchen with them, approximately fifteen minutes to a half hour before the bodyguard called out. Mr. Dodd claims that he left the kitchen a short time after the Monsignor did and was on his way up to the guest quarters, when he heard the bodyguard yelling. His claim, of course, is yet to be substantiated."

Alvarez momentarily broke off to concentrate on making the sweeping loop to merge onto the toll road. "And as for Monsignor Cabrera, I had no opportunity to speak to him at all, before my investigation was halted.

So, I have only the statements of those two monks that the Monsignor left the kitchen with the intention of having tea with the Abbot, before returning to San Juan."

Alvarez briefly glanced over at me, before finally issuing his instructions. "So tomorrow, up at the monastery, I want you to discover Monsignor Cabrera's movements, from the time that he left the kitchen until the time that he left the monastery. And I need to know every gap in that timeline. This I will compare to the statement that the Monsignor gave to Captain Rivera at the General Stationhouse."

"You suspect Monsignor Cabrera of killing Rahim?"

"I wish only to eliminate the Monsignor from my list."

"I guess that's a nicer way of putting it."

I decided to withhold, for the time being, that Monsignor Cabrera had mentioned stopping by the dining hall for a chat with Rahim, prior to taking the tea on up to the Abbot's bedroom. It might end up being the only information I'd have to offer Alvarez at all. Especially, if none of the monks up at the monastery felt open to informing on a priest.

Just to make sure, I asked, "So the only person's activities you want me to try to discover are those of the Monsignor?"

"I could hardly expect from you an unbiased accounting of the actions of your friend Mr. Dodd."

"Well, I mean, what about the bodyguard? Why is *he* not a suspect?"

"The bodyguard, if he so wished, had available to him abundant opportunities to kill Mr. Rahim anywhere along the cart path and dispose of the body in the rain forest. He then would simply take the next plane to Paris, and no one would be the wiser. We cannot assume the murderer was witless."

"Okay, I guess I can't argue with that."

"And consider this. It was reasonable to use the police helicopter to bring the Medical Examiner and Detectives to the scene and to transport the body away. It is a remote area, and time matters greatly in this heat and humidity. But then, as you saw, a mere few hours later, the helicopter returns. And it brings to the monastery Captain Rivera, who proclaims death by natural causes and terminates my investigation. Could the Captain not have used the telephone on his desk, rather than a helicopter, in order to communicate with me? Or was the helicopter necessary to remove the investigation's Lead Detective from the scene of the crime, as promptly as possible?"

I didn't really think he was seeking my input, so I remained quiet.

"This has the reek of politics, Mr. Elton. Strings from high places have been pulled. And who involved in this case is affiliated with such power and influence? I can think of only two. Your friend Mr. Dodd, a Special Agent within a department of the Federal Government, and Monsignor Cabrera, a significant figure within an Archdiocese of the Catholic Church."

"That's a very short list," I said.

"Startle me by making it longer."

***

After leading Detective Sergeant Alvarez to believe that my impending rendezvous was with Alicia and

Ellen, I had him drop me off at the Piña Colada Club in Old San Juan. An earlier glance at my tourist map had shown that the restaurant was located across the boulevard from the San Cristobal Fortress.

Before we parted, Alvarez wrote a phone number on the back of another of his cards and handed it to me. "Use this number to call me when you return from the monastery tomorrow with the information. Do not call the General Stationhouse again."

Having survived a perilous boulevard crossing, I walked up the wide cement ramp, under a punishing afternoon sun, to the entrance of the fortress. As I paid the fee, the girl told me that I'd be the last visitor to be admitted that day, and that I had only 20 minutes to view the historic site before closing. I bought a short bottle of cold water in the souvenir shop and leisurely drank it down, while scanning the crowd that milled about on the parade ground, although not really expecting Dodd to be among them.

At ten minutes to five, I climbed a flight of broad interior stairs all the way up to the highest level. If the fortress were a ship, that's where conning tower would be. And knowing Dodd, that's where he would be – up there, on watch.

He was easy to spot, since the only other people along the upper-level parapet were a pair of elderly tourists. Dodd again wore sunglasses, but instead of a ball cap, this time he wore a full-brimmed straw hat with a gaily-colored cloth band, the kind sold to pale-skinned tourists for sightseeing out in the baking sun.

As I approached, Dodd said, "Quite a nice vantage point up here, Francis. Just look at that ocean."

Dodd wasn't looking at the ocean when he said this. He was looking past me toward the top of the worn steps that I'd just climbed. We now stood well away from those steps and close to a padlocked wooden door, from which, I noticed, the screws, meant to secure the metal hasp to the weathered-gray wooden frame, had been pried free.

Since I wasn't the one being hunted, I took in the panoramic view of the Caribbean Sea, and spoke without facing Dodd. "Alicia and I are going back up to the monastery tomorrow."

"I knew I could depend on you. Just like the old days."

"I don't suppose it matters to you that I had to volunteer to cover my own expenses for the trip down here in order to make this happen."

"You said what you had to say to get the deal done." Dodd's voice held no hint of concern. "That's what counts."

I turned around to look inland. Over the top of the far wall and beyond the jumbled rooftops of the old city, there was a good view of San Juan Bay. In addition to providing protection from a seaward attack, the San Cristobol Fortress had been placed in an excellent position for harbor defense too. And given the superior height of the upper parapet, I judged that the few rusty cargo ships, anchored off the old wharfs of the warehouse district, were easily within cannon ball range.

Dodd turned to where I was looking. "You won't see those freighters there for much longer. They're moving all the shipping down to Ponce. First the Navy's gone, now the freighters. Nothing but cruise ships, after that." Dodd let out a sigh. "I hate to see this. They're selling the soul of the city, just so they can jam in a few more hotels and condos. In the old days, the Headquarters of the Tenth Naval District was right over there." He indicated somewhere off to his left with a wave of his hand. "A few rotting barracks and weeds growing up through the cracked concrete, that's all that's left now. No more Caribbean Sea Frontier, no more Greater Antilles Defense Command. You been out to 'Rosy Roads,' lately?"

"I haven't ventured that far yet." I vaguely knew of Roosevelt Roads, only because it had been a Naval Air training base that had an active horseback riding stable and its own golf course.

"It's enough to make you sick to see it now. I mean, at least it's still there – for the time being anyway. But it's like a skeleton of what it was. Less than that even. Just a few picked-over bones left. The Navy's offered it to the Puerto Ricans, but they don't know what to do with it. You remember 'Papa Joe's' just outside the north gate?"

"We were in the Pacific when we sailed together," I reminded him.

"You remember how there were no walls, except the one behind the bar? Just iron pipes holding up the roof, so free and open. I know you remember slamming down beers and using Joe's phone to order out for pizza, and peeing between the cars in the parking lot, because the can was always backed up, and that big, honking boom box Joe had behind the bar."

"Yeah." I now just played along. "The best of times."

"And then in the morning steaming out for a little gunnery practice and hurling a few explosives at the live impact area on that one little island, what's the name… Vieques?"

"I think so."

"Of course, the people living on the island didn't much like it. Then that security guard got blown up, and the Puerto Ricans really went ballistic. Even the Catholic Church was denouncing us. I think that's what finally did it."

"That's when the Navy pulled out, wasn't it?"

"Enough to make you sick."

We'd begun strolling along the upper parapet.

"You find out anything?" Dodd asked.

"When Alicia and I talked to Monsignor Cabrera this morning, he told us about seeing Rahim, alive and well in the dining hall, on his way taking tea up to the Abbot's room."

"Well, that's a little something I didn't know. Took a little detour, did he? Was the bodyguard there with Rahim, did Cabrera say?"

"Nothing about the bodyguard. He said he left the monastery right after delivering a mug of tea to the Abbot."

"*Delivering* a mug of tea? I thought he was supposed to be *having* a mug of tea with the Abbot. I saw him through the kitchen doorway with two mugs, as he walked off. Two. Plain as day. You've got to dig a little deeper when you ask questions, Francis."

"I got my head bit off for asking just one question."

"I'm going to check into Cabrera. I don't like how he slipped away, just before Rahim turned up dead."

"His first name's Pedro, and he was an Army Medic, during the Vietnam War."

Dodd looked at me with wonder. "I take it all back. You *do* know how to gather intel. Specialist Pedro Cabrera. I'll see if my little honey up in Mayport has a contact in Army Records. Report in to me when you get back from the monastery tomorrow."

"We can't meet here, again. It'll be too late. This place will be closed."

"See that bunch of shanties down by the water?" Dodd pointed to a haphazard sprawl of worse-for-wear buildings down by the water line below the old city wall.

"It looks like a sleepy fishing village."

"It isn't. I'm holed up down there for now. I'll leave a postcard in your hotel room with directions."

"Can't you just tell me now? I'll concede you've been crafty as hell at getting in and out of my room."

"If there's no postcard, something's changed and the meeting's off. Or, if there's a tourist postcard, restaurant flyer, or whatever, that's different than what we discussed, you go there instead. See how simple?"

We had circled back to the wooden door where we'd first met. The elderly couple had wandered off, and on the parade ground below us, I could see tourists being gathered and herded toward the exits.

"Looks like our time is up," I said.

"One last thing. I nosed around in Jaspar Rahim's laptop when I was up in his hotel room yesterday afternoon, going through his stuff. It was all in French, even the e-mails from Monsignor Cabrera. But then I found some recent Google searches for *Inquisition Espagnole*. That's the Spanish Inquisition in French, isn't it?"

"Sounds like it."

"Rahim didn't strike me as the type to dabble in Church history as a hobby. Makes you wonder. Keep your ears open about that, will you?"

Dodd opened the wooden door, revealing a dark, narrow stairway going down. He stepped onto the top tread, but just before pulling the door closed behind him, he instructed, "You go down the stairs you came up. And would you mind pushing the screws for the hasp back into their holes? They must have gotten stripped out, or something. No sense upsetting the Park Service."

***

A taxi dropped me off at the Caserio Inn. In a plastic sack, I carried four bottles of Medalla Light with the intention of stealing a relaxing hour or so with a few well-earned cold ones.

I entered the hotel and climbed the three steps up from the lobby to the small lounge area that I had to cross in order to access the stairs up to my room. As I entered the lounge, two men rose to their feet from out of the wicker furniture. I recognized them as the two NCIS agents who had stopped our rental car with Phil Dodd in the trunk. Their sunglasses were off, but they still wore the windbreakers to cover their side-arms.

"Francis Elton. We need to speak with you."

The speaker stepped toward me, while the other agent circled around to block any retreat.

"I'm in a rush," I said. "I'm meeting some people for dinner."

"This will only take a minute. NCIS. I'm Special Agent Randal. This is Special Agent Briggs." He produced an I.D. that had the same trappings, as the one Dodd had shown us at the airport. "You aren't in any trouble. Have a seat."

I sat on one of the wicker chairs, withdrew a bottle from the sack, and pried off the cap with the opener blade on my Swiss Army knife. These things always take longer than a minute, no sense letting the beer go warm. Randal sat opposite me. Briggs settled on a loveseat, positioned between me and the lobby. Next came the pause, where the person of interest is supposed to ask what's going on. Instead, I took a swig of beer and let the clock run.

Randal finally broke the silence. "We're trying to contact Philip Dodd. Have you seen or spoken to him today?"

While taking another unhurried swallow of beer, I noticed Briggs's eyes, beneath a sweating forehead, following the arc of the sweating bottle.

I lowered the bottle and said, "The last time I saw Dodd was yesterday, up at the monastery. I don't know where he is now. I don't have his phone number."

"We found his mobile phone in a police helicopter," Randal said. "At the old Isla Grande airport. He's checked out of his hotel. Turned in his rental car at the SJU airport. But there's no record of him flying out. We think he's still here on the island."

I briefly wondered if he ever let Briggs say anything. "Maybe you should talk to the Puerto Rico Police."

"The chicken-and-rice boys claim they don't know what became of him. Lost track after they shut down their so-called investigation. But, for the NCIS, the Rahim murder is still open. It's in your best interest to cooperate with us."

It was time to bring this to a close. "Alicia and I did what Special Agent Dodd, as a representative of our Government, asked us to do. For our country, in a time of war. It all fell apart, but that's not our fault. We're out of it now."

"When Dodd contacts you, you call us." Randal produced a business card from a little case.

I tilted the beer bottle to my lips again, while I decided whether to pretend to cooperate, or not. I decided on 'not.' "This is your problem. Keep your card."

"Look, hotshot," Randal said. "We have a rogue agent running around loose. Now, we *will* bring him in. Bet on it. You keep holding back on us, you face a charge of 'aiding and abetting.' That's a felony. And believe me, we *will* pursue it." Randal again pushed his card toward me. "It's always best to cooperate with your Government. Take the card."

"I've got to go." I slid the empty bottle back into the sack and stood. "The ladies will be upstairs, waiting. I don't want to start off the evening with them being pissed at me for being late."

The words were barely out of my mouth, when Alicia and Ellen came bustling into the hotel and up the three steps from the lobby, chattering happily and loaded down with shopping bags.

As they attained the lounge level, Alicia spotted me. "Francis! Look what I got you."

Alicia dropped all but one of her bags onto the half of the wicker loveseat not occupied by Briggs and pulled out a souvenir pirate hat with a purple plume.

"Oh." Alicia now became aware of the NCIS agents. "Oh Jesus, not freaking more of *them*."

"It's okay," I said. "We're done. Let's go upstairs and change for dinner."

I took the pirate hat from Alicia, put it on my head, and gathered up some of the shopping bags that were crowding Briggs.

Randal and Briggs rose to their feet – Briggs remained stationed behind us, and Randal stood encroaching upon, but not quite blocking, our course toward the stairway up.

Randal asked, "Have you ladies seen Philip Dodd today?"

"You mean, while we were out shopping?" Alicia asked in return.

"Or maybe he visited your room."

"Well, naturally we keep any number of men up in our room," Alicia said. "But I don't believe we have a Philip, do we, Ellen?"

"No." Ellen drew her shopping bags up in front of her. "No Philip."

"Now, you secret agents run along." Alicia picked up the remainder of her shopping bags. "You fooled me once with the patriotism gag. It won't work again." She turned to me. "Wrap it up with these two, Francis. We're hungry."

Alicia swung her shopping bags ahead of her, in a groin-threatening manner, as she briskly proceeded on toward the stairs. Randal quickly sidestepped out of harm's way, and Ellen rushed to catch up to her sister.

Laden with the sack of beer on the port side, Alicia's shopping bags on the starboard, and the plumed pirate hat aloft, I followed in the ladies' wake. As I walked past him, Randal reached out and jammed his card into my shirt pocket.

"You see him, you call me. You keep screwing around, you go down with him."

Chapter 7

Alicia and I nursed after-dinner drinks in a picket-fenced, outdoor dining area in front of a small, only-moderately-overpriced, Ashford Avenue restaurant. Ellen had excused herself to "powder her nose."

"What did those two jug-heads back at the hotel want?" Alicia asked.

"They were requesting my cooperation, while threatening me with 'aiding and abetting.' The usual G-man stuff," I said. "So, I guess Dodd's officially a hunted fugitive now."

"And?"

"And they can go screw themselves. I'm tired of being recruited."

Alicia stirred her drink with a pair of narrow red straws for a few moments. "Who else has been recruiting you? Besides your old lieutenant."

"For Dodd, all I have to do is find out where everybody was located when the bodyguard started—"

"That's not what I asked. Who else wants you to nose around up at the monastery?" Alicia now tapped insistent red straws on the tabletop. "There's something more going on, isn't there?"

Ellen rejoined us, took in the situation, and asked, "What have you done now, Francis?"

"Just let me handle it," I responded to Alicia. "It's nothing you need to—"

"Do you want to go back up to the monastery with me tomorrow, or not?" Alicia stopped the straw tapping and bore her ethereal green eyes into my standard issue brown ones. "Who else?"

"Alvarez."

"You're joking. What's he need *you* for? *He's* the freaking detective."

"Alvarez never stopped believing that Rahim was murdered. But, since his Captain declared it death by natural causes, Alvarez can't continue his investigation openly. So he pressed me into his service."

"How do you let crap like this happen to you?"

"Alvarez is holding a criminal trespass charge over Ellen and me, and—"

"What?" Ellen brought a napkin to her chin, as she quickly set her drink down.

"I take it," Alicia said, "that Alvarez doesn't know you're working for Dodd, and Dodd doesn't know about Alvarez."

"For now, it's probably best to let them each think he's getting an exclusive," I said. "Alvarez hasn't crossed Dodd off his shortlist yet. And for different reasons, they're both suspicious of Monsignor Cabrera."

"That's just loony," Alicia said. "Monsignor Cabrera is a saint. And if anybody murdered that Arab, it would be that nut-job Dodd."

"When did I trespass?" Ellen looked worried. "Am I in trouble?"

"No. It's just that Francis can't seem to keep things simple." Alicia's eyes swung back to lock onto mine. "And if he starts pestering those monks up at the monastery, he'll likely get us *both* thrown out."

I noticed the wait-staff in a group looking over at us. I didn't know if was because of the subject of our conversation, or that a small, impatient crowd had begun to build out on the sidewalk.

"Let's go somewhere else for a nightcap," I suggested, signaling for the check while trying to think of someplace cheaper to drink.

***

The sparsely populated lounge at a nearby towering ocean-side hotel featured a two-piece band: a keyboard player, suited in a sequin-trimmed tuxedo, and a castanet-wielding songstress, gowned for a red carpet arrival.

Much less formally dressed, Alicia, Ellen, and I sipped iced Kailua and coffee and leaned in to hear each other beneath the renditions of pop songs from the seventies.

"Are you okay with entertaining yourself tomorrow," Alicia asked her sister, "while Francis and I go back up to the monastery?"

"I'll be fine. I'll take a book down to the beach again. Maybe write a couple postcards to my boys."

A commotion started up in the hotel's casino just outside the glass panels that separated it from the lounge. Within the carnival of whirling lights, shiny primary colors, and electronic noises, an elderly lady attempted to contain the windfall of tokens gushing out of a slot machine. While two of the casino employees assisted the elderly lady, several others kept watchful eyes over the nearby slots during the distraction, on alert for any knavish appropriations from un-minded token buckets.

"That looks like fun," Ellen said. "I think I'll just wander through the casino for a minute."

"Keep in sight, will you?" Alicia said. "I haven't the stamina left to organize a search party tonight."

"I've stayed up past my bedtime before." Ellen slung her purse strap over her shoulder and left us.

"While Ellen explores Wonderland," I said, "maybe you can save me some time up at the monastery tomorrow. Was anyone with you, around the time Rahim died?"

"I'm not sure when he died exactly. Why? Does someone we know need an alibi?"

"Just sorting things out," I said. "So, Rahim's death happened when you were still alone up in the guest quarters, waiting for Dodd to return." Then I had a thought. "But why weren't you in the dining hall, working with the paintings?"

"I was in there earlier, running a flashlight over the paintings, checking the signatures, and jotting down some initial observations. Dodd and Monsignor Cabrera were with me. The Arab had his fat butt planted in that big fancy chair and his henchman was by his side. But we were two separate groups. We didn't talk to them, they didn't talk to us. Of course, it might just have been a language thing."

"So, Rahim wasn't doing anything, just sitting there?"

"He seemed happy enough. But then, Monsignor Cabrera says the Abbot should be finished with his prayers by now, and we ought to go meet him. Dodd and I go with Monsignor Cabrera up to the second floor to the Abbot's room. But just as he's about to knock on the door, it opens and out pops this little three-quarter-sized monk, who looks like he's about twelve. The little monk and Monsignor Cabrera talk in Spanish for a bit in the hallway, and then we go into the Abbot's room. The Abbot is sitting in a straight-back chair with a book on his lap. He looks really frail, and his fingers are so crooked from arthritis it made my own hands hurt. The room is hot and stuffy, but he's got a fan blowing on him, so—"

"Wait a minute. A fan? They have electricity for a fan?"

"It was a small table fan. I guess it could have been battery powered. I didn't scrutinize it."

"That's probably what it was. Just go on."

"The Monsignor talks with the Abbot for a while in Spanish. The conversation starts out with what sounded like pleasantries. And then I can tell Monsignor Cabrera is explaining who Dodd and I are, because he turns toward us and says our names. Well, my name and Dodd's assumed name. But pretty soon, there starts this tense back and forth going on between the two of them. And the Abbot just keeps saying what sounded like 'Me see ya', over and over. Which I know doesn't mean 'I'll see you later', but I couldn't help thinking it."

"He was saying 'my chair.' Probably talking about the one Rahim was sitting on, down in the dining hall. The one they call 'the Abbot's chair'."

"Well anyway, after some more Spanish, we finally leave the Abbot's room and go into the guest quarters. Monsignor Cabrera said he wanted to talk to me about my first impressions of the paintings, before Dodd and I left for Luquillo. But first, he said he had to dash down to the kitchen to tell the cooks that it'd just be the Arabs eating lunch in the guest quarters that day, because he forgot to tell Brother somebody-or-other – I guess that little monk – to do it. Then out of the blue, Dodd offers to go, instead. He claims he can speak enough Spanish to get the message across. And I thought this was really odd, but off he went."

"Dodd told me about that. And that he was still in the kitchen when Cabrera came through to grab a couple mugs of tea."

"I was just coming to that," Alicia said. "So after Dodd left, I gave Monsignor Cabrera a brief overview of the paintings. Well, it had to be brief. I didn't have all that much time with them. But he seemed really pleased when I told him I'd have it wrapped up by the end of the next day. Then Monsignor Cabrera says he'd arranged to bring the Abbot his late-morning tea, himself, that day. He told me to wait in the guest quarters, and that he'd find out what's keeping my husband and send him right back up to take me to lunch."

"So, you stayed there by yourself in the guest quarters?"

"Until I started fuming about being stuck up there for freaking ever, when I could have been making some damned progress with the paintings. So I ventured out and down the hallway, and I bump into that little monk again, who comes rushing, wide-eyed, up the stairs. He herds me back into the guest quarters, before disappearing into the Abbot's room. Well, I knew something was up. And I wished Dodd would get his slow ass back up there, because I really needed to hook up with Ellen and my nasal spray. By then the pressure on my sinuses had my eyes welling up and my nose dripping. And I'm looking around for a napkin, because

I'm out of dry tissues. Then I notice this narrow door, which I'm hoping is a closet with some napkins in it. And I look in there, and what do I see, but a bathroom with toilet paper. Oh, thank you, Jesus."

"I wondered about there being an actual bathroom when we were up there with the police."

"Well, the toilet's kind of funky looking, like it's out of the thirties, and it takes about a year to refill the tank after you flush it, but it works, so who gives a rip? And there's a sink too, but only the coldwater knob gives you anything. Still, it was a lovely sight."

"There's more to that monastery than I thought," I said. "Now, I'm anxious to get back up there and look around."

"Look what I won!" Ellen dumped a double handful of casino chips on our table.

While the women counted the largesse of Lady Luck, I sat back in the soft afterglow of the Kailua and listened to the keyboard guy and the castanet lady dust off an oldie that last had radio airtime when I was in grade school.

As Ellen left to go cash in her chips, Alicia snapped me out of it.

"Francis. That's the same black guy who was at the restaurant earlier. No, don't look."

I stopped my instinctive head swing. "There are lots of black people in Puerto Rico."

"Do they all wear the same Hugo Boss jacket? And did I mention he's wearing a freaking jacket? It's still eighty degrees outside."

Which, of course, practically forced me to now steal a look.

The only man in the room who wore a jacket that wasn't part of a tuxedo sat with a full drink in front of him, as he idly watched the few couples out on the dance floor. In Puerto Rico the races mixed and intermarried to a point that was beyond multi-cultural. So, a black man in a jacket should have just blended into the scenery. But women like Alicia read clothes the way birds read feathers.

On our three-block walk back to the Caserio Inn, I caught several glimpses of the brand-name jacket following us through late-evening sidewalk foot-traffic. I now felt it safe to assume that a third Special Agent had been flown in from Mayport.

***

The next morning I woke with a start. The desk lamp was on, and Phil Dodd sat on the other double bed.

"Reveille," he said.

I swung my legs over the edge of the bed and sat up, facing Dodd. "This had better be important."

"Yeah, I know. It's early."

I felt the first throb of a headache, and pressed the heel of my hand against my forehead, a remedy that achieved only fleeting relief.

"You're quite the hot item," I said. "The team of Randal and Briggs questioned me, yesterday. They were laying in wait, down in the guest lounge. You know them?"

"Randal, I do. Kind of a prick."

"Well, just so you know, they may be watching the Caserio."

"This morning, the NCIS is across the lagoon, over in Miramar, giving their utmost attention to the apartment of an old girlfriend of mine."

"How did you find this out?"

"On the opposite side of the street and just up the hill from her apartment, there's a guy hunched at the wheel of an SUV, drinking coffee out of a paper cup. Was the Briggs guy black?"

"No, but there was a black guy wearing a pricey jacket, who followed us around last night."

"Damn. They're spending some serious man-hours on this."

I woke up my cell phone and looked at the time. "It's not even six."

"The two Middle Eastern boys who followed us in from the airport when you first arrived, I've got them stashed in that apartment," Dodd said. "Decided I had enough players to keep track of, as it was. And didn't especially relish Rahim's lackeys dogging us when Alicia and I went up to the monastery."

"You kidnapped them?"

"I prefer 'benched them.' So anyway, I figured my old girlfriend's apartment was a good safe-house – she still keeps a light on for me. I got her nephew and a couple rough-boy pals of his to help me grab the lackeys off the street. I took a camera off one of them and uploaded its pictures to my laptop. There's several, nice, zoomed-in shots of Alicia at the car rental counter and a couple of you and me unloading the luggage in front of the Caserio. No good face-shots of Alicia's sister, though it wasn't for lack of trying."

"But the NCIS found out about the apartment."

"I guess they had a hunch I'd have to use any old contact I had to evade them. They probably think I'm holed up in her apartment right now. I doubt they have an inkling about the pair of unwilling guests."

"And yet, they did know about some old girlfriend. What do you do, list them on your resume under hobbies?"

"This particular old girlfriend and I have a deep history," Dodd said. "Back in the old days, after blazing my way up through the ranks, I'm a freshly minted, mustang Ensign, hanging around San Juan, waiting for my new ship to get back into port. Naturally, I sought out a little companionship. Anyway, after an amazingly short gestation period, there was this paternity thing. Of course, the kid wasn't mine, but the Navy told me to clean up my mess. Money straightened it all out, but I have to say it pinched me pretty hard at the time. I guess some residue of the incident still lingers in my file."

"None of this explains why you're sitting here."

"This morning I'd originally intended to slip over to her apartment in the wee hours – you know, just after she got home – wake up my detainees, feed and water them, and put them on the can. Then I'd dope them back up and go for a little romp with my old Puerto Rican squeeze. But the situation's changed now. Their fearless leader is dead, so there's no point in hanging on to his lackeys anymore. And I'd be happy to go cut them loose myself, but there's that NCIS agent in the SUV keeping watch, like I told you. I'd be walking into a trap. Therefore, somebody else has to do it. So, I come to you, my old shipmate."

I now wondered, myself, what it would take for me to say "no" to the lieutenant who, ten years earlier, had persuaded the Captain of the Marietta that it would be in the best interests of the Navy not to turn Chief Mossman and me over to the Philippine authorities.

"I don't suppose the old squeezebox could do it," I grumbled, as I was pulling on my slacks.

"No," Dodd said. "It'd be too dangerous. The sleepy-time powder I put in their cocoa will be wearing off by now. And you know how they treat women."

I had my socks on and was shoving my feet into my shoes. "The black Special Agent knows me by sight. My going into that apartment building may well confirm for him that you're definitely in there. How do I explain away your captives, if he swoops in to arrest you, before I can cut them loose and shoo them away?"

"He'll be under orders not to attempt to take me down by himself. I'm supposed to be an armed and dangerous killer, after all. Yes, he'll call Randal and Briggs about seeing you enter her apartment building. But he'll be told to wait for backup. That'll give you time to free the lackeys and get yourself clear."

"What about your old girlfriend?"

"She'll know instantly that they're not local police. And she knows how to not speak English. She'll be fine."

Dodd then held out two envelopes that were decorated with advertisements in French. "These are the lackeys' return plane tickets. I found them in Rahim's hotel room. Also, I've got to get this to her." Dodd pulled out a plain white envelope, added it to the pair of colorful ones, and pressed them all into my hand.

I slid the envelopes into my back pocket and buttoned up my shirt. When I left my room, Dodd had his shoes off and was stretched out on the spare bed.

**

Supplied with the address of the girlfriend's apartment and guided by a city map, on which Dodd had marked its location, I eased the rental car down the steep, one-way street. Cars lined both sides, leaving only a single traffic lane open. I spotted the SUV easily, since the front fender of the big vehicle poked out somewhat from the line of parked cars, its wheels pre-turned toward the traffic lane, like a getaway car for a bank robber. Finding no open spaces along either curb, I circled around the block. Back up at the top of the hill, I snuggled the rental car up to a "no parking here to corner" sign, on the left side, just past the intersection.

The sun had yet to rise above the horizon, but it was no longer dark, as I walked down the steep sidewalk. In passing, I stole a glance toward the SUV, parked on the opposite side of the street. The black Special Agent was engaged in refreshing his paper cup of coffee from a steaming, Styrofoam tankard. Evidently, either Randal or Briggs had been by recently to tend to the morale of their night watchman. I hoped neither of them were lurking somewhere nearby.

Multiple stories of balconies rose in pairs up the face of the girlfriend's apartment building. I mounted the front steps, entered the terra cotta tiled lobby, bypassed an ancient, questionable-looking elevator, and took the stairs.

The smell within the confines of the interior stairway that wrapped around the elevator shaft was more intense than that of the lobby. I breathed through my mouth, hoping the repellant odor was merely from landlord-grade floor soap, and continued on up to the second floor.

The doors of the two front apartments, whose balconies would overlook the street, each featured a large, frosted glass window, which I assumed allowed light to filter into the interior hallway during the day to give the bare bulb in the porcelain, ceiling fixture a rest. I checked the address again, slid the paper back into my pocket, and knocked on the door of Apartment 2B.

The woman who answered the door was still in heavy evening makeup. At this hour of the morning, it was more than a bit unsettling, but then I recalled that Dodd had said she would be only recently home from work. And besides, she was expecting Dodd. Her shimmering, faux-Chinese robe, hemmed to just barely conceal the entrance to the Forbidden City, gave testimony to that.

The woman held the door partway open, fixed me with an unwavering glare, but didn't say anything. From somewhere within the apartment, a television newscaster droned on in a long string of unbroken Spanish.

"Philip Dodd sent me," I said in Spanish. "It is time for your guests to leave."

Without a word, the woman turned away, leaving the door as it was. I slipped into the apartment and closed the door behind me.

The woman picked up a burning cigarette from an ashtray on a side table and settled onto the adjacent chair. She crossed her bare legs, blew out a cloud of smoke, and said in English, "The one on the right speaks Spanish."

Two young men of obvious Arab descent sat side-by-side on the couch, directly across the room from the woman. They seemed awake, but their eyes were only half open and neither one took active notice of me.

The two captives each had his crossed wrists bound with a tie-wrap, which were, in turn, tie-wrapped to an encircling series of end-for-end connected tie-wraps that were fed through their trouser belt loops. Their ankles were hobbled with somebody's out-of-fashion neckties.

"I have come to release you," I spoke in Spanish to the one on the right. "Jaspar Rahim is dead."

"I know," he said in Spanish, now looking up at me. "The whore leaves the television on all day."

The woman spat a profanity at him and flicked her cigarette in his direction. It fell short. I retrieved it from the floor and crushed it out in the ashtray next to her, before returning my attention to the captives.

"I will release your friend first," I said. "Then I will watch from the balcony. And when I see him walk away, down the sidewalk, only then will I release you also. Tell him."

There was a back and forth in what I supposed was Arabic. I waited for it to end and then stepped over to the one on the left and opened the blade on my Swiss Army Knife. As I went down on one knee to cut the necktie binding his ankles, I caught a movement out of the corner of my eye.

I rose quickly back to my feet. The woman had brought a small handgun up from its concealment, probably tucked down at the side of her chair cushion.

"A present from Felipe," she said.

I had no idea how good a shot she was, so I wasn't happy about being downrange when I went down on one knee again and cut through the necktie material. I felt better being back up on my feet when I cut the tie-wrap that freed the young man's hands.

I stepped to the door, opened it, and said to the one who spoke Spanish, "Tell him to leave now."

Following a short burst of their language, the freed young man wobbled through the open door, still fighting through the waning effects of whatever drug Dodd had given him. Like a slow-witted lab rat, he at last found the stairs, and I soon heard his sluggish descending footsteps.

I closed the door, crossed the room, and stood to one side of the French doors that led onto the balcony, keeping myself hidden from view of the Special Agent in the parked SUV. Soon, through the open spaces between the railing's balusters, I caught a brief view of the young man continuing with faltering steps down the hill.

As I moved away from the French doors, the remaining captive's eyes followed me. His lids were almost all the way up now, and he looked hostile and impatient. But I wasn't letting him go without a few questions first.

"Where did you learn Spanish?" I asked.

"In Spain," he replied. "I live there. You are to set me free now."

"In a minute. Rahim lived in France, but you work for him. How is this?"

"Rahim needs two men who speak Arabic and Spanish. His mosque contacts my mosque. It is how it is done. I bring my cousin, even though his Spanish is no good. We need to work. Rahim brings us to Puerto Rico. We watch the people that Rahim tells us to watch. Is this all you desire to know?"

"So Rahim spoke only Arabic and French?"

"I hear him try to speak some English words to the clerk at the shipping company, here in San Juan. But it is no good. And there is another language that he speaks with his bodyguard. I do not understand it."

"Do you know the name of their language?"

"No."

"You said that Rahim tried to talk to a shipping clerk."

"When I translate for them, then they can talk. Rahim wants to send a crate by cargo ship to France. He tells the clerk that the crate will be one and a half meters for each dimension. Fifty kilograms in weight. But Rahim refuses to say what the crate will contain. This makes the clerk very angry. The clerk says that he will not ship weapons for Muslims. The clerk throws us out."

"What was Rahim trying to ship home?"

"I do not know. You must cut me free now."

"You followed us from the airport," I said. "How did you know what we looked like?"

"I call each car rental agency. I am Mr. Elton. I wish to confirm the date and time that I am to have the car. Soon, I know when Mr. and Mrs. Elton are to arrive at the airport. At the airport, my cousin and I have the neckties and the luggage carts. We are the servants of

Mrs. Elton. We check the tags on suitcases at each carousel when it starts to turn. Soon, we find the name Elton. Then we watch. Two men and two women take the suitcases. We follow them. We take photographs. It is what Rahim tells us to do."

"Then later that night you are captured."

"The man who is not you leaves the hotel named Caserio. He takes a taxi. We think it is very strange that he does not use the rental car. We follow the taxi. I call Rahim. Rahim orders us to find out where the man goes. The taxi takes the man back to the airport. The man leaves the taxi. He enters a parking area. He drives away in a car. We follow him back to San Juan. The man stops in the street outside this building. Another car stops behind us. Then there are bandits all around us. Then I know that it was all to capture us."

I cut the necktie from his ankles, but before I freed his hands, I slid in one more question. "Did Rahim say why he wanted to buy the monastery?"

"Rahim tells us only what he desires that we do for him. He buys food for us only one time each day. In the way of all rich men, he treats poor men like dogs. My heart is glad that he is dead."

Once freed, the young Arab was more energetic than his cousin in getting to the door, which he opened for himself. I barely had time to hand him the two plane tickets, as he turned back for a last look.

I told him, "It is best that you fly back to Spain today. You can change the tickets."

"I know." He closed the door behind him.

I was pretty sure the young Arab would gather up his cousin and they'd make their way straight to the airport, but I listened for his footsteps on the stairs and returned to my lookout station just to make certain. As soon as he passed through my line of sight, I again stepped away from the French doors.

The woman rose out of her chair and entered a narrow alcove that housed a cramped kitchen. There, she poured herself a cup of coffee and added a generous splash of rum.

She had left the little gun lying next to the ashtray. It was a five-shot revolver. Small caliber, short barreled, and not something I, myself, would give to a hot-blooded girlfriend.

"And where is my Felipe this morning?" The woman spoke in English, as she returned from the little kitchen with her cup of enhanced coffee.

"He's hiding from his fellow NCIS agents. There's one of them in that SUV parked up the street, waiting to arrest him."

"That is not the sort of thing that would have kept him away in the past." She took a tentative sip of hot black liquid. "Perhaps, we are getting too old for this."

The woman went to the French doors, opened them, and stepped out onto the balcony. After a casual sweep of the street and another taste of rum-flavored coffee, she came back in.

"The SUV must have been there since early yesterday afternoon," she said. "He would not get such a parking space, after the neighborhood gets home from work. My Felipe always brings me trouble."

"So, you and Phil, uh Felipe, have kept up with one another over the years?" I asked.

"Felipe appears magically from the North, bringing little presents, but with much less sense of schedule than Santa Claus. He then disappears again, tearing a hole in my heart. Perhaps, that is what you wish to call 'keeping up'."

She lit another cigarette, blew out a voluminous white cloud, and took in a medicinal swallow of rum-stiffened coffee. "He told you of the trick I played on him when I was young and in trouble?"

"Just by way of explaining why the NCIS would focus on this apartment."

"My childhood sweetheart, the real father of my daughter, chose to flee to the Army. I was pregnant. I needed money. In those days, lonely sailors were everywhere. So, I told a big lie. Other girls in my circumstance had done it. And I had an officer. I thought that I had hit the jackpot. Of course, now, when I think of how it might have been, how I played it all wrong…" She let the rest of her fantasy drift out through the French doors, along with the cigarette smoke. "Naturally, whenever Felipe comes smiling to my doorstep, I cannot turn him away."

She walked back into the restricted confines of her kitchen. On the television, a meteorologist was talking about tropical depressions and wind speeds. The woman came back to the living room with a small white container in her hand. "Here. Return this to Felipe. It is too much temptation."

She placed in my hand what looked to be a labeled, plastic bottle of aspirin tablets.

I squeezed and twisted off the childproof cap. Peering inside, I saw that it was half full of reddish-orange capsules with little numbers printed on them.

"I'll see that he gets them back."

When I replaced the cap and slipped the pill bottle into my pocket, my arm brushed the white envelope. I pulled it out. "Phil asked me to give you this."

The woman looked at envelope, but didn't take it. "Tell my Felipe that he has given me enough money."

She turned away, went into her bedroom, and closed the door.

"What if there's a letter in the envelope?" I asked in a raised voice through the door.

"He knows where I live." Her voice sounded muffled, as though through a pillow.

I laid the envelope next to the little purse gun and let myself out of the apartment.

***

My legs strained up the steep sidewalk. As I passed by the SUV parked across the street, the black Special Agent sipped at his coffee and pretended to ignore me. At the top of the hill, due to a momentary gust of wind, the parking ticket under my windshield wiper waved a cheery greeting. Next to the rental car, a policeman sat astride his motorcycle, refastening his helmet's chinstrap.

Just as I reached the driver-side door, a blue sedan carrying Special Agents Randal and Briggs slowed to a crawl to squeeze past the policeman's motorcycle. From behind the wheel, Randal gave me a hard look, as he inched by. Once clear of the motorcycle, the blue sedan sped down the hill past the SUV, braked hard, and swung into a private driveway, just beyond the girlfriend's apartment building. Because of a closed gate across the private driveway, the blue sedan was left blocking the sidewalk and protruding a noticeable amount of rear fender into the traffic lane, as Randal and Briggs leaped out and charged into the apartment building.

With its brake light brightly glowing, the motorcycle carried the policeman, in a controlled coast, down the hill, coming to a halt just short of the blue sedan's bumper. After leaning the weight of his machine onto its kickstand, the policeman brought out his ticket book and began to write.

With my own parking ticket tucked into my pocket and adding to my woes, I also proceeded down the one-way street. Then it was my turn to slowly ease past the parked motorcycle, which also allowed the SUV to easily catch up and stay with me all the rest of the way down the hill.

The side street ended at a stop sign, where a major three-lane artery crossed in front of it. While I waited impatiently for an opening in the heavy morning traffic, the chromed grill of the big SUV gleamed in my rearview mirror.

I couldn't be sure what the Special Agent's orders were, but I had an idea the aiding-and-abetting check that I'd just written was about to be cashed. And since I was also overdue for breakfast with Alicia, prior to our trip up to the monastery, I decided the time was ripe to add fleeing-and-eluding to my growing list of offenses.

The far two lanes of traffic were bumper-to-bumper, flowing swiftly and unrelentingly down toward the bridge crossing the lagoon. The nearest lane, which headed in the opposite direction, was empty. But, it was also clearly marked "Bus Traffic Only."

Trying for a left turn into a fleeting opening in the far traffic lanes seemed suicidal. So, with some trepidation, given that a "Bus Traffic Only" sign appeared to be the only traffic law that the locals bothered to obey, I turned right, onto the bus lane, and put the gas pedal to the floor.

In my mirror, I noticed that the powerful SUV had no problem keeping up with my anemic rental car, as it strained up the shallow incline. But then I saw, coming toward me, a sizeable break in the opposing two lanes of traffic. And I felt confident that I had room for a tight, 180-degree turn.

Anticipating the passing of the last car in the queue, I eased off the gas, slowing enough to where I figured I could just make it. Hoping my timing was right, I cranked the steering wheel rapidly hand-over-hand into a hard left U-turn. I felt the rear tires break traction and then carom off the far curb with a heavy jolt, as I frantically spun the steering wheel back around and floored the gas pedal.

With the little rental car doggedly picking up speed, I checked the mirror for my pursuer. To my delight, the less agile SUV was nosed into the curb and blocking both lanes of the next long slug of morning traffic.

However, my delight was short-lived, as the previous slug of traffic, whose rear my little rental car was bringing up, now began slowing for a far-up-ahead red traffic signal. And a second anxious glance at the mirror showed the SUV was now backed into the bus lane – poised and ready to resume its pursuit.

But then, to my relief, a final mirror check showed the SUV had pursued me down the bus lane only as far as the side street, out of which the chase had begun – and where it now ended with the big shiny grill busily reflecting the blue and red flashing lights of the equally busy police motorcycle.

***

At the Caserio Inn, as I slid my room key into the lock, Alicia stepped out of her room and fixed me with a withering stare.

"Where the hell have you been?" she demanded. "Do you know what time it is?"

"Well, it can't be much after eight, can it?"

"But you wouldn't know, would you? Because you left your cell phone in your room."

"I must have—"

"Yes, you must have. I embarrassed myself by getting the desk clerk to come up and let me into your room, because I thought you'd died on the toilet like Elvis, and…" Alicia tossed away her bizarre train of thought with a quick movement of her head, flinging an errant lock of hair away to reveal a second hostile eye.

Alicia reached for the doorknob and called, in a remarkably abrupt and sweetened change of tone, "We'll be back, late this afternoon, Ellen." She pulled the door closed.

"I don't suppose we have time for a little breakfast," I said with hope.

"No." Alicia's tone just as abruptly reverted back to 'admonishing Francis' mode. "Isn't that the same shirt you had on yesterday?"

"I was going to—"

"Come on. Let's get a clean one."

While changing out of my shirt, I felt Dodd's aspirin bottle of sleeping pills in its pocket. I tossed the deceptively labeled bottle into my satchel. It'd be just my luck to be caught with *those*.

"Where did you go so damn early in the morning?" Alicia didn't let up.

"I couldn't sleep. I went for a walk."

"I don't believe you. I think you met up with Dodd."

"Can I at least grab something to eat on the way?"

"If you'd been where you were supposed to be, you'd already have *had* your precious breakfast."

***

Alicia was at the wheel, as we drove the highway, going east out of San Juan and toward El Yunque National Forest. I was buckled in the passenger seat, consuming a barely-life-sustaining English muffin and black coffee, hastily caged from the hotel's kitchenette.

"Whatever it is that you're doing for Dodd, or whoever, up at the monastery, you do it without bothering me. I've only got today to bang this all out. You get no help from me whatsoever."

"Actually, I don't really—"

"Just don't ask, okay? I'm trying to be optimistic about appraising those depressing old paintings, but I can't sugarcoat what they are."

"Well, just because there isn't a Rembrandt—"

"And yet, that would be exactly the point, wouldn't it. None of them were painted by anybody even remotely important. I saw that the first day. But I couldn't tell Monsignor Cabrera without first double-checking. So, I made a call back to Chicago, to the Art Institute. Of course, I didn't mention that I had to do a little sneaky cleaning just to make out any freaking signatures at all. The damned things are filthy. Anyway, the Curator confirmed what I already knew. There aren't any lost treasures."

"They can't all be totally worthless, can they?"

"I didn't say worthless. A couple of them should fetch enough to cover the cost of cleaning all of them. But for the rest, there's more value in the frames."

"It sounds like you got more work done on that first day than I thought."

"I was the only one doing anything productive, I can assure you of that." Alicia briefly stopped at a tollbooth and paid the fee for a divided highway without traffic lights. "That worthless Dodd, aimlessly wandering around, when he could, at least, have been holding a flashlight for me. And the Sheik of Araby, enthroned on that big chair like he was already Lord of the Manor. And that creepy-ass bodyguard, eying everybody with deep suspicion. Of course, Monsignor Cabrera wasn't with us most of the time. I'm sure there were very important things he had to attend to."

"So, none of the monks were around?"

"Oh, the little one popped in once. He fussed with the candles and pretended to be checking on something for a few minutes, before disappearing again. And one time I saw a big monk come to the doorway and look in. I don't know what the attraction was."

"You sure it wasn't you?"

"Look at me. I don't have the slightest bit of makeup on, just sunscreen. These are men's trousers and a man's dress shirt that I'm wearing. And this is the same outfit I wore last time I was up there. So, unless they're deep into androgyny, I don't think they saw me as forbidden fruit."

"So you've seen the big monk and the little monk. They're the two who make wine and rum out in the big shed. Dodd said there are two others, who work in the kitchen. So, that's four monks, not counting the Abbot. Did you see any more?"

"No." Alicia cast a penetrating look at me, before returning her eyes to the road. "If you're going to spy for Dodd, the least he could do is tell how many people there are up there."

"He did. He told me four monks plus the Abbot. I was just confirming, because...Look, I don't know what I'm doing. People want me to find things out for them, but they don't tell me how to go about it."

"What you *should* be doing is watching out that somebody isn't setting you up to take the fall for him."

"You mean Dodd?"

"I mean Dodd."

"I don't think—"

"Yes, that's the problem."

Chapter 8

It was a long, humid climb up the zigzagging cart path, which, despite Alicia's grumbling, I found to be considerably easier than blazing my own trail up through the rain forest.

Arriving at the top, damp with sweat, Alicia and I stepped onto the covered stoop that sheltered the monastery's front door. While Alicia took a top-off steroid spray up each nostril, I set down her tote bag, which I was again obliged to carry, and raised my knuckles to knock.

"They don't have a butler." Alicia's words stayed my hand.

"Well, we can't just—"

"But, you *can* just act like a gentleman and open the door for me."

True enough, once inside, we made our way along the dark hallway without seeing a soul, or even hearing any sounds, other than our own footsteps on the worn, wooden floor.

Despite a pervasive musty odor, the hallway held several reminders that, perhaps a hundred and fifty years ago, this had been a grand manor house, fit for a prosperous plantation owner. The details of the handrail and balusters that swept up the open side of the wide staircase, spoke of proud craftsmanship. And the finely honed trim moldings were still elegant, in spite of the cracked plaster walls and ceilings.

After crossing the stone pavers of the central patio area, where a morning mist hid from the rising sun, Alicia and I entered the dining hall. In the dim light, the old Abbot lounged, torpid and softly snoring, in his great chair. His chin rested on his chest, his gnarled hands hung over the ends of the silvered armrests, and wisps of long white hair hung in front of his lined face. The light grey metal of the temple and bridge pieces of his rimless glasses closely matched the old man's complexion. We quietly moved past the sleeping Abbot and toward the paintings on the far wall.

Alicia, making a show of determined efficiency, emptied the contents of the tote bag onto a side table and regimented the multitude of items she'd brought with her. I helped her lift down the first painting and set it on the side table, leaning it back against the wall behind her tool layout. Alicia then went to work.

With critical eyes, Alicia scanned a section of canvas, wrote a note on a pad, and proceeded to the next section. My job consisted of holding the second flashlight and keeping the magnifying glass at the ready. Alicia occasionally made a verbal comment about how difficult to repair some particular damage to the painting would be, but for the most part, I was bored out of my skull and began to look forward to questioning the monks.

I endured my tasks, as Alicia's assistant, for a good hour and a half, before I attempted to squirm free. "If you don't need me for the moment, I think I'd like to take a closer look at the Abbot's chair."

Alicia, who had been flipping through her notebook, looked up and gazed toward the oversized, ornate chair.

"It's really quite lovely. Arabesque, but with some floral designs too. Not just the geometric figures you'd expect. I'd guess late Spanish Renaissance."

"What do you think it's worth?"

"A lot more than all these paintings combined. That's for sure. The chair is the only prize in this room."

As I advanced toward the Abbot's chair, Alicia moved with me. We stopped a yard short of the chair and together took it in, at close range.

Alicia kept her voice soft. "I wouldn't say it's worth a fabulous amount. And it's not really my niche. But still, throw out those ratty cushions with the 'dry clean only' tags sticking out and get rid of the plumbing collection at the back, and you'd have something worth maybe as much as ten thousand."

"Seriously?" I asked in dialed down volume. "For a chair?"

"Well, let me qualify that. Europe's the only market where you'd get that much out of it. So, once you subtract for shipping costs – and they'd be considerable – plus export and import fees, the auction house's commission, and God knows what else, it's not going to add up to the answer to the Monsignor's prayers."

I stepped closer and ran my hand over the intricate sculpted pattern, carved completely through again and again, giving the figures three dimensions and an overall effect of heavy lace. The lacquer finish was dull behind the Abbot's white hair. Under his bony forearms and fingers, the hammered silver, protecting the armrests, was worn and pitted. But even the matted, velvet cushions under the slight weight of the sleeping Abbot couldn't take away from the richness of the chair's design.

And then there was the battery.

I moved around to the rear of the Abbot's chair and directed the beam of the flashlight onto the u-bolt, clamped onto the galvanized steel pipe at the center of the Baghdad battery, where, the day before, I'd noticed the end of a piece of copper wire poking up. The wire, held within the u-bolt's grasp, was solid, un-insulated, and about as thick as a number 2 pencil. With the aid of the flashlight beam, I could now follow the rest of the bare wire's length, as its span passed with ample clearance above the open ends of both the copper tube and the outer white plastic pipe. The stiff wire continued its sojourn, bending to follow along the back of the Abbot's chair and bending again to land on the elbow end of the thin sheet of silver covering the chair's right armrest. There the bare copper wire ended with a soldered connection to the silver armrest cover.

I fully expected to see another bare copper wire, bent in a similar manner but in this instance, connecting the copper tube to the silver cover on the left armrest and soldered at both ends. And that was exactly what the flashlight revealed.

Additionally, on the left armrest I noticed another curiosity. Near the modern soldered connection, the end of the thin silver armrest covering had been folded back on itself and hammered down to capture a short length of beaten-flat copper ribbon, whose natural reddish-brown color occasionally appeared through scratches in the heavy green patina. The hammered joining of the copper ribbon remnant to the silver armrest covering looked (to me anyway) like an ancient craftsman's idea of an electrical connection – supposedly, from an age before there *were* electrical connections.

Also caught in the beam of the flashlight were more green-surfaced copper remnants, this time lining the interior walls of the chair's tall square box that presently housed the modern plumbing pieces. It was a short leap to conclude that the new battery, constructed of scrap plumbing parts, had been inspired by these hints of a Baghdad battery, originally built into the Renaissance-era chair.

From a trouser pocket, I brought out the little multi-meter that I'd used in the demonstration of my battery-making skills for Detective Sergeant Alvarez. I had brought it along to confirm my assertion that the nested plumbing parts, filled with wine, actually constituted a functioning power source.

I set the dial on the meter to read low level DC voltage, as I had in the lowlife bar with Alvarez. I then touched one probe to the copper tube and the other probe to the galvanized steel pipe. The meter registered 1.2 volts. It was a working battery all right.

"Are you actually getting a reading from the plumbing?" Alicia's hushed question came from over my shoulder.

"It's actually a make-shift battery," I whispered back. "And it's connected to the chair's armrests. Come around to the front of the chair. I'll prove it to you."

Alicia followed me to the front of the Abbot's chair. I gave her the meter to hold, while I touched one probe to the silver-plating showing between the Abbot's gnarled fingers, where they curled over the end of one armrest, and touched the other probe to the silver, showing between his fingers, on the opposite armrest.

"Look at the reading," I whispered over my shoulder. "The Abbot's hooked up."

"One point two volts," Alicia whispered back, her eyes on the meter's LED display. "That's not even a flashlight battery. What's it for?"

I caught a movement in the shadows. I quickly took the meter from Alicia's hands, wound the probe leads around it and shoved it all back into my trouser pocket. I then looked more intently at the silently moving figure and saw that it was the diminutive monk, Brother Emilio.

***

Moving out of the shadows and carrying a large pewter pitcher, using both hands, Brother Emilio approached a side table positioned against the wall on the opposite side of the dining hall from the depressing paintings. The little monk set the pitcher down next to a seemingly identical pitcher, except that this second pitcher had a green band of color around its neck. The little monk then beckoned me over to him with a hand gesture.

I moved away from the sleeping Abbot and toward Brother Emilio. When I was near enough, I whispered in Spanish, "I did not know it was you, at first."

"We must be quiet," Brother Emilio responded in whispered Spanish. "We must let the Abbot rest."

When Alicia joined us, Brother Emilio now motioned for us to follow him. He led us all the way back across the spacious dining hall and to where the paintings hung beneath the high dusty windows.

At a normal voice level, Brother Emilio inquired, "May I ask why you are here today? There is no longer to be the sale of the Monastery."

"Monsignor Cabrera has instructed us to continue with the evaluation of the paintings," I said.

"What's going on?" Alicia broke in.

I switched to English. "Brother Emilio wants to know why we're back. I'll try to get him out of here, so you can work."

"Good. I'd like to finish this up today, so we can fly the hell out of here, before something else goes wrong."

I went back to Spanish for Brother Emilio. "You surprised us, when you suddenly appeared."

"I must change the wine in the Abbot's chair." Having evidently reminded himself, Brother Emilio abruptly walked away from us.

With heightened interest, I watched the little monk return to the table on the other side of the dining hall and pick up the pewter pitcher with the green band. Brother Emilio brought the green-banded pitcher to the rear of the Abbot's chair, knelt down, and held it under the spigot that Dodd had noticed at the base of the Baghdad battery. He opened the spigot, drew off the wine, and closed the spigot. After returning to the buffet table and swapping pitchers, Brother Emilio brought the un-banded pitcher to the back of the Abbot's chair and slowly poured its contents into the confines of white plastic pipe.

Overcome by curiosity, I approached for a closer look. The scent of pineapple was now much stronger, than it had been before.

I asked Brother Emilio in whispered Spanish, "Fresh wine?"

"Brother Hugo asked me to do this every morning," he whispered back. "I give the old wine to Brother Carlos and Brother Rafael for use in the garden to help the soil. It is why the marking on the pitcher is green." He displayed an impish smile.

I nodded and smiled back at his little joke.

Brother Emilio returned to the side table, took up the full green-banded pitcher with both hands, and started off in the direction of the dining hall's only door.

Hurrying, I caught up with him. And as soon as we were out of earshot of the Abbot, I asked, "Isn't this, ah, ceremony a waste of good wine?"

"We are never short of wine," Brother Emilio said, before pausing at the doorway to look back toward the great chair. "If the Abbot was awake, I would ask if he would be joining the Brothers for lunch. But because we again have guests…"

"Please, continue with your plans. Alicia and I would rather eat our lunch outside in the garden."

"I do not understand."

"Alicia asked me only this morning, if this was possible. It is a 'picnic'." I gave him the word in English. "A meal in the fresh air. It is better for her allergy, and Alicia loves the view of the mountains and the ocean. We would need only bread and cheese and a bottle of wine." What the hell, they were never short of wine.

"It is a very unusual request," Brother Emilio said. "And yet, I am sure that the Abbot desires to dine with the Brothers once again. However, I am equally sure that the Abbot would not wish to insult his guests."

"On the contrary, it would please Alicia very much. Can we arrange it with the monks who work in the kitchen? I will go with you."

"The woman would be alone, outside the guest quarters." The little monk looked worried.

"She needs to work. And the Abbot is with her. In spirit, anyway."

***

Brother Emilio and I crossed the central patio. The smell of burning wood announced that a kitchen was somewhere near.

A cast iron woodstove was situated in a recessed area off the patio, on the far side of the fountain. A large steaming pot sat next to a teakettle on the stovetop. From under a low roof that sheltered the woodstove, smoke billowed out, free to find its own way up to the open sky. Adjacent to the stove's alcove was an open doorway. I followed Brother Emilio through it and entered the kitchen.

The kitchen, as it turned out, was more of a spacious pantry and food preparation room, since any cooking would be taking place out on the stove and a large bowl of water stood in for a sink. Refrigeration, I assumed, was out of the question. A large wooden table, stained and wounded by, perhaps, many decades of food prep, dominated the center of the room. Against the walls, open-faced cabinets held an assortment of blackened cookware and countless, repurposed coffee cans, labeled with their new contents.

Two monks worked at the large table, one trimming and slicing raw vegetables, and the other cutting wedges from a round of cheese and portioning out chunks from two free-formed loaves of bread. While the two monks continued with their knife work without looking up, I followed Brother Emilio's example and stood silently waiting. As one of the monks reached for the next tomato, he finally noticed us and looked questioningly in our direction.

"Good morning, Brother Carlos," Brother Emilio said. "We have guests today after all. They wish to take their lunch in the garden. May I trouble you to make available bread, cheese, and wine for two guests?"

"It will be here on the table for them," Brother Carlos said.

"And I believe that the Abbot feels well enough to eat lunch with the Brothers in the dining hall."

To this, Brother Carlos gave a nod, before returning to his tomato slicing.

The teakettle, out on the woodstove, pierced the air with its whistle. The other food-prep monk laid his knife down and went out. Mercifully, the high-pitched scream of the kettle soon stopped. When the monk returned, he filled an old-fashioned metal strainer with tea-leaves and placed it in an empty mug, draping the little chain and fob over the edge. He carried the mug out to the stove.

When the monk who tended to the tea preparation returned empty-handed, Brother Emilio explained to me, "Brother Rafael makes tea for our Abbot. It is steeping now, out on the stove edge. I bring tea to our Abbot every day, before he takes lunch. A mug of tea is the one luxury that the Abbot will allow himself."

Brother Emilio smiled at this. I returned a smile, but at the same time, sensed an opening for a little information gathering.

"But on the day that the Arab died," I kept it casual, "I understand that Monsignor Cabrera brought the Abbot his tea."

"Oh yes," Brother Emilio said. "On that day, Monsignor Cabrera offered to deliver the tea when he went up to say goodbye to the Abbot."

Brother Rafael held another tea strainer dangling by its chain. "Brother Emilio, do you require a second mug of tea today also?"

"We have no guests today who require tea," Brother Emilio said. "A single mug for the Abbot is sufficient."

His business in the kitchen apparently done, Brother Emilio simply exited out to the patio. I followed, damning myself for having gathered exactly zero additional information.

Brother Emilio agitated the strainer up and down in the steaming mug a few times, before laying it aside on a nearby shelf and taking up the mug.

"The hot tea will help to wake the Abbot," he said.

I was just arranging the words in my head to reopen the topic concerning the singular departure from Brother Emilio's daily tea delivery task, when the young monk abruptly started off in the direction of the dining hall, again leaving me standing flat footed.

Hurrying, I caught up with Brother Emilio just as he entered the dining hall. The Abbot still slumbered in his great chair, and Alicia was still busy with the paintings.

Brother Emilio stopped at the Abbot's side and gently stroked the old man's arm. The Abbot came to the surface and accepted the mug into his gnarled hands. He gingerly took a sip of hot tea.

Having flubbed my chance with Brother Emilio and figuring that the old Abbot was as awake as he was ever going to be, I decided to try a different source.

"May I ask a question of the Abbot?" I had directed this request to Brother Emilio, but it was the Abbot who answered.

"What is it that you wish to ask?" His Spanish was spoken in a high and weak voice.

"Forgive me for interrupting your tea," I said. "The woman who works with the paintings must answer questions from the police. However, she does not speak Spanish. So, I must ask a question of you for her."

"You may ask."

"Thank you. Do you remember drinking tea with Monsignor Cabrera on the morning that the Arab died, the day that Monsignor Cabrera brought your tea up to your bedroom?"

"Brother Emilio brings me the tea." The Abbot took another sip from his mug.

"Yes, but on that particular day, it was Monsignor Cabrera who brought you the tea. He had a mug of tea, and you had a mug of tea."

"No."

"Are you saying that you do not remember, or—"

"Monsignor Cabrera did not drink tea."

"So, the Monsignor had a mug of tea available to him, but he did not drink it?"

The Abbot's tired eyes shifted to Brother Emilio. "Who is this man?"

"He is a servant of the woman who works with the paintings," Brother Emilio said. "He speaks Spanish for her. He carries her equipment."

I wasn't especially pleased with this summation of my worth.

"He looks hungry. Take him to the kitchen. Brother Carlos will feed him." The Abbot continued to sip his tea. He didn't look at me again.

"We must allow the Abbot time to enjoy his tea," Brother Emilio said. "And I must help Brother Carlos and Brother Rafael bring today's meal to the table."

As Brother Emilio walked to the door, I hurried to catch up with him, once again, and tried a different subject. "The apparatus behind the Abbot's chair, the one in which you change the wine every day, it is an unusual assembly. What is it for?"

"Brother Hugo said that the great chair was built long ago to give tranquility to the person sitting in it. He said that, if we could make the chair function again, it would help the Abbot manage with his arthritis. But some essential elements of the chair had been lost. And we found that we could not barter for the things that Brother Hugo needed to restore it. That is when Brother Hugo said that we must work with what God has given us. And that is what you now see."

"To me, it looks very much like a version of a Baghdad battery," I said, hoping Brother Emilio had heard Brother Hugo use the term.

"The chair is not from Baghdad. Monsignor Cabrera told us that the chair came from Spain, hundreds of years ago. Please, I am needed in the kitchen." Brother Emilio's eyes suddenly brightened. "And after lunch today, we bring the rum down to the city. It is our exciting day."

Apparently rejuvenated by the thought of his upcoming adventure, the young monk rushed out of the dining hall, his footsteps light on the worn floorboards.

I pulled the little voltmeter out of my pocket, as I returned to the rear of the Abbot's chair, and retested the battery's voltage, now that the wine had been refreshed. The meter read 1.4 volts. Brother Emilio's daily replenishment of the pineapple wine, which served as the battery's electrolyte, restored its full charge. A parting glance at the tortured fingers on the silver armrests triggered a hope within me that Brother Hugo was right about the chair's therapeutic properties.

Alicia's head turned at my approach. "Where have you and your little friend been off to?"

"Arranging lunch al fresco for us."

"Francis, I love you. I'm starved."

***

Alicia and I sat in a pair of weathered Adirondack chairs, positioned with a view of the Caribbean Sea through a break in the trees. At our backs and to our flanks, the extensive vegetable garden covered most of the cleared area on the high mountain ridge. Between us, on a low rustic table, the crumbs of thick chunks of bread and narrow wedges of cheese lay littered on a plain, dinner plate. Nearby, a half-empty bottle of unlabeled, pineapple wine gave further testament to a satisfying picnic lunch.

"I'm still on track to be finished with the paintings this afternoon," Alicia said.

"At least one of us is making progress," I lamented, while dividing the last of the wine between the two mugs. "It's taking more time than I thought to draw information out of the monks. Except for Brother Emilio, they're not big talkers."

"You're not really trying to figure out who killed the Arab, are you?"

"I'm only trying to pick up whatever scraps I can. It's up to Dodd to piece it all together. But if don't give him something to work with, his temporary absence from the NCIS will likely become permanent."

"He can get another job."

"I feel responsible for screwing up his Navy career."

"So helping him to keep *this* job is what, atonement?" Alicia set her mug down. "You think you're being all kinds of stalwart, when what you're really doing is helping that scoundrel shift the blame onto somebody else." She poked my arm with a sharp-nailed index finger. "And don't you go trying to pin it on Monsignor Cabrera, either."

I leaned back and gazed at the encroaching clouds. "And on top of gathering intel for Dodd, I've got to feed some tidbits to Alvarez too. Just enough, anyway, to keep him from making good on his threat."

"Does everyone get to cheat off your paper?"

"I can't act on Dodd's behalf without pretending to work for Alvarez, too."

"And who's Alvarez's favorite suspect?"

"He's all focused on toxicology reports and people who pull strings. So, he can't see beyond Dodd and Monsignor Cabrera."

"Another genius." Alicia stood. "I'd better get back to work."

I raised myself out of the deep chair. "It's a small place. Somebody must have seen something."

"Well, if you insist on playing detective, you'd best tear into it. Ellen and I fly out tomorrow, with or without you."

***

Alicia and I parted company in the patio. She returned to the paintings in the dining hall, and I carried the empty wine bottle, dinner plate, and two mugs over to the stove, where I found Brother Rafael using a pair of tongs to successively dunk plates in a large pot of simmering water and Brother Carlos busily employing the drying towel.

"Thank you for a fine lunch," I said in Spanish, as I placed our dinnerware on an open space of the monks' cast iron workstation.

The two monks continued with their work. Neither looked at me, or responded.

I pressed on, as though they had. "It must be difficult to keep track of all your plates and mugs, especially when they sometimes are taken to places other than the dining hall. Like out in the garden for our lunch, or up in the Abbot's room for his tea."

Brother Rafael rinsed the two mugs I'd given him in the hot water and passed them on to Brother Carlos. It was as though I hadn't spoken at all.

I continued my attempt to prime the pump. "It would be a wonder if both those mugs that Monsignor Cabrera carried away the other day made it back to the kitchen at all, considering the disturbance that followed the Arab's death."

Brother Carlos continued with his toweling, but now spoke. "None were missing."

"Ah, all accounted for. Good." Emboldened, I pressed further. "But how on Earth did those mugs find their way back?"

Brother Carlos gathered up the cleaned mugs and the rinsed-out bottle, before responding. "When none are missing, there is no reason to ask."

With Brother Rafael carrying the stack of clean plates, the two monks entered the kitchen, leaving me standing there.

I decided I'd definitely have to work on refining my technique.

***

I walked the path through the garden, heading toward the outbuildings. I wanted to catch Brother Hugo and Brother Emilio, before they left for their "exciting day." After all, I knew they, at least, would talk to me.

While traversing the extensive garden, I decided I'd better take another shot at phoning in to my boss. The downside of this idea was that the call would inevitably be routed through his gatekeeper, Sally. But still, I definitely needed more time in Puerto Rico. And I felt sure, if I could just get through to him, that I could explain. Dreading the one-woman gantlet I'd have to endure, I tapped in the numbers.

"Francis, don't even *begin* to tell me that you're calling to ask for more time off." Sally's voice pierced the airwaves. "We're short of guys. There's nobody to cover for you. You've already made 'bad boy du jour' status."

I went straight to bargaining. "I'm fairly certain I can make it back the day after tomorrow at the latest."

"You've got a fantastic, yet plausible, excuse, right? Because I'm putting you through to the Lord of the Liquid Lunch. And this time I don't think even a doctor's slip will cut it. You might squeak by with a death certificate...yours."

"He seemed okay with it last Friday."

"We're talking about today. And today, he needs a body in Indianapolis at Allison Transmission. And he hasn't got anyone to send. He yells at me, 'Where the hell's Francis?' Did you want me to tell him you're down in Puerto Rico polishing up your ex-trophy? Because that's what I told him."

"Look, don't put me through to him. Just tell him I'll be flying back tomorrow."

Once again our conversation ended with an electronic clunk.

***

In front of the large outbuilding, where I'd first met Brother Hugo and Brother Emilio, there now stood a donkey hitched to the modified rear half of a short-bed pickup truck.

This jury-rigged cart rolled on bald tires, which were openly on display, because the tailgate and outer side panels were gone, leaving only the three sides of the inner truck bed. And while the length of the original truck bed had been retained, it's width had been reduced by some torch cutting and welding handiwork, probably to accommodate the narrow width of the zigzag cart path down to the road. I crouched down for a look at the weld on the altered axle. As I expected, the drive train's differential had been removed, and the remaining axle sections aligned and rejoined.

As I straightened up from my inspection, Brother Hugo emerged from the doorway of the large outbuilding carrying an open-top wooden crate filled with bottles cushioned by straw. The big monk effortlessly loaded the crate onto the cart.

Brother Emilio next appeared in the doorway, his arms strained straight with the burden of another crate. Bending his knees, he eased the crate down onto the threshold and disappeared back into the building. Brother Hugo retrieved the crate from the doorway, placed it gently onto the cart, and then shoved both crates forward on the corrugated bed.

"Good afternoon, Brother Hugo," I hailed him in Spanish, before switching to English. "That's a lot of wine. Can I help with the loading?"

"It is rum." Brother Hugo responded in English. "What do you want this time?"

Brother Emilio struggled into the frame of the doorway again with the next crate and, with obvious relief, set it down.

I stepped over and picked up the crate. It was heavier than I had anticipated.

Handing the crate off to Brother Hugo, I said, "I hoped that you might clear something up for me."

Without responding, Brother Hugo set the third crate on the rear of the cart and pushed all three forward, keeping the weight centered over the axle.

"I wondered," I went on, "if you knew what time Monsignor Cabrera left the Monastery on the day the Arab died." I retrieved the next crate that Brother Emilio had deposited on the doorsill and turned for the handoff. "I'd like to know, because—"

"Because the police had asked Mrs. Elton this question, and even though their investigation is now closed, you feel it necessary to pointlessly assist Mrs. Elton in finding the answer," Brother Hugo finished my sentence somewhat differently than I would have. "Brother Emilio has related to me this curious reason for your roaming the monastery and asking questions, rather than remaining with Mrs. Elton, as her required escort."

Brother Hugo didn't make a move to take the next crate from me. I adjusted my arms and shoulders to another position, but the pull on my tendons was just slightly different, not relieved.

"We have enough rum." Brother Hugo talked over my head in Spanish to Brother Emilio, who had reappeared in the doorway. "Make up a case of wine."

"Oh," I said in English, "then you sell some wine too?"

The big monk returned to English. "The wine's duty is to occupy the restaurant managers, while we barter our rum for their chef's perishable items, nearing the end of their storage. The pineapples that are too old to be served they simply give to us for wine making. And although we must exchange rum for it, the chefs make sure that we have enough molasses and sugar to make more rum."

"No complaints from the Bacardi factory?"

"The lion is not bothered by the mouse." Brother Hugo crossed his massive arms and looked down at me from his superior height. "And as for your curious behavior, I will give you thirty seconds to explain yourself."

Thirty seconds was plenty. The weight of the rum crate was tearing my arms from their sockets. "Detective Sergeant Alvarez asked me to find out where everybody was around the time of the...of Rahim's death."

"How can I trust a man who goes out of his way to avoid the police one day and goes out of his way to assist the police the next?"

Unsteadily, I stepped around the big monk, lifted the crate with the last of my strength to clear the bed, and set it down on the back of the cart, rather more heavily than I'd intended. The donkey brayed in protest.

"It is precisely because I evaded the police that day," I leaned on the crate and drew in a deep breath to finish, "that I am pressured into co-operating with Alvarez now."

The big monk took a few moments, perhaps to mull over what I'd said. "You may tell your Detective Sergeant that I did not see Monsignor Cabrera leave."

"I suppose you were still out here making wine and rum at the time."

"That particular morning, it was candles. And then before washing up for lunch, I tended to the donkey. Of course, this may not come as news to the Detective

Sergeant, since the other detective took this information in my statement, which—"

Brother Hugo rushed to rescue the crate of wine from the faltering grip of Brother Emilio. Returning to the cart, the big monk shouldered me to one side and used the wine crate to shove the row of rum crates forward, before setting it down.

To show that he hadn't discouraged me, I stepped right in to lend Brother Hugo a hand, as he started securing the cartload with a weathered rope. At one point, the big monk had to make a long reach for a rope end, and I caught a glimpse of a tattoo in faded reds and blues on his stout forearm. It looked like a gun lying across a pitchfork, symbolism rather at odds with those typically associated with his current calling.

"It is not necessary that you accompany us today," Brother Hugo spoke past me, in Spanish.

I hadn't noticed anyone's approach, but now turned to find Brother Rafael standing with his hand still on the garden gate.

"This man can lead the donkey back up the mountain for us," Brother Hugo continued. "He seems to have an uncontrollable need to offer his assistance."

Brother Rafael appeared to have some difficulty in suppressing a smile, as he retreated back through the garden.

I wasn't looking forward to trudging back up the mountain, myself. And I suspected that this was Brother Hugo's way of keeping me – and my questions – away from the other two monks. But that was okay. I was fairly certain there were more nuggets to be panned from the stream I was already working.

**

Brother Emilio and I followed the donkey cart, loaded with crates of alcoholic beverages, as we descended the mountainside through the switchbacks. Ahead of us, Brother Hugo walked beside the donkey, not really leading it. The animal seemed to know the routine.

At one point Brother Emilio had to stop and take care of business, off to the side of the cart path. I had waited for him, so when we resumed our journey downward, Brother Hugo and the donkey cart were already past a switchback that Brother Emilio and I were only just approaching. Through the intervening foliage and below us, I saw Brother Hugo's hand on a lever mounted on a metal box that was fastened on top of the donkey's harness.

"What is the device that Brother Hugo has on the donkey's harness?" I asked Brother Emilio in Spanish.

"It is the brake control for the wheels. It is to keep the weight of the cart from overwhelming the donkey. Brother Hugo adapted it from the old truck."

"Where did the old truck come from?"

"Brother Hugo exchanged two bottles of rum for a smashed truck at the repair garage in the village at the base of the mountain. For one more bottle of rum, the mechanic performed the cutting and welding to reduce the width of the cart. The cart path, as you can see, is no longer wide."

Even with the cut down version of the cart, the donkey was certainly going to earn its feed that day.

"We have put to use other parts of the old truck, also," Brother Emilio went on. "The seat is in our work shed. I believe that it is the most comfortable seat on the mountain."

A sudden rain filtered down through the forest canopy. The cool rinse was a refreshing change from my hot sweat.

"How do you get the crates of rum all the way into town?" I asked the young monk.

"It is arranged that, on the days that we take the rum to Luquillo, a pickup truck meets us at the road. Brother Hugo and I ride with the driver and the rum."

"It sounds like you have it all worked out."

"It was not always so," Brother Emilio said. "Before we had the cart, we would take the crates two at a time on the donkey's back, down to the waiting truck. There were many trips down and back up the mountain. It was a very long and exhausting day. And, of course, there was the time with the robbers."

"You were robbed?"

"Almost. I was waiting with the truck driver, resting myself for leading the donkey back up, after Brother Hugo arrived with the last two crates. Three men came walking up the road. This was unusual. Then they were upon us. One had a pistol and the other two each had a big knife. They demanded all the rum and the truck. What could we do against a pistol and knives? I admit that I was very frightened. Then the robbers argue with each other. But the one with the pistol prevails, and they wait for the last two crates."

"So, they knew your routine," I commented.

"It would appear so. And when Brother Hugo and the donkey then arrive with the last two crates, the one with the pistol demands that Brother Hugo load the crates quickly onto the truck. But Brother Hugo works very slowly at the ropes. The man with the gun becomes very angry. He yells at Brother Hugo and waves his pistol. Inside me, I am pleading with Brother Hugo to hurry. But still, Brother Hugo works slowly. Then the robber rushes in and presses the pistol to Brother Hugo' head, and again he threatens. But the robber does not finish his words. It happens very fast. Brother Hugo grabs the robber's wrist. The robber screams. The gun falls to the pavement, and Brother Hugo is now behind the robber. His sleeve is back, and I see his many tattoos. He captures the robber's throat in the crook of his big arm. The tattoos flex hard, the robber's eyes get big, and then he goes limp. Brother Hugo lets him drop."

When Brother Emilio didn't immediately continue, I prompted, "And the other two robbers?"

"Oh. They ran away. Brother Hugo tied up the one who had the pistol and threw him into the back of the truck. After I returned from leading the donkey back up to his shed, we took the robber with us. Brother Hugo set him free along the highway on our way to Luquillo."

"Were you not afraid that the robbers would come back?"

"Brother Hugo said that they were not that type of men."

As we continued down the cart path, I asked, "What happened to the pistol?"

"Our truck driver now carries it. It makes him very happy."

***

An elderly pickup truck and driver, both physically scarred by life's misfortunes, waited for us on the graveled pull-off at the base of the cart path, near where the little rental car was parked. The driver, a corpulent and dark-skinned man, probably in his sixties, climbed out of the truck at our approach and gave Brother Hugo a hearty handshake. He petted the donkey's forehead and bear hugged Brother Emilio. As soon as the driver became aware of me standing behind the cart, his hand darted to the grip of a handgun stowed in a waistband overwhelmed by his generous girth.

"If you shoot him," Brother Hugo said in calm Spanish, "we will be delayed, while one of us takes the donkey back up to his shed."

The driver let his hand fall away from the gun, but he kept an eye on me, as we all pitched in to transfer the crates to the truck.

Brother Hugo took the driver aside to quietly explain my presence, while Brother Emilio gave me instructions to rest the donkey at each switchback on my journey back up the mountain and to brush, feed, and water the animal, before putting him in his shed.

With the transfer completed and the load tied down, the three of them crowded into the truck cab. As they drove off, I took the donkey's lead rope in my hand and started up the cart path.

***

Halfway through my return trip up the mountain, the sudden ring tones from my phone breached the quiet of the rain forest, jangling my nerves and drawing a braying protest from the donkey. The number for Windy City Machinery was on the display. I was hesitant. If my boss can't find me, I reasoned, he can't tell me to drop everything and get on the next flight to Indianapolis. The ring tones sang out again, and the donkey's ears laid back. On the other hand, if I didn't answer, he'd undoubtedly assume I was willfully avoiding his call. On the third ring I relented and brought out my phone.

"Hello?"

"Where the hell *are* you?" my boss demanded. "I gave you a couple of days off to rest up, and you disappear completely. Sally finally came up with a new number for you. She said she'd captured it, whatever the hell that means."

"I lost my old phone in Spain."

"Well, that explains why the woman who answers swears at me in Spanish when I tell her to put you on. Anyway, it sounds like she's swearing. Listen, I'm in a bind here. We haven't had a machine order or even a solid nibble, since GM and Chrysler imploded. Therefore, 'all departments must trim down,' thus came the decree from on high. And so, I dump Old Max. And immediately, it bites me in the ass. I get a call from that plant in Ohio that makes ammunition. They're running three shifts, twenty-four seven, and they can't keep up. The military gets first dibs, of course. Thus, the ammo shelves at Walmart are looking mighty barren. So, they need somebody to breathe new life into some old casing machine that broke down for good about ten years ago. And Old Max was the only one still around who'd ever worked on one, and now he's gone. I bribed a Controls Engineer from Ho Dung's department to cover Allison. Had to set him up with a pair of hookers who'd perform something even *I've* never heard of before. But that put me in the minus column with respect to manpower. And now I've got a deceased casing machine in need of resurrection. And I'm talking to *you*."

"That casing machine must be what, out of the fifties? I've never even seen one. You'd better call Old Max back in."

"The seventies, and if I call Old Max back in, somebody else has to take his place out on the curb." My boss allowed me a moment to conclude who that somebody would be. "So *now*, how does Doctor Francis feel about resuscitating that old casing machine?"

"Okay, but I'll be tied up for a bit longer, down here."

"Down where, exactly?"

"Puerto Rico."

"Oh yeah, Sally said something about that. What the hell are you doing down there?"

"Well, see, Alicia's mother died—"

"In Puerto Rico?"

"Ah…yes. She'd been really ill. Alicia asked me to come down and help with the Spanish to get the remains boxed up and on a plane, and also to deal with the—"

"Alright, alright. I get it." My boss let out a sigh. "Alicia, again. Seriously, Francis, that woman is poison to you."

"So that's why I just need another day or so."

"I can have Old Max in Ohio tomorrow morning."

"Well, see, I'm not exactly *in* San Juan right now, so I'll need some—"

"Call Sally when you're boarding your plane. If she doesn't hear from you by four this afternoon, Old Max is back in, and you're out. Don't drag your feet."

Chapter 9

With the donkey wiped down and brushed, watered and fed, I walked the worn path through the vast garden, heading for the main building.

The newly imposed time crunch weighed heavily on my mind. Assuming there was a direct red-eye flight to Cleveland, I could get there around midnight, sleep in the baggage claim area until the rental car counters opened in the morning, then drive straight down to the ammo factory, maybe get there by nine, or ten at the latest...

The sight of two motionless figures, planted in the Adirondack chairs at the edge of the garden, interrupted my calculations. Brother Carlos and Brother Rafael sat facing the vista of sea and sky. On the small rustic table between them sat a pewter pitcher with a green band around its neck. And on one broad, flat arm of each chair, a mug rested within ready reach of a monk's hand.

Unnoticed – or, perhaps, ignored – I passed behind them, exited through the garden gate, and entered the main building through the back door.

In the dining hall, Alicia sat at the long table, writing on a pad of lined paper. Beyond the far end of the long table, the Abbot snoozed in his great chair. I took a seat next to Alicia.

Without looking up from her work, she said, "You smell like a horse."

"I took the donkey for a spin down the mountain and back. I was helping with a load of bootleg rum."

Alicia flipped to a blank page and in flowing cursive wrote a name (presumably that of a long dead and unheralded artist) across the top of the paper, and immediately began writing a description. I read along behind her graceful penmanship, taking in her unfolding summary of the painted scene – the one where Jesus, with whip in hand, drives the merchants from the Temple. She went on to write another paragraph describing the painting's overall condition, before adding, with the aid of her notes, detailed accounts of various specific areas of damage. Her handwriting was flat-out beautiful.

I waited until Alicia laid her pen down, before I said, "I haven't found out a damn thing more about who might have killed the Arab."

"How odd. The donkey wouldn't open up?" Alicia turned the page to a new blank sheet.

"I mostly get useless responses from the monks. Except for Emilio, they're all kind of reluctant to talk to me."

"They're probably not supposed to talk much at all," Alicia said. "Though I've noticed there seems to be a lot of slack in the leash for a place you'd think would run on pretty strict rules."

"I know. It feels like a couple of factories I've been to, right after the second big round of layoffs and the machinery's being sold off. The survivors are just going through the motions. Hanging around, waiting for the end."

Returning to her work, Alicia briefly referred to her notes and once again began documenting her observations in longhand.

Again, I waited for her to finish with the page. "I checked in with my boss. Things have changed. I've got to get back."

"Well, tonight I'm going to type up what I've written here, import the pictures from my camera, and print it all out. Then tomorrow morning, I'm going to hand in my report to Monsignor Cabrera and get my check. Ellen and I are flying out tomorrow afternoon. Are you coming with us?"

"I'm going to see about a flight out this evening."

"Suit yourself." Alicia plunged back into her work.

"I was hoping to have something more solid to give to Dodd."

"You were also hoping for a night of unbridled passion." Alicia's pen barely paused. "Not everything works out."

"Maybe if I'd had more time."

"If you're referring to your self-imposed obligation to Dodd, you're still at the monastery. Make the best of it."

"And if I was referring to what you promised we'd fit in, somehow?"

Alicia's pen hard-landed a period. "Look, Francis. I'm extremely busy right now. And as I explained to you, I'll be busy well into the night. So, if you're calling it quits, then please just sit there quietly. I've got to finish this."

Sitting there quietly sounded about as much fun as sleeping rough at the Cleveland Airport. And besides,

Alicia was right. My opportunity to gather information was now. I left the long table and headed out to the garden.

***

Re-entering the vast garden, I set a course for the Adirondack chairs. It was clearly evident, during my earlier walk-by, that the Baghdad battery's former electrolyte in the green-banded pitcher was not, as Brother Emilio believed, being used to improve the garden soil – at least, not right away. And I was confident that the pineapple wine still retained enough punch to be of assistance in loosening up a monastic tongue or two.

"A beautiful day for the garden," I said in Spanish, as I neared the relaxing monks.

Neither head turned to the sound of my voice, nor did the monks show any reaction to the light rain that had just begun to fall on them.

However, when I stopped next to his chair, Brother Carlos, still gazing off toward the horizon, did finally respond. "We are blessed with abundant rain and sun. It is as though God encourages us in our labors."

I thought "labors" was stretching it at the moment, but I kept the conversation going. "The plants look healthy with your care."

"Caring for the plants is an enjoyable peace." This time it was Brother Rafael who responded.

Brother Carlos added, "And after our communal midday meal, all of the Brothers are free to do as they wish, until gathered for evening prayers."

I looked off toward the ocean. "So you can relax and enjoy the view."

192

"Today, we look to the sky and the water with a purpose," Brother Carlos said. "We watch for the coming storm."

Since we were facing north, not east, I saw only a peaceful sea beneath a scatter of white clouds. "I see no sign of a storm."

"It is what you do not see," Brother Carlos said. "There are no cruise ships. They are the first to flee." He paused for a drink from his mug. "It is after you no longer see the pelicans and the gulls in flight that the angry dark clouds will roll in above us."

"And it will then be the time to move the donkey down into the shelter of the forest," Brother Rafael said. "But not today, I think."

"No, not today." Brother Carlos again grasped the handle of his mug. "But soon, the pleasant weather will be swept away. Just as we, the last remnants of our cherished monastery, will also, soon, be swept away."

Almost simultaneously the two monks raised their mugs and took another comforting swallow.

This was too depressing to witness. It was like watching a species go extinct.

Still, I was supposed to be gathering relevant information about the recent death of an Arab businessman. And so far, I'd only scored an unrelated account about some local bandits.

Also, there was an unexpected amenity I wanted to explore. Namely, the existence of a functioning indoor sink and toilet, on the second floor of a centuries-old former manor house, isolated up near the top of a mountain.

I broached the subject with, "I was actually out here looking for the bathroom. I thought that there would be some small structure..."

Brother Carlos grinned and pointed back to the main building. "For visitors, there is the bathroom up in the guest quarters. For the Brothers, there is a bathroom in the basement."

"A basement? I would never have guessed it. I would be interested to see it."

"Come," Brother Carlos said, struggling out of the depths of his Adirondack chair. "I will take you there. I too feel the need."

We left Brother Rafael to keep watch on the sea and sky.

***

Brother Carlos shut the garden gate behind us. As we continued toward the rear door of the main building, I could just make out another footpath, cutting through a swath of scraggly weeds and aspiring young trees that ran along the far side of the main building. I'd noticed the footpath before, but because it appeared to have fallen into disuse, I'd ignored it.

Pointing, I said, "That looks like a path to nowhere."

Brother Carlos stopped at the threshold of the back door. "It leads a pool that gathers runoff water that finds it way down from the higher elevations," he said. "Before we had the pipe, several daily journeys were required to bring buckets of water from the pool."

Looking closer at the expanse of weeds – sections of which looked grazed, perhaps by a tethered donkey – I now saw, here and there, hints of a long run of white pipe.

"All those years of carrying buckets of water," Brother Carlos shook a rueful head, "and then we had a plastic pipe glued together in one day."

"I would think such water to be unsuitable for drinking without treatment."

"We use the water from the pool only for flushing and mopping. And naturally, it is pleasant to bathe in the pool." Brother Carlos smiled. "For drinking, there is the rainwater that is gathered by the cistern in the patio."

"Oh, I thought it was a fountain."

Brother Carlos looked at me with merriment in his eyes. "A fountain. You are a romantic, sir. Do you imagine that the Brothers splash and play like the children of San Juan in the Fuente Raices?"

I smiled at the mental image he'd evoked. "I spoke without thinking. A fountain would require a pump."

"Oh, we have a pump," Brother Carlos said. "To raise the water up to the level of the guest bathroom."

I scanned the grounds and looked up to the roof of the main building, searching for a windmill. But Brother Carlos had already proceeded on through the doorway, forcing me to abandon my search and follow him.

But that was all right. Compared to his terse responses, earlier in the day, Brother Carlos's words were now pouring forth like wine from a green-banded pitcher. I needed only the discipline to probe, not with questions, but with casual observations. I had learned what playing the Quiz Master had gotten me.

***

Brother Carlos and I crossed through the interior of the building, skirting what I now knew was the cistern in the central patio, and eventually entered a room off the front hallway, near the front door. The corner room was empty and smelled of damp earth. Daylight streamed from two directions, through tall, unadorned front and side windows. The only feature in the room, apart from jagged cracks that ran floor to ceiling up the plastered walls, was a large, rectangular opening cut into the floorboards, just beneath one of the windows. Within the cavity, a steep stairway led down. I could see the rocks and mortar of a foundation wall on one side and the vertical wooden planks forming an interior wall on the other. I followed Brother Carlos, as he descended into the earth.

The stairs ended just two feet short of the building's front foundation wall, but the wood plank interior wall had ended with the bottom step, leaving an opening to the left. Having made the abrupt turn at the bottom, we entered a basement room, featuring a dirt floor below and barely a foot of head-clearance above.

Apart from the damp earth smell, which was now so strong that I began to taste it too, the next thing I noticed was that the basement's light source was not a candle, as I had anticipated. Rather, a small dome light, perhaps from a car's interior, was fastened to the bottom of one of the floor joists, positioned to dimly shine down on a row of three toilets and a pedestal sink. The rest of the basement room – which ran the full length of the front foundation wall, but had been excavated back for only about ten feet – was cast in deep shadow.

"I did not expect an electric light," I said.

"The little light is from a broken truck that Brother Hugo obtained. It is powered by the truck's battery."

The pedestal sink and line of toilets were mounted on a six-inch high, wooden platform. Just behind the porcelain fixtures, the long foundation wall – which in previous centuries, I supposed, had stoutly supported the front exterior wall of the building – now pitched ominously inward.

The water to fill the toilet tanks was delivered via flexible connections to a one-inch, white plastic pipe. Undoubtedly, this was the terminus of the pipe I'd seen crossing through the weeds outside. For the effluence of the gathered toilet and sink drains, a three-inch diameter pipe poked out of one end of the raised platform, took a sweeping 90-degree turn, and plunged through a hole chiseled out of the inward-leaning, foundation wall.

"I hope that drainpipe does not simply empty down the side of the mountain," I said.

"We made a settling tank and a seepage tank, using cement blocks," Br. Carlos said. "The dirt that we removed to create this basement, we packed around the settling tank. The rocks, we piled around the seepage tank. It was our month of digging." The monk let out a wistful sigh. "There were twenty of us then."

Without a doubt, it was the removal of the supporting dirt and rocks from the inner side of the foundation wall that allowed the relentless pressure from the damp and heavy earth on the outer side to pitch the foundation wall inward. And given that several cracks in the foundation's front wall were already wide enough to accept a man's fingers, the potential for a catastrophic failure was leaning toward becoming imminent.

Opposite the inward-pitched exterior foundation wall, an interior retaining wall had been built of modern cement blocks and mortar to hold back the dry, unexcavated earth beneath the rest of the building. Unfortunately, this strong new wall now acted as a fulcrum over which the monastery's back was breaking.

At the moment, however, biology was trumping caution. Facing the threat posed by the collapsing foundation wall, Brother Carlos and I stood shoulder-to-shoulder on the raised platform with the tops our heads within a few inches of the joists above us, and used two of the three facilities. My zippered trousers were noticeably more practical for this operation, than the skirt of the monk's robe.

Gravity-fed water gradually refilled the holding tanks, and still had enough reserve flow for a rinsing of the hands in the pedestal sink.

"If you have a pump," I said, "you could have saved yourselves a lot of digging by putting this bathroom in the room above us. Not to mention, avoiding the collapse of a foundation wall."

"There was no pump at first. There was only the pipe and the water flowing of its own accord. It was not until the arrival of Brother Hugo that the little conveniences began to appear."

"The installation of a bathroom up in guest quarters sounds more like a major project."

"As it happened, the necessity for a guest bathroom was a matter of considerable dispute."

My ears pricked up with the word "dispute."

"About a year ago," Brother Carlos explained, "the Archbishop determined that the monastery could no longer prohibit women from entering its grounds. We were instructed to provide for their comfort. However, no funding accompanied our assignment."

"Classic," I recognized the ploy.

"The Abbot traveled to San Juan to protest that for the monastery to shoulder this obligation alone was impossible. However, the Abbot quickly found himself defending the continued existence of the monastery itself."

I had a vision of the arthritic and confused old Abbot attempting to be the monastery's bulwark against the might of the Archdiocese.

"Monsignor Cabrera intervened," Brother Carlos went on. "But his influence secured only a brief reprieve. A guest bathroom was still required."

"But with twenty of you and a revival of the bucket brigade…"

"Unfortunately, our numbers very soon began to diminish, as other places were found for our fellow monks, some as far away as Argentina."

"So, apart from the Abbot," I grabbed my chance to confirm it, "you are now down to just four monks."

"Actually, we were reduced to three. Then, curiously, Brother Hugo joined us. And it was he who devised a way to power the little pump that lifts the water to the second floor, as well as the dome light."

Brother Carlos pointed toward a small, plastic pump, fitted between a check valve and a pressure switch along a length of half-inch plastic pipe that tapped into the larger, gravity-fed, water pipe. The truck battery, I saw, provided the 12-volt power for the pump.

"So, a bottle or two of bartered rum produced the answer to your prayers," I made an informed guess.

"After Brother Hugo began making wine for our table and rum for barter, the monastery became much less dependent on the Archdiocese for support." Brother Carlos's palms, perhaps unconsciously, came together. "But then, a delegation from the Archdiocese arrived for an unexpected visit." The monk frowned at the leaning foundation wall and his hands fell to his sides. "And soon after, the structural engineer came up the mountain path…"

When Brother Carlos didn't go on, I finished for him, "And the Archdiocese was provided with a new reason to eliminate the drain on its finances. The repair of the foundation wall would be too costly."

"You are astute, sir. Do you enjoy politics?"

"Not when I am on the receiving end of it."

I returned my attention to the truck battery and spied a small DC-to-AC inverter nearby that was also connected to the battery's terminals. '300 watts' was boldly printed between two sets of cooling fins on the power inverter's cast aluminum cover.

A plug, inserted into a duplex outlet on the front of the inverter, fed two individual wires, both insulated in black plastic. These wires draped up to join two white plastic pipes: a half-inch water pipe and a three-inch drainpipe. Grouped together, the wires and pipes eventually passed through an opening at the top of the interior basement wall, where a concrete block had been removed.

Presumably, the plumbing was for the guest bathroom up on the second floor. What the wires, that carried 120-volt AC power from the inverter, were for, I couldn't guess.

Brother Carlos, having apparently noticed my scan along the black wires, said, "The wires bring power to the electric fan up in the Abbot's room. The fan was a gift from the ladies of the Cathedral's Altar Society. The Abbot suffers so in the heat."

"That was certainly kind of them."

"Truly, it was a lovely gesture. Of course, the Altar Society was not aware of the absence of public utilities up here on our remote shoulder of the mountain."

"But you seem to have solved the problem."

"That again was the work of Brother Hugo. We were all much relieved when he and Brother Emilio pulled the wires up to the Abbot's room for his fan."

"Brother Hugo seems to possess a great store of practical knowledge."

"We have a wizard among us."

I looked to Brother Carlos's face, expecting a smile to accompany his remark. There wasn't one.

I pressed on, "I saw the donkey cart with a hydraulic brake in action when I helped with the rum shipment, earlier today. I was impressed."

"Brother Hugo has distributed the various parts from the old truck so thinly that one hardly notices his little improvements," Brother Carlos said. "It is forbidden to ask, but I cannot help wondering what he was before."

"I would assume that Monsignor Cabrera knows."

"Monsignor Cabrera knows everything."

Again, I looked in vain for an accompanying smile.

I then ran my eyes over Brother Hugo's entire setup, one more time. It wasn't especially tidy, but admittedly, it was solid.

However, a battery needs to be recharged. And I'd noticed that, in addition to the relatively thin wires that delivered power to the dome light and little pump, two sets of thicker insulated wires were also connected to the battery terminals. One set, as I'd previously seen, ran power from the battery to the DC-to-AC inverter. The other set of thick wires, I figured, were for bringing power to the battery in order to keep a charge on it. Those wires ran for only a few feet behind the battery, before terminating at a small aluminum case, bristling with cooling fins. I picked it up and read the label. It was a 36/48-volt DC to 12-volt DC step-down regulator. I remembered replacing one like it on an electric forklift, working nights at a factory when I first got out of the Navy.

Looking deeper into the shadows, I picked out a pair of wires, one white and one black, that came down from the hole, where the incoming one-inch water pipe entered at the top of the building's side foundation wall. These two wires, each about the thickness of a pencil, continued in along the dirt floor and fed the power to the step-down regular. But that only begged the question: where the hell was Brother Hugo getting that kind of voltage from?

While still pondering on this, I unintentionally blurted out, "Does the Abbot give his blessing to all these improvements?"

Damn it. I'd asked a direct question.

But, to my relief, Brother Carlos responded. "With the passage of time, our Abbot has become much less aware of his surroundings. He does not seem to notice the truck parts."

"But one-hundred-and-twenty-volt electricity does not come from a truck part." I pointed toward the inverter that powered the Abbot's fan.

"Brother Hugo did not barter for the apparatus that changes the power only to accommodate the Abbot's fan. There was also the idea to install electric lights in the dining hall. When we gather for evening prayers, we burn many candles into the night."

"And candles are expensive."

"Only in the sense that we were dependent on the Archdiocese for our supply and that their cost added to the financial burden that threatened the monastery's existence. Thankfully, Brother Hugo persuaded a hardware store owner to accept a bottle of our rum in exchange for the twine, borax, and paraffin wax."

"So, you could immediately reduce your financial dependency by making your own candles, which in turn bought you time to install the electric lights."

"Unfortunately, it was during this respite that the failing foundation wall sealed our monastery's fate. Therefore, the task of installing electric lights in the dining hall became pointless."

On that unhappy note, I said, "Well, thank you for the tour."

"Yes, I suppose that you are our bathroom's first tourist." This time the monk showed me a smile.

As Brother Carlos followed me toward the stairs, I stopped to look at a stack of wooden crates, packed full of fruits and vegetables and crowded into a dark corner.

"I had not noticed these crates before."

"The vegetables are stored down here where it is cooler." Brother Carlos explained. "They had to be gathered before the coming hurricane. Just as we must be mindful of the Scriptures to preserve our souls, we must also be mindful of Nature to survive on our mountain."

***

Outside the main building, Brother Carlos and I parted ways. He reentered the garden to languidly read the sky with Brother Rafael. And I, with piqued interest, started off in the opposite direction, along the less trodden pathway that led across the swath of weeds and toward the pool of mountain runoff water.

The white plastic water pipe joined the pathway, just as it entered the rain forest, and continued along at the pathway's side, still accompanied by the white wire and the black wire that had passed through the foundation's wall with it. Once under the forest canopy, from up ahead, I heard the sound of rushing water, and soon spotted the pool with its surprising amount of overflow spilling out through the v-shaped juncture of two massive boulders. From the cascade over the boulders, the water washed down through the lesser rocks, and finally formed a fast moving stream, racing down the mountain's steep slope.

Continually refilling the reservoir behind this natural dam were countless rivulets that fell as a line of showers at the rear of the pool. Given El Junque's daily rainfall, I doubted that the pool would ever cease overflowing.

The white plastic pipe extended beyond where the pathway ended at the rocks and made an up-sweeping bend, thrusting its open end deep into the flow of the spillway. A mound of fist-sized rocks, piled on the pipe, held it in place against the onslaught of the gushing water.

My eyes now followed the white and the black pair of wires, which had parted company with the water pipe, after it was well inside the diminished light beneath the forest canopy.

Strangely, the two wires led to a four-cylinder engine block, plunked down in the swift stream below the pool, as though it had dropped from the sky. But even more weirdly, the engine block had become partnered with the back half of a bicycle, and the engine's cooling fan and the bicycle's rear wheel were both spinning madly.

On closer inspection, the partially submerged engine block had been stripped of almost all internal and peripheral parts – with the notable exception of the cooling fan, whose blades acted as a water wheel with their tips propelled around by the rush of water flowing past, and the engine's alternator, which remained bolted in its place, well above the waterline.

The fan was still mounted on the engine's water-pump pulley, but sandwiched between the pulley and the fan blades was the large diameter drive sprocket that would formerly have been rotated by foot pedals powered by a cyclist. The bicycle's chain circulated around the teeth of both the big drive sprocket and the little sprocket on the axle of the bicycle's rear wheel, which spun within the supports of the bicycle's upturned rear frame-half.

The spinning bicycle wheel no longer had a tire and tube, but it did have a v-belt around its circumference that transferred its rotation to the alternator's small diameter pulley, spinning it in a blur.

The white wire was connected to the output terminal on the alternator, and the black wire was connected to a bolt on the engine block. I brought out the voltmeter from my pant's pocket and touched the probes to the two connection points. It read a little over 37 volts.

He'd lose a couple of volts due to the length of the wires. But I supposed it'd be close enough for Brother Hugo to skip tinkering with various pulley diameters and just use an off-the-shelf, step-down, voltage regulator, in line just ahead of the battery. He would've had to spend another bottle of rum on replacing the alternator's original wire-wound rotor with a permanent magnet one to get that much output voltage, but that was unavoidable, given the distance and wire size he'd had to work with.

This engineering-on-the-fly wouldn't exactly qualify as wizardry, but I had to allow, Brother Hugo certainly knew his stuff.

In fact, Brother Hugo and his various improvised concoctions of junkyard finds and off-the-shelf items reminded me of the farm boys with whom I'd attended high school – the ones who were taught by their fathers to be self-reliant and, in a pinch, be resourceful enough to use whatever was at hand to keep the farm and its machinery operating.

Having successfully found the power source that kept a charge on the old truck battery, I walked back down the neglected pathway. Once out from under the rain forest canopy, I now noticed how close the sun was to the treetops and pulled out my phone to check the time. It was already quarter to four. I quickly punched in the numbers for the Service Department at Windy City Machinery on a gamble that Sally was still on her 3:30 break. To my relief, my call was sent directly to voice mail. I left a message saying that I was presently in line at the airline ticket counter and would soon be on a flight to Ohio.

***

As I entered the dining hall, Alicia stood at the end of the long table with her purse hanging by its strap on her shoulder and her tote bag about to be taken in hand.

Spotting her beast-of-burden, she let go of the tote bag's handle, and said, "I was almost ready to leave without you. I tried to phone. I couldn't get through."

"It must have been when I was leaving a voicemail about being in the ticket line for a flight to Ohio, so I wouldn't lose my job."

"I'm getting tired of lies," Alicia said, as she walked past me, heading for the door. "Come on. We can swing by the airport on the way back and bump your latest fib up to a half-truth. I'd like to see about a flight out tomorrow anyway."

Dutifully, I grabbed up Alicia's tote bag and followed her out. In doing so, I noticed that the Abbot's chair now stood empty. Evidently, the old holy man was devoutly snoozing elsewhere.

Alicia waited until we'd left the building, before saying, "While you were allegedly out sleuthing around, I did a little snooping on my own. And guess what. That fan, up in the Abbot's room, it's a regular plug-in one, not battery powered like we thought."

"When were you up in the Abbot's room?"

"While I was packing up, one of the monks asked for my help to get the Abbot upstairs. It was all in Spanish, but he was pretty good at pantomime, so I got the idea. And it turns out the Abbot doesn't weigh all that much, but I guess you'd risk dislocating his shoulder, if you tried to haul him up the stairs by yourself. Anyway, we got him stretched out on his bed, the monk said 'gracias' more times than I could count, and then I left. But not, as I said, before noticing, for your damned benefit, that it was a normal-looking fan that was plugged into a homemade-looking extension cord."

"That fits with what I found out," I said, as we neared the cart path down.

Alicia stopped and scanned the monastery grounds. "So, where does the electricity for the fan come from? I don't see any power lines."

"Brother Hugo built a little power station out of salvaged parts from a junked-out pickup and a store-bought power inverter that changes the truck battery's direct current to regular household alternating current."

"Brother Hugo. That's the big one, right? He sounds pretty skilled."

"He also can take down an armed robber barehanded, make hard liquor from molasses, and slide back his sleeve to reveal a heavy armload of tattoos."

"What was he, Outlaw Biker of the Year?"

"The unarmed combat part would take formal training," I said. "That will interest Dodd greatly. I don't think Dodd has settled on a likely suspect for Rahim's murder yet."

"Uh huh. So while Brother Hugo is holding his thumb on the Arab's windpipe, what's the bodyguard supposed to be doing, looking out the window?"

***

On the drive back to San Juan, as we luxuriated in the rental car's air conditioning, Alicia said, "Oh, I almost forgot. I did something else for you today. Since you're so interested in the Abbot's chair, I sent some pictures of it, with my phone, to one of my old professors. So he called me back, and I was right about it being sixteenth century Arab-Spanish. And he said that, back then, all the regular people sat on stools. So the fact that the chair had both a seat back and intricate carvings meant it was for somebody who was really important. I guess like a sultan. And he said the chair probably ended up in Puerto Rico during the Spanish Inquisition."

"Why would that be?"

"Because if the Catholic Church found out there was a Muslim chair with a magic box on the back, my old professor says there's a hundred percent chance they'd burn the chair along with the guy who made it and probably his workshop too. So, he figures the Muslims must have decided to hide it, until things cooled off."

"He thinks Muslims brought it over here to Puerto Rico?"

"Yes, but he said they'd have to hire some down-on-his-luck Spanish nobleman for cover. Someone who could petition the King to bring some furniture and a few white slaves over to the New World with him."

"Then how did the Catholics finally end up with it?"

"My professor says that, when the Inquisition eventually came to Puerto Rico, the chair would have to go into hiding again. But how it ends up in some coffee plantation's manor house up in the mountains, that eventually gets sold to the Catholic Church for use as a monastery, is anybody's guess."

"And probably, by that time, the Baghdad battery part of the chair had already corroded away with the humidity and been forgotten about," I said. "Until Brother Hugo recognized what it was."

"Maybe he'd seen something like it somewhere before. Maybe he's been to Baghdad."

It galled me that Alicia could think so quickly. All I could offer was, "Yeah, maybe so. I'm pretty sure he's ex-military."

"Anyway, my professor said the worth of the chair would mostly be for its historic or religious significance. And he agreed with me that you'd take a hell of a hit on shipping costs getting it back to Spain. And that's where you'd have to take it to get any serious money for it. And you know who's going to pay top dollar. The Muslims."

***

We took the toll road to save time. I even managed to coax ten-over-the-limit out of our rented four-banger with pistons about the size of a third-grader's fist. The sky didn't look right at all now. It had become darkly overcast in pea green, where, only an hour before, it had been puffy clouds on pale blue.

"Any chance you could submit your report to Monsignor Cabrera, right when we get back?" I asked. "I think it'd be better, if all of us flew out tonight."

"How many times do I have to explain that I'll be tied up all evening, getting my report together?" Alicia snapped. But she then added a conciliatory, "I know. I see the sky too."

As we neared the exit for the SJU airport, it was hard not to notice that there were no planes in the sky – no take offs, no landings, no circling around. So, it was already too late. But I still had to try. I took the exit.

At the airport, I found a place to park at the far end of a mostly full lot. After a long walk, Alicia and I entered the main terminal and joined the fringes of a restless mob of people. On the screens above the check-in desks, every flight departure time stated 'delayed'. The flight arrival screens were more honest: they were completely blank.

We never came anywhere near to within speaking distance of an airline representative. But that didn't really matter. It wasn't hard to figure out that, like the cruise ships, all commercial aircraft had fled. And they wouldn't be back, until after the hurricane had passed.

With my slim hope dashed, I again tapped in the number for Windy City Machinery on my phone's keyboard. I left an after-hours voicemail, explaining the situation and expressing my regret. It was a voicemail that I knew would cost me my job.

***

Up on the second floor of the Caserio Inn, Alicia entered her room, just as I reached mine. But, before I had my key out, I heard Alicia yell.

"Francis!"

When I burst into their room, Alicia stood over Ellen, who lay curled up on the far bed, her whole body shaking with each sob, her tears soaking a pillow.

"I can't do anything with her," Alicia said. "She won't tell me what happened. Help me get her up."

Alicia drew Ellen's legs over the edge of the bed, and I lifted her to a sitting position. Ellen sat hunched, as Alicia held her sister's head, her palms placed fore and aft.

"Whenever you feel like telling us," Alicia said softly.

Ellen's words were pitched in squeaks. "I lost it. I lost it all. All that money."

Relief swept over me. It was just money.

Her voice still soft, Alicia asked, "What money?"

Ellen managed to get her voice under more control and to a lower pitch. "I maxed out my credit card. At a casino. All that money. It's all gone."

"How much money, Ellen? What's the card's limit?" Alicia gently prodded.

"Nine thousand. But I already had almost four on it. I just kept thinking I was going to win."

Alicia sighed. "Well, it's not the end of the world."

"But, Roger—"

"Roger will be fine." Alicia's tone became more resolute. "You'll just get a little job when we get back. And a year from now, we'll be laughing about it. Your great adventure. Little Ellen, the mighty gambler."

There was a knock at the open door. A handsome Puerto Rican in a stylish suit looked in on us. His pompadour coif matched his black, pointed-toe shoes, both in color and brilliance. If I had to guess, I'd say late twenties.

"Am I early?" the young man asked in English. Even his accent was charming.

"Armando helped me place my bets," Ellen introduced him. "I think I invited him to dinner with us."

Alicia's judgment was swift. "Francis, get rid of him."

I briefly wondered if Brother Emilio's assessment of me, as Alicia's servant, wasn't uncomfortably on point.

However, something definitely had to be done with Armando. I moved purposefully toward the young man, keeping my eyes locked onto his.

We were roughly in the same weight class, but the young man retreated into the hallway without the need to crowd him much. I closed the door behind me.

"The lady is not feeling well." I spoke in English, rather than the more polite-sounding Spanish. "She is sorry about dinner."

"But I must speak with her."

I didn't respond, but remained steadfast between him and the door.

The young man raised a determined voice. "You cannot stop me from seeing her."

"I am not concerned about the damage a fight will cause to my face," I said. "How about you?"

The young man required no further persuasion. His livelihood was at stake. He showed me a scowl and walked away. His man-perfume lingered only for a moment. I waited for his footsteps to descend the stairs, before I reopened the door.

Alicia halted my entrance with, "I've got it from here, Francis."

Back in my own room, a postcard lay on the desk. The postcard had a picture of a descending row of three stucco townhouses on a steeply pitched street, each building painted in a different, yet complimentary, pastel hue. On the back of the postcard was written, "Across street and down. Then first street on left. M."

***

A block away from the Caserio, I leaned on the roof of the rental car, opened my phone, and punched in the private number that Alvarez had written on his card.

After we established contact, I told the Detective Sergeant, "I could find no one at the monastery who saw Monsignor Cabrera leave, the day Rahim died. I talked to all four monks and the Abbot. The Abbot was the last one to see the Monsignor, but he seemed hazy about whether, or not, he even had tea with him."

"This does not help me," Alvarez was gruff. "Has Mr. Dodd contacted you? The NCIS has asked for my Department's assistance in locating their wayward agent. This makes him the one person that I am permitted to question openly. I must get to him first."

"The NCIS asked for my help too. I told them I didn't know where he was." I now wanted the hell off the phone with the Detective Sergeant. "Look, I did what you asked. I talked to everybody I could who was there, including Alicia. It's not like I could talk to the bodyguard."

There was a pause, before Alvarez said, "We cannot talk to him either."

"An eye-witness, and you couldn't question him?"

"I have not been able to discover what language he speaks. It would be unwise for me to use police resources to pursue the matter further."

"I thought that Rahim's corpse and his bodyguard would be back in France, by now, anyway."

"The airlines will not transport a corpse unless it is embalmed, which is forbidden for Muslims. So, despite Captain Rivera's orders, Jaspar Rahim's journey will end here. The Medical Examiner allowed the local Muslims in to wash and shroud Rahim's body, after hours today at the morgue. He offered to release the body for burial tomorrow, but even Muslims will delay a burial until after a hurricane has passed. Rahim will remain in cold storage at the morgue until then."

"Well, I guess that gives you an extra day to figure out—"

"It will do me no good. I am at an impasse. None of the Muslims who came to prepare the body could understand the bodyguard's language. They could say only that it is not a dialect of Arabic."

And then it hit me that I actually did know a guy who could speak the bodyguard's language. At least, I knew *of* him. In any case, I had a bargaining chip.

I took a deep breath. I was about to promise something that I wasn't sure I could deliver.

"If I produce a translator, will you forget about the charges you have hanging over Ellen Van Kemp and me?"

"How can you produce a translator for a language that has no name?"

"Actually, the biggest problem is that the translator is in Cuba. A sailor stationed at Guantanamo. But there's a chance we can still get him here today."

"I assume that you will be speaking to our friend Mr. Dodd."

"Yes, I'm going to go meet with him now."

"If you get me that translator, I will personally provide transportation to the airport and use my influence to put you and all your lady friends on the first available flight to Chicago. Also, I will forget that you lied to me about not being in contact with Mr. Dodd."

"Deal."

"Do you wish to know the consequences, if you fail me again?"

"No," I said. "The implied threat is enough."

Chapter 10

There were no cruise ships tied up at the docks on the lower bayside of Old San Juan. But the sea gulls were still in evidence – some soaring and swooping over the placid bay, others pecking at the bits of washed-up garbage along the shore.

I drove slowly through the deserted tourist area, looking for some local who might direct me to the three pastel-colored houses, pictured on the postcard. Eventually, I spotted a lone street vendor who was packing up, abandoning his day's futile effort. With his directions, I drove up through transmission-straining, cobble-stoned backstreets. After some confusing turns, not mentioned by the street vendor, I spotted the three adjoined pastel houses, their flat roofs ascending in steps as the street rose. The houses looked out on the ocean over the top of the old city wall, just across the street. There was a break in the old wall, almost opposite the pastel houses, where the street forked and its seaward tine plunged downhill, hugging the side of the old fortification. I drove on past and finally found a place to park, two streets away.

Returning on foot, I crossed to the break in the old wall and ventured downward. The ancient walls of the old city rose ever higher above me, as I made my descent through the surprisingly thick foot traffic passing up and down the steeply pitched street. The unbroken line of parked cars along one side left open only a single narrow lane. God only knows how two cars meeting in opposition would sort it out.

I gave room to a seriously skinny man, whose age I couldn't guess, because no human has ever lived to be as old as he looked. In passing, he determinedly climbed the steep street on unsteady legs, concentrating hard on not spilling his shot glass of dark amber liquid.

Descending further, I passed under a massive stone arch, just before reaching the bottom of the steep slope. After taking a hard right turn onto a wide, moderately downward-pitched, main street, I immediately found myself in the midst of an open-air illicit-drug bazaar.

Arrayed along a row of adjoined, dilapidated, two-story buildings, the dope dealers openly sold their wares from opaque trash bags and outer jacket pockets. The buyers and passersby formed a sparse crowd, so my presence drew the attention of an idle drug merchant. He advanced a couple steps toward me, his open hands turned up, silently asking what I wanted. He didn't look Hispanic, but I told him in Spanish that I was on my way to meet a friend.

I continued ever deeper into the down-at-the-heels neighborhood, which was clustered on a spit of land, trapped between the towering wall of stone and the perilous ocean. As Dodd had instructed on the back of the postcard, I took the first street on the left. In doing so, I caught a glimpse of several local men, casually walking behind me.

I kept to the center of the street, because, ahead and off to one side, a woven basket was being lowered by a rope from a second-story window. The basket's descent stopped, and it hovered in the air at waist height near two men, engaged in close conference on the narrow sidewalk. One of the men placed a thick fold of money into the basket. A pair of hands, reaching out from the window ledge above, hoisted the basket up. As I walked by, the basket was already being lowered again to the sidewalk, laden, I assumed, with some forbidden freight from the upstairs wholesaler.

Up ahead, a small group of denizens monitored my approach. From behind, the sound of footfalls steadily followed me. I had a sinking feeling that the critical moment to turn back had already passed.

"Francis, are you going to hang around in the street all day? These boys have business to attend to. You're making them nervous."

I turned to see Phil Dodd standing in a doorway. I lost no time moving past him and getting inside. Dodd closed the door behind us.

"Thanks for the walk on the wild side," I said.

"I believe I mentioned that it was not a sleepy fishing village."

Dodd led the way up a creaky flight of stairs to the single doorway at the second floor landing. We entered a sparsely furnished, studio apartment. Along the wall opposite the door, there was a canvas-slung folding cot, with a yellowing bare pillow. To the right, a small table and single kitchen chair were positioned just beneath an open double-hung window that overlooked the side street below. A closed laptop computer rested on the table, and a hard-covered briefcase was at hand on the floor, next to the chair.

"Bring the other chair," Dodd said, as he walked over and seated himself at the table.

I stepped into a modest kitchen area at the rear of the apartment, where a lone kitchen chair stood next to a base cupboard containing the sink and faucet. As I picked up the chair, I took a quick look through the open rear window above the sink. The view was of a jumble of tarred flat rooftops in the shadow of the towering, old city wall.

I carried the chair over and sat across from Dodd, as he brought his briefcase up onto the table and snapped it open. Dodd carefully stowed his laptop between a spare shirt and a change of underwear, topped it with a toiletry kit, and closed the briefcase lid down on the stack, to secure everything in place with two latch snaps. He then redirected his attention toward the street below.

"Have to keep a lookout for your tail."

"I'm pretty sure I wasn't followed. Not counting the locals, I mean. Coming down that steep street along the old city wall, I checked behind me several times."

"There's only one way in and out of La Perla. No need for them to stick tight. But then once they're down here, they'll have to buy the information about which street you took and then shell out again for which door you entered. That'll slow them up. Gives us a little time. What did you find out?"

I told him Brother Emilio's story about Brother Hugo and the bandits. Next, I described the mini power station setup in the basement bathroom and out by the overflowing pool. I also gave him Brother Hugo's account of having just walked in from tending to the donkey, when he heard the bodyguard yelling.

"Nothing more about the mugs of tea?" Dodd asked.

"I tried to nail down whether Monsignor Cabrera and the Abbot both drank tea together that day, but the Abbot's powers of recall are on the fuzzy side. The general impression I got, though, was that the Monsignor didn't drink any tea, himself."

"See, that could be significant," Dodd said. "When Brother Hugo and I first ran into the dining hall and found that Rahim was dead, there was an empty mug on that big table. I saw it clear as day. Then, well before the police arrived, it wasn't there."

"You think Brother Hugo took the mug?"

"Might have been him. Maybe to cover for Cabrera. You know, so the police couldn't analyze the mug for any residue of poison. Or any priestly fingerprints."

Phil Dodd suddenly stood, getting a different fix on the street below.

"It's okay," he said, regaining his chair. "Not yet."

"Again. I was checking. I didn't see anybody following me."

But Dodd maintained a steady watch on the street, as he said, "I think, from what you said about him, that Brother Hugo used to be Special Ops. You see any ink on him?"

"What?"

"Tattoos."

"Oh, right. Brother Emilio says he has an armload. I only saw a little. A pitchfork and a gun."

"You mean a trident and a flintlock pistol? That's part of the Navy Seal insignia. Was there an eagle and anchor too?"

"I didn't see his whole forearm."

"That's okay. That gives me enough to call my honey in Mayport. Brother Hugo *looks* Hispanic, but there's definitely mixed blood there. Look how big he is. And his English. Did *you* hear an accent? I didn't. I'll bet Spanish isn't his first language. I'll bet he was born in the States. Not Southern, but all the same, someplace where the family farms tend to have a hidden still up in the woods."

"While you're calling around," I said, "any chance of getting that Engineman over from Guantanamo to talk to Rahim's bodyguard? According to Alvarez, no one's been able yet to ask the bodyguard exactly what happened, right when Rahim slumped over. Not even the local Muslims."

"Alvarez is still active on this?"

"He's not buying natural causes, either. And he's whittled the probable suspects down to you and Monsignor Cabrera. And your supplying a translator would go a long way toward taking you off his short list."

"I don't consider Alvarez much of a threat." Dodd's eyes still watched the street below us. "Also, getting that Engineman over here would be a big assed deal. Plus, I'd just as soon not pop up on anybody's radar, just yet. Although…"

Dodd went silent. I gave him space to think.

After a half-minute, he resumed speaking, from mid-thought, "…but the request would definitely have to come from the local cops. And I was kind of liking the free hand I was left with. So, what exactly would I get out of it?"

I'd anticipated the question. "Gauging from the Detective Sergeant's level of zeal, there should be enough latitude for you to bargain your way into the room when they're interrogating the bodyguard. Probably, even to let you ask a few questions. But he needs that Engineman to translate."

"When?"

"Today."

"Are you nuts?"

"There'll be a hurricane tomorrow. And as soon as it's over, the local Muslims will hustle Rahim into the ground and Captain Rivera will have the bodyguard on the first flight out to Paris. So, any chance for you to clear yourself will vanish. It has to be today. Cuba's not that far away."

"You do remember that my current status with the NCIS is somewhat iffy."

"Look, you said yourself the call would have to come from the Puerto Rico Police. So, you just have to advise Alvarez on where to start in the chain of command to get it rolling. You know who's who, he doesn't."

"Why am I even listening to this?"

"Because you don't want to spend the rest of your life hiding among scumbags."

Dodd sat up straight. "Well, there's Randal. And he's brought a friend."

I turned in my seat and peered out the window. Up the street, the two NCIS agents were talking to one of the slum's addicts-in-residence.

"That's Briggs with him," I said.

We watched as money changed hands, and the adequately bribed, disheveled citizen pointed straight to the door below us.

"Time to go." Dodd grabbed up his brief case in one hand and his chair in the other and bolted for the little kitchen.

Taken by surprise, I leaped to my feet and caught up with Dodd, as he exited feet-first through the kitchen window and dropped out of sight. Like Dodd, I used the chair seat to step up on the countertop. I then grabbed the bottom of the raised sash, awkwardly got each leg poked out the window, twisted my body around to feed the rest of me out, and blindly dropped to the tarred rooftop below.

I sprinted after Dodd along the adjoining, flat rooftops, dodging around vent stacks and jumping over hurdles of protruding former outer walls, for perhaps fifty yards to where the back wall of a building blocked our way. However, to our left, an adjacent wall held a window with no glass in the frame, and after handing me his briefcase, Dodd scrambled up and in. I tossed the briefcase up to him and clambered up after him.

We continued, hotfooting it down a hallway that reeked like a city dump, and then clattered down an interior stairway. Dodd never looked around or hesitated at any turn, as we ran what I now figured was his preplanned escape route. At the bottom of the stairway, we ran hell bent along another pungent hallway, before bursting out through an exit door.

The stone archway spanning the narrow street leading up and out of La Perla was off to the right and not far away. The dope dealers stopped their trade and stared, as Dodd and I rushed headlong past them, and up through the archway.

We were forced into a slower, more leg-punishing, pace in our ascent to the less sordid city above. Dodd had me take the lead for the two-block hike to where I'd parked the rental car. I, frankly, wanted to lie down, but Dodd insisted that we'd recover faster and avoid leg cramps, if we kept walking. And admittedly, the eventual sight of the rental car up ahead did wonders for my morale.

"There it is." Dodd impulsively crossed the street to a parked car that blocked a fire hydrant.

I caught up to him. "This isn't my car."

"It's Randal's," Dodd said. "Remember? We saw it from that screened-in restaurant. And look at the plate. It's government."

"So, what are you going to do? Flatten a tire?"

"No. Plant a little GPS transmitter." Dodd reached under the rear of the car, and I heard the clunk of a magnet contacting metal. Dodd dusted off his hands. "Come on. They know I turned in my rental car. So, they'll be making straight for yours. And they didn't have to climb through any damn windows."

Dodd and I hurried back across the street to my rental car. But, instead of getting in, Dodd tossed his briefcase onto the passenger seat, and went down on his hands and knees, getting his head low. Soon, he reached a hand beneath the chassis. When he stood up, he was holding a small, round device that actually looked like it could have been a car part. "You won't be needing this anymore."

Dodd began to brush dirt from his knees, but with the sound of a big rush of air, he left off and ran to the nearby corner, where the door of a city bus had just whooshed open to let off a passenger. When the bus then proceeded on through the intersection, I saw the little round device magnetically attached to its side.

Taking pity on Dodd's legs, I drove up to the intersection and stopped to let him climb in.

"And a job well done," Dodd congratulated himself.

I sped us off in the opposite direction of the bus's heading, without having to be told. But at the same time, I leveled an accusation. "You meant for them to follow me, so you could plant your own transmitter on their car."

"Actually, this was Plan B. I missed my first chance at my old girlfriend's apartment, because a motorcycle cop was writing them a ticket."

Suddenly, I wished I had Officer Saenz's baton in my hand. "Look, let's get this straight. I'm okay with being a co-conspirator, but I object to being an unwitting one."

"You did fine, Francis. No need for a self-critique."

I was still exasperated at being so shamelessly used, but I had my own agenda to promote.

"What about getting the Engineman over here? Yes or no."

We cruised in silence along with the late afternoon traffic leaving Old San Juan, while Dodd considered it.

"Okay," he finally decided. "But bear in mind, the degree of cordiality between Federal law enforcement and the Puerto Rico Police is less like Interpol, and more like an arranged marriage. Also, odds are that

Rahim's loyal bodyguard is unlikely to be a fountain of enlightenment, anyway. Although, it would be a big help to know for sure that the big ox had abandoned his post, during the time when Rahim was killed. So yeah, I'll arrange for an after-hours hook-up between Alvarez and the SAC for the Southeast Region. But don't get your hopes up."

"You want a face-to-face with Alvarez, or are you still the vanishing shadow?"

"I'll meet with him. But only because I want my gun back."

"Alvarez still has your gun?"

"Making a personal appearance at the General Stationhouse to retrieve my gun had, of late, seemed somewhat risky, considering my potential usefulness as a sacrificial political pawn."

"But now?"

"Now, Alvarez needs me. So, don't worry. I'll say it in Spanish, if I have to. No *pistola*, no translator."

Chapter 11

Detective Sergeant Alvarez had agreed to an immediate meeting in his office on the sixth floor of the General Stationhouse in Hato Rey. Dodd had me stop on the way at a self-storage facility, where he retrieved his sport jacket and belt holster from a suitcase, stashed in a rented locker. Thus, late afternoon had become early evening by the time Dodd and I occupied the two guest chairs in the Detective Sergeant's small office.

There had been no handshakes. Through his bifocals, Alvarez now eyed Dodd over the scatter of case files on his desktop, in the manner of a wary tank commander, peering through his binoculars, taking a measure of his adversary across a repeatedly contested battlefield.

"Mr. Elton tells me that you can produce a translator for Jaspar Rahim's bodyguard," Alvarez opened the meeting.

"There's an Engineman at the Guantanamo Bay Naval Station, over in Cuba, who speaks the bodyguard's language," Dodd began, as though giving a staff briefing. "Turns out, the Engineman, the bodyguard, and Rahim all have family among some remote tribe of camel jockeys, out in the shifting sands. But the hurricane is getting damn close. We'll need to bring the Engineman in on a prop plane that can fly through spiral rain bands."

"And you can make this happen?"

"The Commanding Officer at Guantanamo can, depending on who's asking," Dodd said. "And the NCIS Special Agent in Charge for the Southeast Region not only has a vested interest in what the bodyguard might tell us, but also the hefties to call in the play. It's after hours, of course, but I have his home phone number."

"And in return?"

"I get my gun back. Plus, I expect to be the Special Agent who sits in on the interrogation of the bodyguard. I have several questions of my own to ask."

"Your gun will be returned to you when you leave Puerto Rico for good," Alvarez said. "And as for the interro...the interview with the bodyguard, this is a Puerto Rico Police investigation. However, we do occasionally allow outside, interested parties to listen in from behind the glass. I will go so far as to offer that. But I alone will be asking the questions. Perhaps, you will care to take note of how it is done."

"And perhaps, I did not make myself clear," Dodd said. "I get what I want, or there'll be no translator today."

Alvarez pulled a tissue from a small box on his desk, removed his eyeglasses, and made a business of cleaning the lenses. Dodd calmly watched.

The Detective Sergeant restored his polished lenses to a scowling face, but his words took a tactical step back. "It is the impending hurricane that forces my hand. I will need that home phone number." Alvarez pushed a pad of yellow legal paper and a ballpoint pen across the desk. "I will have your gun sent up. You may attend the questioning of the bodyguard, and you may ask one question of your own."

"I'll try to make it one that you hadn't thought of." Dodd held the pen poised over the yellow paper. "I'm trying to recall that number, but I can't seem to think without my gun."

There was a single spasm on the edge of Alvarez's right eye, as he lifted his desk phone from its cradle and ordered Dodd's gun to be brought to his office.

While we waited, Dodd, still sitting, rolled his chair on its swivel ball casters close enough to the Detective Sergeant's desk to rest an elbow on it. Then, to Alvarez's obvious annoyance, Dodd began to idly toy with a glass paperweight that had evidently caught his fancy.

Alvarez put up with this irritant for almost a full minute, before he reached out, roughly snatched the paperweight away, and placed it pointedly well out of Dodd's reach. Alvarez then picked up a business card lying next to his phone.

"You do not completely have the upper hand here, Mr. Dodd. I could easily contact Special Agent Randal and have you detained, pending his arrival." Alvarez momentarily turned the card toward Dodd for his viewing, before replacing it next to his phone.

Dodd leaned back in his chair. "I'll wager that today you want the services of a translator, far more than you want a wet kiss from Special Agent Randal."

A plain-clothes officer entered the office. It took me a moment to remember him as Montero, the other detective who was with Alvarez up in the guest quarters at the monastery. Detective Montero laid a black semi-automatic on the desk.

Dodd picked up the pistol and gave it a little bounce in his upturned palm. "Are we forgetting something?"

Responding to an almost imperceptible nod from the Detective Sergeant, Montero laid the pistol's magazine in front of Dodd. The solid clunk that the magazine made on the desktop suggested that the cartridges were included.

Dodd slid the magazine home with a snap into the base of the grip, laid the pistol back on the desk, and wrote a name and number on the yellow pad. He then slid the pad toward Alvarez, saying, "When you make the call, I'm not here."

With the pen restored to his shirt pocket and the legal pad in his hand, Alvarez stood. "I will make the call from Captain Rivera's office. If I am still a Detective Sergeant when I return, you and I, Mr. Dodd, will proceed to the old Isla Grande airport, where I will direct the Engineman's flight to land. We would not want the hopeful throng of stranded passengers at the SJU airport to suffer from jealousy."

Alvarez and Montero left us.

"Damned toady," Dodd said. "I'd have barreled right on through on my own and sent the old fart a memo when it was over."

"Maybe Alvarez was thinking he'd like to be a Captain someday, himself."

"*I* could have been a Captain by now," Dodd grumbled.

Skirting another rehash of long ago events, I asked, "Aren't you afraid that your SAC will demand that the Puerto Rico Police hang onto you, until they can hand you over to Randal and Briggs?"

"Alvarez will be careful not to upset me, until after he's had his quality time with the bodyguard."

"I understand that, but then what?"

Dodd looked at me steadily for a moment. "I'll have to consult my master plan."

***

Half an hour later, Detective Sergeant Alvarez entered his office with a triumphant swagger and crossed to his desk to face us.

"Mr. Dodd, we are off to Isla Grande."

Dodd stood, picked up his gun, and stowed it in the holster beneath his jacket flap. "Where will the interrogation take place?"

"The bodyguard has been sitting as close to Rahim's cadaver as we would let him, all this time. He will not budge." Alvarez hastily cleared the folders off his desk, as he spoke. "I prefer not to unnecessarily agitate him. We will conduct the interview at the morgue."

Dodd now relaxed against a file cabinet, apparently finding the venue to his liking.

"Mr. Elton, thank you for arranging this." Alvarez locked his desk. "I invite you to attend the interview to assist Mr. Dodd, in case we lapse into Spanish."

As I rose from my chair, I brought my city map out. "If you could mark the morgue's location, I'll be sure to be there."

After a close scan of my map and the inking of an X, Alvarez said, "Oh, it might interest you to know, Mr. Dodd, that at the beginning of our phone conversation, your Special Agent in Charge was exceedingly unhappy to be disturbed at home. However, after we explained our limited time frame and the importance of the bodyguard's statement and how we would, of course, gladly provide the NCIS with a transcript of the interview, he began to warm to the idea. And when he stipulated that a representative from the NCIS be present at the interview, I informed him that we were already working with Special Agent Philip Dodd."

Dodd straighten up and took a step away from the file cabinet.

Alvarez smiled at Dodd's discomfort and went on, "The words were like magic. Suddenly, your superior was confident that the Engineman could be aboard a rerouted prop plane within the hour. And he was very anxious that Special Agent Dodd remain here at the General Stationhouse, until Special Agents Randal and Briggs arrived to assist him."

Dodd slid a quick glance toward the open office door, before asking, "And what did you tell him?"

"It is of more importance what I did *not* tell him," Alvarez said. "I neglected to mention the morgue."

Dodd visibly relaxed. "And what's that bit of negligence going to cost me?"

Alvarez smiled again. "You will tell me all the background information and all the other discoveries that you and your fellow Special Agents have gathered, so far. You can enlighten me on our way to the Isla Grande airport. It is unfortunate, of course, that you cannot remain to greet your associates, but I'd rather you not be out of my sight until after the interview."

"I'd be more than happy to accompany you," Dodd said.

"I thought you might be."

"And as for my fellow Special Agents having discovered anything, they haven't discovered squat. I, on the other hand, with the help of Francis here and a reliable stateside source, have gathered up quite a sizable pile of facts."

"Perhaps, you will delight me with a sampling," Alvarez said.

"Okay, here's a tidbit about that priest you're so interested in. Back when Cabrera was a medic at this field hospital in Vietnam, he notices that the American soldiers are breaking out with these prickly rashes that the FDA approved medicines don't do a thing for. But the Vietnamese soldiers, who the South Vietnamese medics are taking care of, don't have the rashes, at least not for long. Spec Four Cabrera finds out that the Vietnamese medics treat the rash with an extract from some jungle plant, something their mothers used when they were growing up. They showed him what plants to gather and how to process the leaves into a paste, and also what some other jungle plants are useful for. So, Cabrera starts using the home remedies and curing the American soldiers of their outbreaks on the quiet. But eventually, the American Army doctors find out. And Cabrera gets busted back to Private and reassigned to a base hospital in Saigon, as a file clerk."

"So, Monsignor Cabrera has a working knowledge of medicinal jungle plants," Alvarez said. "How very interesting. I am eager to hear more facts that you have uncovered."

I spoke up, "Does all this mean that Captain Rivera has reopened the case?"

Alvarez turned to me. "For the moment," he said. "My Lieutenant suggested to Captain Rivera that it would be unwise, politically, to pass up an opportunity to interview the only eyewitness, now that we are aware of ongoing active interest at the Federal level. So, for the purpose of conducting this interview, today I am allowed to openly gather any relevant information. And tomorrow, while our imperiled island temporarily shuts down for the hurricane, I hope to apprehend Rahim's murderer, before Captain Rivera emerges from his shelter and, in effect, closes the case down again."

The Detective Sergeant brought his wristwatch up for a time check. "Mr. Dodd, we have a plane to meet."

***

Back at the Caserio Inn, I found Alicia typing away at her laptop. Next to her, the little printer sporadically spat out completed pages of her report. Ellen was busy laying blood-red polish on her nails and poisoning the air with noxious lacquer fumes. I found it difficult to breathe, but it didn't seem to bother the women.

"Where do you always disappear to?" Alicia demanded. "I had to go out and get another cartridge of ink for my printer, and the guy didn't speak any English."

"And we've been to church," Ellen said. "Alicia's idea."

"We went to the Cathedral for Mass," Alicia explained. "I practically had to drag her."

"She did drag me. I came down here to cut loose a little before I die, and she takes me to a damn church."

"Did you ever think it might also be fun to be at peace with yourself, before you die?" Alicia asked.

I wondered a little at Alicia's new piety.

"She made me wear a scarf on my head," Ellen lodged a further complaint. "Nobody else was wearing a scarf."

"None of the *tourists* were wearing scarves. Don't be such a Protestant. And quit whining. It didn't hurt you."

Ellen turned to me. "Francis, you're Catholic, aren't you? Were we supposed to wear scarves?"

"It's kind of old-school," I said. "Like if you learned about Catholicism from Wikipedia." Seeing Alicia's head quickly turn away, I hastily added, "But Puerto Rico's heavy on tradition. It probably wouldn't look out of place here."

"Oh, I see. Now you're siding with her." Ellen replaced the cap on the nail polish and shook it furiously. "And you *never* side with her."

"I think Monsignor Cabrera appreciated the scarves," Alicia pressed her defense, "even though we were just taking them off outside the Cathedral, when he came out through the front doors."

"Monsignor Cabrera said the Mass?" I tried to keep up.

"He called and invited us to attend," Alicia said. "And we just bumped into him outside afterward. Of course, I didn't mention that we had no idea what was going on, most of the time. We just stood and sat and knelt when everyone else did."

"It felt stupid," Ellen said.

"But then," Alicia ignored her, "there was a part where Monsignor Cabrera was just talking normally to the people in Spanish, without the half-singing business.

And suddenly, he broke into English. And it was amazing how genuine the Monsignor sounded, despite the ceremonial robe and all the surrounding pomp. He said to just concentrate on what Jesus was trying to tell you. All the other stuff – the altar and the candles and the ritual – that's just to put you in the mood."

"Oh, that's what the scarves were for. To put me in the mood."

"I'm sorry about the freaking scarves, okay? Now, drop it, will you?"

"What did Monsignor Cabrera have to say after Mass?" I asked.

"Mostly he asked about *you*, oddly enough," Alicia said. "He wanted to know what you were up to."

"What did you tell him?"

"Oh, just that this is what you did to amuse yourself, while I'm busy doing my work," Alicia said. "Then he wanted to know how soon we were leaving Puerto Rico. I told him as soon as I hand in my report and get my check. And he told me to get my report to him as quickly as possible."

That sounded like my access to the monastery was over for good. I can't say it saddened me any.

"Listen, something's come up," I said, "I have to bow out of dinner with you two, tonight. They're flying in a translator – that Engineman from Guantanamo – so they can question Rahim's bodyguard. Alvarez is letting me sit in."

"Oh sure," Alicia said. "They can fly in some sailor, no problem, but I have to lose a whole damn day waiting for their freaking hurricane to be over with."

"You'll feel better when you get your check tomorrow morning," I said. "And then maybe you should take the rest of the day off to celebrate. Maybe work off some of that pent up—"

I saw Alicia reach down for her sandal, so I had time to duck. The sandal struck the wall just behind where my head had been a split second before. I was out in the hall and a half step away, when I heard the other sandal hit the door behind me.

***

Alvarez's X on my city map brought me to the Institute of Forensic Science in the Toa Baja district. Because of the late hour, I had to walk around to the rear entrance and explain my business to a security guard. Luckily, I was able to supply Alvarez's cell number, and one phone call later, I was allowed to proceed.

I followed the signs, until I came to a set of double doors on which a large placard proclaimed both 'City Morgue' and the more descriptive '*Depósito de Cadáveres*.' Against the wall and near to the double doors were a straight-back chair and a small folding table, bearing a cafeteria tray, cup, and tableware. Remnants of a meal were evident, so I guessed this was where the bodyguard had kept his vigil.

I pushed on through the double doors and entered a cool and spacious room, smelling of antiseptic and featuring several stainless steel tables with shallow troughs running around their perimeters.

Phil Dodd, Detective Sergeant Alvarez, and Detective Montero stood facing two seated figures: a large, middle-aged Arab wearing a wrinkled white dress shirt and a smaller, much younger Arab in blue Navy dungarees with two black chevrons printed on his sleeve. Jaspar Rahim, I presumed, was in temporary residence behind one of the stainless steel cooler doors that were stacked and arrayed along three walls.

A recording device, alight with LED's, was set up on a nearby autopsy table, and a technician wearing headphones fussed with its knobs nervously.

Alvarez directed his voice toward the microphone positioned in front of the bodyguard and the Engineman. As I approached, Alvarez was making a record of the names of people present in the room, and when I came to stand beside Dodd, my name was officially appended to the end of the list. With the preliminaries over, the questioning of the bodyguard, by way of the young Engineman, commenced.

Alvarez instructed the Engineman in English, "Ask this man who he remembers seeing in the dining hall. Starting from a half hour before Rahim's death and right up to the time of his death."

The Engineman spoke in his forebears' obscure language and was answered, equally obscurely, by the bodyguard. "He says a holy man entered the dining hall with two cups of tea. The holy man gave one cup of tea to Mr. Rahim."

"Wait a minute," Dodd cut in, "There are a lot of holy men up at the monastery. Which one's he talking about?"

"Is that the one question that you wished to ask, Mr. Dodd?" Alvarez glared at him.

"No. I just thought you ought to—"

"Then do me the courtesy of letting me conduct this interview without your help." Alvarez turned back to the Engineman. "Ask him which holy man."

After asking, the Engineman translated the bodyguard's answer, "The holy man who is an elder and conducts business for the Christians."

"Monsignor Cabrera, then," Alvarez concluded. "Ask him if this elder holy man offered the tea, or if Rahim asked for the tea."

"Assuming, of course, that the bodyguard understood what was being said," Dodd spoke, as an aside to me, although not especially softly.

Alvarez directed a nasty glare in our direction, while the Engineman asked the question.

"He says he saw the elder holy man give Mr. Rahim the tea," the Engineman reported, after the exchange. "He did not understand what was said."

"Ah, I will pursue this matter further with the Monsignor, then." Alvarez quickly moved on, "Ask him who else came into the dining hall."

The Engineman asked, and the bodyguard replied at length, before we heard the translation. "The little holy man came in with a heavy vessel that smelled of fruit. He set the vessel down. He then took an empty vessel and filled it with liquid from the box behind the grand chair. Next, he poured new liquid from the first vessel into the top of the box. Then taking the vessel that he had filled, he left the room. This gentleman says he has seen the little holy man do this curious thing many times before. And, as before, he watched him closely, but he saw nothing out of order."

"Which one is the little holy man?" Alvarez threw the question out.

"That would be Brother Emilio," I spoke up. "It's his daily job to recharge the Baghdad battery."

"I have heard quite enough of your Baghdad battery, Mr. Elton," Alvarez snapped at me. "If you wish to remain here, I suggest you keep your strange ideas to yourself."

The Detective Sergeant returned to the Engineman. "Was there anyone else?"

The Engineman went back to work. "No. It was not long after the little monk left that Mr. Rahim suddenly died."

Alvarez asked, "At the moment Rahim died, was there any reaction, or did he just slump over?"

There was another exchange in the obscure language. "He says that, without warning, Mr. Rahim sat up straight and stiff. His eyes became large, as though he foresaw and feared his approaching death. His hands gripped the armrests of the chair, his mouth opened to scream, but he did not make any sound. Only after this, did he slump down. He says he could not revive Mr. Rahim. There was no heartbeat in his chest. He then called for help."

"And I've got to say, this guy has some awesome lung power."

"Be quiet, Mr. Dodd." Alvarez growled, before continuing with the Engineman, "Ask him what happened, after he called for help."

The Engineman asked. And he received a long answer, during which the bodyguard pointed at Dodd and, later, at Alvarez.

Then came the translation. "This gentleman says the big holy man came running into the dining room, followed by the man who Mr. Rahim called the American spy. Here he pointed to Special Agent Dodd." The Engineman's eyes darted to Dodd's face and quickly returned to the Detective Sergeant's. "This gentleman then says that the two men who ran in put their fingers to Mr. Rahim's neck and their ears at his chest. The American spy looked closely at Mr. Rahim's eyes and fingers. And the big holy man checked all around Mr. Rahim's body and the grand chair. They then tried to speak to this gentleman. He says he could tell that they were trying different languages. But he understands no other language. Then, after the policemen arrived, he says the fat man with the eyeglasses – excuse me, but he pointed at you, sir – the fat man shouted at him, as is also the custom of important men in his own country. But still he could not understand anyone. He says that he is glad that he can talk with me."

"I am also glad." Alvarez reached out and gave the young Engineman's shoulder a squeeze. "Because we now have an eyewitness account of the decisive events that occurred during the crucial time period. Excellent." The Detective Sergeant smiled. "And now, Mr. Dodd, you may ask your question."

"Thanks." Dodd pulled a small notebook and a pen from an inside jacket pocket and pushed them into my hands. In a low voice, he said, "Francis, do me a favor and take notes. I get the feeling I'm not going to receive a transcript of this little get-together."

Dodd returned to a normal voice to address the Engineman, "Ask him what he smelled or heard at the time Rahim stiffened up and looked bug-eyed."

Alvarez grumbled, "I already asked that."

"No, you didn't," Dodd shot back. "The man has more senses than eyesight, you know."

Alvarez sighed. "Go ahead. Ask him."

The Engineman and the bodyguard conversed.

"This gentleman says that he does not recall a new smell. By then he was used to the smell of burnt wax and decay. But he did hear something strange. He says that, as Rahim's soul rose from his body, he heard the wind blowing through the caves in the mountains of their homeland and the crackle of far off machinegun fire, as from some distant battle."

"Well, there is your answer, Mr. Dodd," Alvarez said. "And unless you enjoy Arab poetry, you have wasted your one question."

"You're not ringing down the curtain, are you?" Dodd was incredulous. "I told you how little we know about Rahim. Now's your chance. Pump this guy."

The Detective Sergeant's eyes focused an intense glare through his lenses at Dodd's face, while his pulse beat at his temples. It was almost painful to watch him fight to regain his composure.

"I was just getting to that," Alvarez finally stated.

The interview now became a probe of Jaspar Rahim's business dealings: how he represented various Arab consortiums for their investments in the Western World; how his Paris apartment would fill with paintings and antiques, and then just as quickly empty again; how he constantly shifted his money in and out of various banks throughout France and Switzerland. The bodyguard told of traveling with Rahim many times to Middle Eastern cities – Damascus, Baghdad, Riyadh, Amman – where Rahim met with businessmen in noisy cafes and spoke in quiet Arabic and envelopes passed from jacket pocket to jacket pocket.

I had to write like a madman in Dodd's little notebook to get it all down.

Through the Engineman's translation, the bodyguard also related that, when traveling, Rahim ate all the wrong food, that he made all unimportant people very angry with him, and that he had a bad heart.

Alvarez perked up at the last part. "Was he under a doctor's care?"

The Engineman asked, was answered, and interpreted, "Mr. Rahim distrusted doctors and only tolerated dentists. He said they were all bad servants."

I heard the hum of a cell phone vibrating, and immediately, Dodd produced a flip phone from his pocket – probably, a prepaid one that he'd deep-six, after a couple of uses. Dodd stepped to the far side of the morgue with the device pressed to his ear.

A minute later, Dodd rejoined us. "That was the pilot. The plane's been refueled, the crew's been fed, and we're out of time." As the Engineman stood up, Dodd placed a hand on his shoulder and asked, "Ever been to Biloxi, Sailor?"

The Engineman's eyes looked in askance.

Dodd now draped his entire arm across both of the young man's shoulders and guided him toward the door. "That C-One-Thirty you flew in on is a Hurricane Reconnaissance plane. Air Force. That's why their uniforms look so funny. Now, they did us a big favor, just like you did, but we've already made them crazy late getting back. So, they're not stopping at Cuba on their way home. But the good news is they have to come back out for more fun with the hurricane tomorrow. And they'll drop you off just as soon as they're done bronco-riding through the turbulence and collecting their data. I hear the eye of a hurricane is just beautiful, once you get through the rough stuff."

Alvarez spoke to the other detective, in Spanish, "Montero, I must make a slight change in what we discussed. It will be you and Officer Saenz who will take the sailor back to the Isla Grande Airport. And, because the sailor is still under his care, it is required that Mr. Dodd will accompany him. But do not let Mr. Dodd get on that airplane. Shoot him, if you have to."

Detective Montero took determined strides to catch up with Dodd and the Engineman.

Alvarez turned to me. "Mr. Elton, I trust you will be able to find your own way out. I must speak with the Assistant Director of Toxicology, before he leaves."

"An Assistant Director, and he's still here this late?"

"Despite his senior position, this particular toxicologist works late every evening. His work is his life. He will be here tomorrow, even though the whole island will stay at home, waiting out the hurricane. So tonight, I will inform him that I suspect that there is an extract of a poisonous plant from the El Yunque rainforest mixed with the tea that they detected in the stomach contents of Jaspar Rahim. The bodyguard clearly described to us the effects of a poison that quickly constricts the throat, allowing neither a breath in, nor a scream out. And knowing this toxicologist, as I do, these words will be a siren's song to him."

"The toxicologist likes a challenge?"

"He lives for it."

Chapter 12

After a lonely beer and an indifferent sandwich at a backstreet café, I arrived at the Caserio Inn with my head and shoulders soaked from the rain that pelted my mere half-block walk from a fortunate parking space on the opposite side of Ashford Avenue. Just as I gained the second floor hallway, a woman, balanced on spike heels and squeezed into a blue dress, backed out of the room just before mine, taking great care to close the door soundlessly.

Ellen turned toward the stairwell. By that time, I was almost up to her. She quickly stepped in close and pressed an index fingertip to my lips, while making shooing motions with a black leather clutch wallet. I retreated with her back to the stairwell.

"I'm just going out for a drink." Ellen kept her voice low. "Alicia's asleep."

I matched her volume. "Give me a chance to put on a dry shirt, and I'll go with you."

"No, that's all right. I'm sure you're tired. But could you lend me a hundred dollars? I'm tapped out."

I took in the full effect of the mid-thigh length of the tight blue dress, the crimson lips, and the black eye liner. Ellen looked damned fine, but I knew that no good would come of her leaving the hotel, all by herself, looking like she was open for business.

"It's raining. Let me get you a taxi."

Ellen gave me a hard look, but must have decided to settle for cab fare, if that's what it came to. Without another word, she proceeded on down the stairs, her stability on the high heels greatly assisted by a catch-and-release-style sliding grip on the handrail, timed to each descending tread. I followed her down.

I had the clerk at the front desk summon a taxi, and waited with Ellen in the doorway of the Caserio. When the taxi arrived, I dashed ahead in the rain and opened the rear door for her. Within the constraints of her tight dress, Ellen tiptoed across the sidewalk in rapid geisha girl steps, backed onto the rear seat, and swung her legs in. I pushed in after her, crowding her over, and pulled the door closed.

"Where are we going?" I asked.

"*I* was going to the Marriott." Ellen slid further away from me.

"The Marriott, driver," I said to the back of the man's head.

The flag dropped, and taxi pulled away from the curb.

"What's the deal, Francis?" Ellen's voice was flat and hostile.

"I wanted to see what kind of drink costs a hundred bucks."

We didn't have long to ride in silence after that. The Marriott was only a block away.

The big horseshoe driveway brought us up to a wide expanse of sidewalk, across which Ellen and I hurried through the rain. Once inside the glass doors, the splendor of a lobby – that looked like it could swallow the Casario Inn whole – lay before us.

"Let's get you that drink." I brought out two fifties and held them before me, thinking I was taunting her.

Ellen plucked the money from my hand. "Right this way. If I buy a hundred dollars worth of chips, I can drink for free, for as long as I'm playing."

She set a quick pace toward the flashing lights and bright colors of the Marriott's in-house casino. I followed, feeling like a dope.

***

It takes an astonishingly small amount of time to drop a hundred dollars at a craps table.

Ellen and I now sat on high stools at the bar, out in the center of the Marriott's cavernous lobby, watching a band set up on a shallow stage, before which lay a polished parquet dance floor. The broad arc of tables and chairs, between the bar area and the dance floor, gradually filled, as couples and small groups arrived and first rounds of drinks were ordered.

"I was feeling really lucky tonight." Ellen took a sip of her second cocktail of the evening. "I don't know what went wrong."

"The stars weren't right," I offered.

"Are you mad that I lost your hundred?"

"Technically, it was *your* hundred. I gave mine away."

"Well, the important thing is I set a limit. I'm getting savvy."

The salsa band popped the clutch without warning. The beat of the conga drums and the staccato of the horns came off the line at maximum speed and volume. Half the tables emptied onto the dance floor, as the vocalists burst forth with lyrics in rapid-fire Spanish. The pace of the dance was heart pounding, yet the movements of the dancers were amazingly fluid. They spun and dipped in the crowded space, never actually side-swiping each other, but coming awfully damned close.

"That looks like fun." Ellen perked up.

"That looks like about a dozen levels above what I would even attempt." I was content to stay on my perch.

"I want to try it. It looks so provocative. Like flirting at the speed of light."

The band played and the dancers danced practically non-stop for an hour. Then there was an extended interval, during which the band broke down its set and the dancers returned to their tables to sip sweetened alcohol and squeal with delight upon seeing a friend at another table.

A new band began its setup on the heels of the departing one. Hugs and kisses were exchanged between the in-coming and out-going musicians and singers. With their setup complete, the new band left the stage, apparently delaying their performance to give the waitresses adequate time to replenish the dancers' glasses. In the meantime, recorded music in the same genre, but at a relatively subdued volume, filled in during the intermission.

With the delivery of the next round, the bartender, evidently having overheard our earlier conversation, suggested that we ask some of the regular patrons near the deserted parquet floor to show us a few of the basic steps to Salsa dancing. Ellen, of course, thought it was a wonderful idea. I foresaw only the prospect of making myself the laughingstock of the evening. And normally, I would have stood my ground like a recalcitrant mule. But Ellen and I had been drinking steadily for over an hour. And potent cocktails have a way of diluting one's resolve. Which goes a long way toward explaining my unprecedented consent to have a go at it.

Ellen and I threaded our way through the crowded tables to the dance floor. I approached a table at the dance floor's edge that appeared to be populated with an extended family and asked in slightly impaired, but polite, Spanish if someone would show us the rudiments of Salsa. An elderly, yet trim and enthusiastic, couple took on the task. And they soon had Ellen's and my forearms locked together and our feet moving forward, back, and to the side in a basic pattern.

Ellen and I butted heads several times, as we watched our feet and attempted to keep up with the recorded music. This prompted the elderly woman to reach out, lift our chins, and command in vowel-challenged English that we keep our heads up, gaze into each other's eyes, and think of love. True enough, this forced us to lose the hesitation in our foot placements, but at the same time, required a level of mutual trust typically reserved for a flying trapeze act.

My shirt was soaked with sweat and Ellen's skin glistened in the intersecting beams of colored spotlights, when to my relief the salsa beat ended. After profusely thanking the elderly couple, we returned to our bar stools through a boisterous round of applause for the game couple from the Frozen North.

I switched to iced coffee. One of us had to be sober enough to tell the taxi driver where we were staying. Even so, we didn't stay all the way through the next band's set. The evening's bar tab threatened to exceed the evening's gambling losses. Also, Ellen had called me "Roger" at least twice by my count.

Circling around through the one-way streets on our return trip to the Caserio Inn, there was an ardent moment in the back of the taxi, where I was being thanked for a lovely night out. In fact, we were well along the road to thank you very much, when our ride abruptly ended.

***

Having found our way up to the second floor hallway of the Caserio Inn, I dropped Ellen off in front of her room and proceeded, on legs more weary than unsteady, next door to my own. I'd taken perhaps only three steps into my room, when, from the corner of my eye, I became aware that Ellen had followed me in.

As I turned to ask what was up, Ellen moved right on past me, as though sleepwalking. In the middle of the room, she stopped with her back to me.

"Unzip me. I'm going to throw up. Don't want to mess up my dress."

If a woman is going to throw up, I'll do all I can to accommodate her. I ran the zipper down, and Ellen's dress parted revealing a bare back.

"You know," Alicia's voice came from the open doorway behind me. "I feel like a mother who doesn't dare to take a nap for fear of what her kids will get up to."

I turned to Alicia. "She's about to be sick and doesn't want to spoil her dress."

At the edge of perception, I heard Ellen's dress drop to the floor.

"At least, she's managed to keep her panties on," Alicia observed.

I turned to look, but it wasn't news to me that the black panties were all that Ellen wore under her blue dress. I'd touched on that subject during our return trip in the back of the taxi.

"Alicia, I'm going to throw up."

Alicia thumped me hard on the chest, as she brushed past. She snatched up the blue dress and tossed it on a bed, before placing her hands on Ellen's shoulders and firmly directing her sister into the bathroom. The bathroom door swung closed.

"All right! Where is he?" A masculine voice loudly demanded from behind me.

Startled, I half-turned and shuffled sideways away from the open door, as Special Agents Randal and Briggs aggressively advanced into my room, their windbreakers still dripping with rainwater.

"Francis, get rid of whoever it is." Alicia's voice pierced through the bathroom door, along with the squeaks of shower knobs being rotated.

"I *said*," Randal was now in my face, "where *is* he?"

A rush of adrenalin picked up where the iced coffee's caffeine had left off. I actually had to feign slow-wittedness, "Where's who?"

"Phil Dodd. You know damned well *who*." Randal's 'who' was a hot puff of mint-over-alcohol.

Briggs stepped around us. "I'll check the can."

"Oh, man." I moved to stop him. "Don't go in there. You don't…"

Heedless of my warning, Briggs barged into the bathroom.

"GET OUT!" The words were screamed with the ferocity of a wildcat.

"Ow! Jesus! Damn it, bitch!" Briggs retreated hastily out of the bathroom. He brought his hand down from his cheek and stared the blood on his fingertips. "She clawed me!"

The bathroom door slammed shut.

"I tried to warn you," I said.

Ignoring his partner's plight, Randal was in front of me again. He jabbed my shoulder. "You were supposed to call us when you made contact with Dodd. Instead you tipped him off."

"Hey, didn't your boss tell you Dodd was at the General Stationhouse in Hato Rey?"

"Yeah, and we got jacked around pretty good there," Randal said. "Lots of cooperation from *those* assholes. Briggs, go check next-door. He might be holed up in the other room."

Briggs didn't look too happy with his assignment. And I noticed he was quite a bleeder. Four parallel rivulets of blood ran down the side of his face and soaked his collar red. I would have offered him a towel, but I sure as hell wasn't going into that bathroom to get one.

"You got the key to your girlfriend's room?" Briggs asked.

Ellen's clutch wallet was lying there on the nearest bed. I rummaged in the wallet, pretending I hadn't found her key almost immediately, wedged between her I-phone and maxed-out credit card. Meanwhile, I formed a plan to lead my unwanted guests out of my room and, in the process, to swing the door closed to self-lock behind us.

"Come on." I now produced Ellen's key and extended my arms to herd them out. "Let's go next door and find out Dodd's not in there, either, and button this up."

"No." Randal blocked me. "What *you're* going to do is tell me where that screw-off Dodd is."

"And I'm telling you, I don't know. But since we know he's not here, let's go check the room next door."

Randal grabbed the key from my hand and tossed it to Briggs. "Just go check that room."

Randal then crowded me back a step, saying, "You're a real smartass, aren't you?"

I voluntarily attempted a further step back from Randal's breath, but my heel made contact with the wall behind me.

"Why all the fuss about rounding up Dodd, anyway?" I asked. "Even the local police don't think he killed Rahim, anymore."

"Well, there's a little something those dopey cops don't know about Dodd. It just so happens he's got a track record for going postal on Arab mucky-mucks. The guy's a loose cannon. You don't know him like we do."

"As a matter of fact, I do know him, and I doubt that—"

"This Iraqi tribal leader drowns in a goddamn desert. Drowns." Randal poked my chest with the word. "He's Dodd's intel source. And Dodd's right there in the guy's compound when it happened. And Dodd's been known to carry knockout pills around with him. So, how many guesses do you need, as to why this Arab ends up taking a nap, facedown in a fountain?"

"Why didn't you arrest him back then?"

"The invasion started. Everything else got put on hold."

"Then why put Dodd on Rahim's tail, if you guys didn't trust him?"

"To test him. That was the bright idea of the SAC up in Mayport. Plus, Dodd said he knew *you*. Said he could talk you into anything. I guess you're like a *chump*."

"And I guess you both can get the hell out of my room, before I call the *real* police."

"Randal," Briggs broke in. "I don't think this is getting us—"

"I thought you were checking out that other room," Randal snapped.

Briggs looked from Randal to me, and left my room.

"Now, tell me where Dodd is." Mint over alcohol wafted forth again. "Right goddamn *now*."

"He dives and surfaces like a submarine. Squeezing me for information doesn't help you one damn—"

Randal grabbed my unbuttoned collar together, twisted the material tight around my neck, and slammed me against the wall, ramming his fist into my throat hard enough to cut off my last bit of air.

"I'll squeeze you witless, if I have to," Randal said through clenched teeth.

He had a good twenty pounds on me and was holding my right wrist with the hand he wasn't using to strangle me. I flailed at him with my free hand, while in a panic for air.

BOOM, BOOM, BOOM.

"Randal's choking! Randal's choking!"

BOOM, BOOM, BOOM.

I knew it was Alicia yelling and banging on the wall, even though I couldn't see her. But I did see Briggs burst into the room with a drawn gun.

"Randal's choking Francis to death!" Alicia's completed alarm was accompanied by the clattering of wood against wood.

Then over Randal's shoulder, I saw a beefy hand shoot up and catch one leg of a desk chair that was coming down from the ceiling.

"Okay, put the chair down, lady," Briggs ordered. "Randal, this isn't the way to do this."

The constriction on my neck suddenly slacked off, and I slid down the wall, coughing and gasping for air.

"All right, we're done here." Randal's voice came from above me. "For tonight, anyway. But tomorrow morning – hurricane or not – Mister Chump, here, is going to contact Dodd, arrange to meet him, and lead us straight *to* him. Or next time, I'll make sure nobody's around to *save* his sorry chump ass."

Randal turned and he-man marched out of the room, smacking the doorframe with his open hand to punctuate his exit.

Briggs had remained and was taking a sweep of the room, when his scan suddenly stopped. I looked to see what caught his attention.

The silk tunic that Alicia usually slept in was so soaked from her efforts to wrestle Ellen into the shower that Alicia looked as though she were naked and her body drenched with a bucket of violet paint.

With the back of his gun hand Briggs dabbed at the last trickles of blood on his clawed face, before he pushed back one side of his windbreaker and holstered the gun at his hip.

Ellen, wrapped in a white bath towel, appeared with straight, damp hair at the bathroom doorway. "I don't feel good."

Alicia stepped over to the bed nearest the bathroom and pulled back the cover and top sheet. "Just lay down for a minute."

Alicia steered Ellen to the side of the bed. Ellen let the towel fall, crawled onto the bed, and rolled onto her side.

After pulling a modest sheet over Ellen's body, Alicia stood up straight and fixed a pair of defiant green eyes on Briggs. "If you and psycho-cop are done terrorizing us, we're going to call it a night."

Without a departing word, Briggs left the room.

I felt drained of strength, but I forced myself to get on my feet. Massaging my crushed Adam's apple, I attempted to swing the door closed on any further intrusions. But before the latch clicked, the door was pushed back open, and the hotel's night clerk stood at the threshold.

"Who were those men?"

I tried to answer him, but I couldn't make my voice work.

"Government men," Alicia strode forward and spoke for me. "They were looking for someone. But they got the wrong hotel. It's all straightened out now."

The desk clerk focused on Alicia. "You are all wet."

"I know."

"The other guests reported explosions."

"They were mistaken. The government men are gone now. Everything's okay."

The night clerk turned to me. I tried to say something, but still couldn't.

"I will reassure the other guests."

The night clerk stepped back into the hall, and I lost no time in swinging the door closed on him.

Leaning against the door for support, I managed to croak, "How's Ellen?"

"Oh, *now* you're concerned about her welfare."

"We went out for a drink," I painfully pushed my voice further. Spotting a lone bottle of warm beer sitting on the desk, I thumb-nailed out the opener blade on my pocketknife, pried off the cap, and took a medicinal swallow. It tasted awful, but it helped my throat. "And we had a dance lesson. Then we came back. I guess she's not used to—"

"Nice job. Too bad I didn't have nearly as much fun with her in the bathroom. It was like grappling with a greased zombie just to keep her upright under the showerhead."

Alicia started pulling at her wet tunic, but stopped, when she apparently noticed my interest and correctly deduced that she was fanning the flames.

"Maybe I'd better go change out of this wet silk, before you get it into your head to do the rumba with me too." As Alicia passed me on her way to the door, she paused to poke my shoulder with an index finger, tipped with one of her assault nails. "Just drink your beer, and try to stay out of trouble. I'll be back for Ellen in a few minutes."

She was back in ten seconds.

"The damn door is locked."

"Don't you have a key?"

She held her arms out. The wet material seemed to cling even more tightly to her body. "Do you see a key on me?" Alicia pushed past me. "There should be one in Ellen's clutch."

"They took...I had to give Ellen's key to Briggs. They thought Dodd might be hiding in your room. I didn't get it back."

"You're a genius, you know that?"

"You're the one who locked herself out of her room."

"I left the door ajar."

"I'll just go down to the front desk and—"

"Oh brilliant. Right this moment, the night clerk's probably thinking about how he should've ordered us to leave the hotel when he had the perfect opportunity. So let's give him another time at bat, why don't we? We should be out on the street in no time."

Alicia opened my satchel, rummaged through it, and pulled out a dress shirt.

"That's my last clean one," I said. "I was saving it to wear on the plane."

"I'll have it back to you by then. Now go shut off the light. No more strip shows for you tonight."

I set down the half-finished, room-temperature beer, walked over to the switch, and plunged the room into darkness. Moving uncertainly toward the bed, willing my eyes – without success – to rapidly adjust, I bumped into something hard. I felt around to make sure it was the unoccupied bed, before unbuttoning my shirt and sitting down to again massage my throat – a throat as bruised as my ego.

I should have clocked that bastard. It didn't look good, having Alicia come to my rescue. I hated looking weak in front of her. And now I had to thank her.

I wanted to get the 'thank you' part out of the way. At least, it was dark. Some things are easier to say in the dark.

"I haven't had a chance to thank you for saving my butt tonight," I began. "That was quick thinking, getting Briggs to charge back in here with his gun drawn. The gun immediately put him in command." Then to my instant regret, I added, "I couldn't breathe."

"We have our differences, but I don't want to see you dead." There was the swishing sound of a towel being briskly rubbed over skin and then the rustle of dry cloth, as, presumably, Alicia pulled on my last clean shirt. "And next time Dodd calls you, you tell him he's going to get you killed, if he doesn't stop screwing around, and just goes and stands in front of his boss, like a man, and takes his lumps."

"He doesn't call me. He leaves little hints on postcards and brochures there on the desk. I don't know how he gets into my room."

"The maid."

"What?"

"The maid. Knowing him, he chats her up, maybe fondles her uniform a little, probably slips her a few bucks. And then she either leaves the postcard for him when she cleans the room, or just lets him in with her pass key."

"I didn't think of that."

"You think kind of slowly. And if you haven't noticed, you read slowly too. It used to drive me nuts when we were married. Waiting forever for you to get finished with a section of the Sunday paper I wanted to read. I think it's just your way of being methodical. And it's why you can go and fix machines, after the bright boys have jumped to the wrong conclusion, messed it up even worse, and then have to call for help. I doubt it's any fun, being a turtle in a world full of rabbits. But it seems to work for you."

"Except when I'm being choked to death."

"Okay, except then." Alicia's flowery fragrance told me she was near. The mattress jostled under me, as she climbed into the bed. "I need to get some sleep. If Ellen pukes on herself again, it's your turn to clean her up."

I took off my shoes and clothes and slid in next to Alicia. I waited for her to object. When she didn't, I tested the situation further by placing hand on her hip.

"You can sleep there, if you can behave yourself," Alicia laid out her terms. "Otherwise, take a pillow and sleep on the floor."

I rolled onto my other side, facing away from Alicia, and tried to convince myself that her unsociability was a side effect of her allergy medicine.

But still, I should have clocked that bastard...I was *trying* to hit him...I must have looked like a rag doll.

I lay there brooding, craving revenge. I needed Randal to experience how it felt to be powerless. I wanted him on the ground with his gun and his badge gone.

I began to plot. First, I'd have to get him into an environment where he wouldn't be in control. Then, I could exploit a weakness. And I already knew that he drank on the job…Yes, I could make that work…And just as Dodd had used me as a lure for *his* purposes, now I'd be the lure for my own.

I reached down to my trousers on the floor, fished out my phone, and opened it. It was only one in the morning. Plenty of time.

Chapter 13

Down in the lobby of the Caserio Inn, I felt the night clerk's eyes following me, as I made straight for the front door.

"It is very late, sir."

My hand was on the push bar, but I stopped. Much as I wanted to, I couldn't simply ignore him. "Just slipping out to the ATM, while there's still money in it."

"May I remind you, sir, that you and your lady friends are due to check out tomorrow morning?"

"We can't get a flight out until after the hurricane passes. It should only be an extra day."

"There may be a conflict." The night clerk started tapping computer keys.

I didn't wait around for him to invent an imminent influx of storm chasers with confirmed reservations.

Outside, the rain god apparently was on a break. The pastel yellow casts of the streetlamps reflected off the wet pavements and parked cars, and the music and glow of San Juan nightlife still emanated from the cafés and hotel bars. But where the trees and darkened buildings obstructed the nighttime illumination, equally deep shadows concealed shapes and obscured features.

The ATM was part of the façade of the towering bank building, next door to the Caserio Inn. During my brief walk to it, I studied the cars, parked bumper-to-bumper along both sides of the one-way street. I was sure they'd have left someone to watch for Dodd, perhaps sneaking in to crash on my spare bed.

And then I spotted a silhouette behind the wheel of a car parked directly across the street from the bank. The Special Agent in the car probably wouldn't be Randal, himself. But I was betting that, whichever NCIS operative it happened to be, he would call Randal, if I did anything out of the ordinary. He'd need instructions – whether to stay put and keep an eye out for Dodd, or to follow me and find out what I was up to.

I withdrew eighty in twenties from the ATM (the maximum the machine decided I was to be allotted), and retraced my steps, as though returning the Caserio. But instead of reentering the hotel, I walked straight on past, without so much as a glance at the entrance.

As I'd anticipated, a car engine, somewhere behind me, coughed to life. I walked on, but the sound of the engine remained at an idle. No commitment to follow me had been made, just yet.

Next, I walked right on past the rental car, parked on the opposite side of the street. Hopefully, this would also be noticed and relayed to Randal, because my third bit of curious behavior was about to force his decision.

Just ahead, there was considerable activity in front of one of the larger hotels – large enough, in fact, to have its lobby face Ashford Avenue and still provide ocean-side terraces and unfettered beach access on the building's opposite side. By the looks of the sizeable coterie of tanned and svelte men, enveloped in the music and laughter of a party that packed the lobby and spilled out onto the apron of pavement out front, I had come upon the street entrance to the gay hotel, whose guests Ellen had identified on the hotel's beachfront, a couple of days before.

The gay hotel was not my goal. But the two taxis parked at the curb, waiting for practically guaranteed fares, were. I climbed into the back of one of them and told the driver to take me to a strip club.

By stealing a page from Dodd's playbook, taking a late-night cab ride alone, instead of using the obviously available rental car, I hoped that to Randal's mind this suspicious behavior could only mean that I was on my way to a clandestine meeting, undoubtedly with Phil Dodd. However, it took an iron resolve, right from the start, not to peek out the back window to see if I'd picked up a tail.

After crossing the bridge that spanned the lagoon, the taxi entered the Miramar neighborhood, turned onto a side street, and negotiated the typical single lane between the rows of parked cars. As we passed by several clubs, each with its gaggle of smokers out front, it became increasingly evident that there were no women to be found among the various groupings. It then dawned on me that, because of where he'd picked up his fare, the taxi driver had made an assumption about my sexual leanings, and thus, which type of strip club I would find more to my taste. The driver stopped and let me out in front of a place whose neon call letters radiated through the dark glass of the front window: "JR's."

As I paid the driver, I finally snuck a glance back down the street, but saw no following car. I'd hoped for a little positive feedback that things were proceeding at least mostly to my plan, but had to console myself that maybe my tail had hastily nosed into a driveway and doused his lights as soon as he saw the taxi finally brake to a stop at a likely destination.

Even before the taxi departed, a disheveled skeleton of a man shuffled toward me to bum a cigarette. I brushed him off easily enough, but wasn't cheered, as I surveyed the several other homeless men sleeping huddled on the sidewalk against the front of the building, beneath the security blanket of both bright lights and non-threatening bar patrons. Representing the other end of the refinement scale and positioned nearer the club's entrance, a tight congress of well-groomed, well-dressed men smoked and chatted among themselves, a few momentarily casting a critical eye in my direction.

Chalked in a rainbow of colors on a blackboard was the declaration in Spanish and again in English that, tonight, the club was hosting a "Hurricane Party." At the bottom of the chalkboard, "Two Drink Minimum" was underlined twice – which, for my purposes, would be all to the good, if I had, in fact, been followed.

There was only one way to find out. I stepped through the invitingly open door and into a parallel society.

***

From within the depths of JR's, a jukebox blared with the sound quality of a clock radio, pushed to its volume limit. In a solo dance before a backdrop of tinfoil decorations, a well-muscled young man was dropping his garments one-by-one onto the stage. A few patrons were looking the dancer's way, but the majority of them sat shoulder-to-shoulder on tall stools, forming an almost unbroken chain around the long cigar-shaped bar, and engaged in private conversations. From among the many available tables, I selected a table-for-two and seated myself with a good view of both the long bar and the entrance.

Soon enough, I was rewarded with sight of the black NCIS agent entering the club. He brought his phone up to his ear, blended into the crowd, and eventually reappeared seated on a stool on the far side of the bar, facing me.

A bartender finally acknowledged my existence and came over. He began right away in English.

"You seem to have wandered pretty far away from home."

I wasn't sure whether he was noting that I wasn't a regular, or that I wasn't gay. But I felt I could make a safe assumption about what was foremost on his mind.

"Call me curious," I said.

"Then this is the place." The bartender laid a paper doily on the table in front of me. "You know there's a two drink minimum?"

I saw Randal enter the club and meld into the crush around the bar. "Actually, I counted on it. I'll start with a beer. Let's keep it to a Bud Light."

The bartender, whose broad face and sun-damaged skin hinted more of California surf than Caribbean Sea, took an additional moment to consider me and returned to the bar.

Looking between the hunched backs arrayed along the near side of the elongated loop of bar top, I saw, among the line of countenances on the far side, that the black Special Agent's face had been replaced by Randal's pasty white one. Averting my gaze, I pretended to watch, as a new performer mounted the stage to a thin smattering of applause.

The lure had worked fine, but as for landing my catch, I'd have to wait. Of course, I'd missed my chance at Randal's first drink. Nonetheless, I was secure in the knowledge that he had at least one more drink in his future.

It took a while, but eventually the bartender found his way back and placed a bottle of beer on the doily. "You've been in the candy store long enough to peruse what's on offer. Anything to your taste?"

"He's just arrived. The one in the white polo shirt on the far side of the bar."

Without looking, the bartender said, "Dear boy, that's rough trade. He's not looking for love, he's looking for a victim. That one's not for beginners."

"I like a challenge. And I have a surprise of my own." From my pocket, I extracted Dodd's bottle of pills, which had lain forgotten in my satchel until I remembered them, while formulating my plan for revenge. I set the innocent-looking aspirin bottle on the table next to my beer.

Without hesitation, the bartender scooped up the aspirin bottle, twisted off the cap, and looked inside at the reddish-orange capsules with the little printed numbers. "Ooh, Seconals. Talk about tilting the playing field. I'll have to rethink *you*. I'm sensing a dark side. What's your name?"

"Tonight, I'm Willie." I wished Alicia could've heard how fast I came up with a nom de guerre.

"So, what's the plan, Willie? And how am I involved, as if I didn't already guess?"

"You break open a couple capsules and mix them into his next drink."

"A couple? You want to ride the pony, or harvest one of his kidneys?"

"One then."

"And in return?"

I pulled out my wallet and handed him a pair of twenties, fresh from the ATM. "A hefty tip and two capsules for your own use."

"Make it three capsules."

"Three then."

The bartender pocketed the money, shook out four knockout pills into his palm, and set the bottle back on the table. "This should be amusing."

As the bartender returned to his workstation to mix Randal a special drink, I sat back in my chair and poured some cold beer down my still-aching throat. As soon as Randal fell asleep on the bar, I would gather up "my new friend, who went a little over his limit," and whisk him off in a taxi. In the back of the taxi, I'd relieve Randal of his wallet, his NCIS identification, his phone, and his gun. Then I'd divert the taxi to a hospital and dump him there. In the morning, he'd find out how far cocksureness alone would get him with the San Juan Police.

I noticed it had taken only about ten minutes for Randal to polish off his first drink. A volume drinker. That, at least, was encouraging.

Fifteen minutes later, I'd finally nursed my beer dry, as I pretended to be watching the door for Dodd's entrance, while actually monitoring Randal's progress with his second drink, out of the corner of my eye. Thus,

I was a witness when to my chagrin, instead of falling into a gentle slumber at the bar, Randal toppled off his barstool and crashed on the floor.

I was out of my chair and around the bar, as quickly as I could manage through the crowd. As I maneuvered my way closer to Randal, the crowd unexpectedly surged back, and suddenly, I had an unobstructed view of the black NCIS agent kneeling on the spine, pummeling the head, and twisting the arm of a hapless, flamboyantly-dressed man who tenaciously maintained a tight grip on a worn-smooth wallet. Randal slept peacefully facedown, next to the action.

Another commotion started up behind me. I turned to see Special Agent Briggs, bulldozing his way through JR's clientele, as though clearing an access road through a stand of ornamental saplings.

I tactically faded back into the crowd, as Briggs broke onto the open patch, dropped to one knee, and slapped handcuffs on the subdued and badly beaten pickpocket. Briggs then forcefully pried back the cuffed offender's thumb the wrong way and recovered Randal's wallet. The black Special Agent lifted the pickpocket by an upper arm, while simultaneously rising to his own feet, and hauled him headlong through the crowd toward the exit.

Briggs turned Randal over and started checking his vitals. A large, purple bruise was already raised on Randal's forehead and seemed to be growing by the second.

Red and blue flashing lights arrived to pulse through the open door and strobe the smoky glass of the front window. And soon, two San Juan Policemen and two

Emergency Medical Technicians plunged their way in through the outflow of hastily departing club patrons.

As the crowd thinned, I retreated even further back around and nearer to the little stage, where the stripper stood, looking clearly miffed at having gotten only partway through his routine. My favorite bartender, protected within the redoubt of the cigar-shaped bar, appeared innocent and frightened – although when he momentarily caught my eye, he mouthed a theatrical "Oops" in my direction.

I was pondering that perhaps I hadn't done due diligence in thinking my grand scheme completely through, when I saw Briggs barreling straight for me. I had no time to react.

Briggs didn't grip my upper arm especially hard, but there was no question that I was going with him.

"Let's, you and me, get some fresh air," he said.

With the arrival of reinforcements, the San Juan Police proceeded to empty JR's of what few patrons had remained after the initial mass exodus. Briggs and I arrived out on the sidewalk with them.

As the other nightspots along the street absorbed the displaced refugees, Briggs and I leaned against a patrol car. The skin on the left side of his face alternated red and blue in the rhythm of the flashing light bar, but Alicia's claw marks held steady as black parallel streaks on his cheek.

"Randal was duped," Briggs said. "But I knew what you were up to."

My stomach twitched. "Can't a guy go out for a beer?"

"Cut it out. You and Dodd set this up. It's no co-incidence that we're only two blocks from the apartment of that old whore of his. It was obvious to me that you were a diversion. But Randal pulled us off the apartment, even though I told him it smelled like a set-up. By now, Dodd's been into the apartment and got what he wanted and is gone. And all Randal gets is some faggot pickpocket doping his drink. Well, it serves his dumb ass right."

I kept quiet.

"Now I know Dodd's your best friend forever. But he's playing you hard. He's got you convinced that he didn't kill that Arab, even though that's exactly what he did. And I don't know if you're familiar with the term 'accessory after the fact,' but that's what you'll be charged with, if you don't stop helping Dodd elude us. It's a separate offense, so even if Dodd wiggles free, we've still got *you*. And we've spent too much time on this to come home empty-handed." He let me dwell on the threat for a few seconds. "But it doesn't have to be that way. Just tell me now where Dodd's sleeping tonight."

"If he's not at that old girlfriend's apartment, then I don't know where, the hell, he is." I felt better with getting back to the truth. Trying to outwit people is a strain.

"Look...uh, it's Francis, isn't it? Look, Francis, for the time Randal is laid up, I'll be taking the lead. So let's forget about what Randal wants. There's a simple way to get you out of this. And you won't be betraying a friend. In fact, it won't jeopardize Dodd at all." Briggs pulled a business card from his pocket and handed it to me. "Here's all I need you to do. You contact Dodd and tell him I want to set up a meeting. Just him and me. He chooses the time and place. Dodd and I can work it, so it looks like he had no idea that we were looking for him. And as soon as he found out, he contacted me and willingly came in, all on his own. Then just him and me, we fly up to Mayport and hash everything out with the SAC. He'll be all right. He's danced his way out of this sort of thing before."

I pretended to give it some thought, before saying, "Well, if the two of you could work it out. I mean, like along those lines. I guess that would be the thing to do. Next time he contacts me. You know, to just give him that option."

So much for staying with the truth. But I did want to start winding things up for the night.

"That's great." Briggs gave me a little way-to-go punch on the bicep. "We're all on the same team."

"Maybe my teammate will give me back Ellen's room key."

"Oh, yeah. No problem." Briggs searched around in a trouser pocket. As he handed me the key, he asked, "Which one's Ellen? The naked Vogue model, or Victoria's Secret in the wet tee-shirt?"

"The naked one."

"Yeah, she's pretty sweet looking. The trim little body and the sassy hair. She reminds me of my wife, back in the early days." Briggs coughed lightly and then returned to business, his eyebrows set to stern. "That's what gave it away, incidentally. You got the best of both worlds up in your hotel room, but you come over here to fraternize with the fairy brigade. It didn't fool me,

274

because it didn't make any sense at all. And that's also, from what I hear, Dodd's trademark."

"You're pretty quick."

"Maybe now you'll realize what you're up against." Briggs rested a comradely hand on my shoulder. "But I don't get a tingle out of cat-and-mouse games, like Randal does. I like a nice, quiet resolution to the problem. It'll be just Dodd and me, flying up to Mayport to straighten things out. I'll back up his story. And, of course, I'll be sure to mention *your* valuable assistance. See if I can maybe get you put in for a Letter of Commendation." Briggs gave my shoulder a squeeze. "Something to show the folks back home, right?"

***

I didn't switch on the light when I entered my hotel room. I bumped my way through to the bathroom in the dark and closed the door, before turning on the light over the sink. After a hot shower, I found that there were no dry bath towels left. I made do with the several hand towels, having to tie three together to dry my back.

Without a towel to wrap around me, I moved through the pitch-black bedroom, naked and cautiously feeling my way. At last, I found the bed where I'd left the sleeping Alicia and slid in next to her.

"Where've you been?" Alicia remained lying on her side, facing away from me.

"I had a score to settle with Special Agent Randal."

"That doesn't sound like you."

"I drugged his drink, and they took him away in an ambulance."

"Oh, now that I can believe."

"And I got Ellen's room key back."

"Okay, you scored some points there."

I did a little exploring. Alicia was still wearing my last clean shirt, but I discovered that it was unbuttoned.

"You don't have to check any further to see if they're all right. Thanks for your concern." Her fingernails pressed hard into the flesh of my hand, as she removed it. "And I know you're fresh from the battle and all, but the USO is still closed. Trudging up and down that freaking mountain took a toll on me. Maybe if I get a good night's sleep, we'll get around to it tomorrow."

This was bad news for Mr. Lucky, who was presently saluting like a Hitler Youth.

Alicia spoke in the darkness again. "I thought I saw a bottle of aspirins in your satchel, when I borrowed your shirt. Then, after you snuck out, I got up to take a couple. But I couldn't find the bottle again."

"Aspirin's too slow," I said. "Ellen showed me your family home remedy." I maneuvered around and pressed my hands onto the front and back of Alicia's head."

"It's not my head that hurts. The pain is in my back and legs." She pushed my hand off her forehead. "And stop poking me." Alicia slapped back at me, hitting my thigh.

Then, the faintest of giggles escaped from her lips. "Oh hell." She rolled to face me. "Here, let me give you a hand with that, so we can both get some sleep."

Chapter 14

In the morning, heavy rain showered down on whatever was at the bottom of the airshaft, outside my hotel-room's bathroom window. While I shaved and brushed my teeth, a voice from the TV in the bedroom reported that the tropical storm had worked itself up to a category-one hurricane, and its most damaging winds had just made landfall at Fajardo on the eastern end of the island. In the meantime, the outer rain bands were giving the streets of San Juan a thorough wash down.

When I emerged from the bathroom, Alicia was seated on the edge of the bed where Ellen had spent the night. She'd just finished fielding Ellen's morning-after questions, such as how she ended up in my room and in bed and naked. I held a washcloth warmed in hot water to my sore neck and wished Dodd's aspirin bottle actually contained some damned aspirins.

"I have to deliver my report to Monsignor Cabrera this morning," Alicia announced. "So, we're all going to the Cathedral."

"I think I'll skip church this morning, thank you." Ellen's head dropped like a dead weight back onto the pillow.

"I'm not about to leave you on your own again." Alicia made a show of gathering up Ellen's clutch wallet, little blue dress, panties, and heels. "God only knows what you might get up to this time."

After some back and forth concerning whether someone's little sister was entitled to call the shots, I shepherded a victorious Alicia, still wearing my last clean shirt, and a resigned Ellen, wrapped in a still damp bath towel, to their room. After advising them to suit up for foul weather and that I'd return shortly with coffee and rolls, I set out for the breakfast buffet down in the hotel's kitchenette.

***

Across from the breakfast buffet, Phil Dodd sat at a small round table, drinking coffee and reading the San Juan Star – undoubtedly the English edition from the previous day.

I proceeded directly to the coffee urn on the counter and separated three paper cups from a stack. As I filled the paper cups, I asked, "No maid this morning to deliver a message to me?"

"Oh, you figured that out. Congratulations. Faster than I thought you would. Takes the fun out of it, of course." Dodd folded his paper and set it aside. "Bring your coffee over. There's another chair."

"I don't have time." I stacked three jellyrolls on top of a napkin and looked around for something to use as a tray. "I have to run Alicia over to drop off her report and grab her check, before a hurricane blows the Cathedral down, again."

"And I have to run up to the monastery and put some pressure on Brother Hugo," Dodd said. "I'm certain now that he's the one who killed Jaspar Rahim. Feature this. As Brother Hugo is coming through the garden, he sees the bodyguard leave by the back door to go take a pee in the weeds. So, he seizes the moment, slips into the dining hall, and puts a sleeper hold on Rahim's neck. Just like he did to that bandit. Only this time he held on for an extra minute – that is to say, for the rest of Rahim's life."

"Brother Hugo doesn't strike me as a guy who can be intimidated at all. How do you put pressure on a someone like that?"

"You tell him that you know he did it. You lay out all the facts for him, like they're already chiseled on a pair of stone tablets. And then you let him try to explain them away." Dodd lifted his paper cup of coffee. "It'll be like watching a cow trying to do math."

"I can't think of any facts you'd have to lay out."

"Oh, there's a shock." Dodd set his coffee back down, un-sipped. "Hell, it was you and your obsession with the tea mugs that put me onto him. I saw Brother Hugo enter – or, should I say, reenter – the dining hall just ahead of me. So we were the first ones to arrive, after the bodyguard started making this huge clamor over his boss being dead. And while I'm checking for a pulse and so forth, I notice Brother Hugo looking all around the Abbot's chair, like checking to see if Rahim – or maybe, Brother Hugo, himself – dropped something. Then, just as the other monks are rushing in, Brother Hugo leaves, saying he's got to get to his cell phone – I guess maybe to call the Vatican, or something, because Rahim was way past needing medical help at that point. And that's when I noticed that the tea mug – the one I knew for sure I'd seen on the table – was gone. There was so much confusion, monks running to and fro, and whatnot, that I kind of forgot about it. That is until later, when you made such a big issue about the mugs."

"I don't think I really made—"

"And when I tell Alvarez about the missing mug on our trip to the old airport yesterday, he snaps to like a gust of wind just whistled up his tailpipe. That's because Alvarez had already convinced himself that Monsignor Cabrera poisoned Rahim. And given what I told him, he now thinks Brother Hugo was in on it, or at least, was covering up for Cabrera, after the fact. But, of course, there's an even better explanation for his making the mug suddenly disappear."

"Certainly none that I can—"

"Well see, like I told you, I was busy feeling for a pulse at the big arteries on Rahim's neck, while Brother Hugo was busy checking around the big chair. Okay, no pulse, no heartbeat, so he's dead. But what killed him? Well, he's not bleeding anywhere, so I look into his mouth, which is pink and lovely with dull yellow teeth. And then I lift his lids and shine my penlight on his eyeballs. And the whites are good, no off color, just a lot of red veins. And then I'm on to the fingernails, checking for color, when I notice Brother Hugo is staring at me."

"Maybe, he was wondering if you were a doctor."

"More likely, he was thinking I'm law enforcement – the other profession that checks a dead body for cause of death."

"And you're saying that's what caused Brother Hugo to remove the mug?"

"I'm saying that he'd have figured I had seen that mug for sure. No way I'd miss it. And, as a law enforcement officer, I would pass on to the local police the fact that a mug originally present at the crime scene had mysteriously disappeared. Which then leads me to believe that the real reason Brother Hugo took away the mug was to put the Puerto Rico Police onto a false scent. To make some dimwit, like Alvarez, think poison-flavored tea, instead of blood-starved brain."

"No offense, but that's all you've got?"

"It was, until my honey up in Mayport comes through with some juicy shredding-room gossip about this security contractor's employees – you know, mercenaries – and an operation, in the heat of the Insurgency following the Iraq War, gone exceedingly bad. So bad, in fact, these mercs have to vanish. And get this. One of the mercs goes to ground at a monastery. And the Church won't let anybody touch him, because he's all holy now."

"That doesn't necessarily mean the monastery is the one up in El Yunque and the mercenary is Brother Hugo."

"Just hear me out, "Dodd said. "This is why I think Brother Hugo knew Rahim from before. Okay, the operation went down this way. There was this informant in Baghdad who sells these mercs the future location of this high value target – as in, where this Al Qaeda honcho is going to be at a certain time on a certain day. However, the informant also sells the same intel to the Iraqi Police. Now, the mercs, they do the protocol and get the green light from the U.S. Commander, but the Iraqi Police, they don't bother. So, both teams converge on the target simultaneously, but neither group knows about the other. There's a hot-barrel assault and, given the circumstances, an ungodly amount of crossfire. And finally, when things quiet down, the target and his guys are all dead, but so are all the Iraqi policemen. So, you can see why certain employees of a certain security contractor need to quickly scatter far and away to different parts of the planet."

"And you think Rahim was the informant who double dipped?"

"Exactly. So fast-forward to present day. When Rahim stumbles into this monastery deal, Brother Hugo recognizes him and keeps an eagle eye out for the opportunity to exact some righteous retribution by squeezing Rahim's greedy, tea-sipping neck till he's well past blue-in-the-face."

"But you can't confirm any of this."

"But Brother Hugo can. I just have to get him to tell me. Therefore, I need you to get me back into the monastery. So, hurry up with Alicia's business, and you and I will go on up there."

"Why don't you just go by yourself? What do you need me for?"

"Because they're used to seeing you, and they'll assume Alicia must be around somewhere too and that I just came along for the ride. See, I need Brother Hugo calm, so I can explain to him what I know and to emphasize that I have no professional interest in him, other than to get the story nice and straight, so I can lay it all out to my boss. Thus, saving my job, and maybe, just maybe, allowing me to transfer off that God-forsaken prison camp. I'm like the resident castaway there. It rips me apart every time I see a ship put to sea without me."

"So then, what happens to Brother Hugo?"

"I don't feel any obligation to the Puerto Rico Police to hand him over, gift-wrapped. If that's what you're asking."

After a short search, I found a small serving tray in one of the cabinets. "Look, the hurricane will be on top of us by lunchtime. And this morning, I've got to wrap up this deal with Alicia at the Cathedral."

"That's okay, I'll tag along. I'd like to hear what Monsignor Cabrera has to say in defense of Brother Hugo, anyway."

"No!" I felt like throwing the tray at him. "You're not going to mess things up any further for Alicia."

"Francis, what's up? I thought we were working together on this. Now, all at once, you're taking your marching orders from Alicia, when...oh wait, wait just a second. She gave you a little taste, didn't she? A savory lick of the spoon to remind you that Mama can still cook. Damn, if she can't play that thing. She's this close to scooping up her prize, and she just needs to keep you towing the line, until that big old check is safely stowed in her purse. And for insurance, she's made damned sure that you know you won't have to wait for heaven to get your reward."

"Are you done? This coffee's getting cold."

"Hell, now I *have* to go with you to the Cathedral. Once she bags that check and you get her back here, you'll be dug in. A mod-five torpedo won't blast you out of that room."

I topped off the paper cups with hot coffee from the urn. "You are not going with us to the Cathedral. I'm sure you can figure out how to handle things at the monastery all by yourself. And yes, I intend to ride out the storm with Alicia, up in my room. It only makes sense to show up on payday."

I pulled Briggs's business card out of my pocket, stepped over, and dropped it on the little table in front of Dodd.

"Here," I said. "The number scribbled on it is his cell phone. Briggs says if you call him, he'll go with you, without Randal, up to Mayport and explain to your boss that you were just so involved in your investigation that you had no idea that other special agents were looking for you. He said he'd vouch for you, and it'll all be cleared up."

"And you believe that."

"I'm not required to. But now that I've delivered the message to you, I'm supposed to be off the hook for being an accessory-after-the-fact."

"I see," Dodd said. "Did he also mention a possible commendation from a grateful government?"

"Look, I understand that everything Briggs said was a load of crap. But, as of this moment, I'm out. What you do from now on is up to you."

I returned to the loaded breakfast tray and picked it up.

"Don't bail on me now, Francis. Not when we're within hailing distance of resolving this."

I set the tray down again. It was no use pretending that my outstanding debt to Dodd didn't still weigh heavily on me. But that didn't mean I couldn't establish some boundaries.

"Okay," I said. "We both know I can't stop you from just showing up at the Cathedral anyway. So, you can ride with us over there. But you don't say a word to

Monsignor Cabrera, until after Alicia has a signed check in her hand. Directly after that, we'll be coming straight back to this hotel. Alicia and I have our own contract to fulfill, which, with any luck, will take up the rest of the day. Then tomorrow, Alicia and Ellen will fly out, and I'll be available to go up to the monastery with you, if that's how you still want to play it. At least, you'll have someone to bring you back down the mountain, if Brother Hugo decides to re-contour your face. Which, if you ask me, seems likely." I picked up the breakfast tray. "Take it or leave it. We'll be down in a few minutes."

* * *

When I delivered breakfast to Alicia and Ellen up in their room, they were already dressed in blue jeans and hooded, polyester jackets. While they munched their rolls and sipped their coffee, I slipped back to my room to fetch a jacket and ball cap. I ate my breakfast on the way down to the lobby.

I expected Phil Dodd to be waiting for us, either in the lobby or just outside the front door. But he wasn't anywhere to be seen. I didn't know if he'd been delayed, or diverted, or what, but I wasn't going to wait for him.

I left Alicia and Ellen to listen to the morning-shift desk clerk's discouragements about venturing out into the storm, while I charged out into the wind and rain to fetch the rental car.

Receiving a damn good thrashing from the forces of Nature, I huddled my head deeper within my hunched shoulders and upturned jacket collar. I pulled the bill of my ball cap down almost to my nose and only peered out from my tortoise defense strategy to check the street, before dashing across to the rental car.

Just as I slid in behind the wheel and yanked the door closed, I heard a couple of sharp knocks. Turning toward the sound, I saw Dodd's face, framed in the front passenger's window, looking like he was trapped inside a carwash. I pushed the button to unlock the passenger doors.

Dodd opened the door just enough to say, "Give me a minute. I'll be right back," and shut it again.

The drum roll of rain on the metal roof and the constant wash of water over the windows, prevented me from hearing or seeing, what Dodd was up to. Less than a minute later, Dodd, wearing a dripping raincoat and flop-brimmed hat, dropped onto the passenger seat next to me.

"Some kind of rainy day, huh?" Dodd summed up.

"What were you doing?"

"Giving your latest tracking device a new home under the car behind us. You'd think they'd learn. This one wasn't hidden any better than the last one. Still, I score them a nine-point-five for persistence."

I started the car and inched it back blindly, until it made light contact with the car behind us.

"But it's okay," Dodd went on. "None of my valiant cohorts are lurking about. I checked. Must be they're counting on the hurricane to make you stay put. Kind of strange, though. You'd think Randal would post a watch with one of his underlings, anyway. Just to be sure."

I shifted into drive. "Randal's in the hospital. Briggs has the reins now."

Dodd looked at me, as we pulled away from the curb. "I seriously doubt they would freely offer this information to you. And yet, I find it even harder to believe the alternative – that Randal's 'reporting to sickbay' is the result of anything you might have intentionally done."

"Believe what you want," I had the satisfaction of saying.

We had to circle the block on one-way streets to come around to the Caserio's entrance. The windshield wipers couldn't quite keep up with the deluge and their rapid cadence afforded me only momentary glimpses of the lane ahead. As I turned the corner, the wind lifted the wipers out of contact with the windshield, forcing me reduce our speed to a crawl and use distorted color groups to steer by. After spotting the next corner out the side window and taking the turn, the wipers regained contact with the windshield. Now that I could see ahead again, I felt confident enough to take one hand off the wheel, extract from my pocket the aspirin bottle containing the Seconals, and hold it out to Dodd.

"Your girlfriend said she didn't want these around anymore."

Dodd took the little bottle, twisted off the cap, and looked inside for a few seconds.

"Assuming that not all the capsules made it back to me," he said, "should I also assume that the number of missing ones will bear a direct relation to the length of Randal's hospital stay?"

"Randal almost choked me to death – trying to force me to turn on *you*, incidentally. I set him up for a little retaliation. It didn't go exactly as planned, but I figure I got even with the bastard."

"How many capsules are missing?"

"Four."

"Good God, you tried to kill him?"

"The bartender was only supposed to empty one into Randal's drink and keep three for his own recreational use. But I think he doubled down, because Randal took a swan dive off his barstool. His forehead broke his fall."

"Can any of this splash back on you?"

"The San Juan Police arrested an opportunist who had Randal's wallet in his hand, but not before that black Special Agent beat the living snot out of him."

"My honey in Mayport says he's fresh out of training. Working with Randal is teaching him some bad habits."

"Well anyway, Briggs laid it all off on the pickpocket. And I think the San Juan Police will be happy enough to go with that."

Dodd rode in silence for a bit, before saying, "Francis, leave the scheming to people who have wit and guile baked into their DNA. If that pickpocket hadn't taken a chance, it could easily have been *your* manly features that took the beating, and *your* sad carcass that the cops hauled away. Stick to machinery and techno-crap. Play to your strengths."

* * *

As I made the last turn onto Ashford Avenue, a blast of wind lifted the sweep of the wipers clear of contact with the windshield again, and I drove the last fifty feet up to the hotel, mostly by memory.

When I pulled to the curb in front of the Caserio Inn, Dodd leaped out and had both curbside doors open for Alicia and Ellen, as they scampered to the rental car through the pelting rain. Alicia sat up front with me, and Phil Dodd jumped into the backseat with Ellen.

"What the hell's going on now, Francis?" Alicia immediately demanded. "How come we can't simply go get my check without your old lieutenant doing a ride-along?"

"He just wants to ask Monsignor Cabrera a couple questions."

"I promise to be as silent as an altar boy, until after you get your check," Dodd spoke from the back seat.

"You're damn right, you will," Alicia said, as she pulled her phone out of her purse. "And I hope the Monsignor chews your lying ass off, for causing so much trouble." Alicia tapped on the screen, but soon put the phone away. "No service. I guess it's the storm. I wanted to let him know we were on our way over."

As we crossed a broad open stretch that bridged the low land between the modern buildings of the Condado District and the historic buildings of Old San Juan, the wind and rain had their way with the compact rental car. I stayed close to the long metal guardrail, using it as a visual guide, until we were finally within the narrow streets of Old San Juan, where the wind had a more difficult time getting at us.

We abandoned the car in a no-parking zone in front of the Cathedral. Once inside, we created a trail of rainwater down a long empty hallway and entered the administration offices of the Archdiocese.

Sitting behind a chaotic desktop, a lone clerk – pale and bald with an askew, paisley necktie – looked up over his half glasses and blinked hard, as though to clear his vision of the sopping wet aberration that had manifested itself before him.

Alicia pushed forward to the desk with her neatly bound report wrapped in numerous plastic bags. "I'm here to deliver my report to Monsignor Cabrera."

"Oh, yes, I remember you. The Art Restorer," the clerk responded in English. "It is Mrs. Elton, is it not?"

"It is. So, if the Monsignor has a moment…"

"I *am* sorry, but the Monsignor is not here. I have your check prepared, ready for his signature, but he has been called away." The clerk checked his watch. "He should be almost to the monastery by now."

"The monastery? But…"

"We received word earlier this morning that the Abbot's condition has gravely deteriorated."

"Well, that's just…I mean, that's really quite unfortunate." Alicia managed to rein herself in. "And I know how the Monsignor must feel. I can understand why he had to rush to the bedside of his old friend."

"My sister and I lost our mother recently," Ellen put it.

"Oh, I am very sorry for you both," the clerk said.

"And the Abbot," Alicia continued. "Well, you could tell his health was failing him, but I really didn't expect…and after he just got his monastery back. It's all too sad."

"Brother Hugo called on his cellular," the clerk said. "Of course, Monsignor Cabrera rushed right out. The hurricane meant nothing to him. You are, of course, welcomed to leave your report here with me, but…" The clerk tapped his finger on the unsigned check laying on top of the pile in his out-basket. "I am afraid that your check will have to wait, until the Monsignor returns."

"Maybe there's someone else here who could sign the check," I suggested. "The Archbishop, maybe?"

"Unfortunately, the Archbishop is still in New York. A problem with the flights, I am told. The only Auxiliary Bishop who is familiar with this project is presently visiting family in Mayaguez."

"Look," I said. "Mr. Dodd and I were going up to the monastery later on, anyway." My statement drew raised eyebrows from Alicia and a hearty clasp to my shoulder from Dodd. "We could bring the check and Alicia's report along with us. I'm sure Monsignor Cabrera could find a spare moment to look over the report and sign the check." What the hell, I could afford to suddenly be generous with my time. After all, no signed-check for Alicia meant no promised-reward for Francis.

The old clerk looked longingly at the telephone on his desk. "I wish that I could call the Monsignor. The regular telephones still work. But even if the Monsignor carried a cellular, we discovered that the towers on this half of the island were out of service when the policeman was here, a little earlier. He was also asking for the Monsignor."

The clerk picked up a business card lying by his phone and dropped it on the large, heavily annotated calendar serving as his desk pad. The card displayed the contact information for Detective Sergeant Alvarez.

"Usually," the clerk added, "the only policeman that we see, back in these offices, is Captain Rivera, when he comes for the weekly gathering for bridge, rum, and cigars. It stinks up the library. The housekeeper always has a fit, the next morning."

"Well, that's quite interesting," Dodd broke his silence. "Who all does Captain Rivera play bridge with?"

"Oh, whoever is available at the time to make up four players. Anyone from the Archbishop on down."

"Yeah?" Dodd probed. "Do *you* ever play bridge with the Captain?"

"Oh, bless you, no, sir. Nor does the gardener."

I asked, "What did Detective Sergeant Alvarez want with Monsignor Cabrera?"

"I know only that he wished to speak with the Monsignor. He seemed quite upset that the Monsignor had gone to the monastery, but then he seemed strangely relieved when I could not get a call through to Brother Hugo. The Detective Sergeant then said he would try to catch up with Monsignor Cabrera at the monastery and hurried out."

Alicia grabbed my arm. "Francis, what's Alvarez doing?"

"Whatever he's doing, I think we'd better get the Monsignor's signature on that check, before Alvarez does it."

Alicia snatched the unsigned check from the out-basket, saying, "We'll save Monsignor Cabrera some time by running this up to the monastery for his signature."

Before anyone could react, Alicia was already through the office door. From the hallway, she yelled, "Let's go, people."

"She's got spunk." Dodd had a big smile on his face. "I'll give her that." He hurried after Alicia.

I flung a hasty "thank you" at the old clerk and brought Ellen along in Dodd's wake.

Halfway down the hall, Ellen put a hand on my arm to slow me to a stop.

"Francis, about last night." She quickly glanced ahead and behind. "I really had fun. I mean, the dancing – my God, how these people dance – and that music, so fast and so sensual all at once. I never heard music like that. Never in my life. I mean, the way it made me feel. And my skin was so hot. And I wanted to jump you right then and there." Ellen quickly covered her lips with her fingertips. "I didn't mean to say that last part." She placed her hand on my upper arm again. "But that's just between you and me, okay? What I mean is, none of this can get back to Roger. That's understood, right? I mean I do want to thank you for such a lovely time—"

"You already thanked me."

Ellen clutched my sleeve tightly; her eyes anxiously searched my face.

I gathered that there was some missing time in her recall of the previous evening.

"A kiss," I said. "A little kiss, here on my cheek, on the cab-ride back."

Ellen released her grip. "Oh, that's okay then. I must have dreamt…But still, mum's the word, okay? Roger wouldn't understand about the music."

Chapter 15

As we drove east on Highway 66, I gripped the steering wheel with both hands, resisting the wind's relentless efforts to push the rental car across the other eastbound lanes and down into the grassy median. I was grateful for the weight that four adults lent to the light, economy vehicle.

At first, we had shared the highway with several other stalwart drivers, braving the storm, although they were all westbound, wisely scurrying toward the shelter of the city. But not long after we'd passed without pause through the abandoned toll station, our little rental car became the sole vehicle pushing through the sweeping tempest.

An elliptical image of Dodd's eyes and nose filled the interior rearview mirror. "Can you actually see anything, Francis?"

"I can still pretty much make out the lines on the road. Cabrera and Alvarez probably made it through, before it got this bad."

"Is Alvarez going up to the monastery to arrest Monsignor Cabrera?" Alicia posed a question that was also on my mind.

"What that chucklehead Detective Sergeant is going to do is make a monkey of himself," Dodd stated, as his face left the mirror and he resettled in his seat. "Alvarez thinks that Cabrera gave Rahim a mug of poisoned tea. And the circumstantial evidence for that looks pretty good, I'll give him that. But it'll be a bitch to actually prove it."

"Circumstantial evidence, like what?" Alicia asked.

"Well, the bodyguard confirmed that a short time before Rahim died, Cabrera handed Rahim a mug of tea. And we know, from Cabrera's days as a forward base medic in Vietnam, that he has experience in making mysterious potions from jungle plant leaves."

"And just how could you possibly know that?" Alicia demanded.

"Army records," Dodd said. "A lady I know in the Mayport office has a back channel up in Washington. And I passed on the info about Cabrera's dabble in primitive pharmacology to Alvarez."

"Can Alvarez get a copy of that Army record?"

"I seriously doubt it," Dodd said. "But anyway, what Alvarez really needs is a definitive toxicology report and a physical link to Cabrera."

"So he's got nothing." Alicia sounded pleased.

"I didn't say that," Dodd countered. "Alvarez laid out a motive for the Monsignor on our ride to Isla Grande, and it's a dandy. And it goes like this. Through the Archdiocese grapevine, Cabrera gets tipped off that there's an ongoing Homeland Security investigation of Jaspar Rahim. This leads Cabrera to believe that Rahim is fronting for a bunch of wild-eyed Islamic extremists. But, this revelation comes too late to stop the sale of the monastery from going through – unless, of course, Rahim somehow isn't able to make the phone call to release the funds from his numbered Swiss account. And so, Cabrera poisons Rahim with some homemade jungle-leaf extract. And he convinces his pal Captain

Rivera to hastily tidy up an inconvenient Muslim death at a Catholic facility. Thus, a potential Al Qaeda terror plot is thwarted, and the Catholic Church avoids another blot on its permanent record. That's Alvarez's theory, anyway."

"And that's crazy." Alicia said. "Monsignor Cabrera couldn't possibly hurt a soul. He's the most considerate and thoughtful man I've ever met."

"The crazy part is Alvarez not waiting for the final toxicology report," Dodd said. "He's got to give the Lab Coats some time to fire up the mass spectrometer."

"Wait a minute," I managed to get in, while still manfully piloting through the hostile weather. "Alvarez got a temporary go-ahead from his Captain to question people about what the bodyguard said. So maybe, Alvarez just going up there to ask the Monsignor a few questions."

"Without a doubt," Dodd said, "it'd be okay for him to cruise over to the Cathedral this morning to clear up a few minor points, before the brunt of the storm gets to the city. But following Cabrera up to the monastery, heading straight into the approaching hurricane, makes the questions look mighty damn important. And if Cabrera decides to be uncooperative, Alvarez is just dumb enough to haul him back to San Juan and hold him until the test results come back. And if he does that, he'd damn well better be right, because it sounds to me like Captain Rivera is exceedingly protective of his bridge partner."

"Freaking unbelievable," Alicia said. "Alvarez conjures up this vast political intrigue that all turns on a single entry in an Army record from something like fifty years ago."

"Well, that's Alvarez," Dodd said. "I, personally, think Brother Hugo is a much stronger candidate for the title of Murderer in the First Degree. He has the physical power to clamp Rahim's fat neck with his tattooed arm and squeeze off the blood flow to Rahim's double-dealing brain. Not to mention he carries enough weight to hold Rahim down to keep him from struggling too much. That way, there's no noticeable damage to the neck. I just wish that damned bodyguard had come clean about leaving the dining hall for ten minutes to go take a leak, or something. Maybe he would have, if Alvarez had let me pump the truth out of him at the morgue. But the great Detective Sergeant can't see past his precious poisoned tea theory."

"Who made the tea?" Ellen piped up. "I'm sorry. I know you guys are all way ahead of me. But I can't really imagine someone as important as Monsignor Cabrera making the tea."

"One of the two monks who do the cooking made the tea," Dodd said. "There's a wood stove on the patio just outside the kitchen. But it doesn't matter. It wasn't—"

"So," Alicia cut in, "if the tea is just sitting there unattended out on the patio, then anybody could have poisoned it, not just Monsignor Cabrera. Good one, Ellen."

When Dodd didn't immediately respond, Alicia pounced. "Why so quiet all of a sudden, Lieutenant? I heard all about your little bottle of sleeping pills. That guy Randal was talking so loud I think everybody in the whole hotel heard about them. And let me just add that *your* version of how that Iraqi tribal leader managed to drown in his fountain isn't nearly as convincing, as how the other agents from your department tell it."

"Randal wasn't there. And anyway, it was war. And if you haven't been in the thick of one, you can't pass judgment on people who were."

As we neared the mountains of El Yunque, the toll road gave up and merged back into Highway 3's two blacktopped lanes. Through the steering wheel, I could feel the hurricane steadily increasing in intensity. And then came the sucker punch. A crosswind from a new direction smacked the little rental car and followed up with a relentless fury, seemingly determined upon wresting the car's steering from my control. It was as though the storm god had abruptly cranked the hurricane valve open a couple extra turns.

All conversation in the car ceased. I slowed to a crawl in order to stay on the highway and not be blown off onto a flattened field and beneath a stretch of lofty high-power lines that undulated in a turbulent dance, arcing across to one another with the loud crackles and bangs of thousands of volts of leaping electricity.

Thankfully, before my stamina gave out, the little rental car miraculously made it to the beginnings of the rain forest at the base of the mountain range. And as we progressed deeper within the shelter of the trees, my fight with the steering wheel eased, and I could actually feel the tires gripping the wet blacktop.

I recognized the turn-off for the road up through the National Forest. I took it, and we bumped onto the short, narrow bridge that now spanned a swollen and fast-flowing drainage ditch. Another right turn put us on the street that ran through the scruffy village at the base of the climb up El Yunque. But, unlike the rain forest, the opposing rows of storefronts along the corridor of cracked pavement that passed for Main Street did not serve as a windbreak. On the contrary, it formed a wind tunnel.

Trash and roofing debris tumbled like sagebrush alongside our rental car. Worse, coconuts, torn free from the high palm trees, soared as an onslaught of cannon balls, crashing down on parked vehicles and setting off a cacophony of car alarms, like the wail of air raid sirens. Our rental car took a few hits, but blessedly, no coconut missiles struck the window glass.

At the end of the village, the road turned sharply left, and we pressed upward through the weed-choked orchards just outside the village, where the hurricane had already stripped the unpicked fruit from the trees. Soon we were again within the shelter of the rain forest, and the hurricane had to content itself with merely bending the treetops high above us and pelting us with heavy rain. Except for brief openings in the vegetation, where the road hugged a drop-off and exposed us to a blast from the roiling gray storm, I could navigate up through the turns with a slightly more relaxed death-grip on the steering wheel.

***

In the parking area below the monastery, two cars had arrived before us. I recognized the Crown Vic as the one I'd ridden in with Detective Sergeant Alvarez at the wheel. I assumed the black Toyota Camry belonged to Monsignor Cabrera.

Once parked, I took a moment to flex the tension from my fingers, before tugging my ball cap down tighter on my head and zipping up my jacket, in preparation to leaving the womb of the rental car.

Next to me, Alicia sprayed a preemptive shot of allergy medicine up each nostril, before producing zip-seal-type plastic bags from her purse and handing them out for safe guarding cell phones and wallets against the pouring rain.

"Well, gang, I guess we'd better hop to it," Dodd urged us. "Even for a Man of God, it's awfully difficult to sign a check with your hands cuffed behind your back."

That brought Alicia out of the car in a hurry, with her jacket hood up and cinched tightly around her face and her triple-wrapped report held tightly to her body. Ellen was similarly cocooned, and Dodd had his flop brimmed hat back on.

We began the long climb up the slick, leaf-strewn, cart path to the monastery. The rain was an unceasing deluge, even beneath the cover of the darkened forest. The promise of dry shelter up at the monastery was our only solace in the purgatory of our upward climb.

At the last switchback before the final segment of the cart path, there was a new and surprising sight. The monastery's donkey stood patiently without a tether, beneath a tented canvas tarp that was held aloft by ropes tied to tree trunks. Just outside the makeshift shelter, a bucket of water overflowed in continual replenishment.

"Looks like the monks don't have much faith in their sheds," Dodd said, as we all gathered under the tarp and surrounded the docile animal.

"Can't we just hang out with the donkey for a while?" Ellen pleaded.

"I'm with you," Alicia said. "This is beyond miserable."

Dodd touched my arm. "When we get up there, while I'm poking around, I need you to pry some additional scuttlebutt from your pint-sized friend. Brother Emilio's tale about Brother Hugo taking out the armed robber with his bare hands was the initial nugget that broke this whole thing wide open. He's bound to know more."

"Then, you're assuming that the toxicologist hasn't already made Alvarez's case against Cabrera?" I asked.

"Why wouldn't I assume it?"

"At the morgue, after you left, Alvarez told me he was going to talk to the Assistant Director of Toxicology and entice him into searching for an exotic poison in Rahim's blood and tissue samples, today."

"During a hurricane?"

"Evidently, he's driven by a challenge," I said. "And Alvarez sounded pretty confident that the guy would jump on it."

"Damn. I didn't want Cabrera to be cleared just yet," Dodd said. "I need Alvarez kept busy, sniffing at the false scent." Dodd pulled his bagged cell phone out and opened the plastic enough to tap at the screen. "It's okay, the tower's are still out. I've still got time."

"Time for what?" I asked.

"To find something really solid," Dodd said. "Something so incriminating and irrefutable that I can drop it in front of Brother Hugo and absolutely smell his panic. So much panic that he'll be overpowered with the need to talk to someone. And not just anyone, but someone who's worn the uniform and been to the battle. He'll need to explain himself to one of his own. And I'll be right there for him, his Father Confessor."

"You're depraved, you know that?" Alicia said.

"When I start shoving bamboo under his fingernails, then you can complain about my methods." Dodd swung his attention back to me. "I'll do a hunt through the sheds. That's were Brother Hugo would hide any research he'd done in confirming Rahim's identity. That would be A-one physical evidence. And like I said, you concentrate on that little monk who walks in Brother Hugo's shadow. I'll bet you Brother Hugo told him something juicy. And he'll spill it right out if you just get him talking. He's as naïve as this donkey." Dodd scratched the donkey behind the ear.

"Francis, are you blind to what this freaking charlatan's doing?" Alicia's austere features in the oval of the cinched-up hood lent an unearthly quality to her scolding words. "Isn't it patently obvious that he dumped half a barbiturate capsule into each mug of tea. That way Rahim takes a heavy snooze in the big chair, giving his bodyguard a chance to slip out and take a pee, and giving *you*, Lieutenant, a chance to slip in and suffocate Rahim with one of those ratty seat cushions. I bet he didn't even struggle, did he? And so what, if the Abbot drinks from the other mug? He just takes another nap, like always. So good job, it looks like Rahim died a natural death. Except that the NCIS isn't buying it. Gee, I guess maybe they don't trust you. So, that's really why you have to prove it was murder. To pin it on someone else."

"I'd have used something better than a ratty seat cushion. Give me some credit."

"But you screwed up, because you *can't* prove it was murder, *can* you?" Alicia didn't let up. "First, because you did such a tidy job – just like you did with that sheik in Iraq – so there wasn't any evidence of a violent death for the Medical Examiner to find. That forced you to make up that crap about Brother Hugo being oh so very careful not to injure Rahim's neck when he violently strangled the Arab to death. And second, you thought the bodyguard would own up to leaving the dining hall for ten minutes, during the time Rahim slept off his doped-up tea – but the bodyguard didn't own up to it, did he? So *now* how do you pin the murder on Brother Hugo?"

"Aw for God sakes," Dodd said. "Everybody knows that the bodyguard left Rahim alone for a while and then came back and found him dead. If he had actually witnessed the murder, I guarantee he would have said something to the Engineman who did the translations."

"Oh," Ellen said, "so the tricky part is that if Brother Hugo had time to strangle the Arab, then you had time to suffocate him."

The rest of us looked in astonishment at Ellen, who then appended, "Just saying."

"Well, Lieutenant," Alicia challenged. "Tell us Ellen is wrong."

When Dodd didn't immediately answer, Alicia added, "I wonder what the chances are that the Assistant Director of Toxicology will forget to test for barbiturate residue in Rahim's brain tissue samples."

"This is all fantasy," Dodd finally found his voice. "You're just cherry-picking things I've said. Plus, I have no motive."

"The NCIS thinks you do," Alicia said. "Tell him, Francis. You know he did it."

I didn't expect to be called in for backup. "Ah, well sure, it looks bad that the two Arab sheiks, who Dodd was assigned to, both turned up dead. But I don't think a couple of your points quite jibe with—"

"Then let me help you," Alicia took back the lead. "If Special Agent Dodd's only purpose for taking your place as my husband was to observe the Arab, why did he suddenly decide that he had to rush down to the kitchen, *ahead* of Monsignor Cabrera, to tell the cooks that we wouldn't be there for lunch?"

"It was just a courtesy," Dodd said.

"And that's just more of your crap," Alicia batted it away. "You had to get to the tea first, didn't you, Lieutenant?"

"The impression I got," I said, "from talking to the monks, was that the mugs of tea were for the Abbot and Monsignor Cabrera to sip together up in the Abbot's room, before the Monsignor left. No one knew the Monsignor was going to take a detour to the dining hall to say a departing word to Rahim."

"Would it do any good," Dodd asked, "for me to say that Cabrera said nothing to me about intending to drop in on Rahim in the dining hall first?"

"No." Alicia pointed an accusing finger. "Because you're a pathological liar."

Alicia turned and stomped off out into the rain. Ellen hurried after her.

"She'd make a damn fine prosecuting attorney." Dodd watched Alicia's departing figure continue up the last section of cart path. "All her instincts tell her to go for the jugular. She's got a nice ass, too. You still with me?"

"You okay with me having some doubts about you, myself?"

"Sure."

"Well, I'm not really on board about Brother Hugo, but I'll see if I can get Brother Emilio alone for a minute. Maybe he knows something."

Chapter 16

Phil Dodd and I trudged on up the last of the cart path, catching up with Alicia and Ellen just as they reached the clearing on the mountain ridge. With our first steps out of the shelter of the rain forest, I made a saving grasp at the bill of my departing ball cap, as the force of the wind drove all of us back below the ridgeline.

Dodd had to yell over the howl of rushing air. "I'm going to make my way around to the sheds. You folks will have to make a dash for the main building. Ladies, hold onto Francis's belt, and all of you keep low. Your combined weight should keep you from getting blown off the mountain."

Dodd started off in a crouch, keeping well within the dense forest. He held his windward forearm tight on top of his floppy hat, while keeping his elbow forward to protect his face from flying chunks of horticulture, as he circumnavigated the assailed garden.

Alicia and Ellen grabbed the back of my belt, clung to each other, and buried their faces into either side of my torso. As a six-legged hunched composition, we ventured forth into the fierce wind and rain, pressing ever onward with staggering steps toward the front door of the main monastery building.

I couldn't hear what Alicia was yelling at me. I was the lead goose in the formation, taking the brunt of the forces of nature. I had to keep a tight hold on the bill of my ball cap to maintain a face shield, even though it blinded me to all but the soaked ground just in front of my feet.

In the end, it was mindless determination that brought us to the building's front entrance. I saw that the door was not quite closed, so without pausing I pushed it out of our way. The door initially swung freely, as we moved as a single mass across the threshold, but it scraped to an abrupt stop about two-thirds of the way through its travel. Unfortunately, Alicia and Ellen continued to blindly press in behind me, our legs tangled, and we all tumbled into the hallway, landing in a big, wet pile with me face-down at the bottom.

It took a minute to untangle and climb back onto our respective feet, all the while laughing at our pratfall entrance, elated with having made it through the ordeal. With a slam from my shoulder, I managed to un-stick the door. The door continued to swing toward closure, but ended up merely banging onto the inboard side of its misaligned frame. I wondered how much farther out of kilter the building could shift, before the whole weather-beaten edifice finally collapsed.

Alicia untied her hood and unzipped her jacket. "Well, this did a lot of good. I'm sopping wet."

"Maybe we could wring ourselves out in the guest room." Ellen squeezed a splash of water from the tail of her blouse.

"I'll look for Monsignor Cabrera," I said. "I think he'll be up in the Abbot's bedroom."

I followed Alicia and Ellen to the upper floor. They entered the guest quarters, and I walked on to the open door of the Abbot's room.

Stepping inside, I quietly took a position behind and to one side of Detective Sergeant Alvarez, who patiently looked on, as Monsignor Cabrera stood at the old Abbot's bedside, hands pressed together, intoning a quiet prayer. On the far side of the bed, Brother Emilio sat on the edge of the straight-backed chair, continually replacing a rosary onto arthritic fingers that could no longer reliably maintain a grasp on the beads.

The Abbot's long and scraggly white hair lay on the pillow in a halo around his head. His eyes looked up from their deep sunken shadows toward heaven. Then, in thin soprano Spanish, the old Abbot unexpectedly spoke, "You may save your prayers for the moment, Pedro. A drink of water will do me more good."

Monsignor Cabrera poured water from a pewter pitcher into a mug that shared a nightstand with a pair of wire-rim eyeglasses. Abandoning the rosary, Brother Emilio's hands reached out to receive the mug from Monsignor Cabrera. The Monsignor then lifted his frail old friend up to a sitting position. Brother Emilio delicately placed the mug into the Abbot's gnarled outstretched fingers, but kept his own hands hovering just beneath the Abbot's tentative grip, ready to make the saving catch. It wasn't pretty to watch, but the Abbot's initial sip eventually became an eager swallow.

The Abbot lowered the mug. "Tepid."

"I will get cool water." Br. Emilio took the mug from the Abbot's hands, carried it around the bed, and replaced it on the nightstand. He grabbed up the pitcher and hurried right past me, without acknowledgment, and out of the room.

Monsignor Cabrera eased the Abbot back down onto his pillow.

Detective Sergeant Alvarez now noticed me standing near the doorway. He looked anything but pleased, as he demanded in English, "Mr. Elton, why are you here?"

I stepped deeper into the room and responded in English, "I brought Alicia to see Monsignor Cabrera. She has her final report to submit for his approval, and also, the check from the Cathedral's office, ready for the Monsignor's signature."

Monsignor Cabrera turned from his ministrations. "Then I must sign quickly. I believe I am about to be arrested."

"I proceeded on up here," Alvarez said, "only to ask you a few questions. Had I found you at the Cathedral, I would have asked them there. As I have already stated."

"At the moment, your questions and your official presence here are of no importance to me," Monsignor Cabrera said. "Mr. Elton, I have just given my friend Extreme Unction. His time is rapidly coming to an end. You may tell—"

When the Monsignor stopped, I turned to where he was looking and saw Alicia and Ellen entering the Abbot's room.

"Oh, I hope we're not..." Alicia hesitated in her advance, and Ellen bumped to a halt behind her.

Alicia and Ellen had toweled and finger-combed their hair back. Their wrung-out, yet still-damp, blouses kept no secrets about their feminine contours. Alicia supported the folder containing her report, now unwrapped from its protective plastic, in the crook of her arm.

"Come here, children." The Abbot's Spanish words were stronger now, his voice evidently revived by the swallow of room-temperature water. "It is proper that you visit a dying old man."

I translated for Alicia and Ellen.

"Are you sure you got the 'children' part right?" Alicia asked, as she and Ellen approached the Abbot's bed.

The Abbot struggled to sit up again. Monsignor Cabrera placed a hand on the Abbot's shoulder.

"It is all right, Sergio," he spoke quietly in Spanish. "They can see you from here."

The old Abbot settled back onto his pillow. I could see the strain in his unaided eyes, attempting to focus on Alicia and Ellen, and I sensed the struggle of his aged brain, fighting through mental fog, when he asked, "Where do you girls attend school?"

I translated for Alicia and Ellen, but before they could respond, Monsignor Cabrera produced a white lie rather more smoothly than I would've expected from a priest.

"They attend the University of the Sacred Heart. You should rest now, Sergio. The young ladies must go. They will be late for class."

"Such nice young ladies." The Abbot sighed and returned to gazing skyward. "It is very good. They will be Sisters, one day."

Monsignor Cabrera spoke to Alicia and Ellen in English, "The Abbot is very tired now."

"We'll let him rest then," Alicia said.

As Alicia moved past me, following Ellen out of the room, she caught my eye and pointed at something behind me. I looked in the direction she'd indicated and saw that the spinning electric fan was plugged into a makeshift extension cord – an in-line receptacle fed by two single wires, each sheathed in black plastic insulation.

With Alicia and Ellen's departure, it belatedly occurred to me that no report had been read and no check had been signed. I was about to restate the reason for our having braved the perils of a hurricane when Alvarez abruptly moved in front of me, determined, I supposed, to fulfill his own objective.

However, before the Detective Sergeant got a word out, the old Abbot, with reopened eyes and surprising volume, suddenly demanded, "My chair! Take me to my chair!"

"Sergio, my old friend," Monsignor Cabrera soothed. "You are no longer strong enough to leave your bed."

"Monsignor, I have come all this way to speak with you." Alvarez's patience had evidently reached its breaking point. "Surely, Mr. Elton can keep watch over the Abbot for a few minutes, while we talk out in the hallway."

"Pedro. Must I beg you?"

"Detective Sergeant," Monsignor Cabrera said, "if you will allow me to attend to a dying man's wish, we may then find the time to address your concerns. Mr. Elton, if you will assist me."

Monsignor Cabrera slid an arm behind the old man's shoulders and sat him up. I quickly stepped around the

Detective Sergeant, pulled back the sheet, and carefully swung the spindly legs, sticking out from the Abbot's nightshirt, off the side of the bed. I crouched down to slide a pair of worn-out slippers onto the Abbot's red and blue veined feet. Then together, one on each side, the Monsignor and I lifted the Abbot up, as straight as he was going to get.

We easily carried the Abbot's slight weight across the room. However, the awkwardness of maneuvering a three-man unit through the doorway, especially with the Abbot pretty much just dragging his feet between us, had to be performed with much prolonged sidestepping.

It was smoother going along the hallway. Alvarez trailed behind us, blowing out his breath in bursts, his frustration barely held in check. Alicia and Ellen, standing in the doorway of the guest quarters, watched our approach.

"Fall in," I quietly said to them, in passing. "Bring the folder."

Our next challenge was the stairway.

For Monsignor Cabrera and I, maintaining our shared balance, while carrying our delicate load down the stairs, was a study in risk management. Cradling the old Abbot between us, I slid my back along in contact with the wall to give our unwieldy grouping some stability, as we sidestepped downward, counting each descending tread as a victory.

In the end, we succeeded in delivering our fragile cargo to the ground floor. With the side of one foot, I scooted the soles of the Abbot's slippers back into full contact with the wood-planked firmament.

"Mr. Elton," the Monsignor sounded short of breath, "would you mind assuming the weight the Abbot by yourself for a moment?"

As soon as I reached over and supported the Abbot by the upper arm on his far side also, Monsignor Cabrera, who was as elderly as his old friend, stepped away to rest a shoulder against a nearby wall.

Soon after Alvarez, Alicia, and Ellen one-by-one arrived at the bottom of the stairs, Brother Emilio, returning with the pitcher of cool water, encountered the assemblage and halted before us with questioning eyes.

"Brother Emilio, will you be so kind as to manage the doors for us?" Monsignor Cabrera requested. "The Abbot wishes to rest in his chair."

Alvarez took the Monsignor's place for the remainder of the Abbot's assisted journey to the dining hall, which necessarily moved at an agonizingly slow pace. Brother Emilio, holding the dull gray metal pitcher in front of him, solemnly led the procession.

***

At the long table inside the dining hall, Brothers Hugo, Carlos, and Rafael rose to their feet at the spectacle coming through the doorway. Breaking off from the processional, Brother Emilio took the pitcher of cool water over to a side table. Alvarez and I, with our charge supported between us, continued on to the Abbot's coveted great chair.

Once we had the Abbot safely nestled onto the well-used cushions that provided merciful comfort against the unyielding hardwood seat and backrest of the intricately carved chair, Alvarez and I stepped away.

Monsignor Cabrera advanced to the Abbot's side and was joined by Brother Emilio, who held a mug that he had just filled with cool water.

"Has the wine in the vessel behind the Abbot's chair been refreshed, today?"

"As always, Monsignor."

Monsignor Cabrera gave Brother Emilio a smile and a paternal squeeze on the shoulder, as he motioned for the other monks to gather in close.

Once they were all grouped around the Abbot, the Monsignor intoned in Spanish, "One's allotted time in this world is blessedly unknowable. However, for some, it can be sensed when it is drawing to a close."

Each of the holy men, plus the Detective Sergeant, traced the sign of the cross lightly over their chests. Alicia, to my surprise, belatedly followed suit, even though she couldn't have known what the Monsignor had said.

The Abbot looked even smaller and frailer within the confines of the large and ornate chair. As best as his crooked fingers would allow, he clutched the worn silver on the downward turn of each armrest. A wisp of a smile graced his sagging face. Then, the old Abbot seemed to lapse into some private inner zone – his eyes open, but not focused on anything in particular.

Phil Dodd, looking as though recently fished from the sea, entered the dining hall. A puddle of water grew at his feet, as he halted and scoped out the situation.

Detective Sergeant Alvarez viewed the new arrival with a frown and a series of spasms near his right eye. "Mr. Dodd, did Detective Montero and Officer Saenz fail to give you a ride back to the General Stationhouse, from the Isla Grande Airport, last evening?"

"As a matter of fact, once they'd taken my gun off me again, they were quite courageous in unlawfully detaining me. However, by the time we got back to the Stationhouse, Randal and Briggs had already become discouraged and left. So, don't blame yourself. You betrayed me as best you could."

Monsignor Cabrera ignored both Alvarez and Dodd, as he took the mug of cool water from Brother Emilio's hands and attempted to wordlessly induce the Abbot to take a sip. But the Abbot paid no attention to the mug. Clearly, he already had the only thing he desired.

The Monsignor spoke a few quiet words to the monks, and they retired back to their seats at the long table. Cabrera moved with them, but only to set the mug down on the table, not to take a seat at it, himself.

"Monsignor Cabrera, the questions that I came all this way to ask of you can be postponed no longer," Alvarez announced in English. "And since I cannot seem to get a word alone with you, I will settle for an open discussion."

In a low voice, Brother Hugo translated for his fellow monks at the long table.

"Let me begin with this," Alvarez went on. "The significance of where everyone was located, both shortly before and exactly at the moment of Mr. Rahim's death, cannot be overstated. Leading up to the time of death, Brother Hugo has told us that he was engaged in feeding the donkey. Brother Rafael and Brother Carlos were preparing food in the kitchen. Monsignor Cabrera and Mr. Dodd were also in the kitchen, at least initially, but soon left through separate doors. Brother Emilio then entered the kitchen with several bottles of wine. He poured the wine from one and a half bottles into a pitcher in preparation to transporting the full pitcher to the dining hall. Alicia Elton was in the guest quarters, on the second floor and across the hall from the Abbot, who was feeling too ill to leave his bedroom. And finally, Mr. Rahim sat here in the dining hall, in the Abbot's chair with his bodyguard at his side. Can we all agree that this is correct?"

"Everyone has a corroborating witness, except Brother Hugo," Dodd said. "But maybe the donkey will vouch for him."

"Are you building a case against Brother Hugo, Mr. Dodd?" Alvarez asked.

"It's Special Agent Dodd, and I am assisting you in your quest for an accurate timeline."

Evidently, Alvarez had a range of scowls. The nastiest one that I'd witnessed to date, he now directed at Phil Dodd, before continuing, "Monsignor Cabrera next appears in the dining hall carrying two mugs of tea. This was, it would seem, not only a rather curious detour from the direct route between the cast iron stove and the Abbot's bedside, but also a detour of some significance that the Monsignor neglected to mention in the statement that he gave to Captain Rivera. It was only through good fortune that I managed to extract this information from the bodyguard."

"You're welcome," Dodd said.

This rated only a single spasm next to Alvarez's eye, as he barreled on, "It was precisely this unreported occurrence, Monsignor, that I wished to discuss with you in private. However, since you forced me into an open discussion of the circumstances surrounding Mr. Rahim's questionable demise, perhaps you would now care to explain to all of us your sin of omission."

The Monsignor gazed steadily at the Detective Sergeant. "It slipped my mind."

Alvarez glared back at him, before turning away to address the rest of the assembly at large. "Then perhaps it needs to be emphasized just how significant that little detour in Monsignor Cabrera's journey with the two mugs of tea actually was – given that I now have the bodyguard's statement that Monsignor Cabrera gave one of those mugs of tea to Mr. Rahim." Alvarez's eyes returned to the Monsignor, as he added, "A mug of tea that would prove to be Jaspar Rahim's last drink on this earth."

The Monsignor's countenance remained unfazed by the Detective Sergeant's implication. And now Alvarez abruptly swung his focus onto Phil Dodd.

"During this crucial time, you, Mr. Dodd, had also departed from the kitchen, although your exit was through the door leading to the entrance hallway. And from that moment, up until shortly after Mr. Rahim's death, your actions and behavior still remain an open question. Would you care to enlighten us all, at this time, Mr. Dodd?"

"I was on my way up to the guest quarters to collect Alicia and take her to lunch down in Luquillo," Dodd said. "I've told you that more than once."

"Alicia Elton," Alvarez kept his eyes on Dodd, "did Mr. Dodd at any time actually arrive at the guest quarters to take you to lunch?"

Alicia also looked directly at Dodd. "No, he did not."

"Thus, despite what Mr. Dodd claims," Alvarez said, "for the critical period immediately before Mr. Rahim unaccountably died, we have no knowledge, at all, of where Mr. Dodd was, or what he was doing."

Dodd lifted his hands and let them fall back to his sides. "There's no getting through to this guy."

Alvarez spun back to Cabrera, "I now ask you, Monsignor, did you offer the tea to Mr. Rahim, or did Mr. Rahim request it?"

"Communicating with Mr. Rahim was difficult at best. Sadly, my French is rudimentary." Cabrera spoke leisurely, as though recalling some long ago event. "I do now recall that Mr. Rahim asked what type of tea it was and that we then became engaged in a rather confusing discussion in French about tea in general. But whether, during this discussion, he requested the tea, or I offered it to him, or perhaps even if it was merely a result of a miscommunication, I cannot recollect."

"Ah, I see," Alvarez said with a nod, as though he'd received a useful response. "So, Monsignor, after concluding your business with Mr. Rahim, you next proceeded with the remaining mug of tea up to the Abbot's room. Is that correct?"

"That is correct."

"Unfortunately," Alvarez spoke with a note of regret, "when asked about this visit, the Abbot could not recall whether or not he drank a mug of tea at all that morning. However, the Puerto Rico Police do know that an empty mug, a single empty mug, was still on the nightstand up in the Abbot's bedroom, when we arrived

318

for our investigation. So, I will accept the probability that Monsignor Cabrera did, indeed, sit with the Abbot, if only briefly, while the Abbot drank his tea. And that sometime after this brief visit, Monsignor Cabrera departed from the monastery."

The Detective Sergeant took a moment for a quick visual survey of all those present in the dining hall, before continuing, "Meanwhile, down in this dining hall, Mr. Rahim has finished the tea that the Monsignor had handed to him, and the bodyguard has taken the empty mug from Mr. Rahim's hand and placed it on the long table. Brother Emilio now enters the dining hall and completes his daily ritual of changing out the wire in the peculiar container at the back of the Abbot's chair. We have confirmed this with the bodyguard. And, having completed his ritual, Brother Emilio leaves the dining hall. Then approximately ten minutes later, Jaspar Rahim, while sitting in the Abbot's great chair, convulses and dies."

Ellen emitted a slight whimper.

Alvarez quickly spun his head to locate the source of the reaction, but seeing that it was only Ellen, he merely looked annoyed.

"Finding that he could not revive Mr. Rahim," Alvarez went on, "the bodyguard cries out in his strange native language, whereupon Brother Hugo and Mr. Dodd are the first to respond. Is this correct, Brother Hugo?"

"Yes," Brother Hugo answered, "Then, during the time that Mr. Dodd and I were examining Mr. Rahim's body, Brother Emilio also rushed in. I sent him upstairs to inform the Abbot."

"Ah yes," Alvarez said. "I do recall, from Brother Emilio's statement, that he had returned to the kitchen with a pitcher of old wine and was washing his hands there prior to lunch, when he heard the bodyguard yelling. And for your part, Brother Hugo, you had just entered the main building on your way to wash up for lunch, yourself, when you were diverted by the bodyguard's cries. That was in your statement, was it not?"

"Yes, I was just approaching the interior patio area from the rear of the building."

"Very well. But now we come once again to Mr. Dodd - excuse me - *Special Agent* Dodd," Alvarez overemphasized the title. "In our interview, you stated that you were part way up the stairs, when you heard the bodyguard shouting."

"On my way up to get Alicia. That is entirely correct."

"Was this the same stairway that Monsignor Cabrera used to take the second mug of tea up to the Abbot and the same stairway that the Monsignor shortly thereafter descended on his way to exiting the monastery?" Alvarez raised his eyebrows beyond the top of his wire-rims.

"I bumped into Monsignor Cabrera, just as he was leaving by the front door." Dodd spoke the words off-handedly.

"What!" The outside edge of Alvarez's eye twitched furiously. "You are just informing me of this now?"

"I don't think it ever came up before," Dodd said. "And besides, no one was questioning that the

Monsignor had left the building after tea time with the Abbot."

"Is this true, Monsignor?" Alvarez swung to face the priest. "Did you see Mr. Dodd on your way out?"

"Mr. Dodd was there by the front door. Yes, I do remember that. I assumed that he was waiting for Mrs. Elton. Is it important?"

Alvarez clasped the balding crown of his head with both hands for a few moments, before letting them fall to his sides. "It does not matter," he then concluded. "It nonetheless leaves a vast amount of Mr. Dodd's time unaccounted for."

"I think 'vast' might be an overstatement," Dodd put in.

But Alvarez was already on to another point. "Now, let us take a moment to corroborate something that Mr. Dodd related to me on our way to meet the Engineman's plane. Mr. Dodd stated that he clearly saw an empty mug sitting on the long table, when he and Brother Hugo entered this dining hall in response to the bodyguard's call for help. Brother Hugo, do you also remember the mug being there?"

"No. But we were concentrating on Mr. Rahim. I may not have noticed it."

"Well, I can tell you that the mug was definitely *not* there, when the police arrived." Alvarez then performed a slow sweep of the faces in the room, while asking, "Now what could have happened to that mug?"

No one offered the Detective Sergeant an answer. Even Dodd let it pass – holding his firepower in reserve, I supposed, for his anticipated one-on-one with the ex-Navy Seal.

Alvarez soldiered on, "In any case, we do know that Mr. Rahim did drink a mug of tea and that the empty mug did mysteriously disappear." Alvarez's eyes now pierced through his wire-rimmed lenses directly at Monsignor Cabrera, as he asked, "How can I help but suspect that Jaspar Rahim was poisoned?"

Receiving not a glimmer of response from Monsignor Cabrera, Alvarez turned away to announce to all present, "In another hour or so, the hurricane will pass. As soon as the cellular towers start working again, I intend to call for the local police in Luquillo to assist me in searching every square inch of the monastery grounds and performing a search of each person here for poisons, medications, or anything noxious that could have been stirred into Mr. Rahim's final mug of tea."

"A little late," Dodd observed.

"Can I be sure of that, Mr. Dodd? I can have toxicology results almost immediately, if I give the Assistant Director one specific item to test for. And is it not abundantly clear," Detective Sergeant Alvarez started building to a crescendo, his outstretched index finger pointed to where the Abbot now sat, "that a poisoned mug of tea caused an innocent, unsuspecting human being sitting in that large ornate chair to seize up, gripped with the realization of his own impending fate, and then to slump over dead?"

As if on cue, the old Abbot slumped over in his great chair, dead.

Chapter 17

For a man of his size, Brother Hugo was surprisingly quick in rushing to catch the Abbot, before he tumbled onto the floor. As Brother Hugo gently raised the Abbot back into a sitting position, Monsignor Cabrera was already at the other side of the great chair, feeling for a pulse on the Abbot's wrist and neck. Soon, however, he stepped back and released a sigh.

The other monks were now on their feet. They again gathered tightly around the Abbot's chair. Monsignor Cabrera delivered words of prayer with only enough volume to reach the ears of the four remaining inhabitants of the monastery.

"We should call a doctor," Alvarez said, bringing his phone out. But he must have seen on his screen that there was no signal yet, because he simply glowered at the device and returned it to his pocket.

"Did he just die?" Ellen asked.

Alicia reached for her sister's hand and held it.

Alvarez waited until Monsignor Cabrera finished his prayer, before stepping forward.

"With your permission, Monsignor, in the absence of a physician, it falls to me to verify the death."

The Detective Sergeant pressed his fingertips to the main artery on the Abbot's neck and then pressed his ear to the Abbot's chest.

Dodd came forward with a little penlight and silently offered it to Alvarez. Taking the penlight, the Detective Sergeant thumbed it on. He then delicately lifted one of the Abbot's eyelids, checked for a pupil response to the bright LED beam, and gently closed the lid a moment later.

"I am sorry." Alvarez confirmed the Abbot's death softly in Spanish.

Alvarez stepped back and wordlessly returned the little penlight to Dodd.

Brother Hugo lifted the Abbot from his cherished great chair, cradled the slight weight in his heavily muscled arms, and carried the lifeless body toward the door. Led by Monsignor Cabrera, the other three monks joined in the recession, conveying their beloved Abbot out of the dining hall and, presumably, back up to his bedroom.

"Remind me to never sit in that chair," Ellen said.

Alvarez hammered the buttons of his phone with his index finger, as though the electronics would feel his anger and come to their senses.

While Ellen and Alicia hugged each other for support, Dodd drew me off to one side.

"Get rid of this for me, will you?" Dodd whispered, surreptitiously sliding the bottle of Seconals into my pants pocket. "I'm not sure which direction Alvarez is leaning in. I thought he was fixed on Cabrera. Now, I'm not so sure."

As Alvarez put his phone away, he spotted Dodd and me standing in close proximity. "Mr. Dodd, no fair conferring with Mr. Elton, when I am not looking."

"I was just borrowing his penlight," I said. "I need to go down to the bathroom and use the facilities, but I'm not sure if there's still a light on down there, what with the storm, and all." This was nonsense, of course, since the bathroom light ran off the old truck battery, but I couldn't come up with anything better, on the spot.

Dodd, playing along, handed me his penlight and said to Alvarez, "Maybe, you should worry more about Monsignor Cabrera and Brother Hugo conferring upstairs."

The Detective Sergeant immediately took Dodd's point, saying, "Then come with me, Mr. Dodd. The actions and words of people under stress are always interesting. Let us both go up to the Abbot's room and observe."

Alvarez and Dodd left the dining hall together.

With the dining hall once again quiet, I noticed that a lull in the storm had occurred, and, eerily, that it had coincided with the old Abbot's passing. Now, however, the wind was gradually regaining its intensity, although there was a manifestly different sound to it. The old building began to creak and groan and make loud and sudden banging noises, as the wind began to howl anew. Dust floated down from the high ceiling rafters and the candle flames leaned and flickered toward the opposite direction.

"Francis." Alicia's voice startled me. "I don't care who killed the Arab or what happens to Dodd. Let's just get the damned check signed and get out of here. This place is starting to creep me out."

"The Monsignor will be busy for a while," I said. "And in the meantime, I just need to slip down to the basement bathroom, for a few minutes."

"And Ellen and I just need to not be left behind in the Dining Hall of Death."

"Come with me, then."

Alicia grabbed Ellen in tow, and they followed me, practically on my heels.

***

I led Alicia and Ellen down the wooden stairs toward the gloom and musty smell of the basement bathroom. The structure must have shifted with the last wind change, because the bottom step now emitted a loud loose-nail squeak, in response to my passing weight. I took a sharp left at the shallow lower landing and entered the monks' bathroom. Two squeaks later, Alicia and Ellen joined me.

The aged building's groans were transmitted through the exposed floor joists above us, but the little dome light still valiantly illuminated the trio of toilets and the little pedestal sink.

"Go ahead, Francis. We won't watch," Alicia said.

But a bathroom break was not the real reason I made the trip down to the basement. I played the penlight over the small DC-to-AC inverter and swept its little beam along the two black wires that fed 120-volt power up to the Abbot's fan on the second floor.

As I'd noticed before, the wires disappeared through the 12 by 16 inch opening, created by the removal of a cement block from the top course of the interior wall, where it aligned with an open joist bay immediately above it. The free space of this access opening had been lessened somewhat by the water pipe and drain pipe that passed through at the lower-right corner of the opening.

I had purposely borrowed Dodd's penlight in order to peer into the darkness beyond that opening. Maybe, I'd see nothing. But maybe, I'd confirm something that Brother Carlos had almost, but not quite, said.

"Francis, aren't you going to take care of business?" Alicia asked.

"I came down here to check out an idea I have."

I studied the impression left on the dirt floor right below the missing block. It showed the well-defined corners of a box shape. And the only moveable box shape in the basement was the stack of wooden crates filled with hastily harvested fruits and vegetables.

I carried the top crate over, and set it down on the floor directly beneath the opening in the top of the wall. It fit the pattern pressed in the dirt perfectly.

"*Now*, what are you doing?" Alicia demanded.

"I just want to take a look into that opening up there."

I avoided stepping on the harvested vegetables, by placing my feet on the two front corners of the crate to raise myself up high enough to look into the opening.

Even with the highly focused beam of Dodd's penlight, it was difficult to pick out a coil of black wire lying on the dirt floor of the crawlspace, about three feet in front of me. Had it not been for the glint of freshly exposed copper, where a few inches of the black insulation had been stripped away, I might have missed seeing any wire at all.

Also I noticed that there were actually two stripped wire ends, laying on the top of the coil, and by scanning with the narrow beam, I could just make out that two wires trailed off from the bottom of the coil and continued straight away from me along the bare soil of the crawlspace, until they disappeared into the darkness beyond the reach of the pocket penlight's candlepower. Visually gauging the tight space between the bare soil, along which the wires were strung out, and the roughly-hewn floor joists close above, it was apparent that for someone who was not a reptile to move within the crawlspace, that person would have to be pretty damned determined – not to mention also being immune to claustrophobia.

"I've changed my mind," Alicia said. "I think being uncomfortable up in the creepy dining hall is preferable to being uncomfortable down in a underground men's room."

"It smells bad, too," Ellen added.

I reached in, as far as I could, for the coil of wires, but it lay too deep within the crawlspace. And in no fashion could I contort my arms and shoulders enough to even touch the coil with my fingertips. The plastic pipes that narrowed the opening were just enough to defeat me. I jumped down off the crate.

After attempting to brush the dirt off my damp shirt – and succeeding only in smearing it – I explained, "I'm trying to get at a pair of black wires whose ends I see laying coiled up in the crawlspace, but I can't reach them."

"Do you realize how dumb that sounds?" Alicia said. "What do you want them for?"

"I'm fairly sure I know why the wires are up in there," I said. "A lighting project that was scrapped a while back. And it plays into an idea I have. But I can't get enough of me into the opening."

"So, I guess we'll never know." Alicia didn't sound especially disheartened.

But I was now once again visually gauging – this time, the shoulder widths of the two women.

"No, Francis. Don't even look at me." Alicia was quick to guess what I had in mind. She laid the folder containing her report on the sink and cupped her hands under her breasts. "I've got these."

We both looked at Ellen, who then caught on. "Hey, I've got boobs too."

"I haven't forgotten," I assured her. "But you're the smallest of the three of us. You just need to get part way in and grab the wire. We'll hold you steady on the crate."

"No. This is crazy. And I'll get my blouse dirty."

I took my shirt off, and held it out to Ellen. She gave me an exaggerated mean face, but put my shirt on over her blouse and buttoned it up.

I brought over another crate and stacked it on top of the first one. Then Alicia and I lifted Ellen up and positioned her feet onto the opposing edges of the top crate.

Ellen directed the beam of the penlight into the hole. "I see the coiled wire. Lift me a little more, so I can get it."

Alicia and I each took one of Ellen's legs and lifted. The top half of Ellen disappeared into the hole and I could feel her struggling.

"Okay. Got it."

As we guided her feet back onto the crates, Ellen slid out of the hole with a coil of black wire in her hand. She let it drop, but it fell only about a foot and hung in a suspended tangle. Alicia and I lifted her down.

"Next time I need something, Francis," Ellen's eyes stayed on mine, as she took off my shirt, "all I want to hear from you is 'Yes, ma'am'."

Ellen used my shirt to wipe her hands and arms, before throwing it, in a wad, back at me.

Without comment, I restored the soiled shirt to my own torso and returned my attention to the wires. The tangled coil, hanging by the two continuing lengths of wire that ran under the rest of the building, were either connected to something at the other end, or ran for some serious length along the dirt and rubble under the floorboards. Otherwise the weight of the tangle would have pulled the rest of the wire out. I gave the tangled coil a downward pull. It moved with noticeable resistance, but it didn't jerk to a stop. So, the wires were probably unconnected at the other end. Which made sense, if these were the wires for the abandoned lighting project.

It didn't take me long to straighten out the loose tangle and drape the resultant lengths of wire over toward the mini-power station. There was more than enough to reach.

"If you're not going to pee, let's go," Alicia said. "You can play with the wires some other time."

"Just another minute."

I coiled the wire back up neatly, raised the coil above my head, and blindly placed it back just inside the opening.

"I did have one other reason to come down here," I said, as I slid a hand into my pant's pocket.

I pulled out the little plastic bottle of Seconals and started twisting off the cap, as I moved toward the row of toilets.

"Wait." Alicia caught me by the arm. "Are those the barbiturates? You can't flush those. You could be destroying evidence. That's got to be at least a felony."

"Oh my God, you can't risk it, Francis," Ellen said. "I know he's your friend, but—"

A loud squeak drew all our attention toward the stairs. Detective Sergeant Alvarez stepped into the basement bathroom, his gun out and leveled at my chest.

"Listen to the ladies, Mr. Elton," Alvarez said. "Step away from the toilets, or I will drop you where you stand."

Chapter 18

I moved back from the row of toilets. Keeping his gun arm retracted and his semiautomatic pointed at my center mass, Detective Sergeant Alvarez stepped in just close enough to reach out and snatch the bottle of Seconals from my extended hand.

Again the bottom step loudly squeaked, and a second later, Brother Hugo entered. His presence disturbed me, even further. I couldn't think what it meant.

But Alvarez barely glanced in the big monk's direction, before explaining, "When I announced my intention to search the entire monastery and everyone in it, I had hoped to provoke someone with a guilty conscience into action."

Alvarez holstered his gun, giving him a free hand to complete the removal of the aspirin bottle's cap and receive a couple reddish-orange capsules, shaken into his palm for inspection. He grunted with apparent satisfaction and continued, "Therefore, when Brother Hugo quietly left the solemn group, gathered around the late Abbot up in his bedroom, I followed him. But when I saw where Brother Hugo was going, I overtook him at the top of the steps leading down to this bathroom – a toilet being the disposal unit of choice, for eliminating small incriminating evidence. It was then that I heard your voices, below us. Specifically, I heard the word 'barbiturates.' Happily, the ancient building's loud protests against the storm assisted my stealth, as I hurried down the stairs. I do so love to catch culprits red-handed."

Alvarez scooped the capsules from his palm, using the mouth of the aspirin bottle, and restored the cap. He produced a narrow, paper bag from his trouser pocket, dropped the little bottle inside, and penned a notation on the outside. The bagged and tagged bottle disappeared into Alvarez's front trouser pocket. It was evidence now.

"Mr. Elton, you will either tell me who gave you the barbiturates and instructed you to dispose of them, or I will have you jailed for the unlawful possession of narcotics."

Now here was a threat with some teeth to it. But still, I hesitated. I almost had it figured out – how Rahim was killed – in theory, anyway. But I needed time. It would require major physical proof to actually convince anyone. And if I now confirmed to Alvarez that the pills were Dodd's, he would jump on that single fact and run with it. Any contrary solution that I later presented would be summarily dismissed, just as he'd dismissed the Baghdad battery. I willed myself to think faster.

"Tell him, Francis," Alicia ordered. "Tell him, or I will."

Alvarez turned to Alicia. "Did you actually see who gave Mr. Elton the aspirin bottle that contains the barbiturates?"

"Well no, but—"

"Hearsay and conjecture do me no more good than fingerprints on a container with a misleading label. Prosecuting Attorneys do not like evidence that can easily be thrown out." Alvarez turned back to me. "I am testing your willingness to testify truthfully in court, Mr. Elton. Your freedom depends on it. Give me the name."

Pushing myself to think faster just made me dizzy. I knew what parts had to be there to make it all work. But I needed time to confirm their existence.

"I am not a patient man, Mr. Elton."

"I will give you the name on one condition."

"You are not in a position to dictate terms."

"Look, you recruited me to help you find Rahim's killer. So give me some time to show you what I believe really happened. Just give me until the phones start working again. You can't get the toxicologist's report before then anyway and—"

And then I had it. The connection that I sensed was lurking somewhere in the back of my brain now leaped to the forefront. When I was a teenager, fooling around in my father's basement workshop, I'd powered up a lemon and produced little jets of steam and a flurry of sharp little snaps, as though my mother were making popcorn, up in her kitchen. What phantom neuron triggered this memory, I couldn't guess. But it made me bolder.

"Detective Sergeant," I said, "Jaspar Rahim was not drugged or poisoned with anything. And the bodyguard never left his side. I will convince you."

Alvarez turned to Brother Hugo. I couldn't see the questioning look on Alvarez's face, but I knew it was there, because Brother Hugo raised his hand to pantomime a double-touch of an index finger to his temple, as his assessment of my grasp on reality.

Alvarez next tore a tissue of toilet paper from a nearby roll, removed his wire-rimmed glasses, and slowly polished them.

After a half minute of polishing, Alvarez held his glasses at chest level and looked at me without the aid of corrective lenses. "Mr. Elton, if it is Mr. Dodd that you are protecting, you are a fool. If it is Monsignor Cabrera, your faith may lead you to think it a noble gesture to protect a Man of God. But the Law does not allow for noble gestures. We must follow the Law, no matter where it leads us and regardless of how uncomfortable we may feel about the outcome."

Alvarez raised his glasses to the dome light for a brief inspection, before sliding them back onto his nose and moving on to another threat. "And let me be plain. When I descend this mountain today, I will do so with the murderer in my custody. If it turns out that I have arrested both the murderer and his accomplice, so much the better." The Detective Sergeant's brows lowered and drew closer together. "Do not miss your chance, Mr. Elton, to align yourself on the side of the Law."

But it was too late for threats now. I'd already decided to play out my hand. "Just let me show you the significance of some wires I found."

"Some wires that you have found." Alvarez again looked to Brother Hugo, as though beseeching him to witness the sort of thing a Detective Sergeant has to deal with.

But instead of rejecting my appeal out of hand, Alvarez pulled out his phone and stared at the screen. I stayed quiet, noting Alvarez's tightened lips, as he put the unfaithful device away.

"All right, Mr. Elton," the Detective Sergeant said with a sigh. "Your earlier demonstration, the one where you conjured a battery from pocket change, was entertaining. I will admit it. And since it appears that we have some time before I can communicate with the toxicologist, show me your fascinating wires, Mr. Elton. Delight me again."

"Francis." Alicia's eyes signaled a mixture of disapproval and warning. "This had better be good."

Chapter 19

In the musty-smelling basement bathroom, four expectant faces waited for me to perform. I was used to troubleshooting machinery while people stood around and watched, but this was different. Yes, I was confident about the basic principles involved, but still, there were those elements that I wished I'd had the chance to verify beforehand.

"The most relevant thing," I began, "is the presence of the two wires running under the floorboards of this building. If you will take this penlight and climb up on these crates, Detective Sergeant, you'll see a pair of wires running from where they are coiled near the opening to some distant location under the back portion of this building."

Alvarez looked up to where I was pointing, then down at the stacked pair of crates, and finally back at me. "Tell me where the wires lead."

"I believe they lead to the dining hall. That's what Brother Carlos told me. That's right, isn't it, Brother Hugo?"

Alvarez turned to the big monk, and I held my breath. Brother Carlos had not actually said that the wiring for lights in the dining hall had already been run.

"A pair of wires were strung under the floorboards in anticipation of installing a few small lights in the dining hall, along the wall where the paintings are hung," Brother Hugo said. "They were to be powered by the truck battery, like the dome light here in the bathroom. The project was abandoned, after the announcement that the monastery was to be sold. The wires were left where they were, forgotten."

Alvarez turned back to me. "I presume there is more."

"With your permission," I said, "I would like to pull the two wires out from under the floor and lay them out, going up the stairs and along the top of the floor, all the way to the dining hall, so I can demonstrate to you that these wires were not forgotten about, entirely."

"Do what you wish with them," Alvarez said. "I cannot see how discarded wiring for automobile dome lights are of any importance at all."

I set the top crate to one side, stepped up on the remaining crate, and grabbed the coiled wires from the opening. Stepping down, I unwound the coil of paired wires, laying them along the basement floor, until I was holding the two free ends, each stripped of the final couple of inches of black insulation to expose its inner copper strands. I laid the wire ends on top of the little power inverter, for the moment, and returned to where the two wires emerged from the opening above the crate.

In successive pulls, I began drawing the rest of the paired wires out of the opening, a few feet of wire at a time, draping them in big loops over my arm, as I did so. It took almost a full minute to complete this operation, and I was greatly encouraged when I saw that the far ends of the two wires had also been stripped of the last three inches of their insulation. If they hadn't been, I might as well have stopped the demonstration right there and then.

I slid the gathered loops of wire off my forearm, laid them on the floor, and returned to the little power inverter, where I picked up the other ends of the two wires.

Holding the wire ends on display, I addressed the onlookers, "I'm sure you've noticed that the insulation at both ends of the two wires has been stripped off. But further notice that the wires, encased in the plastic insulation, are actually made up of many individual thin strands of copper. That's for flexibility. But, look how the bared ends of the two groups of strands, that I'm holding here, have been twisted to make each more solid and stiff. Like someone was testing the circuit and wanted to make the bared ends more rigid, in order to insert them into the receptacle slots of a power source.

I tapped the heat-dissipating fins on top of the little power inverter, adding, "Such as this DC-to-AC inverter that changes an old pickup truck's twelve-volt battery power to the hundred-and-twenty-volt household current, needed to power the fan up in the Abbot's room."

"Did you test these wires, Brother Hugo?" Alvarez asked.

"It was some time ago that the wires were run." Brother Hugo paused, as though to think back. "I do remember that we were concerned about a loss of voltage level, using battery power with such long, slender wires. We were worried that, after all our hard work, the new bulbs might glow more dimly than the candles they were replacing. But I do not remember any test, such as Mr. Elton is describing."

But I remembered what Brother Carlos had said about the proposed electric lights in the dining hall – that Brother Hugo hadn't bartered rum for the inverter solely to accommodate the Abbot's fan. Brother Hugo wasn't exactly lying, but he sure wasn't coming clean either.

"Your revelations are getting you nowhere, Mr. Elton," Alvarez said.

It was time to just do it and not worry about the consequences of being wrong. I shoved one twisted wire end into each power slot of the unoccupied half of the 120-volt duplex receptacle on the inverter's front panel, just below where the wiring for the Abbot's fan was plugged in. Then I picked up the wire loops that I'd pulled out from beneath the floorboards and hung them again on my left forearm.

"Francis, are those wires you're holding live now?" Alicia asked. "Are you crazy?"

"I'll be okay, as long as I don't come into contact with both wire ends at the same time."

I kept the two live wire ends separated by holding the black insulation of each just behind their three inches of exposed copper, clamped between different pairs of fingers on my left hand. This separation maintained a relatively safe, two-finger-width distance between them. To maintain a tight grasp on the wires, I clenched my hand into a fist – which made the two protruding sheaves of copper strands look like antennae on a giant bug head.

With my right hand, I paid out each successive loop off my forearm, lifting the loop carefully over the electrically live antennae of the bug head, as I walked backward toward the stairs and then step-by-step up.

The others followed me as a column, trooping up the basement stairs. I noticed that, except for Brother Hugo, they all were careful to avoid stepping on the wires, even though there was no danger.

Our odd column moved through the empty room above the basement and into the entrance hallway. Over my shoulder I saw Phil Dodd, Monsignor Cabrera, Brother Emilio, and Brother Carlos in their own column descending the stairway from the second floor. Evidently, Brother Rafael had remained in the bedroom to watch over the deceased Abbot.

I also noticed that Dodd had stopped part way down the stairway, keeping tight to the railing and allowing others to pass behind him. And I could feel his eyes observing me, as I continued to carefully pay out each loop of wire.

"Francis," Dodd's voice came from above me, "this is not what we discussed."

I paused in my backward journey, but instead of responding to Dodd, I asked in Spanish, "Brother Carlos, as a favor, would you bring the Abbot's fan down to the dining hall? With these wires, I will make it operate there. With so many of us all in one room, the fan's breeze will provide us with some relief, much as it did for your Abbot."

Brother Carlos wordlessly turned and climbed back up the stairs.

"Detective Sergeant," Monsignor Cabrera had also taken an interval in his descent, "is this curious business being done with your approval?"

341

"Mr. Elton wishes to convince me that I am wrong to think that a deadly drug was stirred into Mr. Rahim's tea," Alvarez said. "I am indulging him. At least for the time it takes the cellular towers to return to service."

I saw Monsignor Cabrera exchange looks with Brother Hugo, but he said nothing further.

And evidently, Dodd decided that my casting doubt on the poisoned tea theory could only work in his favor, because he now descended the rest of the stairs, shouldered his way through the crowd, strode purposefully down the hallway, and held open the door that led out onto the central patio.

Continuing to pay out the loops of wire, I proceeded, still walking backward, down the hallway toward the open door. The rest of the gathering followed en masse behind me.

Out in the more open area of the patio, where the roar of rushing wind had now noticeably diminished, my position within the moving column continually fell back, as one-by-one each of the others overtook me. Thus, I became the last to filter into the dining hall.

Brother Hugo, Brother Emilio, and Monsignor Cabrera formed one loose group. Dodd, Alicia, and Ellen formed another. Detective Sergeant Alvarez stood off to one side, again checking for a signal on his phone.

The load on my arm had become progressively lighter and now had almost no discernable weight to it, at all. I began to worry that, because I'd added extra distance to the run by having first to jog in the wrong direction over to the basement stairs, I was going to run short of wire. In fact, I would have, if my destination had been the original termination point of the wires – all the way over to the wall where the old depressing paintings hung. But, to my relief, I had about two feet of wire length left when I stopped at the rear of the Abbot's chair and laid the two bare wire ends on the wood floor with a prudent distance between them.

However, my relief was immediately replaced with anxiety. Alvarez now held his phone to his ear and was speaking into it. The cell towers were operating again, and I was out of time. I could only hope that Alvarez would become absorbed by the information he was receiving, and I could quietly proceed with my setup unnoticed.

Brother Carlos arrived with the fan from the Abbot's room. I removed the fatigued cushion from the seat of the Abbot's chair and had Brother Carlos place the fan on the resulting bare wood.

I then returned to the rear of the great chair, dropped to one knee, and studied the floor beneath the Baghdad battery. I was missing one last detail that I knew had to be there. And within the shadows and among the litter of dust balls, bits of wood, and a fuzzy length of dark thread, I spotted it.

The little hole bored down through the wood plank floor was only about a quarter of an inch in diameter, but a small passage through the floorboards was all that was necessary.

Alvarez closed his cell phone. "I have spoken to the Assistant Director of Toxicology. He is just finishing up with his verification of the initial drug screen from the preliminary autopsy report. He will next test a sample of Mr. Rahim's brain tissue. We will have his results very soon."

"By now, his tests will probably indicate that Rahim overdosed on embalming fluid," Dodd said.

"Let us not be diverted by a discussion of the relative competency of our two organizations," Alvarez said. "Especially since yours doesn't even seem capable of controlling one of its own."

I blocked out the verbal exchanges, while I concentrated on using my Swiss Army knife to cut the plug off the fan's power cord and then to make an initial slice to separate the bonded pairing of the cord's two insulated wires. I finished separating them into two single wires by ripping them the rest of the way apart by hand, all the way up to the fan's base.

"Your poisoned tea theory is stupid," Dodd's voice broke through my concentration. "What was it? Only like fifteen minutes after Monsignor Cabrera left Rahim with his tea that the bodyguard started shouting?"

"I regret that I had already departed the monastery," Monsignor Cabrera inserted, "before any shouting had begun. Had I not, perhaps the situation would not have escalated beyond rational control. But I can state that I spent about ten cordial minutes with the Abbot, between taking leave from Mr. Rahim and passing you at the front door on my way out, if that helps any."

"Yes, Monsignor, it does," Dodd said. "Because after being alerted by the bodyguard's hue and cry, Brother Hugo and I almost simultaneously arrived at the dining hall in what? Half a minute?"

Dodd looked to Brother Hugo and waited for him to finish translating for his fellow monks.

"That seems about right," Brother Hugo finally replied.

"So, let's be generous," Dodd said, "Let's say twenty minutes from the time Monsignor Cabrera last saw Rahim alive, until Brother Hugo and I found Rahim already dead. Not just experiencing symptoms. Dead. No pulse, no breathing, no eye movement, nothing. Now, what the hell could Jaspar Rahim have possibly ingested from that tea that would have killed him so quickly, without it being something that would also chemically burn the crap out of the lining of his mouth and esophagus?"

Having stripped six inches of insulation from the ends of the fan's two separated cord wires, I splayed the resultant thin, stranded, copper wires of each and press-formed them, one onto each silver-plated handhold of the chair's armrests.

"Before we become mired in such variables as speed of toxic effect," Alvarez said, "perhaps, I should mention that I suggested to the toxicologist that he concentrate foremost on substances that cause death by asphyxiation – such as an overdose of barbiturates."

I looked up from my work just in time to see Alvarez closely observing Alicia and Ellen, as he said the word "barbiturates." I also saw both women turn and stare directly at Phil Dodd.

Alvarez smiled. "What do you say to *that*, Mr. Dodd?"

"Barbiturates? Are you kidding me?" Dodd performed an eye roll. "You actually suggested to the toxicologist that his techs missed a common drug like that? Like maybe they can't run a routine drug screen, for God sakes? I'll bet that toxicologist chewed your ass just for even asking. You were better off with your rare jungle poison fantasy."

A vein at the side of Alvarez's left eye danced with rapid pulsations, as he fought for control. The Detective Sergeant paced over to where I now knelt at the rear of the Abbot's chair and worked with the two wires I'd strung up the stairs and along the floor from the basement bathroom. Alvarez's exhalations of breath came out in venting sputters, during the few moments he observed me from above, as I bent the bared copper end of each electrically live wire into the form of a hook, before laying one apart from the other on the floor again.

As Alvarez paced away from me, I finally stood, ready for my demonstration, hoping that my opportunity had not already passed.

Having recovered his mental footing, Alvarez now stated, "Drug tests can produce false negatives, as any professional criminal investigator would well know. Especially, with trace amounts. Also, we have been informed that Jaspar Rahim had a bad heart. So, even a relatively tiny amount—"

"And *when* did you find out he had a bad heart?" Dodd demanded. "There weren't any medications in his pockets, or in his hotel room. I know. I looked before you did. I went straight to Rahim's hotel, while you were off joy-riding in the helicopter. So, we both found out that Rahim had a bad heart only yesterday, from the bodyguard, through the Engineman's translations. And furthermore, how do you know that by 'bad heart', the bodyguard didn't mean 'evil heart'? You know, as in 'he treated his employees like crap,' or 'he didn't give a damn who got killed, so long as he made money off the deal.' So how could the murderer, days before, have possibly guessed that Rahim's heart had something medically wrong with it and then somehow calculate just what tiny amount of whatever drug would tip the scales and instantly kill him?"

When Alvarez didn't immediately respond, an emboldened Phil Dodd skated out to where the ice was, I thought, much thinner.

"And I don't think the bodyguard is such a reliable witness anyway," Dodd said. "It's pretty plain that he was covering up for having slipped off to take a leak, or something, and when he got back, the guy he's supposed to be keeping alive is dead. Mostly what we got from the big oaf was some pipe-dream about the blowing wind and a far-away battle."

Because I'd written down in my notes the translation of the bodyguard's responses to Dodd's questions, I remembered the exact words. "The bodyguard said that when Rahim's soul left his body, he could hear the wind blowing through the caves in the mountains of their homeland and the crackle of far-off machinegun fire from some distant battle."

That earned me quizzical looks from all the English speakers in the room.

"Yeah, that's wonderful." Dodd batted it away. "What's that from, the Koran or something?"

"Even a Christian knows that the Koran would contain no mention of machineguns," Alvarez said.

"Okay, Ali Baba and the Forty Thieves then. The important thing is that the bodyguard said nothing about Rahim getting all dreamy-eyed from a sedative, or puking and choking on some exotic jungle-plant concoction."

With exaggerated weariness in his voice, Alvarez said, "I take it, Mr. Dodd, that you have your own scenario of the murder."

"As a matter of fact, I do. But, unlike you, I like to have my facts all nailed down first, and I've got a couple more things to check out. Plus, unlike you, I'm not up against a deadline to arrest somebody – anybody – today. In fact, I have no intention whatsoever to arrest anyone at all. Not my jurisdiction. I'd just like to get the story straight, that's all."

Dodd didn't look Brother Hugo's way, but he sent the message.

"And you, Mr. Elton," Alvarez now returned his attention to me, "with your theory of the black wires. If Special Agent Dodd can think of nothing compelling to challenge my conclusions, perhaps you can explain the point of your curious activity."

All right, here was my chance. And although I was fully conscious that it might all blow up in my face – quite literally, in fact – it was too late now, not to be all in.

"As I said before," I began, "Jaspar Rahim was not drugged or poisoned. And the bodyguard never left him alone in the dining hall."

"Francis," Alicia broke in. "None of this is our business. Just focus on why we came up here today. Let them arrest whoever they want."

"No, that's all right," Alvarez said. "Go ahead, Mr. Elton. Do not let the inferences derived by a seasoned homicide detective dissuade you. Tell us what you think you have deduced on your own."

I knew Alvarez was setting me up to look like a dope for marching brashly into his field of expertise and then flopping miserably. But, no way could he trip me up, if I kept to my own turf.

"Okay," I said, stepping to the front of the Abbot's chair and pointing, "the fan on the seat here is going to stand in for Jaspar Rahim. The fan's motor will be his heart and the fan's power cord wires will be his blood stream in his hands and arms, as they lay on the worn silver veneer covering the armrests. So, think of the area where the bare copper wire strands contact the silver veneer as his skin contact."

I returned to the rear of the Abbot's chair and picked up the two live wires by their black insulation, one in each hand.

"Sometime before the day Rahim was killed, these two wires were poked up from below through a little hole that someone has drilled through the floorboards, here." I tapped the toe of my shoe beneath the Baghdad battery. "Looking closely, you'd see fresh wood on the sides of the hole. On the morning that Rahim was killed, each wire was attached to one of the opposing terminals of this homemade battery, installed behind the Abbot's chair. But the other ends of the two wires were not yet plugged into the one-hundred-twenty-volt outlet on the power inverter down in the basement. Not yet. That would happen sometime after Rahim had finished his tea. However, they *are* plugged in now. And to save time, I will hook them up live. The end effect will be precisely the same."

I hung one live wire by its hooked bare end onto the thick copper strand that connected the positive terminal of the Baghdad battery to the hammered-silver veneer covering one armrest. Before I hung the other live wire onto the other thick copper strand connecting the negative terminal to the silver veneer on the opposite armrest, I said a silent prayer to the ghost of Nikola Tesla. And just as I made contact with the second hooked wire, I witnessed an assuring spark as his answer.

Within the Baghdad battery, the surges of alternating current repeatedly arced through the wine between the copper tube and the galvanized steel pipe, producing a furious staccato of pops and snaps – a miniature version of the high power lines out on Highway 3, thrashing and arcing in the throes of the hurricane. The energy from the snapping arcs soon heated the wine to a boil, and the resultant steam rushed up through the nested pipes of the Baghdad battery, producing a low octave moan, as though from a breathy bassoon.

"The wind blowing through the caves." Ellen lightly clapped her hands with childlike delight. "And the popping noise is the crackle of distant machine gun fire."

"Exactly," I said. "This is what the bodyguard heard. And what sounded to our ears like Arab poetry was just the bodyguard's attempt to explain these odd accompanying sounds, when he believed he was witnessing Jaspar Rahim's soul rising to heaven in a wisp of steam. He was simply referencing sounds he was familiar with, growing up in some remote mountainous tribal region. I mean, it sounds like popcorn popping to me, but I didn't come of age in a war zone."

I moved around to the front of the great chair. "And this is the electrical current that surged through Rahim's heart and in a matter of seconds killed him."

I flipped the switch at the base of the Abbot's fan, and the blades took off spinning. I looked toward Alicia, as strands of hair blew across her pretty face – a face that also held a smile and approving eyes for me. I felt like, for once, I'd chalked up a win.

"If you are asserting that Mr. Rahim was electrocuted," Alvarez said, "the Medical Examiner would surely have seen burn marks on his hands and arms from the electricity."

"Rahim would not necessarily get a burn." I was back to business. "He had a huge contact area of metal to skin, and his salty sweat would only help with the energy transfer. With such relatively little resistance, it would take more time for it to get hot enough to burn Rahim's skin. And the electricity didn't need to be on all that long to take him out. When you're that firmly attached to the circuit, it doesn't take many seconds of household current to kill you." With my confidence on the rise, I ventured into less familiar territory. "But sure, at a minimum there'd be redness on the skin under the forearm and on the palms of the hands where Rahim was making contact. But that would have been obscured by the time the Medical Examiner got here, because, after Rahim's heart stopped pumping, the blood would settle, gathering at the low points of his forearms and hands, as they lay on the armrests of the chair."

"You are referring to livor mortis," Alvarez said.

"Okay. I didn't know the term," I said. "But I know that's what happens. So, that's all someone examining the body would see. And as for Rahim's reaction, he stiffened up, because of the electrical current surging through him, contracting his muscles. And yes, his mouth was wide open like he was screaming, because inside his brain, he was screaming his damn head off. But no sound came out, because you need airflow to make a sound, whether you're a bassoon or a businessman. And at that point, Rahim had convulsed and stopped breathing, altogether."

There wasn't going to be any applause drowning out the crackling arcs and the haunting moans from the Baghdad battery. So, I finished with, "Well, anyway, that's all I have."

I stepped back to the Baghdad battery to disconnect the wires. "Oh, one more thing." I checked to see that everyone's eyes were on me and then gave a slight downward jerk to each wire and let it fall to the floor. With the disconnection of the circuit, the wind ceased blowing through the mountain caves, and the distant machineguns fell silent. There was only the diminishing whisper of the fan gradually coasting to a stop. "I could have just as easily pulled these wires off the Baghdad battery from the basement, and made them disappear, down through the little hole."

I didn't feel like trudging all the way down to the basement to pull the wires out the inverter's receptacle. I picked up the two live wires from the floor again and gave fair warning, "A hundred and twenty volts of alternating current is deadly powerful. This going to be loud."

I touched their bare-copper ends together. The resultant flash and bang was like a fired revolver. Everyone in the room jumped – even me. And I knew what was coming.

During the ensuing murmuring and nervous laughter that people engage in, after they've shared a moment of fright, only to find they are safe after all, I touched the two wire ends together once again, just be sure I had successfully tripped the circuit breaker down at the inverter. However, the circuit breaker had done its job, the first time. The bare copper strands were now perfectly harmless.

"Well, Mr. Elton, finish it," Alvarez said. "Who do you believe did this and why?"

"I don't know," I stayed in my lane. "I can only tell you the technical part. I'm not a detective."

"That, at least, is true," Alvarez said. "However, as it happens, I *am* a detective, and I am not convinced. What you are, Mr. Elton, is clever. And that makes me rather suspicious of your little demonstration here. Remember that I have seen you perform an electrical trick once before. The little battery made of coins and wine. You may hold these others in awe, but I will not be deceived by the art of the magician." The Detective Sergeant gestured with a dismissive backhand wave. "This does not persuade me. This is theater. We will wait for the results from the toxicologist."

Chapter 20

Everything had worked, just as I'd imagined it would, and had been summarily dismissed, just as though it hadn't. I dropped the dead wires, their exposed copper sections now blackened and partially melted at the contact points, where I'd shorted out the circuit.

Having dispensed with me, Alvarez now moved around to the other side of the long table to launch a deeper inquiry about times and tea mugs with the Monsignor and the monks, in Spanish.

Phil Dodd joined me at the back of the Abbot's chair. "You said something about a little hole in the floor."

I retrieved Dodd's penlight from my pocket and returned it to him. Dodd dropped to one knee, clicked the penlight on, and aimed it from various angles at the little hole. Dodd then picked up and began examining the length of coarse brown thread that lay among the other bits of litter under the great chair. I left him to ponder its significance and joined Alicia and Ellen.

"You did great, Francis." Ellen patted my arm.

"And to hell with that Detective Sergeant." Alicia kept her voice down. "I mean, the part about it being good theater was true enough, but he just wants *his* idea to be the solution. He's probably told all his policemen friends how he has it all figured out."

I looked back at Phil Dodd. He was standing now, holding the two black wires in one hand and running his penlight over the Baghdad battery with the other. Even though I hadn't convinced Alvarez, maybe my demonstration was, at least, swaying Dodd. And I wondered if, in Dodd's mind, Brother Hugo was about to undergo a secular conversion, from strangler to electrocutioner.

I turned to Alicia. "Maybe we should get that check signed."

"Amen to that."

Alicia and her folder led the way, as the three of us maneuvered around the long table and approached Monsignor Cabrera. When Alvarez came to a pause in whatever he was officiously droning on about, Alicia quietly asked the Monsignor for a moment of his time. Ellen and I followed, as the two of them stepped to the other end of the long table, where Alicia, at last, laid open her folder for Monsignor Cabrera's viewing.

"As you see, Monsignor, on each page there is a photograph and a detailed description of the scene of a painting, along with my assessment of its condition and the estimated cost for its restoration."

Monsignor Cabrera gazed without comment, as Alicia moved page-by-page through her meticulously prepared sheets, stopping only briefly at each.

"I sincerely regret that there was no priceless masterpiece by a world renown artist among this collection." Alicia laid a sympathetic hand on the Monsignor's arm. "Not even a sought-after work by a second tier painter." Her hand left the priest's arm and was back to business, flipping to the final page. "This last page deals with the packing and shipping costs. And here in the folder pocket is the check that your office clerk was kind enough to let me bring to you, all ready for your signature. There's a pen there too."

Without hesitation, Monsignor Cabrera leaned in, slid the check out of the folder pocket, and signed it. As he straightened up and handed Alicia the check, he said, "On behalf of the Archdiocese, I wish to thank you so much for your efforts, under some rather trying circumstances. And although the monastery's future has again entered a time of uncertainty, at least concerning the matter of the artwork, we now know where we stand."

"I enjoyed working with you, Monsignor. And we're so sorry about the passing of the Abbot. I've told Ellen and Francis that he was your lifelong friend."

"It was his time. And he would have been miserable, had he been forced to leave his monastery before his final heartbeat."

"I'm sure there'll be a lovely service at the Cathedral for him," Alicia said. "Regrettably, we can't stay for it."

"I understand completely." Monsignor Cabrera took Alicia's hand and held it between both of his. "And as you are undoubtedly aware, the Catholic Church has also established itself in the faraway metropolis of Chicago. I believe you will find the façade of the Holy Name Cathedral much more artistically pleasing to your finely trained eye."

Alicia smiled. "Whenever I see it, I'm sure to think of you. And I guess it wouldn't hurt for me to view the interior, from time to time."

"Let us settle for that, then," Monsignor Cabrera had the grace to concede.

Alvarez had been eying us from the other end of the table. I walked over to him.

Even though I was pretty sure that Alvarez's pledge to use his influence to get us aboard the first Chicago-bound flight had evaporated as quickly as my passing usefulness, I thought it was worth a nudge.

"Alicia, Ellen, and I will be leaving for Chicago on the first flight we can get aboard."

"Rest assured that I will take it from here," Alvarez said without moving his eyes off of Monsignor Cabrera.

I stepped past Alvarez to speak with Brother Hugo. "If one of you is about to attend to that poor donkey and lead it back up to its shed, I'd be happy to help whoever it is to pack up the shelter on our way down the mountain." I then suggested, "Maybe, Brother Emilio?"

As we stood face-to-face, I sensed that Brother Hugo was taking an estimate of me. He then turned to his two fellow monks. "I think it is time, Brother Carlos, to relieve Brother Rafael from his watch over the body of our Abbot. Brother Emilio, the donkey will wish to be in his stall. Mr. Elton desires to help with the loading, one last time."

Together, Brother Emilio and I walked toward where Alicia and Ellen still stood with Monsignor Cabrera.

The Monsignor stepped forward to intercept us, saying in Spanish, "If you will excuse us for a minute, Brother Emilio, I wish to speak in parting with Mr. Elton, concerning a private matter."

"Of course, Monsignor."

Monsignor Cabrera took me aside, well apart from the others, to a spot beneath one of the dark neglected paintings – the one where Jesus first shoulders his cross. I presumed that I was about to be informed of the Monsignor's displeasure that I had unveiled the actual cause of the Jaspar Rahim's death.

But again Monsignor Cabrera blindsided me. "It was not jealousy."

"Jealousy? Oh, you mean about the divorce and—"

"When you married the beautiful young Alicia, the feeling that you derived was not one of pride in winning her hand, but rather of unworthiness in having won such a great prize. By dissolving the marriage, you freed yourself from the burden of maintaining a supposed undeserved victory. This also freed you to endlessly pursue her, to unceasingly strive to win her over once again. My impression is that you are much more comfortable with this arrangement."

I tried not to let my jaw go slack. "Have you said any of this to Alicia?"

"It is a false conceit to think that she does not already know."

I didn't thank him for the rabbit punch.

"If the two of you are content with this relationship," Monsignor Cabrera concluded, "who among us may say that it is wrong?"

I just stood there, fixed in place.

Thankfully, the Monsignor moved on, "Do you remember our little discussion concerning moral dilemmas, where right and wrong may not be absolutes?"

"I remember you saying I wouldn't find guidance in a technical manual. Why? Am I about to engage in some internal conflict?"

"When you withheld the name of the person who attached the deadly wires to the Abbot's chair, you already entered the arena. I pray that you will find the wisdom—"

"Monsignor!" Sgt. Alvarez raised his voice from the other end of the table. "If you would indulge me, I cannot have people breaking off into little conspiratorial groups, while my investigation is still active. Mr. Elton, were you not just leaving?"

***

Once Brother Emilio and I linked up with Alicia and Ellen, the four of us departed from the dining hall. Just as we entered the hallway, leading to the front door, Phil Dodd came galloping up behind us and grabbed hold of my arm.

"Francis will catch up in a minute," Dodd informed the others.

"We're in hurry to get the hell out of here, Lieutenant," Alicia said. "Whatever you have to say to Francis can be said while we're walking. The little monk can't understand you, and Ellen and I are way past caring about any of this, anymore."

So, the group kept moving, although Dodd and I lagged some distance behind.

"Okay, first of all, I'm signing on with your electrocution theory," Dodd said. "The more I thought about it, the better I liked it. It's got physical evidence, which gives the SAC a woody. It makes the police look stupid and me brilliant, which I'm loving, and...say, you don't mind that I've got to make it, like I just recruited you to help out with that little physics experiment, with the popping noises and the steam blowing a note through a pipe?"

"You're welcome to it," I said. "Just tell me we're even now."

"We're even now. You saved my job. Thanks, Francis."

"You're not worried about Randal and Briggs?"

"Agents who don't complete their assignments don't have much to say. And Randal knows I'm perfectly capable of officially submitting his name for a Purple Heart for falling off a barstool in the line of duty."

We exited one at a time through the stuck-half-open front door. Alicia and Ellen had their phones out and were tapping and swiping away, as they walked toward the edge of the rain forest and the cart path down. Brother Emilio followed innocently behind them.

As Dodd and I stepped clear of the monastery's front stoop, I asked him, "What were you doing by the front door when Cabrera walked past you, leaving the monastery? What couldn't you tell Alvarez?"

"I was on my phone, talking to my old squeeze in Apartment 2B. Just setting up a little after-hours frolic."

"You had an alibi and someone to back it up, and you wouldn't tell the police?"

"I couldn't have Alvarez send a couple of his guys up to her place to check out my story. Remember, at that time I still had prisoners there, drugged and tied up. And later, after you turned them loose, I still didn't want the local police up there. You know they wouldn't treat her like a lady. They'd do their tough guy routine, and you may have noticed a certain rebellious streak in her. It'd be a mess, and…and I didn't want to bring her trouble. That's what she tells me I always do."

"Well, your ploy certainly made trouble for me. It cost me two extra days down here."

"I heard you lost your job. Alicia told me. Well, more like blamed me. So, I guess I'm responsible."

I tried to savor what it felt like to have Phil Dodd owe *me*, for a change. But it didn't give me any particular joy. "Well, you're going back to your island prison. So, you didn't come out of this especially well yourself."

"Actually, this didn't work out too badly for me." Dodd said. "See, I'd been putting in for a Special Agent Afloat assignment on a regular basis for years now. But I'd already done two stints back-to-back on an aircraft carrier when I first got out of agent training. I was told I had to move on. Then after that business in Iraq, it looked like I going to be stuck there at Gitmo, forever. But finally, this latest SAC agrees to another carrier stint for me, but first I have to do this assignment in Puerto Rico, up at a monastery that's being bought up by some Arab businessman. Okay, it was a test. And another Arab Sheik turning up dead sure wasn't any help. But now, I've solved a murder. Now, I'm looking good. Hell, I'm looking great. And I'm going back to sea."

"Well, I'm happy for you then."

"Look, I seriously do feel bad that the way things played out cost you your job."

"You don't owe me anything. I've got a couple connections back in Chicago. Been thinking about going solo for a while now, anyway. I'll be fine."

"Back to Chicago, huh? With a whole world full of broken machinery out there." Dodd affected a sigh. "It's her, isn't it? It's Alicia."

Hearing her name, Alicia, walking out in front of us, turned her head. She'd slogged up a mountain and had her face turbo-washed by a hurricane, and yet Alicia managed to sustain a defiant beauty that I couldn't take my eyes away from.

"Maybe I'm working on something," I said.

"Okay. It's way too far inland, if you ask me, but suit yourself." Dodd momentarily glanced back at the monastery. "Listen, I've got to tidy this thing up. I'd still love a confession out of Brother Hugo. He's the only one with enough brains to pull off an electrocution, right under the bodyguard's nose. But I didn't stumble across anything incriminating out in the sheds. Although I did try out some of that rum he makes. Damn good stuff. Run it through the donkey a few more times and you'd have *vodka de primera*. That's Spanish for—"

"I know what it's Spanish for," I said. "You're still zeroed in on Brother Hugo, then?"

"He conjured up all the other feats of engineering-on-the-fly around here. I'm sure he could wire up the Abbot's chair without overly taxing himself. Now, I'm going to go back and check out that basement men's room with new eyes. I'll catch a ride back with Alvarez or Cabrera." Dodd again put a hand on my arm to stop me. "You won't forget to pump our little friend up ahead there, will you? I still need that golden nugget that'll make big Brother Hugo open up." Dodd pulled out his notebook and pen, scribbled on a page, and tore it out. "Here's the number for my burner. Call me if you get something interesting."

I took the page and also the pen from his hand, before reaching in and writing a number on his open notebook. "That's *my* phone. How about we knock off with the cryptic notes."

Dodd smiled, we shook hands, and he loped off up the rise back to the main building. Despite his way of viewing life from the third angle, Dodd's mind was sharp. He wouldn't be in that basement for long, before he'd have the rest of it worked out. Once again, I was running out of time.

Chapter 21

I caught up to Brother Emilio at the tree line. Ahead of us and already on the cart path down, Alicia and Ellen chatted about flight times and last minute souvenirs, oblivious to the Spanish being spoken behind them.

"I think the donkey will be pleased to see me," Brother Emilio said. "It will do me good to tend to him. I will repair the damage to his shed."

"I have no doubt that you will easily repair the shed. Brother Hugo has taught you so much."

I hesitated for a moment, before continuing. But I knew that it would be better if I were the one who drew the information from the young monk. I could edit it later for the consumption of others. No need for everybody involved to take a fall.

"I am sure," I continued, "that you were of great assistance to Brother Hugo in constructing the battery charging system from the old truck parts – not only powering the bathroom dome light, but also producing household current to run the Abbot's fan."

When Brother Emilio didn't respond, I went on, "You must have been a great help in running the wires up within the walls to the Abbot's room. And I am sure the Abbot enjoyed the relief from the heat that the fan gave him. Just as he gained relief when he sat in his big chair, and the trickle of current from the pineapple-wine battery behind it soothed his arthritic hands."

Brother Emilio kept his eyes focused on the ground in front of him. "It no longer matters. I do not wish to look at the chair again."

"The chair served its purpose," I said. "I could see that it made the Abbot very happy when he regained possession of it. He seemed so at peace."

The young monk looked at me, briefly, but again didn't respond. We continued down the path toward the donkey's shelter without conversing further.

I helped Brother Emilio take down the makeshift shelter. Ellen and Alicia watched us, as all women watch men at work – arms folded beneath their breasts and impatient with the progress. Brother Emilio's efforts were hampered by the donkey, which kept butting him with its head and rubbing its nose against the coarse brown cloth of his robe.

I waited to reopen our fairly one-sided conversation, until we had the tarp folded and tied to the donkey's back and the bucket strapped on top. "I hope that the donkey's home is not too badly damaged."

"I will repair it."

"When I was young like you, I worked in construction during summer breaks from college. Mostly it was running new wiring in old houses. I crawled around a lot of attics and drilled holes to lower a string with a weight tied to its end, within the wall cavities, in order to pull the wires up to the attic to make the electrical connections. It was hot work."

Brother Emilio had the donkey's lead in his hand, but he didn't move.

It was time to lay it out for him. "You saw my demonstration, where I showed how the Arab was actually killed by electricity, not by poison. And you saw that I had to run the wires on top of the floor to make the connections at the back of the Abbot's chair. But to run the wires *beneath* the floor, someone had to be small enough to fit through the opening at the top of the basement wall, and to crawl under the floorboards and redirect the abandoned wires up through the little hole that had been drilled through the floor, just behind the Abbot's chair. But the wires could not be left sticking up through the floor where they might be seen. So, someone had to tie the ends of the wires to that length of dark thread that I saw lying there and then lower the wires down again through the hole and out of sight. So, all anyone would see in the dim light, was just a stray piece of course thread from the frayed hem of a monk's robe lying in the dust."

The diminutive monk looked at the ground again, as his ears reddened.

I went on, "And on the day the Arab was killed, when someone's daily routine brought him to the rear of the Abbot's chair, he could furtively pull on the string to bring the ends of the black wires back up through the little hole and hook them over the bare terminal wires of the chair's built-in battery. All without disturbing the Arab businessman, or exciting the bodyguard's suspicions. Then all someone had to do was to go down into the basement bathroom and stick the other ends of the wires into the hundred-and-twenty-volt receptacle on the electric power inverter."

I paused, but Brother Emilio continued looking at the ground without responding.

"The person who stuck the wires into the receptacle did not have to be you, but it could not have been Brother Hugo, because when he ran through the patio and into the dining room, Mr. Dodd saw that he came from the back door of the building, not from the direction of the basement bathroom. And Mr. Dodd also witnessed Monsignor Cabrera come down the stairs from the Abbot's room and depart from the monastery, a short time before the bodyguard started yelling."

Again I paused and again garnered no response.

"And you, yourself, told Detective Sergeant Alvarez that you were returning from washing your hands before lunch," I pressed forward. "But you let Alvarez assume that you washed up in the kitchen, using a bowl of hot dishwater…not in the basement bathroom, using the sink's cool pond water."

The donkey startled me by shaking its head hard enough to fling water from its mane, as though hotly denying my assertion.

"And, in fact," I continued, despite the donkey's advocacy, "you were still in the basement when the bodyguard started shouting. Because you still had to pull the far ends of the wires off the homemade battery behind the Abbot's chair and back down through the little hole. And then coil up the other end of the wires and throw them out of sight into the opening at the top of the block wall. And then move the crates of vegetables back to the other wall."

I waited for a protest, or a denial backed by a feeble lie, or even a plea that I not tell anyone. But all I got was a bray from the donkey, undoubtedly impatient to return to its shed.

"Francis, are you done fooling around with that animal?" Alicia echoed the donkey's sentiments.

"In a minute," I said in English and then returned to Spanish. "The Arab came every day and installed himself on the Abbot's chair. And the Abbot with his arthritic hands could only sit in his bedroom and suffer. And you loved the old Abbot, like he was your grandfather. So, something had to be done. Someone had to act."

Brother Emilio stroked the donkey's nose, calming the animal. He didn't look at me.

"Now, allow me to speculate," I said. "I think that you received a momentary shock of electricity, back when you were helping Brother Hugo with the wiring for the Abbot's fan. And that shock hurt like a serpent's bite. I too am familiar with the pain that it causes. In my work, I routinely test electrical circuits with the machine power switched on. And I think that it was your memory of the pain of that electrical shock that gave you your idea. You knew that if you momentarily shocked the Arab, while he sat in the Abbot's chair, he would never want to sit in that chair again."

Brother Emilio now looked at me. I couldn't read people anywhere near as well as Monsignor Cabrera, but in Brother Emilio's eyes, I could see the bond of shared experience.

"I also think that Brother Hugo knew right away what you had done," I continued. "While Mr. Dodd was busy examining the Arab's body for signs of life, I think that Brother Hugo spotted the little hole that you had drilled and the length of dark thread. And he knew that there were wires strung beneath the floorboards and that you had helped him test the circuit by sticking the twisted wire ends into the receptacle on the power inverter. So, Brother Hugo knew, and it is apparent to me that Monsignor Cabrera also knows. But none of us think that you actually meant to kill the Arab."

Brother Emilio was again looking at the ground, but at last he admitted, "Monsignor Cabrera heard my confession."

To even it up, I also admitted, "I am sorry that I had to reveal that Mr. Rahim was actually electrocuted. It was my obligation to help Mr. Dodd prove that Mr. Rahim was murdered, but not by Mr. Dodd. When we were in the Navy together, Mr. Dodd intervened, at a great cost to himself, to keep me and another sailor out of a Filipino prison. I was in his debt."

My phone's electronic music sounded loud under the rain forest canopy. The donkey's head swung up and the animal brayed even more loudly over the ring tones. Brother Emilio reached up and pulled the donkey's muzzle down.

I opened my phone. "Yes?"

"Francis, you bastard, you knew," Dodd's voice accused. "You couldn't tell me? You couldn't say, 'Hey Phil, that access hole in the basement wall is kind of small for that big burly ex-Seal to get through. It must have been the little guy.'"

"I needed a little time to confirm it."

"He's still with you? Hold onto him. I'll be right there."

"Stop. You don't need him. You've got the full story to tell now, with hard evidence to back it up. He didn't mean for it to happen. He just wanted to give Rahim a friendly jolt to get him out of the Abbot's chair and keep him out. He just misjudged how long the guy could take it, is all."

"What are you, his mother now? And what about Alvarez?"

"He's still busy with Monsignor Cabrera and the jungle-plant-poison-in-the-tea fable. And I doubt he'll have the final toxicology report today, anyway. It takes forever to find nothing. So, we have time before Alvarez finally tumbles."

It went quiet on the other end for a moment. Then Dodd said, "Okay, I'll hold off for today – even though I can't at all fathom how the little fellow became your special worry. But listen up, Francis. Alvarez is not as dumb as he looks. Do not drive the getaway car."

"I know." I closed my phone.

"Francis, can we go now?" Alicia insisted.

"I need another minute."

I returned my attention to Brother Emilio and spoke in Spanish. "It is becoming more difficult to contain the truth. Now, Mr. Dodd also has determined that it was you."

Brother Emilio fussed with the donkey's rigging. "I must ask Brother Hugo what to do."

"Brother Hugo and I have gotten you away from Detective Sergeant Alvarez, for now anyway, and Alvarez is the only one that you need to worry about." I took time for a breath, before reprising my role as accessory after the fact. "This is your opportunity to run away and hide from the police, until the situation quiets down. Neither Brother Hugo, nor Monsignor Cabrera, will have any problem standing up to a police interrogation. They will be threatened, but they will not be afraid. They will be offered a bargain, but they will not take it. They are strong men." I allowed Brother Emilio a moment to gauge his own inner strength, before I put it into words. "The police would have a confession out of you in ten minutes."

Brother Emilio looked up the path toward the monastery. He swung his gaze to the path down. Finally, his eyes returned to my face. "You must take me with you."

"I cannot involve these ladies." I also didn't want to get further involved myself, but Br. Emilio looked so like a puppy in a cage that I couldn't stay cold. "You will not get very far wearing your robe. Are there any regular clothes around here that you can change into?"

Brother Emilio spread his arms wide. "These are our clothes."

I stopped myself for a moment. How far did I want to go with this? Yes, if it had been a premeditated murder, then Brother Emilio should be punished. No question. But since it was an action born of a naïve miscalculation that caused the death, should his penalty be as harsh as what the judicial system would surely have in store for him? And as for my part, the easiest thing was to do nothing. But that seemed as wrong as anything else.

I looked at the artless young monk and thought about what would surely happen to him in prison, even during a relatively short sentence for involuntary manslaughter.

"Okay," I said in Spanish. "Do you know that little waterfall, where the stream meets the road below us?"

"I know of it."

"Take the donkey back up to its shed. Then go directly to the stream up where the old engine block sits in the water. Do not say goodbye to anyone. No one can know anything about your leaving. Follow the stream down. At the top of the little waterfall by the road, you will find a shirt and a pair of trousers and a baseball cap waiting for you. Put them on, leave your robe in the rain forest, and walk down the mountain. Get off the road and hide when you hear a car coming. When you get to Luquillo, stay away from your friends and family and the churches. If the police look for you, they will look there first."

"My only friends are here. I have no family."

"Well, stay away from churches, then. You must be nowhere to be found, and you must survive on your own for a while. The Medical Examiner will not be able to determine for certain that Mr. Rahim was killed by electrical shock. Without your confession, Detective Sergeant Alvarez has nothing. But it may take several days for Mr. Rahim to have died by natural causes again."

"How can I know when I may return?"

I gave it some thought. "Brother Hugo brings a load of rum to Luquillo every Thursday, right?"

"It was our routine."

"Good. This coming Thursday, go to one of the restaurants where you and Brother Hugo always went to barter, and wait outside for him. Brother Hugo will then contact Monsignor Cabrera, and he will find someplace to keep you hidden away from Detective Sergeant Alvarez forever."

Brother Emilio still looked sad.

"Damn it," I swore in English – because the war in my head was held in that language. But I returned to the more polite Spanish to tell the young monk, "Just take the donkey up to its shed and run away. Just do it."

"Thank you. I will do as you say."

I turned, stomped past Alicia and Ellen, and continued on down the cart path, not looking back. Alicia and Ellen hurriedly caught up with me.

"What the hell was that freaking boatload of Spanish all about?" Alicia demanded.

Emotion constricted my throat. It felt as though Randal had a hold of my neck again. It took me the better part of a minute to regain my voice. "I was just telling Brother Emilio that I knew he hooked up the wires to the Abbot's chair and electrocuted Rahim."

"The little monk did it?" Ellen asked. "Are you sure? I thought maybe the big one. He looks kind of tough."

"Brother Emilio didn't mean to kill him," I said. "He only meant to give Rahim a motivating jolt to get him out of the Abbot's chair. Like the remote control collars they put on dogs to correct bad behavior."

"He zapped the Arab to keep him off the furniture?" Alicia put it somewhat more harshly.

"He seemed like such a sweet little guy," Ellen said.

While the three of us proceeded carefully down the muddy and slippery leaf strewn path, I explained, "Sitting in the great chair eased the old Abbot's arthritis. The Baghdad battery provided the stimulus. I can only speculate that, back around the year zero, somebody figured out that holding onto two different metals that were stuck in a jar of wine was therapeutic. Maybe it interferes with the pain signals going up to the brain, I don't know. But Brother Emilio couldn't stand to see the old Abbot suffer by being denied access to his arthritis-soothing chair. He really loved that old man. I guess he felt that he had to do something."

"And once the monks were chucked out of the monastery," Alicia said, "that would be the last they'd ever see of the Abbot's chair."

"No way Rahim was going to leave that chair behind, after he closed on the monastery property and headed back to France," I said. "He was making a pig's breakfast out of the shipping arrangements, because of his arrogance. But I think the chair was his bonus for brokering the deal. Your professor friend said it was valuable."

"He said it was valuable for its religious and historical significance," Alicia said. "He said nothing about medicinal purposes."

"I can't believe someone was killed over a damned chair," Ellen said.

"And I can't believe Monsignor Cabrera conspired with that police captain to cover up for the little monk," Alicia said. "But I guess, that's what he did."

"I'm pretty sure Brother Hugo knew right away what had happened," I said, "but he waited until he could inform Monsignor Cabrera by phone, before he notified the police that the monastery had a dead Arab on their hands. That's when the cover-up began. But still, a Muslim's sudden death in a Catholic monastery was bad optics for the Church. So, when the Monsignor rushed over to the General Stationhouse to do damage control with his bridge club pal and the preliminary autopsy came back as 'undetermined,' Monsignor Cabrera was right there to suggest to Captain Rivera that a quiet death by natural causes was preferable to attracting an uninvited involvement from the Federal level and an unflattering media blitz raining down on the Church. Of course, neither the Captain nor the Monsignor was aware at the time that Dodd's assignment already constituted Federal involvement."

"I was in the dark too," Alicia said. "Before the police arrived, I had no idea what was going on. All I know is Brother Emilio came flying up the stairs when I started out to go look for Dodd. He shooed me back into the guest quarters and hurried on to the Abbot's room like Satan, himself, was chasing him."

"He'd just come from the dining hall and seen what he'd done," I said. "Brother Hugo had sent him up to the Abbot to keep him from blurting anything out in front of Dodd. At the time, Brother Hugo wouldn't have known if Dodd understood Spanish or not."

"If the Arab was electrocuted, then why all the fuss about the tea mugs?" Ellen asked.

"Dodd was right that Brother Hugo swiped Rahim's tea mug off the table to misdirect the police into thinking the mug was important – but to cover for Brother Emilio, not for himself."

"But that just shifted the spotlight onto Monsignor Cabrera," Alicia said.

"But it also allowed Monsignor Cabrera to really step up to his role as the High Priest of Jungle Poisons, today, in order to run out the clock for Alvarez."

"So, you're saying Alvarez still doesn't know that the little monk did it?" Ellen asked.

"He's still hoping the toxicologist will come up with some exotic poison in Rahim's blood sample. But, when *that* pretty sparkler finally burns out, he'll get around to rethinking what I'd said about the Abbot's chair being hot-wired. And once he's on the right track, he'll quickly figure out that it was Brother Emilio, just like Dodd just did. Hopefully, by that time, Rahim will be officially dead by natural causes again, and Brother Emilio will be safely out of Alvarez's reach."

"You told Brother Emilio to run away and hide, didn't you," Alicia was quick to accuse me.

"He didn't mean to kill Rahim," I said.

"You don't care about justice?"

"That's somebody else's job. I just fix things."

Alicia whacked me hard on the chest. "Stop fixing things that you know you shouldn't."

***

After backing the rental car around to face the road that wound its way down through El Yunque's rain forest, I turned left instead of right and drove up the mountain toward the little waterfall.

"You went the wrong way," Alicia said.

"That may well prove to be," I had to admit. "But I've already committed myself."

"Damn it, Francis, we're done. Done with all of it."

I swung the car in a U-turn at the pull-off in front of the little waterfall and put it in park.

"This will only take a minute." I left the key in the ignition and my phone on the console, before getting out and scrambling up what was becoming a trail beside the falling water.

I took off my shirt and ball cap, and after I shook my legs out of the wet trousers, I retrieved my wallet. Following a moment's hesitation, I took out the thirty-three dollars I had left in cash and shoved it into a trouser pocket. It was a grand gesture for an unemployed engineer. And I briefly wondered if Brother Emilio had any experience with actual cash.

I rolled the clothes up, placed the bundle in the shelter of an overhanging rock, and topped it with the ball cap. With my wallet clenched in my teeth, I slid down past the waterfall, wearing only my boxer shorts, shoes, and socks.

"I take it that someone is about to impersonate you again," Alicia said through the open window, as I approached the car. "Won't your clothes look a little big on him?"

"He'll be wearing my costume, but playing a different part."

"Is Francis going to be driving us around in his underwear?" Ellen asked.

"Not freaking even." Alicia climbed out and pushed her way ahead of me. "Ellen, sit up front with me, and let Everybody's Favorite Accomplice take his rightful place in the backseat."

Alicia slid in behind the wheel. Ellen moved up to the front passenger seat, and I climbed into the back. The women were safely buckled in, but I barely had my last foot inside, when Alicia stomped on the gas, and we rocketed down the twisting mountain road.

"So, you expose the killer and then help him escape," Alicia said. "Brilliant, Francis."

"It wasn't an easy decision. Sometimes you have to do something wrong to set things right."

"Sounds like you've been hanging out with your old lieutenant too long."

"That one wasn't from Dodd."

***

We didn't go straight back to San Juan. Instead, Alicia drove to Luquillo. At a souvenir shop, once again happily in the throes of shopping, Alicia bought t-shirts and shorts for all three of us. From there, we found the restaurant overlooking the ocean, where we were supposed to have had a pleasant lunch with Phil Dodd five days before. The sun was low in the sky, and the electricity wasn't back on yet. But the owner had found some table candles and an old, mechanical, credit card imprinter. So, we dined on sandwiches, featuring yesterday's chicken, and sipped room-temperature cocktails.

We lingered till dark and, cheered by many after-dinner drinks, resolved by unanimous vote to take our last round of rum and cokes in plastic cups for a nighttime stroll on the beach.

Our enhanced celebration at having survived the storm broke the stillness of the deserted, brightly moonlit beach. The pelicans, undisturbed by our rowdy behavior, had returned to roost out on the wood pilings that staked out the swimming area. Alicia and Ellen, taunting and daring each other, decided it was time for a swim. We abandoned our new clothes under a palm tree and ran laughing for the water. And then we were the three of us again, floating and splashing in a placid, warm Caribbean Sea, skinny-dipping in the moonlight.